Mercury's Son

Copyright © 2017 by Luke E.T. Hindmarsh

All rights reserved. This book or any portion thereof may not be reproduced or used in any manner whatsoever without the express written permission of the publisher except for the use of brief quotations in a book review.

This is a work of fiction. Names, characters, businesses, places, events and incidents are either the products of the author's imagination or used in a fictitious manner. Any resemblance to actual persons, living or dead, or actual events is purely coincidental.

First Printing, 2017

ISBN 9781521082089

TLTQ Publishing

www.lukehindmarsh.com

To Mum for feeding my imagination.

To Dad for teaching me that hard work gets you what you want.

Most of all to Maiken, my beautiful wife, for believing in me and supporting my madcap pursuit of a dream.

With love, always.

α

FERE LIBENTER HOMINES ID QUOD VOLUNT CREDUNT.

MEN WILLINGLY BELIEVE WHAT THEY WISH TO BE TRUE.

-GAIUS JULIUS CAESAR-

The Murder

A change of air pressure came like a breath on his neck, stiffening his flesh and running cold fingertips down his back. He felt a presence looming over him — a phantom conjured from all his misgivings, from being forced to take this way. Diving into the reeking, mechanical bowels of the Plenum. Logic told him it was just the cycling of the megastructure's pressure doors — the closest to wind he would ever know — but his heart jumped and bounded in his chest all the same.

Eugene Fisher scurried down the narrow way between the tangles of machinery at the base of the towering habitation blocks. High above, clouds swathed the latticework of the uppermost levels — the drudges had left the great fans of the air recycling system idling again.

Oily water spattered the ground around him, leaving multi-coloured puddles that shimmered in the rain. Each raindrop that ran down his face with a nauseating tickle was a filthy cocktail of condensed breath, sweat and pollution. His every panting breath drew in bitter air that left a greasy film on his tongue and filled his mouth with the tang of bile.

He was late. The Conclave of the Centra Autorita would be waiting with all their usual patience. No doubt, relishing the chance to tear him apart. The latest test results didn't add up, and it made no sense. No sense at all. Someone had made a mistake somewhere and, as Project Head, he was going to feel the bite.

The warning his grandfather had given him about the fatal price for failure nagged at Eugene, as he hastened through the murk. His hand caught the corridor wall coated with mats of greyed g-moss and came away slick. Even these plants, modified to process pollutants, had been overwhelmed by the contamination down here. Out from another narrow passageway, a shadow approached in the gloom of the under-levels.

'Just what I need,' Eugene said, under his breath, as the hunched figure came closer.

Fear that the figure might attack him rose fluttering in his chest — but it was just a tatty indigent, stooping in the downpour and hurrying along to shelter deep in the innards of the Plenum. It was only then that he considered the other downside to the route he'd taken: security monitors in the under-levels would cover vital areas — nowhere else. He'd be without the protection of the watchful eyes of the kensakan for most of his journey. If the ragged man *had* accosted him, there would have been no record of it; no kensakan patrol sent in to rescue him and arrest his assailant.

Eugene wasn't surprised that most people never set foot groundside. Only those with no choice came here: the maintenance drudges and few outcasts within the Plenum. He couldn't help but recall the look on the faces of a couple of maintenance drudges he'd passed on the way. One leaning over to the other and shaking his head, saying '*baka*' as he looked up at Eugene in his pristine lab coat. With so many leftovers from the languages of dead nations, he'd had to search his memory. *Baka* — idiot, fool. Well, they were wrong. He had a purpose to fulfil, and if that meant slogging through the under-levels, then so be it.

When an artificial rain wasn't falling, the constant dripping of condensation kept the ground sodden — as if the stench alone wasn't enough. Not even the ubiquitous g-moss could cloak the fetid odour of waste from ten million human bodies. Down here every moment was an inescapable reminder that they — the Enclosed — were all crushed together within Arcas Plenum. It was bad enough visiting, never mind trying to live in the poisoned underbelly.

He was regretting the decision that brought him to the ground, of all places, but taking the under-levels had been a necessary shortcut to the inner sanctum of the Conclave. If he wanted them to listen to him, he had to get there in time — taking a more civilised route just wasn't an option. The choice had been made for him.

His surroundings were a far cry from the sterility of his destination: the administrative level. Down here though, he could move, avoiding the permanent crush of the higher levels' neverending rush hour. So many people crammed into a space conceived of for less than a quarter their number — all on a rotating work schedule, where night and day were matters of choice and labour demands. Where the Sun was a dictator no longer.

Rushing on, his hands grew clammy from the atmosphere or tension: probably both. There was so much riding on this meeting. Eugene worried about the consequences for future generations if they closed his program down. The leather briefcase he carried — an antique affectation that once belonged to his grandfather — was fit to bursting with hardcopies, test results from before this latest anomaly. They were too sensitive to trust to wireless transmission, what with monitoring by the Temple.

Something fell from above, plopping into one of the pools of stagnant water ahead of him. Eugene stared upwards — nothing. Feeling the skin of his scalp tighten — almost prickling — he stood still: looking, listening. All he could see above was the haze of the air and the sparkle of lights in the buildings and along the crisscrossing walkways. Eugene picked up pace, hustling along so he was almost jogging. There wasn't time for paranoia — he had real problems to solve.

Whatever the nature of the mistake, it was a major setback, but he refused to accept that he'd wasted his efforts or that his life might be forfeit. He hated living in a Plenum, but the idea of a Martyr's Preserve was worse: being a savage, scrubbing out a life in the dirt of the dead world. He was in the minority who still held that humanity's destiny was greater than just squatting on Earth's decaying corpse. Now, in the skoler, they taught the children that cyclic decline was fact: civilisations were doomed to rise and fall; this was both predictable and inevitable. Last time he'd visited a skoler to deliver a lecture to the young students, he'd had to wait while the teacher spun the lies she'd been told to teach.

'Humanity is a macro-virus, and like all viral clades, the harm that it does to its host diminishes that host's ability to provide an environment that will sustain the virus. We destroy ourselves,' Eugene recalled the words with growing wrath. *'Look to the cycle of human history. The rise of a powerful empire, for example, and you will see it will use its resources to grow to such strength that its existence becomes unsustainable. Like a viral infection — which spreads through every part of its host — eventually, it kills the host and thus itself.'*

He expected such ideas in the Temple seminaries, but to see even the secular skoler adopting that thinking filled him with resentment. Poisoning the minds of children. He'd watched the young faces, attentive to their teacher and ignorant of their own true potential — the beauty inside them. Addressing them afterwards, he'd abandoned his prepared, dry lecture on the role of science in repairing the damage done by previous generations. Inspired by his anger, he'd drawn on some of the oratory his grandfather had possessed that up until then had lain dormant inside him.

The reaction? Well, most of the children had worn bored expressions. They'd switched off the first time the word 'science' had left his mouth. An awkward expression somewhere between a frown and a blush had battled on the teacher's face. He'd dismissed her — the kensakan weren't going to be sending any officers to get *him*, no Moderator to probe his thoughts. But the failure to connect with these young minds, fired up though he'd been, had eaten away at his belief that he could make a difference.

When he'd turned to leave, the smallest child — no more than seven — had approached him.

'Sir, do you mean we can leave the Mother? We don't have to stay here to purge our sin?'

He remembered thinking, *What have we done to our children? They think of the damage to the Earth as sin and don't even know its name. How can we have let the Temple do this to us?*

'What's your name, son?'

'Sadiq, sir.'

'Sadiq, I know what you've been taught. But their truth isn't the only truth. Don't close your mind to other possibilities. Remember that. You'll understand when you're older.'

He'd wanted to say more, to share the hope his project might bring, but he'd said too much already — there was a limit to what even he could get away with. The boy had seemed to understand — he'd nodded in respect and walked slowly from the classroom.

Now, one thought stole centre stage in his mind: ending the toxic dominion of the Temple of the Wounded Mother. The hypocrisy of religious fanatics: kept alive only by the technology they abhorred. None of it would matter — if he succeeded in his project. Gave them a way out of the trap they'd all made for themselves — a way off this dead rock. He would prove the philosophy of despair wrong. He would save them all.

Eugene approached the base of the looming block where

the Conclave had based themselves. The area around its pressure door illuminated, as the security monitor detected his presence. The white door was reassuringly clean of the filth and g-moss smothering all the other surfaces. He stepped up and looked into the narrow slit of the door scanner. It glowed green as it flickered a beam over his face.

A noise behind him — the splash of a footfall? — made him look up, interrupting the scan. He whirled round, expecting to see that same tramp coming at him, after all. Where were those damn kensakan when you needed them?

Nothing.

Eugene snorted. Here he was jumping at the sound of rat or roach, acting as if he really was some kind of quaking *baka*. He turned back to the door, the scanner's green light still shining in expectation.

A hand, covered in a rough glove, clamped over his mouth from behind. It smelled so clean. Searing pain pierced the back of his head — a twisting spur of fire. Before his nerves could deliver the full extent of exquisite agony, his world whited out to nothing.

PART I

DURA LEX SED LEX

THE LAW IS HARSH BUT IT IS THE LAW

-UNATTRIBUTED-

Chapter 1

The transpod stopped with a jolt at the staging platform. Valko jostled for position like the rest of the crowd: men and women in grey, brown, blue or black wearalls, some a fashionable cut, others not. Drudges from B-shift rushed out, as his similar, C-shift crowd pressed forward to get on board. The masses. Stinking, wretched workers on their way hundreds — if not thousands — of miles to work, day in day out. All angling for better status and dreaming of joining the elite. To live and work in the affluent administrative core of their home Plenum. Either that or the privileged yet dangerous calling of the Martyr.

The dose of NOTT he'd had to take in the early hours while investigating what had turned out to be a simple suicide, was still making its presence known — the feeling of a blush in his cheeks and a shiver down his spine told him so. Knowing the drug's effects so intimately, he tried and failed, to control the upwelling of his — no its — feelings of kinship for the human detritus surrounding him. His mind could call them what they were, but right now, his heart was telling lies: he was one of them — base and ruled by squalid emotion.

Valko pressed on board with all the rest, squeezing his rail-thin frame into the mass. The trick was to find a space where he wouldn't have his face too close to someone else's sweaty back. Transpods were the same the world over. Cramped, worn down and with a distinctive grimy layer on every handhold. Temple sutra's scrawling across the displays on every surface, demanding the attention of the faithful.

The transpod began to slide forwards on its magrail as the last passengers squeezed through the closing doors. They rushed to find an anchor point for their wearall's harness. Valko's ears popped as the craft transitioned through the inner skin of the Plenum, into the departure blister. Strapping in, he readied himself for the burst of acceleration when the launcher would hurl the 'pod through Arcas Plenum's skin and out in flight mode towards Berlin Plenum. Outside the dirty viewport at his left elbow, the shimmering green-gold haze of the blister's surfaces looked sickly to him, not the glistening foxfire of his home he expected to see once they were out in the pre-dawn darkness. The so-called advantages of the job; he smiled in grim recollection of his recruitment:

'You'll travel the world; meet people from all the surviving cultures; make a difference. All for the Justeco Centro.'

It had sounded so good back then. He snorted and received an irritated glare from the middle-aged woman — in a once fashionable, and far too tight, office wearall — packed in against his left side. So much for travelling the world. The reality had turned out to be an endless procession of Plena; each an uncanny likeness to the last. The different cultures were a tweak of the flavour of 'food' from the processors and variant language, nothing more. The latter was mostly just accent these days since the surviving SuperState languages — CantoJapanese, RussoPolsk, DeutschoScandinavisk, TransArabic and Neo-Punjabi — had been subsumed into the Centra Autorita's preferred AngloEsperanto. No doubt, Swahili would be next. Still, travelling was better than being stuck in one Plenum, or the constant cycle of bouncing back and forth between two Plena: at least he had the illusion of change.

The transpod slowed and lurched to a stop. The smooth shift of the magrail over to the launcher interrupted before the 'pod could angle for its launch vector.

The transpod's false, vaguely female voice flooded the compartments — too loud and sharp to be soothing, 'We are sorry for the delay on this service and hope that it does not inconvenience you. We will launch as soon as the vessel in front has cleared,'

Valko craned to see what was going on out of one of the forward viewports, but there were too many bodies packed in front of him.

The wave of nausea that always accompanied an insight washed over him: the woman next to him was depressed — maybe even suicidal. That was the thing with being a Moderator. It opened you up to people in a way most others could not understand; at least, it did so some of the time. More often, he would have seen the woman's irritated look, heard her sighing and dismissed her as nothing: another administrative worker, a fraction above a base grade drudge. Now, with NOTT still sparking through him, he could feel her desperation like a strong odour — his mind using familiar concepts to interpret the sensory impressions. She wasn't simply a sullen drudge, but a person brimming with despair. He sought in vain for something cheerful to say to her; then settled for the next best thing: solidarity.

'Never met a machine that was sorry for anything. Useless fake apologies. And what's this with the 'We' anyway?' He said, adopting a mock grumpy tone that risked becoming genuine as the delay dragged on.

She looked at him, her tired face almost grey under the make-up, and grunted her assent. Then she seemed to realise what he was and her expression shifted to apprehension. He thought about saying more but realised he could no longer smell her misery. Either the feeling had diminished, or his dose of NOTT was wearing off. Besides, he was damned if he was going to start flirting with some worn-out, middle-aged drudge. Compassion bled away, as did his insight.

It amazed him, sometimes, how his sensitivity to others changed his perception of them as much as his ability to discern truth from lie. It made him more humane — was that an advantage or not? And it made him question things: not always a good thing in his line of work. Since his first dose of NOTT, years before, he had started noticing hidden subtleties in the world around him. He saw the subliminal messages that screamed from every broadcast or service announcement. Even the impersonal voice of the transpod seemed to carry a message concealed within it:

'You, human — you are the problem. A miserable, short life is your just reward for your species treatment of this planet. Know this!'

It was doubtless the work of the Temple; trying to ensure adherence to its doctrine. No one else ever showed awareness of it.

With a lurch, the transpod cleared the end of the magrail and entered the acceleration coil. Valko joined in the collective intake of breath as everyone on board clenched up for the sudden burst of launch. He was treated to the view of one of the sections of the blister folding back, like the petal of a flower opening with the sunrise. A kick of acceleration threw everyone about in the packed confines of the 'pod. A stray datapad, let go by someone in the press at the front of the vehicle, flew backwards, bouncing off the shoulder of the man in front of Valko, and striking the stanchion to one side of his head.

There was a general murmur of disapproval and a shout of '*Sha bi!*' from the man who'd been hit, but no one took the blame or asked for the return of the now fractured datapad. The transpod banked, supported by its EHD impellers — their crackle was barely audible to Valko as he watched Arcas Plenum shrink below them.

Dawn had come, robbing the structure of its glow, but those same rays of light brought out the golden hue of the outer skin. Though he'd never seen one save in history vids, the towering form of Arcas always reminded Valko of a tree, something like the majesty of an oak but shorn of its foliage and most of its branches. The skin appeared smooth at this distance, nothing like bark but the shape spoke of something organic. Seen amongst the green stain of life that surrounded it — in contrast to the blasted landscape all along the horizon — it was easy to believe that his home was the centre of the fragile web of life that still clung to the face of the Mother.

The miles flew by, the broken remains of Warsaw were just visible in the distance, and the ground below the 'pod was nothing but scoured earth. Valko focused on the work to come. He took his headset-hub out of his breast pocket and wiped the contacts clean, then ran a hand over the stubble of his head, tracing the old scars that crossed his scalp. Looking around as he fitted the grey metal band round his forehead, he saw others with their hubs on, eyes closed with looks of concentration, amusement or lust on their faces.

Despite the gold kanji of his rank and title printed on the shoulders of the black wearall that served as a uniform, almost no one on transpods ever noticed his presence. The reaction he might have got if they had — a sudden recoiling in fear at the Moderator in their midst — would have suited him fine or at least given him some more elbow room. Everyone was as good as blind in a transpod — their eyes might see, but their attention was always elsewhere, shutting the world out with the screen of a datapad or the direct connection of a headset-hub. In every other setting his appearance screamed Moderator, but here he was anonymous.

He switched the device on and closed his eyes — taking seven breaths — as it ran through the standard calibration. His mind filled with the device's program and he began reviewing the files on his latest case.

The hub was department issue, a Moderator's special: top of the line in functionality, but uncomfortable despite all its extras. Contacts pressed into his skin, rather than having the feather-light touch of the quality versions reserved for the whitecoats and the elite.

He exhaled slowly and allowed his mind to wander over the data the hub transmitted into his cerebral cortex. After doing the job for a couple of years, he had developed the ability to let his mind flow through the information his kensakan sent to him and seize on anything anomalous. Back to his more focused, less emotive, rational self — *good*.

The hub connected to that worn by one of the kensakan at the scene: Davidson. Third in seniority after Valko and Satoshi, yet one of his least efficient subordinates. He was competent — barely.

Valko's attention turned to the case as images coalesced in his mind: live crime scene observations recorded straight from Davidson's visual cortex. Valko had found it disconcerting, at first, to see the world through someone else. The different spacing between eyes in everyone's face combined with mild myopia, colour blindness or other vagaries of human sight, to reveal subtle changes in the world. There seemed to be less variation with hearing but, if he focused on it, there were more elusive differences: shifts in tone and volume.

Many of the Enclosed still preferred to use the datapads, whose development predated the War by several generations, though hubs were becoming the mainstay. Most users were limited to receiving perceptions of sound, sight, and conscious instructions to their hubs, but some of the 'background noise' of the mind was sent along too. Still, they could not perceive — let alone interpret — the extra signal.

Moderators were different. Their implants allowed a clarity of perception denied any other user; a distinction that he — like the other Moderators — should have revelled in. A normal user could choose to share images, thoughts, and memories but they could not stop involuntary emotional responses riding along with the signal. Reading those responses was the main benefit of a dose of NOTT, alongside the increase in general empathy even without a hub connection. Like with the depressed drudge, he hadn't needed to access her hub feed to pick up on the subconscious cues she was broadcasting with every shift of posture and facial expression. Now — clear of the drug — his implant was inactive, and it afforded him no deeper insight than anyone else would receive. He preferred it this way.

Valko's attention snapped on to the audio. He could hear a muffled conversation between other members of the crime scene team and a background hum, like tinnitus. The sound started and lasted a short time — perhaps four or five seconds. The visual feed showed nothing of note: another dim hallway in one of the poorer areas of the reprocessor section. Kensakan Davidson walked down the corridor and entered a small apartment, a techspert drudge's home from the look. There was grime outside, the internal lights were jury-rigged and flickering, yet the cleanliness was surprising and the general state of the cramped room was tidy, though old and worn.

Most conspicuous was the corpse: lying face up, with a small pool of blood by the head and the jaw clenched. The body was not that of a drudge. It was dressed in the pristine white wearall Valko would expect from a lab technician. The clothing had repelled the blood, remaining unstained and suggesting it was a high-quality smart fabric: something no drudge of any grade would need or have the rec allowance to procure. The body did not belong to the apartment. Of the usual occupant, there was no sign.

One kensakan — Rennard, Valko thought — set up a spectral analysis system, which scanned the room for the blood spray and any fibres or DNA that a killer might have left. The other kensakan was taking samples of the blood: using a small chemical analyser to check for drugs or toxins.

'What do you think a whitecoat's doing in a hiveroom like this?' The kensakan taking the blood samples asked.

This one was Vincent Chang... probably — Valko did not have the time or inclination to get to know his kensakan, they were Satoshi's problem. What else was his sergeant good for? Though there were special cases who drew Valko's attention: Davidson, for example.

The tone sounded normal if a little muted, like Davidson — who Valko was tuning into — had some mild hearing loss. Too much time down the firing range, perhaps.

'Search me — looking for a hookup, you know. Stims, 'pop, zigzag? You name it. Maybe she got bored of the usual simulations and thought she'd try some real rough and ready drudge stimulation. Something a bit more solid than the limpdicks she'd been getting in the lab,' Davidson said.

He gave an unctuous chuckle. The visual feed flickered, and Valko realised it was because the kensakan had winked.

'Shit, don't say stuff like that, Jack. You're being monitored, right? No disrespect, sir,' Chang said, cautioning Davidson even as he was being obsequious to the superior or superiors who might be watching; kensakan at a crime scene could never be sure who was accessing their transmissions. Still, they must have some idea he was monitoring; otherwise, they would have used the gender neutral 'senior'. Chang, at least, had the right attitude. A whitecoat's murder, if murder it was, would attract a lot of higher-level attention from people who wouldn't appreciate Davidson's lack of respect.

'I'm sure there's a legitimate reason why a whitecoat would be down in this area. Probably part of some project monitoring the effect of being this close to the recycling plants, or something,' Chang said.

Though it pained him, Valko thought Davidson had hit closer to the mark, or, at least, had a better theory.

'Wise up, Vince. Since when does a solitary whitecoat do experiments without running it past the plant managers. You know, greasing the wheels a little? Besides, Gangleri's a bloodhound — he's not squeamish. Are you, Chief?' Davidson raised his voice as if to make sure Valko could hear him.

Idiot, Valko thought to himself and sent a short message to his subordinates' hubs, «*Get on with it. I am thirty minutes away. I want cause of death and scene analysis when I get there.*»

'Yes, sir!'

Both kensakan snapped to it, only breaking silence to spout some data at each other. Nothing else leapt to Valko's attention. He would catch up with matters when he arrived, besides the damn headset was pinching. Removing it, he blinked a few times as his brain adjusted to the input from his own eyes once more. A *bloodhound*. Davidson had an unusual vocabulary. Still, it was true he wasn't squeamish. Murder was Valko's speciality because he had made a virtue of being able to disconnect from the lives involved. When it came down to it, he did not care. It was a problem to be solved nothing more. If his psych profiles all showed a lack of compassion and empathy... well, neither was much regarded as an advantage in the pursuit of justice. Whatever that was.

The return of this mindset was a sure sign that he had completed withdrawal from his earlier use of NOTT. He was better like this: free to be calculating. Callous, was what Satoshi called him, but Valko was not bound by the burdens that weighed on his Sergeant; always whining on about his bondmate and their child. The little brat occupied Satoshi's every spare thought. He could not believe that a veteran would be so wet about an ugly, talentless child.

Valko had seen Satoshi's War record — what the Centra Autorita had salvaged of it anyway. Twenty-three confirmed kills: more than half in close combat. On paper, the man had coolant for blood. What with the retrogening he had undergone and the synthorganic mods that surviving vets still carried, he would be a veritable killing machine — if he ever got going. Yet, he had a heart as soft as the mush that the recyclers produced each morning as so-called breakfast.

The transpod slowed as it approached Berlin Plenum, the faint crackle of the EHD impellers dropping to the point Valko could no longer hear them. Looking out of the grimy viewport by his elbow, Valko could just make out the surface details of the megastructure, as it squatted like a fungus of titanic proportions. The outer skin shimmered, responding to the weather: reorganising itself to maintain the optimum structure. It looked so different from his home — an irregular green-gold disc shape that conformed to the old city's limits, as opposed to the almost tree-like, soaring structure of Arcas Plenum — yet the difference was cosmetic, nothing more. Valko held on tight to the handhold as the transpod completed its descent and slipped into the station — its alignment with the magrail so perfect that there was no vibration. Daylight gave way to the wan, grey light of the Plenum as its outer skin sealed shut again.

The same smug computer voice started up again,

'Welcome to Berlin Plenum! Enjoy your stay and remember we came third in the list of low polluters this year. Keep us in the first league.'

Underneath, came the subliminal message, undetectable to him, now his implant was dormant but evident in the sudden slump of the shoulders of the passengers as they disembarked, carrying the miasma of despair with them.

How many Plena claimed to be near the top of the list of low polluters? When you travelled to so many, as Valko did, you realised there was no top or bottom of the list. He exited the 'pod, shouldering through the oncoming passengers and made his way out onto the staging area. The gantry rose from the structures below up to the underside of the Plenum's skin. Like everything else, it was choked with modified vegetation, though this close to the magrail docking points, overgrowth was kept back with ruthless efficiency.

The polluted miasma of the upper levels hid half of his view out over the old city. Berlin as it had been captured on Enclosure. Like other Plena, its architecture had been preserved, though shrouded in greenery. Criss-crossing struts and walkways between the skyscrapers — shorn of their tops by the enveloping Plenum skin — weaved streets and plazas hundreds of feet above the old ground level. Both the old streets and the new were overgrown with modified moss and grasses. Weeds, that would have once been removed, spread everywhere and plant life smothered even the gangways between the levels.

Hand covering his mouth and nose against the foul air — a gesture he knew was futile — Valko hurried as fast as the crowds would allow, down from the staging area and into the main concourse of this level.

The last step before setting foot off the gantry was to pass through the security arch. Its façade may have been marked with *Welcome, Wilkommen* and *Bonvenon*, but he knew it's real purpose: scanning the beacon of everyone who arrived. He'd passed through so many times that the distant memory of his first ever visit to another Plenum no longer even tingled in the back of his mind.

Through the upper-level sprawls and down via packed ramps and F-shafts he finally reached the main plaza on the level above the crime scene. More swimming through the stinking mass of the Plenum's inhabitants. In the crowded environment, you spent much of your time squashed up against your fellow Enclosed. If money had not finally become obsolete, it would have been a pickpocket's dream.

The perceived wisdom for travelling through the large crowds was to see a course and drift towards your destination, trying to correct for being carried one way or the other. He had heard it was much like navigating at sea — with tides and currents — but he had never met anyone who had ever set foot on a real ocean-going vessel and doubted it was true.

The ground was littered with rubbish leftover from the recent Remembrance of Enclosure ceremonies. All the waste material would need to be cleared for recycling: so much for the claim of being high on the list of low polluters. Berlin was no better than any of the others. Now, two days after the ceremony, he could still hear the Plenum address system broadcasting one of Erasmus Fisher's famous speeches from every security monitor. The words echoed from the dark hemispheres mounted under gantries, on the sides of the blocks and nestled in the corners of every corridor and passageway. It was probably the speech he gave when Enclosure happened.

Valko found himself listening despite himself; the vestiges of his indoctrination triggering the compulsion to attend to the half-heard words, *'On this day we hide our faces from the Sun and enter the shelters. Like a return to the ancestral caves. Perhaps, within, we can find an answer to our folly?'*

The voice was strong, cultured. The voice of a time before all of this. Might as well call it 'Fisher Day' and be done with it. Still... the grandson was doing fine work. Valko had him to thank for his implants, after all.

He reached the entrance to one of the habitation blocks and dragged himself inside — taking hold of a convenient patch of g-ivy to avoid being swept past his destination. Catching his breath, he inhaled the heady aroma of the plants festooning the walls — they did a good job of concealing the taint of second-hand air.

In most northern Plena, the cooler external climate allowed regulation of the internal air temperature at a comfortable level. The efficiency of the insulation meant that human body heat was enough to keep a Plenum warm, even when the outside temperature plummeted; overheating was the problem.

Valko thought back to a case he had worked in SingaPlenum. Located on the rough site where Singapore had been before it submerged, its latitude meant that even with efficient insulation the internal temperature was uncomfortable and high. In theory, the amount of solar energy available at such a latitude would have been enough to power cooling systems, but with its hasty construction, SingaPlenum lacked such facilities.

He had sweated for three months on a nasty multiple murder committed by one of that Plenum's governing Weiyuan. Despite his discomfort, the case had absorbed his attention to such an extent that he had been able to ignore the constant sweat rashes and the sharp reek of human bodies in every open space. It was incongruous that a city that had been ultraclean, beautiful and efficient was, post-Enclosure, anything but.

What had intrigued him most, though, was how the Weiyuan had tried to use his position to protect himself, drawing Valko to him and being no bar to the inevitable mental probe — interview was the official euphemism. It was as if the Weiyuan believed that his selection to the Centra Autorita granted him some sort of privileges. His belief had echoed through Valko's mind throughout the interview. Common enough though it was within the Plena for such ideas to remain, not even the governing elite were above the attention of the Moderators. Only those the Temple deemed pure enough for Martyrdom could ever be said to be above the law... or rather, outside it.

He descended to the levels bordering on the tangled pipes and machinery of the Plenum's vital organs. At this level, Valko had left behind open spaces and was deep inside the linked structures of the drudge habitation modules. They squatted like cancerous eruptions on the side of sleek towers that sent pseudopods out to corrupt the clean lines of the cities old skyline. Other lumps grew out of the ground between crumbling buildings of an even earlier age — decay next to new and malignant growth. Though the corridors linking the modules were little more than two-metre by two-metre square tubes, covered on every surface by g-moss, there were still crowds. A press of people moving in both directions, stepping around or over those who paused to crouch or those who fell. It was said that you could die in one of these corridors and be swept along for long minutes before dropping by degree to the floor. The drudges would get the body to a recycler before it became too ripe; at least they would most of the time.

Through the unending press of bodies, Valko found his way to the quarters, suffering the familiar déjà vu caused by visiting a crime scene through the hub link to one of his kensakan before he first set foot there himself. Not allowing himself time to feel relief at escaping the tidal flow of humanity, he ducked inside.

His kensakan stood by the door, but Valko made his way past his team — ignoring their sloppy salutes. Without preamble, he squatted by the corpse, beginning his examination. The room was pokey, with thick g-moss covering floor, walls and hanging from the ceiling; the smell of vegetation cloaked the underlying scent of death.

His team had completed their work and retreated to the small kitchen unit, where they drank strong, almost acrid, coffeine: using up the meagre supply before it was requisitioned along with the deceased's belongings. *Filthy scavengers*, he thought, but it was more from reflex than genuine feeling. His team saw it as a perk of the job. He saw it as an inefficient waste of the resource. Satoshi would have been appalled, sentimentalist that he was. The two parts of Valko warred with conflicting reactions: wishing his sergeant was with him to keep the kensakan in line, versus cold satisfaction at the lack of distraction. For the moment, the absence of NOTT in his system let the dominant, cold side win. He returned to the job at hand, looking at the almost serene body. So little blood.

The speculation of his men had included all manner of salacious suggestions about motive. A whitecoat dallying with a drudge — their 'interaction' getting out of hand during an inventive session — was one of the most interesting. Valko sneered: his team did their jobs but lacked imagination beyond the base.

Every investigation should follow the proper process: analysis on the facts. The diagnostic tools that the Justeco Centro provided its investigators did little to lessen his belief that human observation, and the ruthless application of logic, far outstripped the supposed reliability of the kensakan's semi-forensic, semi-medical tools. Their computing power was limited — all they could do was compare the data entered into them with previous crime scenes. Naturally, they relied on having the right data entered, so his team had to be up to scratch. Something he doubted.

He began, as he always did. Look at the physical signs: pallor mortis — so death was not very recent — and clear signs of rigor mortis too. He had seen worse cases of lividity, but it had clearly set in — so not as long as eight hours but more than two. The body had lain undiscovered a long time, despite the death triggering a beacon alert that had notified the kensakan of the death. The quarters' location must be close enough to some of the Plenum's machinery to disrupt the signal for so long. That did not bode well for the chance of getting a trace on other beacon activity in the area at the time.

He checked the kensakan reports. They had been able to download the beacon's data. Time of death had been several hours earlier, nearly six, which corresponded with his own assessment. The computer suspected cause to be head trauma from blunt force. Never one to trust the scene analysers, he continued to examine the corpse, but he could not see any sign of an injury to match the computer's assessment.

The arms and legs lay against the floor, and the head had lolled to one side. It had stiffened in that position — it made him doubt that the body had been moved — so the murder must have taken place here, which at least was in accord with the report.

'What have we got here?' He said aloud, attention caught by a small mark on the edge of the victim's hairline at the nape of her neck. Something the tools of his — supposedly efficient — team had missed.

It looked like a tiny puncture wound — like one would expect from an old hypodermic needle entry, except there was some blackening and blistering of the skin. Was it poison? Not an air bubble delivered into a vein or artery: it was in the wrong place for starters, but Valko did not need medical confirmation of that — there was the blood around the nose and mouth. It was obvious that his less than bright staff had not considered the meaning of the way the body lay. If this were murder, whether she had been aware of her killer's presence or not, death had been unexpected.

The precision suggested a degree of skill in the murderer — perhaps, more than it suggested that the victim had known them. He noted the dead woman's athletic physique: she would have been strong enough and quick enough, perhaps, to put up a fight, maybe leaving defensive injuries on her assailant — but there was no sign of a struggle. Fingernails were clear of any skin cell deposits from scratching an attacker. If this were murder, someone schooled in deception or stealth had committed it.

There were no other visible injuries, but the difference in the size of each of her pupils was vast: one blown the other constricted. She had a fixed expression as if she died at the point of gritting her teeth. Taking professional care, which made the action almost reverent, he tried to open her mouth. Her jaw was clamped shut, held by rigor mortis suggestive of a penetrating head injury. He had been told that sudden trauma to the brain could cause the jaw to bite down hard. Whether this tension would remain long enough for rigor mortis to set in or not, he did not know — that was a question for the lab — but the site of the mark and the lack of any other apparent cause of death satisfied him. This was, without a doubt, a Class 1 murder scene.

There was no way, even if the victim — for that was the way he thought of her now — was a user of some strange new drug, that she could have injected herself at the angle required to cause the mark. Likewise, he knew of no sex act that involved the insertion of needles into the base of a lover's skull — though given some of the perversions he had encountered when raiding Hotbeds, it would not have surprised him. This could not be a mere lover's tiff or over-enthusiastic, fetishist intercourse. Raucous laughter came from the back room as his men rifled through the belongings there.

Sometimes, Valko wished he could get rid of his staff altogether. In his experience, they were cretins, their education poor and their genes deficient. The average kensakan scraped through the low requirements of the entrance exam. Criminal justice was not a high priority, but they needed a rare few — like he and Satoshi — to examine higher-level matters. They had an unusual job description and even more unusual qualifications.

If you had the wits or the skills to be other than a manual drudge, you stood a good chance of finding a better position than that of a kensakan. Valko thought of the many slang names for the kensakan beyond the simple alternative name of Inspector: Crows, Crackers, and Fiddlers to name but a few — all too appropriate in his opinion. He did not mind the monikers they attracted as he found his own — whether the official Tantei or Moderator or the colloquial Raven or Shivers among the drudges — more flattering. It was strange that the Enclosed used bird names when avians had died out — with the rest of Earth's wildlife — nigh on three generations before. When they existed only in vids now. So many craved contact with some element of the dead past: he had no time for it himself.

Something about the corpse's injury nagged at him. He closed his eyes — took seven breaths — and rubbed the bridge of his nose. The other withdrawal symptoms of NOTT were kicking in, a dull ache behind his eyes and a slight vagueness in his thought process.

He called out, 'Davidson, pour me a coffeine shot and bring the gear back over here. I need a closer look at this puncture wound.'

Jack Davidson grunted his assent and, with some clattering in the small kitchen unit, prepared a shot of the synthetic coffee. A short time later, he came over with the strong smelling liquid. A short, florid man with acrid breath who came close to failing his physical every time, Davidson was at least semi-competent but still suffered from the same lack of discipline and diligence that riddled all the kensakan.

Before Valko's arrival, he knew Davidson and the others would have looked for anything of value and pocketed it — like narc addicts in a medcentre. The scene would have been disturbed and proper procedure ignored. Of course, the need for thorough investigative work was far less. Why bother with forensics when the victim's brain could be stimulated and a Moderator could sift through the fractured, degraded images and feelings it put out? Then, all that needed to be done was to put a suspect in the same room as him — with the mindlink equipment set up — and leave the Moderator to pick through their mind and 'feel' their guilt.

Still, it was sloppy and foolish to rely on the technology and NOTT stimulated powers of the Moderators alone. The splintered sensations from a dead brain were disturbing: prone to disorder and thus confusion or misinterpretation. The level of tissue degradation and brain trauma would lead to a dramatic decrease in efficiency. Nonetheless, this death was recent enough and the angle of the entry wound did not suggest damage to the portions of the brain that would connect to the hub. He would have to try it and see.

'Here you go, Chief. It's not bad stuff,' Davidson said, setting down the small egg-cup sized cup of coffeine, its sharp, acrid odour rising from the syrupy back surface.

A pang for the smell of real coffee rang through Valko, an unusual longing from his half-remembered childhood when old-world luxuries were easier to come by.

'Do you want me to, ah, retrieve her head now or are you going to jack her up here?'

'Davidson, leave the kit here. Take the others out and do a door to door,' Valko said, not bothering to look up.

Davidson muttered something as he walked away — quiet enough that Valko could not hear if it was a — *yes, sir* or a *fuck you* — then called out, 'Chang, Rennard, chief says door to door. See if anyone's seen or heard something. Maybe one of them can tell us if she was a regular.'

A flash of irritation went through Valko at this, even as the other kensakan laughed. It was not the disrespect to the victim — he felt no particular sympathy — but for the effect of his underlings' assumptions on the gathering of the facts. Even if they were right, the consequences would damage his investigation. No doubt, they would make suggestions and allusions that would taint any witness's perceptions. He considered reprimanding them again, but it never worked. His reports on their lackadaisical conduct and contamination of crime scenes always went unanswered. Murder thinned the numbers: the body quickly recycled, the murderer — once identified — rendered the same.

Sometimes Valko thought that the primary interest of his superiors in the Justeco Centro, and the governing Centra Autorita as a whole, was in doubling the reduction in population caused by murder, not in any kind of justice. It was efficient; he almost approved, but something about the casual disregard for the truth offended him. Those times when he delved into the feelings of others — when NOTT was running cold through his veins and arteries, firing parts of his brain otherwise dormant — the injustice stung him.

It was curious to feel the emotions that others felt, of which he was devoid. The irony of his abilities never escaped him: he had no natural empathy or real sympathy for others, yet he could reach into their minds and endure their fear, desire, guilt, sorrow, and joy. Freedom from such emotion was boundless, or so Valko thought whenever the drug wore off. Each time, as it did so, the part of him imbued with the intangible weight of feeling, wept.

With a start, he realised that he had been staring at the cadaver in front of him for several moments — eyes resting on the g-moss: the thick carpet covering every part of the floor and creeping most of the way up the walls. He admired its efficiency, its clarity of purpose: hair, dead skin, sweat, breath — all would be absorbed by the moss and converted; some to oxygen and some to high-energy sugars that would go to a single tuber-like root deep in the floor. The root itself would be harvested periodically and recycled — the fate of all of them, this young woman just sooner than most. Then he noticed something incongruous — g-moss kept the air dry it was so efficient at absorbing moisture, yet there was a perfect droplet of water resting on the surface of the moss by the datapad still held in the dead woman's hand.

He fumbled in the forensic kit next to him for a probe and reached out with it. It could not be water — the moss would syphon it up in an instant — but still, it lay glittering in the biochemical light coming from the ceiling. The probe touched a hard surface and the small, perfect sphere rolled away. He used the probes tiny grippers to pick the small sphere up.

A flash made him jerk back and, an instant later, pain rushed from his hand. When his vision had cleared and the burning pain in his hand had hit home, there was no sign of the globe. Instead, half the probe was on a patch of exposed floor surrounded by burnt moss. The probe was steaming and had melted clean away at one end. An angry red burn mark lined Valko's palm. The datapad was still intact, lying outside the small circle of charred moss.

Valko cradled his injured hand, gasping out a string of obscenities as the pain overrode his normally stiff and formal control. By the time the last expletive left his lips, his auto-hypnotic training had begun to take effect, suppressing the scream from his nerves. He felt a dislocation of the pain, the injury to his hand became just a fact, without the distraction of the agony, which had affected him moments before.

He took his time to reach forward and retrieve the datapad — it did not respond to his touch, yet appeared undamaged. Puzzled, Valko tried to activate the datapad again. The majority of such devices did not rely upon internal power but linked into EATS, the Plenum's energy transmission system. There was no response. Another one for the whitecoats in the lab, perhaps.

He looked again at the face of the murder victim. The contrast between her one blown eye and one constricted was disturbing, but she had once been pretty — beautiful even. In a distant, quiet part of his mind, something stirred, maybe a fragment of compassion. A feeling of the value and fragility of human life strove with the programmed enforcement of the idea that humanity was no more than a sentient virus. In the moment this short and pointless war raged in the depths of Valko's psyche, his analytical mind concentrated on the scene in front of him. There was more evidence here than what was stored in the victim's degrading brain, but if he viewed her memories, it would all fit together.

He applied the sensors and stimulators to her at her temples, crown and the base of her skull before placing a single purpose headset on her. Linking it and the sensors to his own hub, he reached into his case for a dose of NOTT. *PSTS117* was visible, printed in small white letters down the side of the vial. A quiver ran through Valko — he dismissed it as his body's reaction to the suppressed pain of his hand but knew deep inside, it was with anticipation for the drug. He placed the vial on the valve installed in his wrist for this very purpose and pressed down hard, breaking the seal and sending the mixture of raw emotion and ice-cool clarity that was NOTT into his bloodstream.

A rush of sensation overcame him. The pain in his hand returned in a flash, and he cried out with pain, physical and emotional. Looking at the young woman in front of him, he could feel the downward pull of one who's lost a dear and pure love, a child killed in an accident or a beloved sister or mother. Tears sprang to his eyes and, in their suddenness, felt like pinpricks in his fallow tear ducts.

Before he'd been able to describe all the ways in which death might affect the human body without once considering the cost in grief at the loss, the fear and pain of the victim, the end of precious life — now, it was all too poignant. His rational mind began the programmed responses to this overwhelming surge of emotion, but it wasn't up to the task. The emotions had never been so strong before. He remembered with a lurch his contact in the pod on his journey to Berlin Plenum. The middle-aged woman. Despite the feeling of full-on withdrawal from NOTT, had he got it wrong? Had that dose still not worn off?

He'd overdosed before. It was never pleasant, but this deep despair — the consuming pain that was pure emotion and yet felt so physical — was something new and terrifying to him. He was spiralling out of control as if lost, adrift on a sea of emotion. Passion or compassion floored him, and as his agonies reached their apex, his control crashed back down, blocking the raw emotional charge.

His tears dried and some measure of professional detachment returned. He could still feel sympathy for the dead girl in front of him, but it was in proportion. For a short time, he was possessed of an ordinary man's emotional responses. The relief of freedom from his hard, uncompromising nature surprised him, as always.

The precise moment he came to terms with the injection of sentiment, his hub completed its start-up protocol and connected to his mind. He flowed down a dark tunnel into the dead brain of the girl. As he approached connection he struck a blank wall; his mind felt as battered as his body would have.

Stunned for a second, he was back in himself — the hub flashing alerts in his mind. When his thoughts cleared, it became obvious what had happened. The brain that he'd tried to connect to was too damaged. That made sense given the blown pupils, but he'd seen no other external sign of such significant trauma. Most times a small penetrating injury wouldn't prevent retrieval. He switched off the sensors and the stimulators — there was nothing left to stimulate anymore. Gentle, reverent, he removed the device from her head, brushed her hair away from her face and tried to close the lids of her staring eyes.

Such a young woman, killed for no good reason.

Then the clarity of his rational mind took over as he continued the careful process of detaching the sensor/stimulator package. Removing the last probe, he considered again the almost bloodless hole at the base of the victim's hair. Had some sort of toxin that would destroy brain mass been used? A necrotoxin? He pulled out an optical probe and examined the hole. Greater magnification didn't help. It showed cell damage but — being no medical expert — he wasn't any wiser as to the cause of the injury, though he began to think that it looked like localised burns. Linking his hub to the forensic kit's probe, he asked for its analysis. After a short delay, it interpreted the damage to the cells referencing previous crimes — all involved thermal damage at high temperatures.

The wound was too small to insert the probe into, so Valko consulted the hub's weapons directory. A search for the terms *thermal* and *needle* produced no answer. He sat back and thought again. One of the other side effects of the NOTT was a mild increase in creative thinking — he imagined a weapon or device that could break the skin and generate such great heat without creating a larger area of thermal damage. It'd have to be able to penetrate the cranium and damage sufficient mass of brain tissue to prevent stimulation. Grim revulsion at the coldblooded efficiency — an efficiency he might approve of but for NOTT — made him look away while he settled himself.

Finally, he recalled the glass bead — he was unfamiliar with the technology. Like the process of designing new synthorganics, it must have been lost after the War. Adding the final parameter — *Lunar War era weaponry* — he set the hub to working. Then reconsidered and added an addendum search: *thermal bomb, glass-like bead*.

The hub display strobed as it searched; he watched as it exhausted catalogue after catalogue. Abruptly, the software-generated display transmitted into his visual cortex flashed red and alarm sounds that his ears would never hear blared through his mind. The flashing words '*ITF Restricted*' projected on the illusory mental screen. He'd never encountered such a restriction before and — letting curiosity override prudence — Valko tried to bypass the system, only to be met by another wall of red light, this time accompanied by a sharp thrust into his mind.

The pain was like nothing he'd ever felt before. It was only as he tried to pick himself up that he understood he'd fallen flat. There was a dim awareness of voices in the background, but he couldn't focus. His headset was gone and, as he tried to pull himself up, the world started to slip away from him.

Eyes struggling to focus on the real world, his mind still felt like the flashing words were burning there. Davidson rushed over to him, coming in and out of focus, and picked up the hub that still had 'ITF Restricted' flashing away.

'Shit the bed,' Davidson whispered.

The other kensakan began to gather around, looking like the carrion birds that were their namesakes. Valko thought he saw Davidson perform a system dump from the hub into his own unit, but he could not focus and hold onto what he was seeing.

'Take the Chief to the nearest medcentre,' Davidson said. 'He might be permanently fucked. I won't have anyone saying it happened because I didn't get you *pendejo* bastards moving fast enough.'

Valko tried to lock eyes with Davidson, to show he knew what the man was doing, but his mind was draining out of his skull: he couldn't hold on. Had Davidson performed a surface level wipe on the last few minutes' access to his Moderator's hub? He couldn't be doing it to protect his superior. It would be typical of Davidson to try to hold on to some leverage over him. Next time he made a complaint about the kensakan, would he be threatened with this? Would Davidson try to curb his authority with blackmail — to use it to creep up to the rank of Sergeant?

Black lines were forming at the edges of Valko's vision. They snaked inwards towards the centre, all the while creeping down into him, extinguishing his consciousness piece by piece. The last thing he thought of before all fell back into oblivion, was the harsh penalty for trying to access War-era material. Should he survive, even a Moderator of his talent might have to pay for the mistake. The last thing he saw, as blackness rose up around him, was Davidson's smile of low cunning.

CHAPTER 2

Satoshi grunted as he strained against the ever-increasing resistance of the machine. The pressure of blood in his head rose, almost blocking out the faint beeping from the monitoring equipment. He fixated, again, on that strange effect — as if the sound were slowing the more he strained.

'I'm engaging your synthorganics,' said the medtech, her voice soft yet with clipped pronunciation.

He concentrated for a moment — using the techniques he'd been drilled in for so long that sometimes it seemed they alone remained from a forgotten childhood. Lower your consciousness. Relax. Separate all worries from the here and now.

When the here and now was all you had left, it wasn't hard. Except a hollow past was still difficult to escape, wasn't it? This life, the last fifteen years, didn't really count as a past, not compared to the eight decades of nothing that had come before it, and the twelve years of War before that. That time was at worst a blank, at best a blur of scraps and snatches, taunting him just out of reach.

Forgetting the need to be present, here in the moment, his mind flowed backwards. Seeking. There it was, that perfect crystallised memory of his eighteenth birthday, spent surrounded by his family — aunts, uncles, grandparents. Mum and Dad. All gone, now. Then, after that day of joy, there was a jagged black hole.

At the strangest of times, the sound of gunfire would come to him — the rapid clicking of lasers and the rhythmic thudding of ballistics. The crackle of a radio screaming orders. The whistling squeal of air escaping into vacuum.

Then that blinding light in his eyes, and searing heat. The face of someone he knew but couldn't remember, covered in blood. Another's face twisted in horror as air was torn from lungs and eyes were pulled forward in their sockets.

The banging sound. *Was someone coming?*

He didn't remember the Battle of Armstrong or the mop-up exercise of hunting the Lunar Terrorists. Those survivors who'd fled to Earth. He didn't remember what they'd done to him, the hack of his, now dormant, medical nanotech. The same thing they'd done to all his comrades — switched them all off. Course, he'd had only the word of the people who'd defrosted him and the others — these Enclosed. What choice did he have but to take their word for it? Sure, there were murmurs among the others that their memories had been wiped to hide wartime secrets. A little bit of paranoia was no surprise after what they'd been through, but there was no proof of any of the conspiracy theories. So, he accepted the official story at face value.

Unlike the less sophisticated cyborgs that had proceeded them, the naukara, at least he and his fellows hadn't been turned into puppets. No, they'd just fallen down, as good as dead — empty bodies that would go on, ageless. That catatonic state, the medtechs had told him when they woke him, had lasted eighty years. The solution had eluded them so long that he and the others had been put on ice. An end to their drain on resources in the difficult days after Enclosure, without ignoring the legacy of their heroism.

Heroes. What a joke. He knew he'd been a soldier and soldiers do their duty. That didn't make them all heroes. Not in his mind. Waking without a clue about where he was and how he'd got there hadn't been as hard as hearing the truth of it.

They'd named it Lunar War Syndrome — the theft of his and his fellow veterans' memories. The same medical nanites that had laid the foundations of his synthorganics had betrayed him. It should've been impossible, but the Lunar Terrorists' skill exceeded all projections. Military intelligence — Situation Normal All Fucked Up. Those moonbug *kuso yarō* hadn't been able to turn the soldiers, so they'd turned the soldiers' tech against them. Overridden their very selves as the nanites tried to rewrite their brains. It hadn't worked, so they'd sent a pulse that had frozen every synapse. The cryofreeze to keep them safe while a cure was found could hardly have done more damage. It was no wonder they were all screwed in the head. The whitecoats called it amnesia. As if one word could convey their loss.

He remembered when they'd told him what had been done, the only question he could ask was, 'Can you fix it?' The expression on the whitecoats' faces said it all. Fisher himself had come — the grandson not the original. He'd saved the vets from their eight-decades trapped under ice. Without him, the medical nanites would have destroyed their minds on waking, leaving them as empty shells or worse: sending them back to fighting an enemy in a war long ended. But he couldn't fill in the holes in their memories. Couldn't fix their broken, bottled-up psyches. Any attempt to do so had opened the floodgates. Sometimes it'd happened on its own. An instant overload of flashbacks. They talked of PTSD, psychosis, Amok Disorder. Veterans called it going killcrazy. Fisher had called it berserkrgang. That was Lunar War Syndrome.

Satoshi was one of the lucky few. So many of the other vets — the ones who hadn't gone off the deep end and been put down — had had their implants cut out. It'd left them crippled for life. But lucky? Fuck lucky.

Here he was, a new Satoshi Tomari. He'd never know who he'd been before this second life. Never be able to look his son in the eye, when the boy asked him if he'd been a hero during the war. Whatever the records said about him — lauded veteran of the Lunar War — he felt like a fraud. Eight decades on ice, lionised for things he'd didn't remember, all the while kept alive because you don't simply recycle heroes. When you're capable of what the records said he was capable of, it was no surprise they'd feared to revive him. The others were the same. Until Fisher. Before all that, before this new life, deep down there'd been a boy who'd loved training with his grandfather. A boy called Oshi who'd learned everything a proud old man could teach. Those techniques were there — written deeper than any memory.

Lower your consciousness. Relax.

The pressure in his head eased, his muscles relaxed and the beeping sound became both clearer and yet even slower. His implants were coming online and under his control. The resistance of the machine continued to increase, but it came as an afterthought, without strain.

Running amped up like this, even for a routine medical, brought back the vaguest echo of memories. He remembered feeling the buzz of his implants. That feeling that he could do anything. How much of him had been sacrificed for that artificial power?

Thinking of sacrificing the self for power brought Valko to mind. The man was an enigma to him much of the time. He'd volunteered for a process that saw hunks of brain tissue removed and replaced with synthorganic structures.

Satoshi grimaced — and it wasn't with the exertion. When army doctors had improved his muscles, bone, and skin — given him enhanced sight and hearing — they'd known what they were doing. He stopped himself: *it's not like Fisher doesn't know his business*. But the grandson could hardly be expected to live up to the genius of the original. Erasmus had introduced the tech, though if the great man himself had been part of Satoshi's own implantation process, it was one of the many memories that'd been lost to the scouring of the medical nanites from his body. Maybe if the grandfather had been around when he'd been brought out of storage... things could have been different. He could still have had his past.

Eugene, well he'd tried to improve it — to bring back what was lost after Enclosure, the memories and the tech both. Satoshi shied away from thinking of the butchery Val and the other Moderators had undergone. Implants forced into their skulls. At least in his own case, he knew that there'd been no surgery. Instead, the doctors — back when they still called themselves doctors — had injected minute tissue samples that had grown fast to bond with his body in symbiosis. But it was all the same, somehow. The same done to the Moderators as what had been done to him and the other veterans. Some doctor, some whitecoat playing God.

Satoshi realised the resistance of the machine he was in had reached the point where it would have crushed an unaltered human flat. His arms were beginning to register fatigue warnings. Even with retrogening of his natural muscle tissue and skeleton taking him beyond human norms, he would not have been able to sustain this level of pressure without the synthorganic tissue overlaying it. Now that combined synthorganic and retrogened organic tissue could no longer maintain the pressure indefinitely. Still, he was well within safety limits. He concentrated on the medtech's various instruments: heart rate was a fraction above resting but increasing, skeletal stress negligible, muscular stress increasing, and synaptic activity accelerated but otherwise normal.

He inhaled a sharp breath, enjoying the clean air of the examination room — the only odours, beyond the sterile tang of lab equipment, coming from his body and the delicate fragrance of the medtech. Turning his head, he looked at her. She always seemed so delicate to him, but he knew that she was both stronger than she appeared and possessed of staunch determination.

Orla was not a classic beauty — in fact, some would not even regard her as pretty — but she had an inner fire that shone through and made her exquisite. At least, that's what Satoshi thought. So different from his bondmate: Iona was a eugenicist's dream, a perfect physique, gorgeous, and possessed of a fierce intelligence, far beyond his. Yet for all her physicality, she lacked that inner beauty Orla possessed: the sensitivity and kindness. Iona might smile, but there was little warmth in it. When Orla smiled, even his austere Moderator would lighten up — if but a little. He'd always thought that Valko needed more contact with someone like Orla, someone with compassion.

'Alright that's enough, for now, Oshi,' she said, bringing the test equipment down in intensity. 'No need to stress anything. So no problems to report?'

'All fine, thanks, Doc.'

The pressure reduced at a steady rate.

'I'll disengage your synthorganics.'

The feeling of superhuman power slipped away.

'You think I'll ever be free of these checks, Orla?' He asked.

'Maybe. It's better than the alternative, though, right?' He couldn't help notice that Orla was quick to change the subject: she'd have strict instructions not to engage in too much discussion with any veteran about their implants. 'What about Iona and Sadiq? She must be happy with him scoring so highly on his tests. Have you heard where he's being allocated to?'

'Urhh, well sure they're both well. Sadiq's been selected as a possible environmental engineer, or maybe even for the Temple. Personally, I don't want him selected for Martyrdom but... Iona's pleased enough.'

'Still some tension between you two? You should be proud of her involvement in the Temple.'

'I am proud of her; it's just... I don't know. I always thought pair bonding would mean sharing my life and my feelings with someone. Not just breeding a better genetic specimen and then using him for advancement. And nothing I do seems to please her. I don't know. She's always accusing me of being gone too long. Hates it when I spend time training.'

'You're hand-to-hand combat practice?'

'Yeah. Kata. It's like boiling water, take the heat away and... well, you get what I mean. Anyway she's always telling me I'm gone for hours with it — it's true I lose a bit of time, but...'

'You lose time?' Orla asked.

'Not blackouts.' *shit, the last thing I need is for the Doc to start thinking I'm going killcrazy!* 'I just get absorbed. It's called *mushin* — means no mind.'

'That sounds like meditation,' Orla said, and Satoshi nodded. 'Tell her you're doing it on medical advice, if that helps.' Orla winked.

'Thanks, though she's not going to listen.'

He sighed, a sound that rumbled deep inside him, even as the physical pressure ceased. Looking at the cardio trace, he could see his heart rate was elevated. Strange how emotional stress showed more than the physical.

'Sorry,' he said. 'You don't need to hear my problems.'

Orla smiled at him and laid a soft hand on his forearm,'It's alright Oshi. That's part of my job.'

His throat tightened as he found himself admiring her curves under the sterile white coat and wearall. He thought of Iona as hard as he could, but that just made it all the more difficult to look away from Orla. A smile touched her lips, and his hand reached out to touch the hem of her labcoat.

His hub blared as the alert on Valko's collapse came through. Within moments, Satoshi was flying on automatic, dressed and ready to travel to Berlin Plenum, thoughts of Orla buried deep underneath duty.

Common sense kicked in, and he realised that he could do nothing. The Centra Autorita would treat the three-hour roundtrip from Arcas to Berlin as a waste of resources and refuse it while he was on duty.

Still, he couldn't help worrying. Valko was his friend first of all. A strange concept. Friendship with a man who could describe all the ways that it might influence a person, but not feel a shred of attachment himself — to anyone... ever. Satoshi sometimes feared that his own feelings of friendship were a facet of his latent Lunar War Syndrome: some throwback to the brotherhood he'd felt during the War. A part of him always wondered whether it was a side effect of the treatment he had received or if he had been selected, in part, because of his strong sense of loyalty.

That camaraderie — the warrior bond — remained even after the ghosts of memory had been culled from his mind. When he thought of the comrades he'd lost to battle and those who might yet survive, there was only a blank. Maybe it'd been a price worth paying to shut down the medical nanites that had coursed through his every tissue, but it was a cost he could never count.

Whenever he saw one of the other surviving veterans — broken shells stripped of all that had made them special — there was no recognition. All he felt was a rolled up mess of pity and relief. But the call was there: that need for someone to stand shoulder to shoulder with. Maybe, that's why he'd allowed the manacle of his friendship with his Moderator to snap so tightly around him — the frayed ends of feelings seizing on duty and twisting around it into a knot called loyalty.

What he did know was that when Valko was under the effects of NOTT, there was no more dear friend in the world. The sense of brotherhood was repaid, and he could share any fear, worry, joy or hope with the knowledge that he would be understood.

In some ways, it was a relationship that he could never dream of having with his wife. If he and Val had been lovers, it perhaps would be a different dynamic, but he knew that — despite the general encouragement of homosexuality — neither man had that advantage working in their favour. It was sometimes difficult to think of Val as a Breeder like himself rather than a Celibate, given the other man's chill manner.

He might wish that his superior would bond with Orla, but — unless Valko took a dose of NOTT every few hours — it would be a joyless and sterile thing for a young woman of such tenderness. Fighting with his own thoughts, Satoshi battled back his memory of her leaning over him earlier, adjusting medical equipment.

He stopped his idle musing and focused on what information had come through from Berlin Plenum. Realisation of what he was seeing swept aside any self-recrimination for his absence from his friend's side. A report had come in, more than a half hour before, about a charred body down in the lower reaches of Arcas Plenum. Two things struck him. The delay in identifying the corpse was unusual given the ease of DNA profiling. And the appearance of the crime scene itself.

The circular burn on the floor of the room in Berlin-Plenum, where Davidson and the others were moving Valko's limp form, matched that found at the under-level murder scene. He'd need to confirm the link to establish jurisdiction. Otherwise, there'd be another Moderator assigned before his could get a look in. The journey to Berlin was not a waste of resources on his own over-emotionalism after all — not going would be the waste. He made the request — holding his breath — the Centra Autorita granted consent.

Strapping on his sidearms, the standard issue tranqgun on his left hip and his Veteran's omni-pistol at his back, Satoshi dashed from the medcentre and out into the plaza in front of Arcas Plenum's Justeco Centro. Like every open space, it was packed with Enclosed — but here there was less of a chaotic melee and more of a dignified queue. Not a drudge in sight. The freshness of the g-moss on the buildings and the proximity to the seat of justice created a calmer zone than the hustle everywhere else.

Satoshi felt no sense of decorum restrain him. Tugging on his jacket and his sergeant's skullcap, he shouldered his way towards the nearest transpod staging area. He was so lost in his thoughts that he felt no pang of remorse about knocking people in their immaculate wearalls out the way of his broad form.

†††

Valko floated in a dream state. His mind grasped the concept of unconsciousness, but as he tried to hold onto the idea, it slipped away from him. He was drifting in a liquid that was thinner than air. There was no sense of body, weight, light, heat, time. Images flickered on the edge of his awareness, fluttering as if a breeze had caught them. He tried reaching for them, but he had no hands with which to reach. He tried following, but he had no legs with which to run. Memories stirred of the countless times he had travelled down the tunnel between his mind, and another's with the help of NOTT and the neural interface. As if the memory of it were enough to trigger its effect, Valko's consciousness surged forward down a shaft of nothingness, towards the nearest flickering image. He entered that single fractured thought and found there, like a frozen frame of vid footage, a field of green g-moss. In that instant, he saw, reflected in the tiny globes of moisture held by the moss, an image of the young woman's face locked in terror. Then — like the shock of plunging into cold water — he was once more in the emptiness in which he had first found himself. A weight pressed on him and with awareness of his body...

...pain pounded through his brain. He was strapped down on some sort of board with the gelatinous membrane of a respirator clogging his mouth and nose. Its synthorganic body was regulating his breathing while microscopic tendrils penetrated the skin above his carotid and linked with the artery, assisting in oxygenation of his blood with the device's gills helping his body's own efforts to keep him alive.

What was going on? He could make out a vague, fuzzy shape, the rough size of Davidson, but the membrane that covered his face prevented clearer vision — something to do with a combined need for measuring pupil dilation and avoiding excessive external stimuli for someone in shock. The momentary panic he had felt at regaining consciousness was already receding, and calm lassitude swept over him. Allowing himself to float again on the edge of consciousness, he felt strange as if the moments before his injury were as dream-like as floating in the void.

With that same detachment, he questioned what was happening to him. Without the mental haze of panic, the answer came bubbling to the surface. The membrane. It made subtle alterations to his blood chemistry, dulling pain, sending calming neural impulses into him, and triggering a deep response buried in his unconscious mind: much like the memory of a mother's heartbeat from its time in the womb would soothe an infant.

Behind this somnolent musing, he reflected on what had happened. What was he investigating that it involved ITF material restricted at the terminal level? Logic and ruthless self-interest reasserted themselves as the last of the NOTT drained from him. He had allowed his emotions over the fate of the young woman to induce him into reckless action. What foolishness: jeopardising his career and his life. Then it registered: ITF restricted. A device that would destroy the brain as it killed. Some sort of localised incendiary. Assassination. There was one problem: why would anyone want to assassinate this young woman?

The board under him moved, and he heard a voice, dulled

by the membrane yet identifiable as Davidson, 'Don't stew Chief. I'm sure you'll find a way of repaying me.'

Valko struggled with this for a moment but, with the lassitude growing stronger, he gave in to the allure of deep, dreamless sleep.

✝✝✝

Satoshi arrived at the medcentre and straightway found Davidson loitering outside the treatment room. The sour odour of the man reminded him of cheap bourbon. Davidson must have maintained contacts with someone running an illegal still in the upper sectors. What was wrong with him? Satoshi suffered from his own disillusions about the control of the Centra Autorita and the Temple, but he never let those feelings lead him into crossing the line as Davidson was. Poor bastard. Must be the hardship of selection for compulsory sterilisation.

'What's going on Jack? What happened to the Tantei?' Satoshi said.

Davidson didn't respond but motioned for Satoshi to follow him a few steps to an area of the medcentre overgrown with g-ivy. Satoshi followed, somewhat reluctant, his patience with Davidson limited.

'It's like this, Sarge. Moderator Gangleri was looking at ITF constricted material. Like Lunar War stuff. Kind of thing protected by Terminal doo-dah security.'

Davidson leant in to say this to Satoshi in a harsh whisper. The smell of poorly distilled whisky on his breath was almost overpowering. One-handed, Satoshi seized Davidson behind his neck. To an observer, it would come across almost as a reassuring gesture between colleagues, but the big man's hand was exerting a degree of force on Davidson's fat neck designed to send a clear message. Discomfort could turn to agony with one twitch of a hand.

Satoshi ignored the liquor fumes and leant even closer to Davidson, 'What have you told them about it?'

'Nothing Sarge, nothing,' Davidson said, spittle flying from his loose mouth. 'Honest. It's why I waited here for you. Didn't want our man getting trouble. Don't think the chief meant to get into it. I told them it was neural feedback from the corpse.

You know, like what happened to that Tantei over in Tokyo Plenum, a few years back.'

'Zalinsky. Yeah, I remember. Quick thinking,' Satoshi said. His attitude changed and he reduced the pressure on Davidson's neck, letting it become more of a friendly squeeze. 'Not that you'd be thinking of holding this over our Moderator's head, now would you?'

'No, no. Of course not,' Davidson said, licking his rubbery lips. 'Look, Sarge. I respect the chief. You know that. But… he's a scary bastard. I mean, he'd feel nothing squashing me. You know, sending me to a dead end posting, the kind where you end up… well… dead. I wouldn't fuck with him any more than I'd fuck with the Old Man.'

'Davidson. Word of advice. Don't call Tantei Gangleri 'chief' and whatever you do, don't call Pravnik Odegebayo the 'Old Man'. Now do your job, keep your mouth shut and I'll stop you getting dead ended, right?'

'Yes, Sarge. Thank you. I'll get back to it — we've had no luck on the door to doors yet,' Davidson said.

He started to fill Satoshi in on the progress of the investigation.

Satoshi held up one hand, 'Wait.'

Davidson spluttered to a stop, while Satoshi grabbed one of the medtech's coming out the medcentre's door.

'You. Let me know the moment Tantei Gangleri regains consciousness.'

He let the man go and watched as he rubbed his arm and scuttled into the building. Turning back to Davidson, Satoshi fought back the desire to give the *bakayarō* some more physical motivation.

'Get on with it, Jack.' He said.

✟✟✟

The air in the recovery room was heavy with the antiseptics released by the modified g-moss coating every wall, but Valko found the smell familiar, even comforting. He was sitting propped up in bed, irritated by the unaccustomed softness of the surface and the spongy pillow behind him. When Satoshi stepped into the recovery room, Valko was still trying to shift to a better position for reading the scene report on his datapad.

Satoshi, his scarred face coming alight, spoke first, 'Val, I worried you'd been hurt. I'm glad to see you're alright.'

'Oshi, I'm fine.'

For a moment, Valko appreciated his friend's concern. No, not his friend's, his subordinate's concern. The hard cage around his heart slammed down again.

'You forget yourself, Sergeant. If you keep up with these emotional outbursts, it will cloud your judgement. Now, what has been happening while I was incapacitated?'

'Sorry, sir. It won't happen again.' Valko knew Satoshi's answer was reflexive — it would happen again. 'I've had the scene preserved, and the deceased sent for autopsy. We've identified her as Iduna Vinnetti. She's a whitecoat who works with Dr Fisher. Your attempt to identify the explosive device triggered an old ITF security protocol; it nearly fried your brain. Davidson scrubbed records of that from your headset-hub, but I don't trust his motives. I've warned him off.'

'Thank you, Sergeant. You have been doing your job after all,' Valko said.

Vague memories stirred of Davidson smiling down at him. He dismissed them — he would deal with Jack Davidson... later.

'Yes, sir. I've identified the owner of the quarters: Darius Actur. He's a drudge, but with techspert status, hence the better quarters.'

'You have identified him? Then why have you not apprehended him already?' Valko said.

'Sir, his beacon can't be located. The Centra Autorita lost tracking on him some days ago. He was last stationed in Outpost Theta outside the ruins of New York, on a maintenance job that needed his specialisation.'

Valko frowned, 'Strange, beacons don't simply disappear unless the carrier wave is blocked or the beacon itself is destroyed. Any report of a lost transpod?'

'No. It's not clear whether he boarded one. Retrieval of Outpost records is as unreliable as normal, and that's doubly true of Outpost Theta: it's still under construction,' Satoshi said.

He was standing at attention, ramrod straight, though he managed to look comfortable — no, natural — in the position. Valko massaged the bridge of his nose — pulse throbbing behind his eyes.

'Actur must remain a potential suspect. He may have chosen to remove his beacon to come back here and kill Vinnetti.'

'I agree, sir. It's possible someone who had been out in the ruins of New York could have obtained a flashburner,' Satoshi said.

'A flashburner?' Valko fixed Satoshi with a keen stare as his mind whirred through the implications: flashburners had been the type of bomb used to devastate the Mother in the Lunar War. 'What use would a bomb be?'

'A miniaturised version, sir. I think that was the explosive you encountered and it would explain the ITF security. All information on flashburners would be restricted,' Satoshi said.

A medical whitecoat came in and began to check Valko's vital signs. He fussed about for a few minutes, without saying a word, before marking something on a datapad and stepping out.

'I thought you didn't remember the War — what with the Syndrome and all that,' Valko said. He had adopted the tone he used when conducting a verbal interrogation.

'Yes, sir. But I do remember some things about the equipment. I must've come across flashburners in one form or another — I just don't remember it. I just know that what you found was a flashburner without being able to tell you how I know. Sorry, I can't be clearer.' Satoshi broke eye contact, intimidated by the much smaller man — inside, Valko smiled.

Even without his synthorganic musculature active, Satoshi would have had little trouble breaking Valko in half. The sergeant was almost twice his size, had been retrogened for strength and endurance and had extensive training in hand-to-hand combat. Despite all of that, he was, once again, cowed by the impact of the Moderator's gaze.

Valko's datapad sounded a soft chime. He checked it and saw two new messages. One was from the chief medtech informing him that he was fit to be discharged. The other was from his superior, Pravnik Odegebayo — the troubling summons urgent.

'There's been a report of a second corpse found in sector seven-delta-niner of the under-levels over in Arcas — burn marks on the scene suggest a similar weapon used, and the same MO,' Satoshi said.

'ID?'

'Not come back yet. First kensakan on site wasn't with a homicide team. Looks like she decided not to tread on anyone's toes.'

'Get one of ours on it — I don't want to have to squabble with another Moderator over jurisdiction.'

'Already done, sir. Chang and Rennard are en route.'

'Good. Set Davidson to investigate Actur and have him check the records for beacon traffic in and out of both loci: if there was a witness to the murder we need to find them. Who knows, perhaps the murderer's beacon will have been recorded at the scene. If he cannot locate Actur in Berlin Plenum, I want him to head out to Outpost Theta. You supervise the autopsy. I know you are familiar with our seconded medtech, get her to do a thorough job. I want her to check a wound I saw on the base of Vinnetti's skull. Have her do a full cranial exploration. And let me know as soon as we have ID on the second body.'

Valko talked as he dressed in his moderator's uniform and strapped on his tranqgun. He took a moment to assess his appearance in the small mirror on one wall, its reflective surface emerging from the surrounding g-moss. His gaunt, amber eyes stared back at him, but he noted with satisfaction that they added to the severity of his appearance, his pallid skin over hard features made sharper by the close regulation crop of his black hair. He was ready to see his superior.

'Where will you be if I have any results, sir?' Satoshi asked.

'They will have to wait. I'm seeing the Pravnik.'

Valko left the medcentre and, after navigating the surging crowd outside, managed to make his way to the nearest transpod dock. He rushed onto an Arcas Plenum bound 'pod and wedged himself in a corner to get some space. Recent events ran through his mind. What had he done that might trigger a summons from the Pravnik, save accessing ITF material? Satoshi's efforts to conceal his activity should have prevented the Pravnik from finding out. Valko had heard some wild theories about the Centra Autorita's ability to monitor the inhabitants of a Plenum. None of the investigations that he had been involved in — and some of those had been high level — had ever revealed such a source of information. The Old Man could not know.

Unless it was Davidson? That worthless moron might

have sold him out for a short-term advantage. Or revenge? Getting back at Valko for a less than glowing, albeit accurate report on his work. No, Davidson would not want to risk his anger. If Valko received a minor reprimand or even no reprimand at all, Davidson would risk permanent deployment to one of the less pleasant Outposts.

Life in a Plenum was cramped and unpleasant, but it was infinitely preferable to the Outposts. There was no guarantee that an Outpost was secure from radiation, nanodestroyers or even mundane environmental risks from turbulent weather patterns. Hundreds of people died every day in the average Plenum but the mortality rate in an Outpost — even the nominally secure ones — was ten times higher.

The worst places were those where groups of survivors who had missed Enclosure had eked out an existence. Most were savage and prone to frequent attempts to raid Outposts. What with all the War-era tech still lying around in the ruined cities of places like North America, the Remnants — the official designation of such survivors — were a genuine threat to small Outposts.

Davidson was many things, but he was not so stupid as to risk a permanent deployment. No, if this was about his unwise access attempt, then the Pravnik had found out in a different way — if not that, then Valko had no idea.

He settled back and, reluctant to use his hub again so soon, began drafting a report on the investigation using his datapad. It was far slower than direct thought typing, but he felt uncomfortable with the idea of linking his brain to the headset again. It was a weakness. One he should not tolerate, but, for the moment, he allowed himself some human frailty. The transpod, packed with its human cargo, sped on through the dark sky.

┼┼┼

Satoshi took his time as he readied to return to Arcas Plenum. He didn't much care for it, but the duty of making sure the corpse of the young woman, Vinnetti, was preserved fell to him. Looking around the crime scene, he felt the itch of memory, like severed synapses trying to reconnect. The quarters were familiar, familiar enough that he began to wonder if maybe he'd been to this part of Berlin before Enclosure. The feeling faded. It'd happened to him more than enough times over the last fifteen years, but it never came to anything — no matter how hard he tried, how much he hoped.

Once he'd satisfied himself that they'd scanned the whole scene and could revisit it via a hub replay at any time, he had one of the other kensakan prep the corpse to be flash frozen. As he looked at the cold face, with its staring, mismatched eyes, a bubble of nausea started to rise in him. He tried to close the eyes, but the lids wouldn't stay shut. Turning away helped and he gestured at the other kensakan to get on with it — desperately holding onto his composure.

Pull yourself together,' he told himself and went to double-check the accounts of the occupants of the neighbouring quarters, some were in, some he had to contact by headset. Like they'd told Davidson, Chang and Rennard, no one had seen or heard anything, and no one knew that there had been any visits by a Whitecoat. The local residents all described Actur as being an ordinary guy, nothing more. Neither a nice nor a horrible neighbour. The answers he'd expected. Living so close together bred a tendency to pay no attention to one's neighbours as often as it encouraged a sense of community. There were no leads here.

Next, he checked the background of Vinnetti. She was mid-twenties. Intelligent. Highly skilled and well educated. Attached to confidential research projects led by the enigmatic Eugene Fisher, grandson of the late, great, Erasmus Fisher who had made Enclosure possible. Satoshi had the vague sense that he had known the older Fisher, but so much of his past was blank he couldn't be sure whether he had only been familiar with the name.

His recognition of the flashburner preyed on his mind. There it was again: the pulling sensation from his memories. When he tried to think back — to follow that pull — he came up blank, the memory a word on the tip of his tongue: so close yet out of reach. He wanted to remember. But Lunar War Syndrome had robbed him of so many years, just as it had taken them from every survivor.

Yet here he was: strong, healthy, preserved in his early thirties. The medtechs had told him he didn't look a day older than he had when he'd gone into stasis. Freezing wouldn't have stopped the process completely and then there'd been the fifteen years since his awakening. The mirror told the lie that time had been suspended, but he felt those years inside. Synthorganics had done more than make him strong — they seemed to have stopped his aging process. But what was the point of living forever if you couldn't remember the most important parts of your life?

Still, the medtechs regarded him as rehabilitated — aside from regular check-ups to activate, test and then deactivate his synthorganics — he could live what passed for a normal life in these blighted days. A life that would last, perhaps, another hundred or more years without intervention.

He could still do some good in this world — he'd been given time for a reason, he knew it. It would be hard to bring some of the old values back into the bleakness of life within the Plena, but he could do it in a small way. He could teach his son, and maybe, just maybe, he could reach Valko. Why did he feel such genuine affection for his superior? Perhaps, because he saw someone who was — in his own way — as fucked up as Satoshi was himself. Or it could just be his mind, screwing with him.

Satoshi shook off his navel-gazing and returned to the task. He commandeered space on a freight transpod for Vinnetti's corpse and rode with it, back to Arcas Plenum. On the way, he identified her quarters. She had lived and worked in Arcas Plenum. Why had she been in Berlin Plenum?

Davidson's theory was still the best explanation — but how had she met Darius Actur in the first place and why had she been so taken with him that she had travelled to the drudge's quarters in a different Plenum? From looking at his file, he was twenty years older than she was. Rugged looking, not handsome. Had it been more about a rebellion from what was expected of her?

He checked the files but could see no sign that the Centra Autorita had selected them as compatible mates — she wasn't even marked as a Breeder. No sign that either Plenum's internal eugenics program had requested a mixing of their DNA. This was all beyond him, but that was why Valko was the Moderator, and he was the sergeant.

His hub buzzed with an update, and Satoshi nearly dropped the device.

'Chikusho!' Satoshi swore. 'No, no, no — it can't be. It

fucking can't be!'

The DNA test had come back, confirming the ID of the second murder victim. Satoshi tried to connect to Valko's hub, but there was no reply. He must already be in the Old Man's office.

Chapter 3

Valko arrived at the core of Arcas Plenum — the bustling green heart with its g-ivy cloaked towers extending vertically in both directions, almost to the edge of sight. A walkway — one of dozens forming the web between buildings, festooned with modified plant life and crammed with people — lay between him and the tower that housed the Justeco Centro. After an age of flowing through the crowds, he broke through to the clearer area surrounding his destination.

In theory, he had an office here but when he stood up his head brushed its ceiling, and it did little more than house a secure store for backing up his case files. The occasional case review took place within Justeco Centro, but it was, in truth, just a focal point for processing all the information flowing in from kensakan and Moderators across the Plena. On the other hand, it did house the portion of the Centra Autorita's data network dedicated to criminal analysis, making it more than just a data warehouse — that and being the base for the Pravniks. Twelve of the most experienced Moderators — from before regular use of the implants and NOTT — were the final arbiters in every case within their remits. Life and death were decided by a quick reference to a Moderator's Pravnik.

Valko had never known Odegebayo to do anything other than sanction a swift execution of an offender. He doubted the Old Man ever spent more than a couple of minutes reviewing a case file before ordering a death. Which was the way it should be.

By the time a case file reached the Pravnik, the Moderator in charge would have been certain of guilt and have identified any extenuating circumstances. Valko had never composed a report until after he was certain that he had no remaining NOTT in his system. Absent the millstone of compassion, he consistently failed to identify any extenuating circumstance for the Pravnik to mitigate sentence or defer execution.

That said — his adherence to a logical process of investigation had saved more than one innocent from the bungling of his kensakan seizing on the most probable suspect, instead of seeking the true culprit. Valko slept at night with a clear conscience — at least he never felt bad about anything he'd done — even when plagued by dreams made from leftover memory fragments. He told himself it was because he did the job right — on those days when he was unwilling to acknowledge the truth about himself.

He made his way to Odegebayo's office and settled in to wait with the twenty others in a cramped room; yet, after a few minutes, the ubiquitous computer voice called him in.

'Gangleri, come in. Sit down,' Pravnik Odegebayo said.

The Old Man, Valko had never learned his first name, sat behind an old-fashioned desk covered with the omnipresent fine layer of g-moss — though this variety had taken on more of the parched look of lichen. The desk was stacked with hardcopies, assorted datapads, and three different headset-hubs. This dried out husk of a man, whose dark face was seamed with deep lines and his beard and hair were shot through with grey, held a tight rein on all the Moderators beneath him.

'I see you have recovered from your misadventure. Anything you want to tell me?' He gave the impression that he was affable and even concerned, but the question cut straight to the heart of Valko's fears.

'Yes, Weiyuan,' Valko said, using Odegebayo's political title — each of the Pravniks had a seat in the Conclave of the Centra Autorita. 'I stumbled across a device which, when I sought to identify it, turned out to be under ITF restriction.'

If he had been discovered, the best thing to do was be honest. It was his sole chance.

'Strange and unexpected.'

The Old Man acted taken aback, and his convivial demeanour broke for a moment. The usual broad smile on his face faded, the deep seams around his eyes shifting as he scowled at Valko.

'And so you sought the answer and paid the inevitable price? I suppose I should expect nothing else of you, should I, Gangleri?'

'Weiyuan, I...' Valko began, but Odegebayo cut him off.

'Don't interrupt me. You were lucky. Lucky that your attempt to access the data was ITF restricted and not restricted by the Centra Autorita. Your inability to let go of a lead usually does you credit, but you strayed close to the line this time,' Odegebayo said, as his face resumed its genial mien. 'At least you had the sense not to try to conceal it from me. I will overlook your transgression, for now, because you will not repeat your mistake, will you?'

'No Weiyuan, I…'

'Good. Now as to why I summoned you here. There is a matter that I need you to deal with. It is sensitive in the extreme and, I think, connected to your current investigation,' Odegebayo said and stroked his beard, fixing Valko with his startling, green eyes — a side-effect of retrogened macula repair. 'Eugene Fisher has been murdered.'

†††

Valko stepped out of the service lift. The smell of rot was overpowering. The source of the stench of decaying flesh — that thing so rare in the Plena — was obvious. A body. Its lower half was scorched away, the rest part-devoured by vermin. Rats and cockroaches, the only true survivors of the War save humans. The corpse was dressed in what must have once been a white lab coat. Its self-cleaning fabric was so damaged that it could not cope with the dirt and had greyed far faster than he would have expected. There was a scorch mark on the floor around some burnt scraps of hardcopies and the remains of what looked to be an old-style briefcase. The kensakan on the scene cleared out of his way as he walked closer and squatted down next to the corpse. Most of the legs were missing, and the flesh was charred. The head was still intact, although the face was unrecognisable. Decay was minor, though accelerated by the humid conditions, but the vermin had done their work.

He held out a hand to the nearest kensakan — Chang he thought the man's name was — and said, 'Probe.'

Chang hurried to retrieve a probe for his superior and stepped back as quickly — though whether to get away from the smell of the corpse or to avoid him, Valko did not know and did not care. He used the probe to turn the head and saw, almost obscured by the rapid decay of the surrounding flesh, the small burn mark and entry hole. The same modus operandi as the murder of Vinnetti, or at least the same choice of weapon.

Given the conditions the body had been exposed to — the humidity and constant dripping of contaminated water and the attention of the local rodent population — his best guess put the time of death close to that of Vinnetti, maybe a couple of hours before, at most. She'd lain undiscovered because of a blackout of beacon signal. But the disappearance of someone of Fisher's status should have been noticed far sooner. The foremost whitecoat in all the Plena couldn't lie dead in the under-levels with no one realising it. Yet, here he was.

'Chang, have you found anything else?'

'No, sir. Nothing but what you see there.'

Valko glanced around, 'Who found the body?'

'Routine maintenance sweep by a drudge. He reported it immediately. He saw nothing and knows nothing, so he says.'

'Check his whereabouts for the approximate time of the murders.'

Thoroughness paid off. Although, there were times it meant unnecessary work.

'Yes, sir,' Chang said and hurried off to make enquiries.

There did not appear to be much else of use at the crime scene. It was an area to avoid. Despite the cramped nature of the Plenum, most of the Enclosed shunned the under-levels. The machinery that made the Plenum's systems function — the recyclers for air, water, biomass and all other waste — needed the space down here. Part of it was also that the recyclers would be where corpses ended up: it made the under-levels take on something of the air of a graveyard. Not that any bodies were kept there. All were fed into the recyclers to be broken down into the basic organic chemicals that made up every living thing and were used to synthesise all the organic products available in the Plenum: from food to soap and clothing.

No one lived down here, except the few illegal entrants to the Plena or those whose parents concealed their births for fear of sterilisation: the wei-zhuce, trying to evade detection. Even they tended to remain as close as possible to the inhabited areas. Drudges tasked with maintenance would travel through at times, but if there was an accident, if some of the machinery malfunctioned while being repaired, it was an isolated place. Help for a trapped worker would be far away, and data communication was blocked over a few hundred metres for large sections of the under-levels.

No, there was no point in looking for living witnesses. 'Rennard. What about security monitors? Where is the nearest?'

The remaining kensakan blanched at being spoken to by Valko — *good*.

'Tantei, the only one within range of this location is by the door but... it's just a light, sir. No sign of a camera. I checked the wider area. No alerts were triggered around the time of the murder so no footage will have been recorded,' Rennard said, his words tumbling out in a torrent.

Valko looked around once more and his gaze settled on the elevator. They were rare in Arcas Plenum, but this building was one of the few that had internal access to all floors. Fisher had been heading into the building that housed the Conclave of the Centra Autorita. The importance of the location explained why the elevator required the security of a door scanner. A thought occurred to him, the door scanner was old, like a model that still relied on visual recognition. If so, there was a chance that Fisher accessed it before he died. It might, just might, have captured an image of his murderer.

'Rennard, get a techspert down here. I want access to the last images recorded by the door scanner.'

┼┼┼

The image was distorted. The lens of the door scanner had been designed to afford greater focus on the eyes of anyone approaching, so there had been a clear read of Fisher's irises. The result matched his file and, despite some abnormal markers on the gene test — an unexplained rapid degradation of his DNA post-mortem — Valko was satisfied that this was the real Dr Eugene Fisher.

'Is this all there is to it? A single frame of vid? No headset compatibility?' Valko asked.

'No Boss,' Davidson said, his face illuminated by the light from the screen in the otherwise dark techroom. 'It's just a flat image, no hub link to feel like you're there, no three-dimensional projection to walk around. This is it. I mean there's more vid, but it's real low quality. I've got the tech working on bringing it up to watchable quality, but, so far, this is the clearest shot of the murderer.'

Part of the distortion of the image appeared to have twisted the shadows under the nearby Plenum stanchion, but the other half of the image was clear enough. There was a male figure: a mass of dirty blond hair and beard coming out from under a tattered hood. The quality of the image was poor beyond those details.

'Can we enhance this any further?' Valko asked, leaning close to the screen.

'I can't guarantee that there's no distortion from the enhancement,' the tech said.

Valko ground his teeth, but the tech carried on, seemingly oblivious, 'No matter what I do I can't get the shadow to resolve when I use light amplification. I can get you a clear view of the vagrant's face, though. Well, as good as you'd get with all that beard and hair.'

The tech, clearly wary of Valko's remorseless reputation when it came to assessing his subordinate's performance, seemed to be doing his utmost. His work was sterling, enough that Valko almost began to forget that he was there. He gave no thought of praise or recommendation, but for the tech, avoiding criticism should be as good as high praise from another Moderator.

'Strange. What's special about that shadow?' Satoshi asked.

'It's likely a data artefact. I've checked the scanner itself, and there is no problem with the camera despite its age. Old systems sometimes suffer temporary, unexplained glitches. I'll keep at it until I have a definitive answer, though, sir.'

'Relax; you're doing an excellent job. And I'm only a sergeant, no need to call me Sir,' Satoshi said.

Valko glared at Satoshi, 'Sergeant, are you quite done with the small talk? Tech officer…'

'Doolan, sir,' the young man interrupted, nerves apparently making him misinterpret the pause in Valko's speech.

Valko took full notice of the young man, and his icy expression made the tech swallow hard, 'Tech officer, show me the rest of the footage. We will return to this still — if it is the best image you can produce.'

The tech's voice broke like a teenage boy's as he answered, 'Yes, sir. But...'

'Just do what the Boss says, you dumbfuck,' Davidson said.

Valko stared at Davidson — one of his dead-eyed stares where his eyes widened, just a bit too much. Davidson backed up a step and looked away mumbling what sounded like an apology — *good*. He didn't need that moron interfering with the key details of the investigation. A curl of amusement — a foreign feeling to him without chemical assistance — flickered deep inside him. He caught Satoshi's eye and saw the feeling mirrored there — ah, so it was not his feeling but a reflection of his sergeant's. From the NOTT dose, he'd taken... wait, no that had worn off.

'Sir, sir! It's ready, sir!' The tech's voice cut through any further introspection.

'What?' Valko said.

'The footage, sir. Look.'

The screen filled with low-quality vid footage. It was grainy and overlaid with flickering lines and blots of colour, but it was continuous, not skipping from second to second. Like the still photo, the focus was off, but the tech made a couple of adjustments, and the image tightened up — a bit.

Valko stared at the scene unfolding before him, his face getting closer to the screen as he tried to make out what was happening.

'Slow it down to twenty-five per cent,' He said.

Fisher was nearing the door, briefcase in hand and a tense look on his face. Not the fear of someone being stalked but definitely the look of extreme stress. Behind him, creeping from shadow to shadow, came the bearded man from the still photo — little more than a hazy image but getting clearer every moment, as he approached Fisher. The man began to take something from under his ragged clothing but then stopped dead. The bearded man's expression changed from a narrow-eyed look of greed to something else — something to check on the still.

Valko's attention was drawn to Fisher — he'd frozen. Blood trickled from his left nostril. He started to slump, was caught and lowered to the ground. His killer — not the bearded man but someone who appeared as a blotchy dark silhouette — kept out of the light from the scanner and removed a thin wire from the back of the dead man's skull. The filament still glowed white hot — the incandescence blurring the display for a moment before it coalesced once more. The weapon was smoking with blood and brain matter, while the wire itself was curling this way and that, almost as if hunting for another victim.

The vague, dark shape of the killer straightened. With one flex of the wrist, the cooling wire retracted, snapping into a black cylinder held in its gauntleted hand. Then the silhouette crouched over the dead man, deftly checking pockets. They found something — it must have been the key — and opened the old briefcase, rifling through it.

The killer took a hardcopy out and — with a nonchalant gesture — flicked something away, then tucked the hardcopy into the dark haze of their body and began to walk away. There was a bright flash, which whited out the image for a full second of the recording.

When it cleared again, there was no sign of the indistinct figure of the murderer. Fisher was sprawled on the ground — what was left of him. His legs and the lower half of his torso had burnt away. The briefcase was no longer visible; there was just a charred patch of ground and rising steam.

The bearded man had remained fixed in position, his face as rigid as his body. Now, he moved with quick, furtive movements — whatever had been in his hand was tucked away again. He picked over the remains, snatching up items — the image quality had degraded significantly after the flash, Valko couldn't make out what was taken. Then the bearded man reached down to something on the ground, just out of the camera's field of view. He reacted as though it had hurt him — cradling his right hand and opening his mouth in what must have been a scream of pain. After doing something with his clothing — binding his hand perhaps? — he reached back down to whatever it was he'd reached for before. Picked it up. Turned away and scuttled back off-screen. The footage ended.

'Play it again. One-tenth speed.'

Valko watched it again, then at full speed, and then slow again, demanding pauses and rewinds.

'So the shadow is a data artefact, is it?' Valko asked.

'Er... no, sir. Sorry, sir. It's some kind of camouflage system. Probably a fixed matrix program imprinted onto the surface of a skinsuit, maybe with a stealth weave as well,' the tech said.

'What?' Valko asked.

Satoshi stepped up. Trust him to try to protect some inept tech incapable of explaining a theory in layman's terms.

'Sir,' Satoshi said. 'He means the suit uses a pattern which contains a program stored in it as a quick response code. Any optical device — camera or security monitor — that records the code inadvertently uploads that program. If I understand correctly, that program then alters the image as it is stored or transmitted.' The tech was nodding. 'A stealth weave is...'

'Yes. Thank you, Sergeant,' Valko said.

Satoshi saluted and stepped back.

'You...' Valko turned back to the tech. '...is there any way to circumvent the effect?'

'No, sir. Not to my knowledge. At the point where the image is converted to a binary signal, the program is already at work. After the image is captured, you could no more get behind it than see through a physical block over the camera lens.' The tech looked like he was going to say more but apparently thought better of it. Good.

'Bring up the still image again.' It leapt onto the screen. 'Can you get an iris scan or facial recognition on that man?' Valko jabbed a finger into the image of the bearded man.

'Yes, sir. Comes back negative. Unregistered, no indoctrination file. He must be wei-zhuce.'

'Wei-zhuce. Interesting. Why burn the suitcase?'

'Maybe it was an inbuilt security system to prevent the loss of sensitive data?' Satoshi said.

'Maybe, but why would such a thing be necessary?' Valko asked.

'It looked old enough to be War era, sir. In those days all data was treated as sensitive,' Satoshi said.

Remembering his recent, near-fatal brush with the old security systems, Valko grunted and turned back to the image.

'Could the murderer have used a miniature flashburner?'

Satoshi asked. Valko had been considering that very thing — if so, the parallels with the Berlin Plenum case were striking — , but the footage was just too poor to be sure what caused the second flare of light — the briefcase or something else. He ignored Satoshi and focused on the glint of something metallic in the bearded vagrant's left hand.

'Is that a knife?'

The tech adjusted the settings, and the image displayed the object at life size proportions. It had caught the flash of green light from the door scanner, and it made it difficult to see.

'Accounting for the high albedo,' the tech said, sounding for a moment like the ubiquitous Plenum computer voice.

The image resolved and they could see that it was a small, narrow bladed knife. It looked like it was made from discarded scrap metal.

'A shiv,' Valko said. 'Too wide to match the entry wound. Definitely not the murder weapon — that much is clear from the footage. Besides, there's no sign of it having a thermal element to it.'

The last was not a question, but the tech clearly felt compelled to respond.

'No, sir. In accounting for the albedo of the knife, I was careful to preserve the object's thermal profile. Look,' he said as he adjusted the settings again; the colours changed as the image shifted to the infrared. 'The blade is only marginally warmer than air temperature like he'd been holding it up his sleeve for some time.'

Valko turned to fix the tech once more with a look. He nodded slowly, turning things over in his mind, 'He's not our murderer, but he clearly had a crime on his mind. Since he's unregistered and without a beacon, he may be hard to find, but I have questions for him. Well done,' Valko said, then turned and left.

Satoshi hurried after, and out of the corner of his eye, Valko caught the stunned look on his face. Was it because he had praised someone? Acknowledged the hard work of yet another barely competent underling? Must be a remnant of NOTT in his system after all, though he felt no other sign of it.

☦

Satoshi led Valko to the Arcas Plenum lab complex — buried under the affluent, green zone like a dirty secret. Getting to it required going through the localised power and environment management systems, lighter versions of what could be found at ground level and below. It kept the level, only a hundred feet under the Administration and the Conclave, clear of anyone without business with the whitecoats. A strange location for the grandson of the greatest hero of the Plena to choose for his base. Still, it made sense to Valko — why attract unwanted attention if you could avoid it. The Temple was also a reassuring distance away. No proximity to the elite for that edifice, in any Plenum. Either it was in the perpetual fug of the upper-levels or else buried deep in the lower level habitation blocks. Never in the green zones.

The lab itself was remarkable only for its light, almost turquoise hue of g-moss. That and an absence of the sort of odour he'd expected — a place like and yet very different from a medcentre. In his years as a Moderator, this was the first time he'd needed to conduct an investigation in the sanctum of the whitecoats. Satoshi, on the other hand, seemed almost at home as he led the way through the building's pressure door.

The big man beckoned a young woman over to them, 'This whitecoat was on one of Fisher's teams. Miss Rhea, please tell Tantei Gangleri everything you can.'

She was tall, a shade over Valko's own height, but nowhere near as tall as Satoshi. She wore her hair — a warm brown tone — tied up, so it was hard to say if it was within regulation length or not. Her skin, a light tan, offset her bright, violet eyes. What was natural — and what came from retrogene therapy — it was impossible to say. Ethnicity was such a variable thing amongst the Enclosed. No one identified as any particular race anymore: the concept had long since fallen out of favour. Everyone was a mix of different backgrounds compounded by the level of genetic manipulation before Enclosure, and indeed some of the retrogene therapies still in use. It made determining someone's ancestry difficult in the extreme if not downright impossible.

Satoshi was a prime example: with features and a name

suggesting Panasian ancestry, he was of hulking proportions, with darker skin suggestive of the former African states and grey eyes one might expect in a northern state's Eurussian. Valko's own ancestry was equally complex, though his pallid skin and dark hair gave him the misleading appearance of having a Eurussian or United American origin. The truth was that such things had ceased to matter the moment Enclosure had taken place — national divisions had died the same day the world had. Whatever her genetic makeup, the result had made Miss Rhea alluring, even to Valko's sterile passion.

When she spoke, her voice was soft but strong, with a confidence that belied her age. Valko had guessed that she was in her early twenties, but he reassessed that upwards by a few years when he heard her.

'I will help all that I can. All of us are in shock over Dr Fisher's death and poor Iduna too. If there is anything that I, or any of the other technicians...' Valko noted her avoidance of the term whitecoat '...can do then please let us know.'

'First, what was Dr Fisher working on?' Valko asked.

'I'm sorry, but I don't know all of his projects. He headed much of the work here. The Temple has ensured a very tight control over who was involved in each project. I'm sure that you can speak to any of his assistants and they will be able to help you. He had been working on plant retrogening, to make seeds provided to the Martyrs more resilient. I know that many of the other projects were of a similar nature, but some did involve improvements to the technical specifications of the Plenum, such as security from nanodestroyers or improved efficiency of the recycler systems,' she said, delivering the stream of information in a clipped, no-nonsense voice.

'I see. I will have all of your colleagues spoken to. But tell me, what was Dr Fisher's own major project?' Valko asked.

'I don't know if he had a current project, Tantei. He may well have been spending his time equally on all the projects, for all I know,' she said.

'We may need to speak to you again. One of my kensakan will ask you some further questions about your recent movements. Thank you.'

Valko turned away from the young woman and squinted at Satoshi.

'Sergeant, speak to the Temple oversight committee and see if they can tell us anything about Fisher's research,' he said.

'Yes, sir,' Satoshi said, heading off to make a start.

Valko wandered through the twenty labs, each teeming with whitecoats. Most were dealing with plant life or technical systems, as he had been told. Some had no obvious explanation, but short enquiries with the whitecoats present revealed nothing of any particular interest. Valko made his way to the late Dr Fisher's office.

It was spacious and strewn with hardcopies. They were of the old style — actual sheets of physical printouts on smart-paper. Diagrams and text shifted as he examined the nearest ones. It was unremarkable that someone like Fisher would have these sort of idiosyncrasies. He had a stronger link to the old way of doing things than almost anyone else in the Plena.

It was a common enough trend among whitecoats for them to cling to the old world, but Fisher had more reason than most, given who his father and grandfather had been. For a moment, Valko wondered why he had never heard about the man's mother or grandmother. Even with the prejudice against breeders, both women must have been unremarkable, to say the least, not to warrant retention in the public memory alongside their celebrated bondmates.

He picked up a datapad, scrolling through the entries until he read the last one:

'The main difficulty in establishing a workable theory, let alone a practical application of superluminality, is in overcoming the restrictions of Causality. The only way I could conceivably approach the problem is by setting aside the wisdom of generations who have come before me and starting with a blank page. I aim to prove that information can be transmitted faster than light without causing paradoxes. I must rewrite 'spacetime'. Is that hubris? Only if I am wrong.'

Fisher's journal. Something about the passage struck Valko as profoundly wrong. Some twitch of the artificial conscience constructed by his indoctrination made him want to reject the words, but he could not quite work out what it was. He put the datapad back down, but he would note it for the attention of Odegebayo in his report.

None of the other smart-papers made any sense to Valko either, though he saw a number of hardcopies that had moving diagrams of human organs and brain structures. He had a vague recollection that Fisher had been involved in perpetuating his grandfather's work on implants, as had his father before him. Was Fisher responsible for the current Moderator implants? Valko needed to check, but he thought it likely. Nothing from the office itself attracted his attention. It revealed something about Fisher, in that he had felt attached to the old world, but otherwise gave little sense of the man — save perhaps that he was disorganised. Valko returned to the main lab area and found Satoshi waiting for him.

'I've managed to speak to the Temple overseers. Well, one of them at least. He's provided me with a list of the projects that Fisher was heading. It's long, and it doesn't look like he was working on anything particular. You'll note his involvement in the Moderator implant program tailed off, but he still maintained direct oversight of the Veteran rehabilitation research,' Satoshi said. He was managing to keep his tone neutral, but Valko knew that the research into the syndrome suffered by Veterans of the Lunar War had a direct impact on his sergeant. 'I've sent you the list of projects and all the information I was just given by the Temple.'

'Yes. Nothing here of immediate interest Sergeant. Get Davidson and meet me outside,' Valko said, and then headed for the door, without waiting for a response.

He glanced at the young whitecoat, Miss Rhea, as he left. She smiled at him, sphinx-like; he thought nothing of it and carried on out of the pressure door.

†††

'Where next, sir?' Satoshi asked once they were outside.

'We need to chase down leads. There are several possibilities as to who the murderer was. Given who Fisher was, he might have been the target of a jealous underling, a jilted lover or he may have attracted the attention of a zealot,' Valko said, disturbed at explaining himself: he should be giving orders — not inviting input from his subordinates.

'So Boss, was Fisher murdered by the Temple?' Davidson asked.

Valko didn't dignify the idiotic suggestion with an answer, though he couldn't help but look askance at Satoshi, who seemed to take it as a prompt.

'Davidson, use your head. The Temple doesn't just murder people. If they want rid of you, they might put pressure on the Centra Autorita to have you shifted to one of the Outposts. Somewhere like Antarctica perhaps. Religious fanatics, though...' Satoshi sounded taken with the idea.

'Simply because Fisher was lead researcher does not automatically mean that he was the target of a fanatic,' Valko said.

He was struggling to control his irritation — investigation was not about guesswork. The idea that intuitive leaps solved crimes was anathema to him. He never played a 'hunch'. Instead, fierce application of logic yielded his results.

'So a religious vacjob, eh?' Davidson had retained an almost old-world vernacular. It spoke of an overfamiliarity with surviving media — vids and books that were controlled. Something else Valko would need to investigate, in time. 'Boss, he has to be someone like that. Why else kill Fisher and Vinnetti?'

'Davidson, you were the one so enamoured with the idea of a jealous lover. What disproves that theory?' Valko asked.

'Sorry to agree with Davidson, sir, but how would a drudge with a grudge get access to War-era tech like those mini-flashburners?' Satoshi asked.

'Same place we'll find our wei-zhuce witness. A Hotbed,' Valko said, as if speaking to a stupid child.

'But the autopsies revealed no sign of sexual activity by Vinnetti for the last couple of days,' Satoshi said. 'Torrid affairs usually require more frequent encounters.'

Satoshi gave every impression of being embarrassed at arguing with Valko, or was it something else? There was a definite sense of his discomfort, almost as if he was involved in an affair himself — or was contemplating one.

'Boss, I want to volunteer to sweep the Hotbed,' Davidson said, salivating at the possibilities.

'What we're going to do is locate either our sneaking wei-zhuce or Darius Actur, our jilted drudge, but preferably both. Then I will interrogate them. Davidson, you will get back to finding out why the Centra Autorita can't find Actur — even if his beacon had been removed, you should be able to find it. Sergeant, you will come with me.'

Valko dismissed Davidson with a wave of his hand, feeling rather than seeing the quick pulse of anger that flowed through Davidson. The sensation dissipated, but as it fled Valko caught a flash of something else — the edges of Davidson's slippery plotting. Whatever it was would need to be squashed when it arose and maybe Davidson with it. The man was becoming more than just an irritant.

Satoshi and Valko walked side by side down a narrow corridor. They were still away from the overcrowded areas, but instead of feeling relief from the crush, the even more cramped surroundings of the industrial zones created a deeper feeling of oppression in Valko.

'What's the latest intelligence on active Hotbeds in Arcas, Sergeant? Still just the one?' Valko asked.

'Sir, current briefing says only one, or at least we know of only one. It's grown larger than they usually get because we've lacked the resources for a full raid. Spot checks haven't picked up anything out of the ordinary, so it's gone down the list of priorities,' Satoshi said.

'They might be more relaxed, but if we try storming it, I'm sure all the rats will scurry down their boltholes. No, we need to be sure that he's there before raiding it,' Valko said, his customary scowl darker than usual.

'Forgive me for asking, sir, but why do you think he'll be there?' Satoshi asked.

'For the same reason any wei-zhuce would go there. Buying and selling. He's obviously a buzzpop or zigzag user. Probably both, from the looks of him. No easy way to get a steady supply, other than going to a Hotbed and plying your trade. Maybe he has things to sell — goods or services. It's lower risk when you go to a place where you know everyone is looking to trade. Imagine if he approached a drudge, out of sight of the monitors, say. There's a risk that even making an approach would lead to someone reporting him. How do you know — merely by looking — whether someone is fully indoctrinated or only partially, like most of us?'

It was a rhetorical question, and Valko didn't expect an answer.

'The eyes,' Satoshi said. 'There's something different in the eyes of those the indoctrination works on fully.'

'Maybe. Still, what are the chances that they are going to want what you are selling and have what you want to buy? It's not like we use money anymore.' Valko was beginning to get irritated. 'The Hotbed is the best place to start. I'm going to check it out. I want you to have a team standing by to raid it if I signal you.'

'Sir, I mean no offence, but you stand out as a Moderator. How are you going to disguise that?' The sergeant asked.

'I'm not going to try. Since when do Moderators involve themselves in raids on Hotbeds? They would expect a team of kensakan dragging them off for interview. Now, if you've finished questioning my orders, perhaps you'll follow them,' Valko said.

Satoshi saluted. It was plain on his face that any feeling of camaraderie with his superior had gone. He spun on his heels and moved off to make the necessary arrangements.

Temper still flaring, Valko sought solace in the cool familiarity of the investigative process. Maybe focusing on the facts, as he had always done, would help him shake off this cloud of emotion that tried to fog his every thought. If it kept on, he would have to endure a psych assessment. His teeth ground at the possibility that he was as psychologically fragile as anyone else; that the trauma of his near terminal mistake at the Vinnetti murder scene could affect him so. He would not believe it. Could not believe it.

Running over the reports, his own and his teams, he began to establish the old rhythms. His mind jumped to details as his subconscious seized upon facets of the case he had not yet considered. Then he noticed the redactions. Part of some of the reports had been excised; it was done without a record of any correction. No one else, not even the kensakan who had filed the reports, would have detected the tampering. Someone had removed all mention of the fragments of hardcopies: the charred remnants of smart-paper that had survived. They had been the link to the possibility that the murder was motivated by the research; a key strand of a potential line of enquiry gone, but for what reason? Who had done it? It could not be one of his team. Not even Satoshi had access permissions that would allow him to edit Valko's reports or reports that he had signed off on, for review by the Old Man.

Valko returned to the hub's central access point, letting his mind strip away all the additional simulated architecture of the programs until he was visualising a simple text-only root menu. This was as close as his mind could get to the source code of the hub, but it should have been enough to let him see some of the data that was usually hidden deep in the background. He found access logs. There at the top of the list was his own unique user code, the hubs recognition pattern for his particular brain waves. He had accessed the reports most frequently, below him came Satoshi, then his team. Below them, was Pravnik Odegebayo: he had accessed the reports only three times. Then below that another code. Where there should not be one. No one else could access the reports unless they had Pravnik-level clearance or the Moderator in charge had released the files to them. Valko did not recognise the code, but saved it, retreated to the easier-to-navigate standard program architecture and queried the code identity.

The hub flashed back the answer: «*Hampton, Eva Maria. Pravnik.*»

Valko removed the device. Pravnik Hampton was accessing his reports. Why? Pravniks did not interfere in cases they were not assigned to. Not ever. Why would Hampton be willing to step on Odegebayo's toes? It went beyond a mere breach of protocol, an embarrassing lapse of etiquette. There was no good reason for her to have accessed the reports in the first place, but then to edit them?

Questions whirled fast through Valko's head and a migraine followed hard on their heels. He had no time for this; whatever internal politicking was going on must not get in the way of his investigation. When he had made some progress — caught the wei-zhuce witness and reported to the Old Man — then he would find out what Hampton was doing, messing with his investigation.

Chapter 4

Valko took a deep breath of stale air. It was redolent with a mixture of the spicy scents of narcotics, the reek of spilt alcohol and the soured bile smell of vomit. This area was on the floor below the lowest of the habitable areas: where living spaces gave way to the Plenum's supporting machinery. The sporadic g-moss and g-ivy growth — greyed rather than rusty or verdant — revealed that it was a more industrialised section, as did the bare pipework. The air was dryer and staler.

There was a small, but persistent, group within the middle-zone breeders who sought locations to meet with the upper-zone drudges. Their descent into vice started with sex. An attraction to the roughness of those who were forced to travel through the height of the Plenum they lived in — if not to another one entirely — to work in the under-level. An attraction that led, as often as not, to a spiral of excess until the former elite found themselves floating to the top of the Plenum like scum rising to the surface of dirty water. While they degenerated, they brought a surge of income for the pits they wallowed in — the Hotbeds.

Valko had never understood the illogical way that the average Plenum was laid out. Under-levels filled with machinery yet woven through with the remnants of the old cities that had been there before the Enclosure. Middle-levels that, by some trick of the Plenum's internal atmospheric dynamics, always remained the most comfortable and least choked with the various pollutants released from the under-level machinery and those produced by the populace. Finally, the upper-levels. At first, people had regarded them as the ideal place to live. Close to the surface of the Plenum, they allowed easier egress and some areas even had external views, but the closer you got to the top of the Plenum, the worse the air became. G-moss and g-ivy grew thicker as they fed off the effluvia and could halve the space in a drudge's quarters.

The least valuable members of the Plenum's populace, except the wei-zhuce, lived, squashed together, at the highest altitudes — which was the way it should be. Those who slipped through the Centra Autorita's monitoring programs and avoided having the standard tracking devices, beacons, implanted in them during indoctrination — they could slip through the gaps. They could find spaces to live in areas of the under-levels, which — because of their proximity to the Plenum's machinery — avoided the overcrowding. Such people were the worst kind of filth; it was not even the lingering hold of indoctrination that made Valko think so. Not only could they avoid revealing their impact on the environment of the Plena, but they also avoided mandatory contribution.

The system was fair: the worst polluting drudges ended up losing more of their time to labour. Those who lived the cleanest lives had time to spare. The wei-zhuce did nothing, except scavenge and prey off those who kept them safe. The penalty for being wei-zhuce was as severe as their damage to society — they were executed on discovery and sent for recycling.

All this made it far harder for him to locate the down and out they were pursuing. He was a wei-zhuce. The best chance of catching him was to try to trace him through one of the Hotbeds, where the saying was *'anything goes until the kensakan turn up'*. There would always be the inevitable trade in Pre-Enclosure items — even War-era tech. No matter how hard the Justeco Centra of each Plenum tried, the kensakan could not locate all of the contraband. Valko recalled his frustration working smuggling cases, relying on the so-called efficiency of the kensakan raid teams.

Someone always slipped through — with the aid of a bribe or two — carrying their tainted goods into the heart of the Plenum. The regular commute of drudges between Plena, to where their labour was needed — not to mention the movement of more skilled specialists — ensured a healthy black market trade.

Every Plenum had its Hotbed area, some had several. Every time the kensakan cleared one out, another sprang up somewhere else. Although the Centra Autorita could track the Enclosed, where the machinery was dense enough it caused beacon signals to drop out. Associating with other registered members of the Plena was no crime, but fabricated charges were a kensakan speciality — Valko hated their corruption, almost as much as he hated their bungling. Unless caught in the act of dealing with a wei-zhuce or obtaining envirocrime contraband, a registered inhabitant — an Enclosed — committed no terminal offence purely by visiting a Hotbed. Their best defence was to adopt an aspect of innocent ignorance — *No, Kensakan, I just happened to be in the general area, trying to avoid the crowds. I had no idea that there was any illegal activity going on.* It would work, particularly if there was some flirtation or a little greasing of the hand — kensakan hadn't earned the nickname 'fiddlers' for nothing. Unless, for some reason, a Moderator became interested in the case. He and his fellows were above bribery; though, he could not help but remember the occasional aberration who'd fallen to a different kind of excess.

Valko had double-checked that his headset-hub's neural linkages were operating as normal. He had begun to doubt the device's reliability after his encounter with the ITF security protocol. Neural buffers were meant to protect him from any such attack, to protect him from any feedback when connecting to unknown devices or other augmented brains. They had let him down badly.

Now, he was going to have to find a fitting candidate for information — and if they would not give it to him through his use of subterfuge or persuasion — then he would call in Oshi, and they would restrain the unlucky Enclosed, while Valko jacked him or her up, then and there.

He stepped through the open pressure door and glared around in the dim crimson light that drove all other colours away as if at war with them. The smugglers who ran the Hotbed had installed a bar; a single white light shone on it from above, driving back the scarlet air. Behind it, a thick-necked man with non-regulation length, greasy hair, was pouring exotic liquids into containers of various sizes. The drinks ranged through the spectrum of colour: from the shimmering to the fetid. Some distorted the air above their glasses with heat, some with rime. Arrayed along the bar and spread out at tables and tattered couches around the room were about a hundred people. Every section of Plenum society — save for the top echelons and the kensakan — was represented.

A few of the Hotbed's patrons gazed up at him but seeing that he didn't have a crowd of kensakan equipped with knockout sticks backing him up, they relaxed, no doubt assuming this wasn't a raid. Valko had no illusions about the aura he radiated — it screamed Moderator to everyone who met him. Only the late Tantei Bezant had a more abrupt effect on the social temperature of a room.

'Don't often see your type in here, sweetie,' a middle-aged woman said.

She was dressed in the typical regulation wearall of a low-level drudge but with the clothing's seals undone to her waist.

'Come looking for some fun, Shivers, or something to take your mind off it?' She asked, giving him a suggestive smile that said, *I'll do anything*.

Valko assessed her in an instant: 'pophead — he could see from the involuntary jaw movements she kept making. Other than that, she hid it well. She would be desperate enough that she would tell him whatever she thought he wanted to hear but was still with it enough not to give him anything useful. He knew the sort. He fixed her with a stare until she licked her lips and backed away — muttering something almost inaudible under her breath as she turned, '*Waj ab zibik*.'

He let it go, though there was a sanction for saying such things to a Moderator, even if it wasn't in Anglo-Esperanto.

Valko approached the makeshift bar and found that the occupants of the two stools there had vacated them, at high speed. He sat and glowered at the bartender. After a slow moment of eye contact, the man's left eyelid twitched, and he looked down.

'Sorry about that *vushka*, her type are worse than the *chi bai* roaches. What can I get you?' he asked.

'A regulation whiskey.'

It would be bad enough to be almost undrinkable, but at least the recyclers had produced it, and not an illegal still — or worse. Many of the substances being consumed in the room were smuggled in from outside. Transpods could be diverted, and every Plenum had vents and pipes for pumping excess organic waste outside where it would make excellent fertiliser. Those same pipes could be crawled up — if one was willing to swim against a tide of shit — and given the desperate existence of those who had survived outside the Plena, people prepared to accept the risks and discomforts involved in smuggling were never in short supply. The Martyrs — alone — stood immune from temptation.

The wall processor extruded a short, bioplastic cup and it filled with the burnt-umber liquid. The barman placed it in front of Valko without meeting his gaze.

'Anything else?'

'Murders.'

'What?'

'I work murders. Not smuggling. Not anymore. I'm not interested in where you got the rest of your stock and why you're providing non-regulation substances.' Valko picked up the tumbler and without hesitation knocked back its contents. 'Another.'

'Right... No offence but why drink here? You could get this from your own processor at home.' The barman poured another.

'Yes, but that's recorded and limited to four shots a day maximum. I'd rather use your allowance than mine.'

The barman relaxed. He seemed to accept that Valko was just another person wanting to be free — for a while — from the restrictions of this life: of being told where to live; where to work; when to sleep; when to eat; how much to drink. The criminal scum wasn't stupid enough to let his guard down, but at the same time, he gave every impression that he'd stopped worrying that he was going to be taken in for interrogation. He went back to serving his other customers.

The economics of the place were so complicated that Valko sometimes wondered how anyone could run a Hotbed. Without the need for money, it all came back to favours and trading luxury rations or other goods. When one Hotbed closed, another sprung up — sometimes debts carried over, sometimes they were lost. Raids were rare and typically followed a noticeable shift in efficiency within a Plenum. The 'off the record' view was that you had to turn a blind eye, on occasion, until the problem became significant. It fell under the bracket of 'unavoidable slippage' that the Justeco Centra — and through it the Centra Autorita — allowed. Temple zealots would have stamped out all traces of every Hotbed as soon as they were located — one of the few things they called for that Valko agreed with.

He scrutinised the clientele, not trying to hide his appraisal — no clear sign of any wei-zhuce presence. There must be a backroom housed in a storage annexe, where smugglers and other lowlife made serious deals. Several smaller storage rooms would surround it, where other — more intimate — deals were being negotiated.

He was in the public face of this Hotbed, hence the lack of security. No terminal crime was being committed in this room: the non-regulation material would all be explainable. Although the barman and some customers might risk losing status, it was doubtful that a search would find any patron with a worthwhile standing in possession of anything compromising. So long as they didn't give too much backchat to the kensakan. Everyone else was probably close enough to damned that it didn't matter anyway. When they were done here, they'd be heading up to the top of the Plenum, to choke in the stifling brume of their homes.

Were any wei-zhuce in the backroom? If he waited long enough — became part of the background — there was the chance the Hotbed security would slip up. On the other hand, he'd have to keep sinking reprocessed whisky until they did…

No, waiting was a bad idea: he needed to act. If he called in a raid on the backroom, by the time that the pressure door at its entrance could be unjammed, all the occupants would have fled. There was the same problem in every Plena: there were too many alternative exits in the industrialised areas for the thinly-stretched kensakan to cover. Anywhere lacking reliable signals from the security monitors fomented the ulcerous growth of Hotbeds.

What he needed was for someone to leave the backrooms with the signs of having recently used 'pop, zigzag or one of the other narcs — the Hotbed's crew would have saved those for consumption in the back. Anyone he grabbed would have seen the occupants. He'd jack them up and see what, and who, they'd seen. Armed with that evidence — and given the importance of this investigation — he could demand access to enough kensakan to cover all the numerous exits and vents in the Hotbed.

Past experience told him that flooding the place with tranq gas might work, but that technique was often ineffective. Most doors had pressure seals — paranoia about breaches in the Plena had been high in the early years.

Why couldn't the Enclosed just follow the regulations? Why did they have to be forced? He knew — in an abstract intellectual way — that there was a limit to how far you could restrict human beings. Even with the tenets of the Temple drilled into every Enclosed — indoctrination which made them believe they were part of a viral species — they still sought a better life for themselves. They found freedom in excess.

Tighten the limits too far and you risk rebellion. It had happened early on in one of the Plena before the rest had accepted the Centra Autorita's way. Melbourne Plenum had been a lesson to all the others — not even Erasmus Fisher had been able to talk them down. People would accept the limitations of life in the Plena because they had no choice. They would accept the tenets of the Temple because it was pumped at them from every angle and indoctrination — whether a full or partial success — enforced that quiescence. But deny the last illusion of freedom? There was one result. At least, that was the Centra Autorita line. Valko saw no reason why the lesson from Melbourne should be *loosen your grip* and not *apply ruthless force early, tighten it if need be*.

A sigh forced its way up from deep inside him. Whatever his feelings, the only way to succeed here was by flushing the wei-zhuce out. Storming in would be counterproductive. If they failed to get their target, he — and any other wei-zhuce scum — would hide deeper in the Plenum's underbelly. This softly, softly approach was inefficient but necessary.

Valko noticed another lull in conversation, turned towards the entrance and saw her. It was the young whitecoat from Fisher's lab, Miss Rhea — the one who had been keen to stop her experiment from being ruined. Skimming over the room, her eyes settled on him and her lips gave the barest twitch of a smile. She came over to the stool beside him and sat down.

Turning her head, she swept her dark hair back over one ear and breathed, 'Do you come here often?'

He could not believe the ludicrousness of the line. No one serious about a pickup would ever use such a tired expression. Unless, they were trying to play the brazen card, but then why not say 'let's get a room'. He stared at her and realised she was making a joke. There was humour scintillating in her eyes. He felt both disappointment and relief. She was beautiful but also a potential witness. It was a line he dared not cross.

'No, my first time,' he said.

'Mine too. When we last met, I don't think I introduced myself properly. I'm Xiang, but my friend's call me Jean. I didn't catch your first name Tantei Gangleri,' she said, offering him one hand, palm down.

He took it and wondered whether he was supposed to shake it or kiss it.

'And I didn't tell you. It's Valko. What are you doing here?' He asked.

He had no time for this — though the timing of her arrival was... What? His train of thought broke off. Any curiosity about her presence in a Hotbed felt suddenly suppressed. By... by the needs of his investigation? Yes, that was it: he needed to stay focused.

'What with all that happened, I needed a break. The experiment finished, so I have some free time. I'd heard about this place and I wanted... I don't know; something to distract me,' she said in a matter of fact way.

Was this flirtation or something else? He wished he had taken a dose of NOTT.

She started talking again, telling him about the shock of the deaths: Vinnetti had been a friend and Fisher an inspiration... Valko tuned it out as just meaningless chatter — but his eyes never left the soft recurve of her lips. The barman brought her a drink and not one from the processor. While she was talking, an idea was forming in Valko's mind. Maybe there was a way to get into the back room without having to call in the kensakan.

He interrupted her as she continued gushing about her feelings over the deaths.

'If you want justice for your colleagues, I need your help,' he said.

She stopped short. 'My help? What can I do?'

Was that a playful tone? She was hard to read.

He leant in to whisper in her ear, noticing the clean scent of her hair, 'I need to get into the backrooms here. You can give me that excuse.'

She pulled back and eyed him, a look of surprise on her face. There were the faint beginnings of a blush on her cheeks.

'You want me to go into the back rooms with you?' She asked, loud enough to be overheard.

At first, he thought she was going to refuse, taking his genuine plea for assistance to be a cheap line, but she surprised him.

Laying one hand on his upper arm, she said, 'I'd love to, Valko.' and began to get up.

The bartender looked at Valko and raised an eyebrow. The look on his face said — *Now I've seen it all* — as clear as any words.

Out loud he said, 'No charge for you. Remember that, if you come back here with any of your friends.' A smirk spread across his face.

How could it be this easy? Valko stood; hesitating a moment, then decided: he took Jean's hand and headed towards the back of the room. The door there was open with no light in the corridor behind. As they passed through, Valko saw the guards waiting out of line of sight of the entrance. Both were armed with heavy lengths of pipe, meant more to discourage disgruntled patrons than to resist a raid by the kensakan. They eyed Valko and Jean but did not move to interfere.

The corridor branched in two directions, one of the guards gesturing to the right-hand side. Without a word, Valko and Jean walked down that hallway. The lighting was the same subdued red as in the bar area. It was no great loss — there was little to see except a series of closed doors. Muffled sounds were audible from behind some, while others had the fumes from assorted narcotics drifting out of them.

How was he going to be able to check the rooms for the wei-zhuce he was looking for? Improvising in situations like these was tricky, but experience had taught him the simple solution was best. He turned to face Jean.

'Keep an eye out down the corridor. I need to know if anyone is heading our way,' he said.

Did she look disappointed? He checked his rising desire — now was not the time for self-delusion.

Valko listened at the nearest door: no noise came from within. It was unlocked — no surprise there: those who ran the Hotbed would need access to the rooms to get rid of customers overstaying their welcome. He eased the door open and checked inside, wary of discovery. There were three men and two women inside, four lying on pallets, one in a beaten up chair. All five were comatose.

The room had the acrid sweet stink of buzzpop and a smoky miasma clotted the air. He took a guess at which one of the unconscious 'popheads was the most regular — in other words, who looked the worst. One of the women was missing teeth; eyes open but rolled back in her head showing yellowed sclera and clumps of her hair had been pulled out — probably self-inflicted. A sure-fire candidate. She was skin and bones and would be the easiest to muscle out of the room into a vacant one.

He glanced over his shoulder to see Jean watching the corridor; she looked round at him with one eyebrow raised. Ducking back into the room, he grabbed the 'pophead he had chosen. She groaned but did not wake up. None of the others stirred. If the guards were monitoring the room, he would have a matter of seconds before they were storming down the corridor.

While not in any way muscular, Valko was strong enough to pass the regular and demanding Moderator's physical; strong enough to hoist the woman over one shoulder and carry her out of the room. Jean's eyes widened, but it was her only reaction.

'Find me an empty room,' he said, keeping his voice low.

She turned and put her ear to a door a few strides along the hallway. Opening the door a crack, she peered inside and turned back to him, nodding.

'This one's empty. It's small — a bed and enough room to stand on one side of it,' Jean said, her voice just above a whisper.

'It'll do.' He followed her to the room but did not go inside. 'Here help me with her a moment.'

Valko leant the unconscious, moaning woman up against Jean. She held the 'pophead under the arms, the only sign of her discomfort being a wrinkling of her nose at the smell. She had confidence, he admired that; nothing fazed her.

Valko entered the cramped room and checked it out, with professional precision. Locating the spyholes and audio snares, he covered them — making it look casual and unintended. That done, he grabbed the 'pophead from Jean and laid her on the bed. The woman's moaning slowed, then stopped as her breathing became deep and regular again.

Valko thought for a moment. He was going to need to attempt a mindlink with the 'pophead: to jack her up in front of a civilian — something he'd never done before — but there was no choice. If he left Jean standing in the corridor, someone would notice before long and come looking for him. He ushered her inside.

'Don't be alarmed,' he said, in as reassuring a voice as he could manage. 'I need to find out what this woman knows. I will not harm her. Please sit still,'

'That's ok,' Jean sat, demure, on one corner of the bed. 'This is fascinating. Please do what you need to do.'

For a moment, Valko wished that they were there for a liaison of their own. With an effort, he shook off his distraction and focused on the job in hand. Maybe there'd be time to get to know her later when his job was done. She didn't act as if it — or he — put her off.

Valko pulled his headset-hub out from where he had concealed it, tucked into the top of one of his boots. It was undamaged. Good. He took out the connectors and placed them in the appropriate places on the 'pophead's skull. She didn't react. This would be a lot easier if she remained unconscious. What he was about to attempt was one of the hardest techniques a Moderator could try. While he could sift a deceased brain for recent memories, and encounter little difficulty so long as it had not degraded too much, doing the same with a living brain was harder — often impossible.

There was a degree of hardwired protection in the human mind that rejected outside probing. He could pick up thoughts freely framed by a person he was interrogating, and catch a strong sense of their emotional state and level of truthfulness, but extracting their recollection of events was another thing. An unwilling subject could block him from even the most recent, strong memories. Sometimes he could persuade them — in one way or another — to relax those mental blocks, but this woman was comatose and should remain so. Without her conscious mind resisting him, he would only need to manage her subconscious reaction to his intrusion. That subconscious mind was probably dealing with enough from the amount of 'pop she had diffused — it might help him or just make things harder, he would soon find out.

When he had secured his headset, Valko took out a dose of NOTT — his hand trembling in anticipation — and placed it into the valve in his wrist. On automatic, he checked the batch code and saw *PSTZ211* printed on the vial. Jean watched, apparently rapt, and — as the first rush of NOTT reached his implant — he was overcome by a strong desire to explain himself.

'It allows me to use the headset-hub to read her surface memories,' he said.

'What is it?' She asked.

'Nitric Oxide α-Trimethyltryptamine. We call it NOTT for short.'

Valko felt a bone-deep trust for Jean sweep over him. They shared a connection: he knew that now. There was no reason not to tell her everything about it, to reward her interest.

'It's a drug that this valve delivers directly to an implant in my brain. The Nitric Oxide encourages greater blood flow to the implant; the alpha-Trimethyltryptamine activates the implant fully. It only works like this for Moderators. Long ago people used it as a narcotic because it could cause hallucinations. Don't worry, it's isolated within my implant and won't make me start having any delusions.' He smiled at her, warmth spreading outwards from his NOTT flooded core.

'You seem... different. Does it always have this effect on you?' She asked, leaning forward as if inspecting him.

A flush of heat rose in his face. He wasn't embarrassed by how attractive he found her, was he?

'Yes, it increases empathy, a useful side effect. Not every Moderator gets it to the same extent and it takes training to control. Mothers Tears, you are beautiful,' He said. Why had that slipped out? He'd better watch himself — repeated blasphemy was a class two offence and flirting with a witness was ill-advised. He was a Moderator, dammit, not some kensakan on the lookout for whatever he could get.

Jean smiled at him. 'Why thank you, Tantei Gangleri,' she said, almost coy before shifting and becoming serious. 'If you're going to read her you'd better do it before we run out of time.'

She was right. Feeling like an idiot, Valko regarded the poor woman lying on the bed and thought what a dreadful waste of a life it was. Steeling himself, his natural self — a sharp, unyielding edge — dragged his mind back to business. He closed his eyes and activated the hub.

With his mind sinking down into the device, the sensations of the addict assaulted him. The ravages on his own dormant emotions were more intense than normal. At once uplifted, he fell in despair and blew through fear to rage, in hurricanes of feeling. Then he was through the barrier and his birthing scream, as he entered her mind, cut short.

She was flying through pink clouds in her mind's eye, the world around her distorting to her every whim and oh, what a pleasant rush everything was. She felt weightless, yet every part of her body had a comfortable heaviness. The contradiction was wonderful; sensual; delicious… Oh!

Valko pulled away from her surface thoughts — it would be too easy to get swept away in her drug-driven dreams. Instead, he focused his mind on the man he was looking for. Forming the image in his own mind, he dove into the maelstrom of flickering visions that whirled through her short-term memories. He encountered sights he wished he didn't have to see: memories of what she'd done to earn her hit of 'pop.

There he was — the man Valko was looking for. In one of the backrooms. They'd shared a diffuser. His name was Joey. It was hard to tell, but the memory was deeper than immediate short-term. It'd slipped into that middle stage, where her subconscious would discard it, not make it into long-term memory. It could be a day ago or a week. He strove to pull her memories into focus so that he could see some sort of order to them, but the 'pop wasn't helping.

Bang.

He was in the memory of sharing the diffuser with Joey again. Before the sweet, sweet dreams had come for them both, Joey had been talking. Rambling, using the argot of the Remnants — oh, it was so sexy.

Valko reasserted himself; it was hard to piece together what Joey was saying. The memory was decaying and what he said had been part-obscured by the way he talked and by the fug of the drug. Something about him having hurt his hand. She had noticed a ragged bandage on his hand. Saying he'd got it from a piece of gold taken from a body. She had perked up at that, if he had gold, he'd be getting more 'pop…

Valko turned away from the memory of her thoughts. She had considered all the things she'd do for Joey to get him to give her more 'pop. That record of her thoughts suggested that the memory must be recent. He strained to find anything else of use and, as he was going to give up, he stumbled upon an errant memory. She'd talked to someone about Joey when she'd woken up and found him gone. Asked where he was, desperate not to be robbed of her chance to get more 'pop. The person she had spoken to — she couldn't remember who they were or their gender — said Joey had left to go see someone. A name. What was it? It was just there. He could almost grasp it, but it kept slipping away from him — the memory was too degraded.

Valko calmed his mind — felt his own body at a distance taking seven breaths — and willed some of the calm that flowed through him, into the memories that surrounded him. The name became clear to him. Slim Jan. A fence. Her memories of the man bubbled up from her subconscious and Valko felt a surge of triumph. She knew where she could find Slim Jan, and now so did he.

Valko broke the connection with a sigh of relief. What a feeling: this gambit had paid off. Most of all, he felt relief at being free of the poor addict's narc dreams. Jean had moved and he had the sense that she'd sat back down only a fraction of a second before. Perhaps, she'd begun to get worried about the time it was taking.

'How long was I gone?' He asked her.

'About ten minutes, no more. Did you find what you needed?' She was staring at him. 'This has certainly been a… fascinating meeting, Valko.'

'We must do it again soon,' he said.

She hesitated for a moment and then gave him a wide smile.

'Yes, I think I'd like that. Perhaps without our friend here though?' She said, indicating the still comatose 'pophead.

Valko felt a heat rise through him. Not knowing if it was the right thing to do, he leant forward and kissed Jean on the cheek — no more than a brush of his dry lips on the swell of her flesh. She didn't pull away but gazed at him. Her lips parted as if to say something — or maybe to kiss him back — when they heard a loud crashing sound coming from outside.

They both stood in alarm: the shouting was coming from a nearby room. Valko risked a look out from their door and saw the two guards barrelling through the door two down from theirs, on the opposite side of the corridor. A young woman was standing in the corridor, in a state of undress and holding her face with one hand, all the while screaming curses in half a dozen languages. An instant later, the guards were dragging a semi-conscious man out of the room and down the hallway. Satisfied that it was nothing to do with them, Valko closed the door and turned back to Jean. The moment between them was gone and the nature of their surroundings sunk in. What he was feeling towards her needed to be expressed somewhere other than a sleazy backroom in a Hotbed.

The cold, rational part of his mind sneered at him. What he was feeling was a side effect of the NOTT working on his implant — nothing more. He had no room for emotional distractions, never had. The voice strove to cut through the churning emotions and physical excitement that he was experiencing. Either way, it was time to get out.

'Come on. Let's go before our sleeping beauty wakes up,' he said.

They rose and left the room, eyes and ears straining for any sign of alarm. Valko — feeling self-conscious even as he did so — reached out and touched Jean's shoulder.

When she'd turned to face him, he leant forward and whispered into her ear, 'You should leave first.'

She didn't answer him, but her eyes held his, their heads still close. He felt her breath almost caressing his lips — the softly spiced scent of the drink she'd had at the bar teasing him with the imagined taste of her kiss. She turned away — slow, reluctant, almost sensual — and was gone through the door.

Valko waited for a couple of minutes, in silence. He found himself feeling like he was beginning to float free from his body — some after-effect of linking with the 'pop user, perhaps. A pleasant enough sensation, but self-discipline kicked in and pulled him out of it. His mind had been smothering under its own weight, thoughts muted and fogged. Now, a fresh breeze blew in, restoring him.

Valko rounded the corner and emerged into the public room, to see the bartender smirking at him. There was no sign of the guards, but Valko didn't want to wait for their return. He nodded at the leering barman and hustled out of the Hotbed; within eight hours his kensakan would wipe away the smirk when they executed their raid.

Chapter 5

Once he was a safe distance away, alone amongst the cramped industrial machinery and pipework, Valko donned his hub to contact Satoshi and Davidson.

«*I've got a solid lead on our wei-zhuce. We're looking for a smuggler's fence called Slim Jan. Based in the backend of D-level.*»

Not quite in the industrial zone, like the Hotbed had been, D-level was the lowest of the main plazas — this rat was seeking safety in numbers, for all the good it would do him. The crowds there would impede kensakan access, but Valko's team was used to dealing with situations like this. Incompetent as they were sometimes, right now there was no evidence of it. To Valko's satisfaction, they replied straight away when he signalled them as he made his own way there.

Pipework and machines began to give way to signs of habitation and the g-moss thickened underfoot. The stuff had always had trouble growing on the metal walkways of the industrial areas and was kept to a minimum around the machinery.

Drudges passed him by, on their way to work in the industrial sections or returning to their small rooms on this level. Their quarters here would be more like a cell than a room: communal toilets, processors and cleaning rooms would be the norm this low down. Valko — NOTT still tearing open his perception — could sense the almost palpable mood of hopelessness around here. Still, it was better than being a resident at the top of the Plenum: here, at least, the air was comfortable to breathe.

The design flaw — that gave the quarters nearest the industrial heart of the Plenum cleaner air than that at the top — was symptomatic of all the problems with Enclosure. Even without synthetic emotions telling him to be angry for the suffering of the masses, Valko might have regarded the failing as inexcusable inefficiency — toxic living conditions reduced productivity — if he bothered to consider the problem at all.

All the waste fumes tended to rise, as did the humidity

generated from human breath, sweat and machines' steam. A predictable problem that had been glossed over — yet the intakes to the internal atmosphere regulators were all located on the inside of the Plenum's outer shell, the pipes arcing down the sides until they reached the recyclers at its base. It was clear that someone had foreseen the problem but had done nothing to protect the people — it was the monstrous attitude typical of the elite. Now he shook his head in sympathy; when NOTT wore off in an hour or two, he'd cease caring.

Soon enough, he was back in the press of bodies, all trying to get somewhere. He made slow progress. There was some kind of problem with the transpods causing an overloading of walkways and plazas, as large numbers of people waited for them to start running again. It took him almost an hour to get near to D-level — he had to go up to a higher level to get around the chokepoints. When, at last, he got there, he found Satoshi waiting for him. Without a word, the Sergeant handed him back his tranqgun.

'We're in position, sir. Davidson reckons he's dealt with this guy before. Jannick Del. He's wheedled his way out of any serious violations and has somehow managed to secure a high enough efficiency rating to live in the lower mid-levels. Seems he's smart enough to know when to help the kensakan without a fuss. How do you want us to deal with this? Kick his door in and drag him in for interrogation?' Satoshi asked.

'Maybe. I'll speak to Davidson,' Valko said, then added, almost under his breath, 'Can't believe he's actually being of use for a change.'

Satoshi grinned at him. Valko turned on his hub and contacted Davidson.

«*Davidson, you know this "Slim Jan"?*»

«*Yes, Boss. I picked him up a couple of times when I was working envirocrime. He'd been dealing fresh vegetables smuggled in from outside. Petty enough that I didn't have to sanction him. Word was, he was the man for whatever you wanted, but I never caught him for any of it. He did give me a couple of leads on a smuggling ring, when I put a bit of pressure on him.*»

«*So, he's worth talking to, rather than interrogating?*» Valko asked.

«*I'd say so, Boss. He's a weasel.*» Valko wondered what he meant but didn't ask, used to Davidson's occasional archaic phrase. Davidson continued, «*But he'll squeak nice and quick.*»

Valko broke the link. He had felt a degree of apprehension coming from Davidson that would have been virtually impossible to detect if they had spoken face to face. With the mindlink and the NOTT still driving his implant, it was obvious to Valko. What wasn't clear, was the reason.

Was Davidson concerned about the reliance they were placing on him — worrying that he might screw up? It wouldn't be the first time. Was it something else, like perhaps this 'Slim Jan' knew something about him? Whatever it was, it was unimportant for now, but — combined with his other suspicions of the man — it made Valko determined to bring the issue of Jack Davidson to a conclusion, sooner rather than later.

'Satoshi, you're with me. Have the other kensakan ready, in case we meet resistance.'

Valko began to move even as he was giving the order. Satoshi repeated the orders using his datapad and took up position at Valko's right.

They entered the small metal structure, little more than a hut attached to one of the towering blocks, but well situated. It was laid out as a shop, of sorts: curtains of material flowed from the ceiling, creating the illusion that the building was a tent. Goods, big and small, bright and dull, were laid out in arcs on tables and the counter. There were sprays of vid modules scattered amongst tech arcana of every sort — none controlled but all available only to the elect.

The place managed to extract a profit from sourcing materials that were out of the reach of anyone without an elite-level processor or a supply of old-world oddities. No doubt, for the truly discerning customer there were other luxuries — more difficult to obtain and dangerous to own — available for the right price.

Valko set his jaw. He'd worked at cracking smuggling operations, back when he first became a Moderator. Exposure to the seedier side of the Plena was seen as a good way to get some experience before dealing with homicides or more serious envirocrime cases. Most of the time, crimes of one sort overlapped into the milieu of crimes of another — vice bred a lack of respect for the Mother and for life: murder often followed.

In all his time scouring records, sweating witnesses and

chasing leads, he'd never managed to catch a fence. They were slippery: always too clever and too far from the source of the smuggled goods to be easily caught. Part of him itched to get this man into an interrogation room and grill him until all his wrongdoing lay open. That would take time, though. The longer they delayed, the harder it would be to catch the murderer, assuming that he was still in one of the Plena. It might be Actur, but until the kensakan traced him, they needed to leave nothing to chance. An eyewitness, like the wei-zhuce they were pursuing, could make all the difference.

Valko strode up to the counter and glared at the man sitting behind it, with his body overflowing the chair. He was using a diffuser pipe to imbibe chillax — a mild sedative that did not have the status of a narc like 'pop or zigzag. The sight of the man disgusted Valko: he represented the worst of those who got ahead through illicit means.

Obesity was rare in the Plena because all food came from communal processors or the reprocessors in one's quarters. A calorific limit was set centrally, so the dietary sludge that the machines produced would never provide enough nutrients for a man to put on the sort of weight this so-called Slim Jan was carrying.

The man's clothing was another sign — of a quality only available to the elite in the Temple, and with bright colours not usually seen in these days. Again, not prohibited, but there was no way that this man could have obtained them by legitimate means. It wasn't like medical causes for obesity were hard to treat, even now, but here was this man: flaunting his corpulence — and his luxuries — heedless of the stigma attached to anyone who appeared to be taking more than their hard-won share. No, not heedless: revelling in it.

Valko gritted his teeth and took deep breaths until the seventh relaxed his jaw. He sought out his inner self. It was still there: a chill, hard lump behind the warm fuzz of the implant, but it took him a moment longer to find it than usual. Perhaps, he'd been letting go too much recently, perhaps it was a side effect of neural shock. Whichever it was, control returned and the gaze that met Slim Jan's could have frozen lava. Valko said nothing but simply held the man's eyes locked on his own for a long, drawn out moment that seemed to drag on with excruciating slowness as if it would last through the remaining aeons, lingering until the very end of time itself. Then... snap.

Slim Jan looked away, swallowed and said with a sybaritic lisp, 'Salutations, Tantei. I'm not sure why I've earned this distinct honour, but please, please, be welcome in my small shop.' He gestured to overstuffed pillows that matched the one on which he lounged. 'Please tell me what I, Slim Jan, can do for you. You know what they say, small shop, small price.'

Valko could feel the man's fear radiating. What was it Davidson had called him, a weasel? The term puzzled him until some echo of memory from his days in the skoler returned and he formed a mental image of the creature. It should be sleek to the point of being almost slippery. Not like the repugnant trader's physical appearance then — more like his mind.

'You have had recent dealings with a wei-zhuce called Joey. You are in violation of code seven one beta of the Articles of Registration and thus liable to execution and recycling,' Valko said.

His every word carried a tone of final certainty as if sentence was about to be carried out immediately — a bluff. What they had wouldn't hold up to scrutiny and code seven one beta didn't even carry mandatory death as a sentence. But this vermin didn't know that.

'I, I, I don't know what you mean Moderator. I beg you to reconsider...' The man's speech trailed off. All trace of his lisp had disappeared — just a part of the act.

'I suppose if you were to volunteer the location of the wei-zhuce, Joey — right now — I might be able to view your interaction with him as unintentional and this the first reasonable opportunity that you have had to report it,' Valko said.

The speed at which Slim Jan gave the wei-zhuce up came as no surprise.

'But of course. You're quite right — that's exactly how it is. He's two levels down, hiding in a broken-down water reservoir. One of a cluster undergoing maintenance. Allow me to copy the precise location to your datapad.'

He did so and Valko forwarded it to all of the kensakan on his team. Davidson responded first: he was closest and would hurry to the location. Valko dispatched Chang to assist him and then stood stock-still, locking the squirming fat man in place with his gaze. Slim Jan licked his lips but had the sense to say nothing more. Valko couldn't shake the feeling that the man, though his fear was real, was still putting on an act of sorts — a pretence at fright more than any true dread. They waited for Davidson — the menacing presence of Satoshi adding another level of intimidation to the threats, yet Valko began to see Slim Jan more as an anxious gambler, than as scared prey.

†††

Davidson was already close to the reservoirs. Thick mats of g-moss covered the gigantic tanks, making it difficult to be sure of the serial number on some of them — he was in the right section, though. Signs of renovation on several of the reservoirs — this must be the cluster under repair. It wouldn't be possible to have more than one cluster out of operation at any given time. Without the grey water stored in the clusters, the Enclosed would have to rely on water coming straight from recycling to their processors — either that or, if they were of sufficient status to have a closed water loop, they could use their own recycled fluids instead of the common pool.

'Fuck that,' Davidson said to himself.

He shuddered as he strained his imagination to consider the consequences of a system-wide failure: external water filtration systems would struggle to meet the need, what with the infrequency of rain and the length of time it took to remove fallout, toxins and sift for nanodestroyers. If the Plena didn't run with a large surplus of water, they would soon fail. Important work then, but there was no sign of any drudges. Slim Jan had done his business — no one in Davidson's way, no one to confuse things or alert the wei-zhuce. This would damn well go his way, for a change.

Davidson located the right reservoir, as easy as Jan had said it would be. He'd begun to climb the external ladder to the reservoir's top when he saw a mass of filthy, blond dreadlocks appear out of the large hatch at the top of the tank. The rest of the owner of the dreadlocks followed, springing up and — with little concern for the drop — jumping down onto the nearby walkway. He began to sprint away from Davidson.

'Come here, you little shit!' Davidson bellowed, dropping

from the ladder to the walkway and giving chase as fast as he could.

The filthy man ran from Davidson. Malnourished and a regular substance abuser, he was nonetheless in better physical condition than the kensakan was — departmental physicals were things to be dodged or faked with narcs, after all. Davidson wheezed along behind him, doggedly refusing to give up. This was his chance and if he blew it, another one wouldn't come in a long time.

They were sprinting down the winding maintenance area, the walkways twisting around vast machinery and narrowing as heavy-duty piping took up space. The wei-zhuce clattered down a short flight of metal stairs and, for a moment, Davidson had a clear line on him. He pulled his tranqgun and fired three quick shots at the man. Maybe his time down the firing range hadn't been wasted after all — he managed to hit the greasy fucker with one shot. It was enough, the small, hardened mass of tranq punching into the fleeing man's arm and twisting him around. In under a second, the drug had dissolved into the wei-zhuce's bloodstream and he collapsed onto the metal mesh of the walkway. Holstering his tranqgun, Davidson went over to the now unconscious man and delivered a swift, spiteful kick to his ribs.

'Make me chase you, will ya? Bastard,' Davidson shouted, kicking again.

Not bothering with his headset, he sent a short text-only message to Satoshi.

«*Got him, Sarge.*»

This was going to make the difference, after trying so many different things to advance. He couldn't help who he was — faking it hadn't helped. When he first became a kensakan, he'd had hopes of making rank. He'd tried to pass himself off as a celibate and even thought about trying to become homosexual so that he could get advancement. It was no use: his sexuality was what it was and he couldn't change it.

The first few times he'd busted some young woman, and had a chance to make her misdemeanour disappear, he'd taken it. Every time he'd found booze on a raid, he'd drunk it. He couldn't steal credit for solving cases so all that left him was to abuse his powers. Sometimes, when he watched the old vids on his datapad or read the books that he'd stashed away, he dreamed of being like the old kensakan, the Police Officers that he'd read about and watched. That world was dead though and this one was gone to shit.

Still, no reason not to make the most of it. Life would never be like the world of his books, but he could make the most out of what the Plena had to offer. Davidson delivered another kick to the prone man and felt better. Maybe he would make Sergeant if this case were important enough. If only smug fuck Satoshi and that pitiless bastard Gangleri would let him.

†††

The stink coming from the wei-zhuce was overpowering: a potent mix of every conceivable human body odour, all underpinned with the smell of infected flesh, which crawled up the nose. There were things living in the matt of thick blonde dreadlocks and the scraggy beard was discoloured in places by the diffusing of one narcotic or another. Maybe several.

Valko grabbed Satoshi's shoulder and said, 'Well done, Sergeant. Have Davidson hose him down and prep him for interrogation. Tell him no rough stuff; I need to know what this man saw.'

'And after, sir?' Satoshi asked, his discomfort with the inevitability of the man's execution and recycling, plain on his face.

'If he cooperates, I'll recommend that he is indoctrinated and sent to an Outpost to earn his way,' Valko said.

For once, he couldn't regard the man as a non-entity. He hadn't even taken a dose of NOTT yet — though he could feel the need nagging at him — but still the pathetic nature of their prisoner struck him. Then there was camaraderie with his sergeant: Valko didn't know what to make of the feelings. He shook his head and turned to leave but, to his surprise, Satoshi followed him. Out of earshot of the wei-zhuce, Satoshi faced his superior.

'Sir, it's one thing to know that we will have to execute him, it's another to dangle a false hope in front of him.'

It was the strongest admonishment Satoshi had ever

delivered to Valko.

'Relax Oshi, I meant what I said. We've done well today. If he provides us with the information that we need then even Old Man Odegebayo will sign off on a reprieve,' Valko said, surprising himself with the familiar tone he was using and his apparent sincerity.

'Yes, sir. Sorry to have doubted it,' Satoshi said.

He bustled away and began directing Davidson to deal with the unenviable task of cleaning up the prisoner.

Now the tricky part. How to tell Odegebayo that he'd allowed a civilian to tag along with him at the Hotbed? Worse, as one of Eugene Fisher's team, she was a person of interest. There was no way he'd reveal the scale of her involvement or that he had allowed her to witness a mindlink, but he couldn't omit her from his report wholesale. Taking care, he composed his report to put a spin on the encounter that wouldn't make Jean look more suspect while at the same time explaining away his lapse in professional judgement. Removing references to a nickname was a start — she'd just be Xiang Rhea in his report. It took three attempts to get it right, but as he sent it, he knew there'd be hard questions to answer.

†††

Pallid skin scrubbed clean, with beard and hair shaved and sent to the processors, the man looked — and smelled, like a different person altogether. The stink of ordure and rancid human sweat had given way to the tang of medicated scrub. His hand had been treated and — once cleansed — the nature of the suppurating wound was revealed: a burn. That burn had contained the letters E, M, F, I and S branded into the flesh. Without a doubt, this human refuse had witnessed the murder of Eugene Fisher. Quite how some of the initials of the victim's grandfather were branded onto the man's hand was but one of the many questions Valko would ask.

Rennard secured a single purpose headset on the prisoner's head, then left. When it was clear that the headset had synchronised with the man's brainwaves, Valko donned his own headset-hub.

Without a dose of NOTT adding its particular haze of purple to his musings, he considered the device dispassionately. There was no fear of a further failure in the feedback prevention protocol. Besides, the wretch in front of him hardly had any fully functional neurones as it was, let alone augmented ones. No, with his old clarity fortified by the ritual of donning his Moderator's hub — ready to sift the suspect's recent memories — Valko felt calm, confident, in control. He knew his capabilities and that of his equipment intimately.

There was no better expert at using the subtle language of mind-to-mind communication to prod, goad or downright terrify a subject into complying — into giving up their deeper, darker secrets. His satisfaction wasn't simply at being able to do what an unaltered human could never achieve — the best they'd get was the voluntary sharing of inflectionless words and hazy images — no, it was at being a true professional and unmatched even among his kind. If the whispered stories about the Moderator's had been true… If they could bore into the mind and steal any memory they chose — the way it was with retrieving memory fragments from the deceased — then blunt instruments like Bezant would have been the paragon for all Tantei and not just a brutal tool for scaring the drudges. Valko knew he was a subtler instrument by far, but then there was always the test of riding the surging wave of NOTT. Sometimes even the most subtle mind could be undone by emotion — artificial though it was.

Valko took the final step in readiness for the interrogation and prepped a dose of NOTT, noting the serial number of the vial — PSUG291 — out of habit. He slid it into his wrist valve and the familiar, slippery rush of added awareness cartwheeled through his mind. Valko turned his attention to the subject.

Looking at him with NOTT ramping up his humanity, Valko felt a flood of fellow feeling for the man — malnourished and leading a desperate existence. Why anyone would choose to live this way was beyond Valko. It must have been some dreadful tragedy or else a mental instability that drove this wretch to his fate. Valko took care as he reached into the man's mind and detected thoughts of pain. He sent a mental command to the subject's headset for it to dampen that pain, then formulated his first question.

«*Who are you?*»

The thought flashed back at him, «*No bod*»

What a terrible way to think of yourself. Valko got a grip of his emotions with the equivalent of a mental slap to his face, as he felt the urge to weep — this was worse than usual. He tried again.

«*Tell me your name. If you help me, I will be able to protect you.*» Valko allowed sincerity to go with the message: near subconscious, not faked.

«*Joey. Mai handle Joey Koewatha*»

Valko broke off and sent a quick message to Satoshi who was monitoring the exchange with his own hub, «*Oshi, any trace within the records?*»

The response was swift and decisive and carried in Satoshi's unique inner voice, «*No, sir. But Koewatha sounds like a Remnant name to me.*»

Valko returned to the mindlink with Koewatha, «*Alright, Joey. You saw someone being murdered, didn't you?*»

«*When ya mean?*»

«*Joey, I can only help you if you give me the information. You do know what will happen to you otherwise, don't you?*»

«*Yo, mai ken. Why you help mai?*»

«*Because I know what it means to feel hollow inside, I understand your pain and if I can end yours maybe there's hope for mine.*»

The thought flowed out of Valko like it were a truth he had been hiding all his life, but the genuine human part of his brain rebelled. *Liar*, it said. He knew who he was underneath and this nauseating sympathy was purely the product of the implant and the NOTT. Sure, he meant it now — had no choice in the matter — but he, the true Valko, carried no inner pain, only a relentless drive, forcing him forwards.

«*Ok. Mai feels ya man. Looks, mai want no badness, mai jest gon tap him threaded dude for some chump.*»

«*We can forget about that, we know you had a knife out and ready, but that's not what killed him*»

«*Mass-mass, man. Mai never tried stick him. Blest Merica, mai jest wanted him help. But… that other one. Like jook him and burned what left with fire.*»

«*What other one?*»

«*Shady one, all sooted up, like ink, man. Her had spike of fire in *him. Her took all him thing from him, burn rest.»*

«*Then how did you get the brand on your hand.*»

«*That from another thing, man.*»

«*Don't lie to me. This is being recorded. The man who was killed was called Fisher. You have his initials branded on your hand*»

The grandfather's initials were close enough, this human ruin wouldn't appreciate the semantics. The familiar process of manipulation was providing a distraction from the enforced solidarity that kept making him forget his role: drawing out the truth not making friends. Even as the thought formed, it was tinged with guilt creeping just behind his full awareness — he was preying on this man's hopes and fears with this manipulation.

Joey stared down at his hand, the dressing now concealing the mark.

«*Mass-mass, man. Mai no know it was portant. Shiny thing off hims bag was gold, man. Gold.*» Avaricious thoughts filled Joey's mind. «*Go burn me crook.*» The pain from his hand returned, as if on cue, before the headset suppressor switched it off once more.

«*You said it was a 'her' that killed him?*»

«*Mai no wanna think bout her, man. Her have the badness in her.*»

«*You must. Are you sure it was a woman? Show me an image of her in your mind*»

«*Mai can't, man. Her darkness, her come get mai if mai be conjure her.*»

«*Being wei-zhuce carries a sentence of immediate execution and recycling. Give me this and I will have you spared. Indoctrinated. I promise.*»

Valko could feel Joey's mounting terror, as the man tried to summon an image of what he had seen in his mind. He was about to prompt him again when the images came in a flood. Joey had surrendered himself to the memory and Valko relived the murder through his eyes.

Dude up front of mai, looks good for some chump — all threaded end with them case. Sure be swank in them for sell the man: swank mai gone get 'buzzin on, 'zaggin on.

Caught up as he was in what he was seeing through Joey's mind, Valko, at first, took no notice of how real the memory was to him. He wasn't only experiencing it as a vid playback with sound, image, and smell, like normal — he was occupying Joey's body; in his mind — losing himself.

Him better have them good stuff for mai. Git deep mai burnin for some buzzin. Doc's in mai crook — him give mai backbite mai gone cut him... cut him deep to that white.

Bar de Godbless! Darkness step outta wall...

Drawing on all his training — all his years of breaking down the will of others — Valko dragged back control to himself. He was there — not Koewatha. Valko — not Joey. He saw the figure dressed in blurry black appear, stepping out of a shadow. He held the image of her: terrifying; fascinating; sensual.

The skinsuit caused her form to waver like thick smoke roiling in the air, but *he* could see her — see the suit, striated with glyphs and symbols and code to blind the electronic eye. She moved with a light step that said one thing to him — power. The power of great strength and physical control. Here was someone who knew her body's limits and capabilities. She seized Fisher and drove a cylinder against the back of his head, as he peered into the door scanner. Valko saw the spike of fire she withdrew, that steamed and smoked with the profane but sacred contents of Fisher's skull. He watched as she popped the catches clean off the briefcase with one thumb like it was nothing; rooted through the briefcase; and found what she sought: hardcopies.

The surfaces of each page of smart-paper ran with charts and equations that shifted as their edges were touched, showing all their stored data. One switched images between a page of equations, some technical drawings of a device and a simulated astrolabe. Another was different, it looked older; its contents were streams of data and text. The killer took this one and — with a nonchalant gesture — flicked a small bead, clear like glass, into the remaining contents of the briefcase. In the first microsecond of the flash from — what had Satoshi called it? — the flashburner, light illuminated her face. It was a single moment of time so short he could hardly comprehend it, yet he found he could control the memory and lock onto the instant like he'd never been able to before. He was seeing a fragment of memory so small that Koewatha could never find it. The wei-zhuce's mind lacked sufficient discipline.

She was wearing part of the skinsuit pulled up over her nose and mouth and small black goggles protected her eyes, to prevent retinal identification. He got the vaguest impression of her face in profile: strong nose over a sharp jawline; broad forehead; tan skin. She'd concealed her hair under the hood of the skinsuit, but a strand spilled out along the right side of her face. Black or brown hair it was hard to say, but neither hair colour nor skin colour was unusual for a citizen of any Plenum anywhere in the world.

Valko let the memory flow on — feeling his awareness of Joey reassert itself, becoming dominant again. *Fear. The trickle of urine down his leg. In the moments following the incandescence, as the violet afterimage on his retina blocked his sight, he cowered in the shadows, his small blade hidden once more up his sleeve. Plans for a quick knifepoint robbery had fled and he blinked, trying to clear his vision. When the purple haze cleared, he looked around. There was no sign of the indistinct figure that had materialised out of the dark. Looking upwards showed nothing, save the fall of constant drizzle and the bright lights on all the towering blocks and walkways crisscrossing the internal structure of the Plenum. The slim shadow had vanished, as silent as her arrival. He breathed again, his heart still beating painfully in his chest. Would she come back?*

Fighting his fear, he crept to the scorched remains that sizzled as water spattered on them. The smell of burnt flesh — something unknown to him — made him gag. He fought his gorge down and, holding a dirty rag over his face, rummaged through the debris removing an antique watch from the corpse's wrist, and an old-fashioned pair of wire-framed glasses tucked into the clothing covering the remnants of the charred torso. Turning to the smoking ash that was once a briefcase, he poked through the cinders with the tattered toe of his left boot. There was a light metallic tinkle, as something skittered across the ground.

A small piece of golden metal — still attached to a scrap of blackened leather — caught his eye. Greed and desperation came before sense — he grabbed the metal shard... and howled. The still hot sliver burned his fingers and his palm where he had grabbed it tight in his need. He prized the offending piece of metal off his hand with his knife, tears running as he cradled his injured hand to his chest. It hurt so much. The metal dropped to the ground and lay hissing softly in the rain. He needed it — NEEDED *— it. With some difficulty, he ripped a strip of smart fabric from the jacket of the corpse at his feet and picked up the hot metal, wrapping it up before stuffing it in his pocket. Turning he ran, hunched over, protecting his hand.*

The flow of memory stopped dead and Valko found himself looking at Joey's emaciated and careworn face.

'What just happened?' Valko asked, pulling off his hub and standing with difficulty, his legs shaky.

Satoshi answered over the interview room comm, 'Everything alright, sir?'

'Yes... No. Oshi, you were monitoring the link, what did you see?'

'The murder. It was grisly, but at least we know for certain that the killer used a flashburner. That's a strong link to the Vinnetti case — it's got to be the same person.'

Valko shook his head, trying to clear it.

'So, you saw nothing unusual about the memory feed over the mindlink?' He asked.

'No, sir. Looked clearer than I expected from a narc user, but that's it.'

'Let me review the recording.'

Valko watched the backup copy that had been made of the mindlink. It was normal: sight; sound; smell, but no more. Something strange had happened, but it had helped him. Confirmed the detail of the killer's gender, which wasn't clear in the backup recording. Right now, he had a case to solve; he'd think about this when it was done.

Valko donned his hub again and returned his attention to Koewatha. The man was looking at him dully — no sign he recognised that anything unusual had happened showed in his sallow eyes. Valko touched his mind again.

« *Can you tell me anything else about her?*»

«*Only what man saw,*» Joey said in the foreground of his mind — Valko detected nothing hiding behind that, no lie or deception.

«*Fine. We're nearly done, then I'll have one of my kensakan get you some food.*» Valko had become acutely aware of Joey's hunger. «*What did you do with the metal nameplate?*»

«*Mai went sold it, man*»

«*To whom?*»

«*Some threaded dude in the hotbed. Said him had a case like it once. Him give mai judds man. Him real intense. Bought mai some zigzag with it, you be sure.*»

«*Was it Slim Jan?*»

«*Ah, not that juice off, man. Him not interested in it, says it 'hot property', mai thought him meant mai crook.*» The image of his burned hand flashed across his mind.

«*Can you give me a name or send me an image of the man then?*»

«*Mass-mass, man. Mai done put him out of mai head straight with them zigzag. The real good jolt. After, mai bar buzzing to help mai crook pain.*»

Valko removed the headset, glad to be free of the pinching contacts — they'd given him a headache. He ran through the pain suppression exercises, waiting for them to pull the sparking pins out from behind his eyes. Pain bled away, drip by drip.

'Davidson, get this man something to eat. Something hot.' Turning back to the witness, he said, 'Thank you, Joey. I'll recommend that you be indoctrinated, it might mean having to head to an outpost but it's better than…' Valko left the unpleasant thought hanging.

'Mass-mass, man. Can't yo be blessing mai back to free town? Mai plain good bar buzzing.' If anything, the man's argot was even more difficult to understand when spoken aloud. The thoughts had not had a heavy accent with the added blur of a mouth lacking most of its teeth.

'That I can't do, but you'll find that life as one of the Enclosed, is better than you think.'

The words rang hollow, even to Valko's ears.

†††

Valko adjusted his hub and took seven breaths, before sending a connection request to Odegebayo's office. It was a mark of how seriously the Pravnik was taking the investigation that Valko was kept waiting less than a minute, instead of upwards of an hour. He'd have to be careful, even without a Moderator's implant Odegebayo was cunning and he could smell lies.

It didn't help that the connection was different from the usual hub-to-hub communication — one of the privileges of a position in the Conclave. Instead of having a simple mind-to-mind link, where thoughts were sent as direct messages to the other user, Odegebayo's headset-hub had a filter, giving him a slight delay to review all outgoing messages and assess how they'd be received. With a normal link, there was emotional overspill —

the strength of a person's feelings on a matter would come along with their words. A normal user could discern that undercurrent, only when the person they were communicating with was in the most extreme of emotional states: homicidal rage or suicidal despair being the most likely.

Moderators — at least those still under the influence of NOTT — could pick out all the subtle inflections. Odegebayo's filter prevented this — it gave him the advantage, even over his Moderators. The information he sent was the information he chose: no overspill unless he constructed it. His words, when they eventually came, carried the confident but warm timbre of the man's voice. They conveyed authority but with a touch of an indulgent grandfather. Considering the ruthlessness of the man behind the fiction, Valko couldn't help but wonder what a true read would be like. A thought to make him shudder — case hardened though he was.

«*Ah, Valko. You have something to report?*»

«*Yes, Weiyuan. We located the witness and I have satisfied myself that he is not culpable in Fisher's death. He provided useful information about the murderer and did so voluntarily.*»

«*Excellent, responsible Enclosed are why the system works. He may merit a reconsideration of his rec allowance,*» Odegebayo sent.

«*Yes, that was another matter I wished to discuss with you, Weiyuan.*»

«*Hesitancy, Valko? How unlike you. What is it?*»

«*The witness is unregistered, a wei-zhuce. To ensure his co-operation, I suggested that he might be spared execution and recycling and would instead be granted indoctrination. Clearly, starting in a low rated position, until he could prove otherwise.*»

«*Suggested or promised? Valko, I am surprised. I would expect nothing less of you than to use whatever means necessary to obtain the information, but if this man has given you all the information he has...*»

«*I believe that he has, yes,*» Valko sent.

«*Then he is of no further use. Promises to wei-zhuce do not matter to me. The law is clear. Anyone who wishes to petition to become Enclosed must do so before entry to a Plenum. Those who are not indoctrinated at their point of entry have compromised the security of the Plenum. There is one sentence and no exemptions.*»

A strong sense of finality pervaded his words.

«*I understand, Weiyuan.*»

Valko felt an upwelling of emotion — an attack from an unexpected quarter. His shame at his broken promise and pity for Koewatha were not so great as to make him protest Odegebayo's order. He felt sorry for Koewatha, didn't want to join him.

«*And Valko. Do it yourself. I want to be sure that you haven't lost your edge*»

Odegebayo broke the link and the impact of the order struck Valko like a punch to the gut. He ripped the headset off his head and threw it across the small chamber, not caring if its delicate components shattered. He had looked Koewatha in the eyes and told him — in the silent candour of mental contact — that it would be all right. He had been so stupid, so confident. The unfeeling part of him — the true Valko — whispered that emotion had clouded his judgement. This was the only possibility he could have expected from Odegebayo.

There had to be another way. He picked up his hub, relieved to find it was undamaged — its impact with the floor no doubt softened by the thick layer of g-moss. Putting it back on, he sent a message to Oshi. His sergeant was quick to respond.

«*Sir?*»

«*Oshi, I need to deal with Koewatha. Bring him to me.*»

«*Yes, sir.*»

Valko couldn't detect any particular undertone from Satoshi's mind — in spite of the NOTT that was altering his mental state, the link was curiously flat. Satoshi must be occupied in some tedious task.

Waiting, unable to focus on anything else, Valko made his decision. After twenty minutes, Satoshi arrived; Koewatha dragged behind him in restraints, head bowed and silent.

'Sir, what do we need to do to register him? I thought we'd need a medtech and someone from the Office of Registration to install his beacon and a Hand of the Mother to indoctrinate him?'

'All in order, Sergeant. Secure the prisoner here. I need to discuss another matter with you, first,' Valko said, trying to give no hint of his inner turmoil.

'Yes, sir.'

Satoshi sat Koewatha down and activated the restraints'

proximity limiters. Koewatha could move freely within two metres of his current location but any further would lead to immediate paralysis. Valko left the room and Satoshi followed close behind.

'Oshi, can I trust you?'

'Val, you should know that by now,' Satoshi said.

'Good. The Pravnik ordered Koewatha's execution and recycling.'

'What?'

'I should have known. He's a ruthless old bastard, without an iota of compassion.' Neither of them commented on the absurdity of the statement: Valko Gangleri, regarded as the most cold-blooded Moderator, criticising someone for a lack of compassion.

'What are you going to do?'

Valko sighed and said, 'He ordered me to execute Koewatha myself. Legally, as Moderator with responsibility for the prisoner, I can choose the method of most efficient execution. Recycling is merely assumed as the next logical step.'

'Yes, I know. Tantei Singh favours having a kensakan give the prisoner a tranq overdose, while Tantei Bezant used to take them straight to the recycler and have his sergeant kick them in.' Satoshi grimaced at the thought.

'Bezant was a violent psychopath, we're better off without his brutality now. But… it gives me an idea.' The Moderator stared off into middle distance for a moment.

'Val? You're not just going to recycle Koewatha, are you?' Satoshi said.

'No. No, that's not what I mean. The recyclers connect to external outlets don't they?'

'Yes, but that's only for sending organic waste out to those Martyrs working to re-fertilise the soil around the Plenum.' Satoshi squinted at Valko, puzzlement plain on his face.

'Only organic material is allowed through but it's not monitored. The recyclers run on a schedule, don't they?' Valko asked.

'Yes, I think so. Something to do with needing sufficient material to warrant them charging up, doing it in dribs and drabs is just too inefficient.'

'So there is time between a recycler finishing its cycle and starting a new one,' Valko said.

'Yes, that's part of the horror of what Bezant used to do... They could be left waiting for death long minutes before the process started, knowing that they were going to be stripped apart as soon as the level of waste being piped in was high enough.'

'If someone could bypass the release valve leading to an external outlet before the cycle started...' Valko let the thought trail off.

'They might be able to get out. I understand. Not a definite release but a chance. Problem is, if he fails, it's supposed to be one of the most agonising ways of dying.'

'Some hope is better than no hope.' Valko could begin to feel the edges of NOTT wearing off. It had lasted much, much longer this time. 'It's not without risk to us, too.'

'If Odegebayo ever found out he'd have us both recycled as punishment,' Satoshi said, his expression grim.

'We must act quickly. Before I change my mind.'

Valko couldn't keep a hint of his desperation from showing. If he didn't do this before the NOTT wore off, he'd shoot Koewatha and that would be the end of it.

'I'm with you, Val,' Satoshi said, as he went back inside and returned with Koewatha.

'Mass-mass, man. What the stress?'

Koewatha looked frightened. He wasn't so stupid he couldn't tell that something was up.

'Do as I say and you have a chance to live. Anything else and you will die. Do you understand?' Valko said, allowing a little of his usual iciness to enter his tone. Koewatha nodded and followed along.

The Moderator, his sergeant, and their prisoner swiftly descended to the recycling level at the bottom of Arcas Plenum, where only vermin and the occasional drudge doing repair work moved. The system was self-maintaining for the most part and the majority of the input was piped directly in — an efficiency that, in the absence of people, conjured a sepulchral air. It was easy to imagine that they were winding their way down into a tomb where the dead lay, while unliving guardians continued their thoughtless vigil.

Valko caught himself in the rising melancholy of this line of thought. Dark thoughts were not a new thing to him, but this maudlin reflection was a product of the drug. His emotions — synthetic though they might be — didn't have much of a battle with his rational, reptile mind over saving Koewatha. It wasn't that his authentic self was concerned with quaint ideas — keeping to the honour of word — his true identity simply didn't care enough about this. Awakening it with despondency or even childish indulgence in a fear of the dark would rouse his ruthless mind to hasty action — he might execute Koewatha to avoid the risk.

They found one of the recyclers located closest to the edge of the Plenum where the large outlet pipes were visible. Eyeballing it, Valko figured the ducts were big enough for a man to crawl through, but he knew they'd fill when a cycle was complete. The recycler had a large hatch — currently sealed — at its top for disposal of oversized waste and occasional maintenance access. A message, displayed on a small screen, warned that a recycling process was in progress with an estimated fifteen minutes before completion. Long enough to prepare Koewatha.

'I can't have you indoctrinated. I've been ordered to kill you and have you recycled, but the choice of how I do it is up to me,' Valko said.

Koewatha dropped to his knees, shaking, 'Don't, man. Don't. Mai begs, mai do what you want.' There was the sudden stink of urine as the pathetic man lost control of himself.

'Stop that, we don't have time. We will open the valve to the external outlet. You must go through it as fast as possible; we can only keep the valve open for a short time before it will trigger a delay of the next cycle. If that happens then what we're doing will be logged and we'll all go in a sealed recycle unit.'

'Yo blessing mai home?' The look of sudden hope on Koewatha's ashen face was almost mad in its intensity.

'Yes, but if you don't move fast then you will drown in the sludge that is pumped out after the cycle. Do you understand?'

'Mass-mass, man. Mai ken. Mai remembers this all days.'

Koewatha got to his feet. Satoshi disabled the restraints but left them on. Valko took the trembling man by the shoulder.

'I can only take these off the moment before I put you in.'

'Val, what are we going to do about the report? Satoshi asked. 'Odegebayo will want proof for the file.'

'Davidson will be here any minute. He doesn't know what we're doing, I'll have him monitor it on his hub and send that for the file. You need to go to the valve now, Oshi. Listen out — when I put Koewatha in you'll hear a shot. You need to open the valve, count to ten then shut it off. Any longer and we risk upsetting the cycle.'

'How do you know all this, Val?'

'I worked a case where a drudge was using a recycler for smuggling contraband. We caught him with the recycler logs. Now move. Davidson mustn't see you.'

Satoshi dashed off, moving with great speed and grace despite his size. A matter of minutes later, Valko heard Davidson's heavy tread as the kensakan — as always pushing the borders of acceptable physical condition — wheezed into view. He'd probably run the last fifty feet or so before walking round the corner to give the impression that he'd tried to get there as fast as possible.

'Boss, I'm here. Sorry, I took so long, I was, er, dealing with some of the perps we caught after the Hotbed raid last night.'

I bet you were, Valko thought. 'You're here now. I need you to help me deal with the wei-zhuce. He's to be recycled.'

'Woah, Boss! You mean you're going to Bezant him?' Davidson was a little apprehensive, clearly reassessing his superior and realising that he was on even thinner ice than he'd thought. *Good.*

'No. I'm simply going to put him in, then shoot him. It's efficient and clean.'

Valko stopped himself from saying more, he'd normally never justify himself to Davidson or even Satoshi — so why was he doing so now? He should've given Davidson his Moderator's stare and then written him up for insubordination later. This damn NOTT episode was really playing with him. 'Get your hub on and record it for the file. Maybe, you can finally learn some efficiency yourself.'

Joey Koewatha had broken down in tears again. Either because he believed that Valko would shoot him or the man was a much better actor than he'd have credited before. Valko opened the pressure door on the recycler and moved Koewatha into position. With the restraints turned off, it should have been much harder but the weeping man moved as if they were still active: quiet and compliant.

Once Koewatha was positioned on the edge, Valko drew his tranqgun and adjusted it — instead of firing the standard pellet of neuroshock tranquiliser it would instead fire a solid resin round designed to soften in flight to impart massive trauma on impact by expanding on contact, before behaving like a non-Newtonian liquid and hardening. The effect was an almost guaranteed kill: a single round would leave a fist-sized or bigger hole wherever it hit. He glanced back to make sure that Davidson was capturing the staged execution.

Adopting his most formal tone, he said, 'Joey Koewatha, wei-zhuce, you are guilty, under section three hundred and seventy-eight, subsection two of the Penal Code of the Centra Autorita and section seven one alpha of the Articles of Registration, of crimes committed against this Plenum and against the Mother. May you repay in death that which you took from Her in life.'

When he had finished the formal pronouncement, he seized the restraints and disengaged them at the same time as he pushed Koewatha forward. The man fell into the recycler with a cry but Valko could see that he landed on his feet and sprinted for the sealed outlet pipe. Valko raised his gun and mimed taking careful aim, before firing one round into the chamber below. The shot was the cue for Satoshi to open the valve sealing the outlet pipe, and, sure enough, it opened — swift and soundless. Valko began to close the pressure door to the chamber one-handed, with the tranqgun still in his right hand. He saw Koewatha disappear down the tunnel then he sealed the door and holstered his weapon.

Turning to face Davidson, he said, 'Sentence executed. Recycling will commence shortly.'

Right on time, the indicator on the pressure door warned that a cycle was starting and waste pumped into the chamber at high speed. They had avoided triggering the automatic delay. So long as Koewatha got out of the outlet pipe before the recycler completed digestion and pumped out, they would be in the clear.

If he didn't, well, he would be dead and one of the Martyrs would find a body washed up in the organic fertilisers pumped onto their Preserve.

Davidson removed his headset-hub. 'What now, Boss?'

'Any update on Actur or the beacon traffic?' Valko asked.

Davidson took a moment before answering, his face a little pale. 'No, Boss. No read on Actur's beacon and we've got zero on beacon records. I was hoping to get somewhere with those 'popheads we picked up from the Hotbed we raided last night.'

'Kensakan, since when have 'pop addicts been good for anything? You'll be lucky if they remember their own names until their doses wear off. Leave them in the holding cells — wherever you were *getting* with them. I want you to head to Outpost Theta; Actur is a lead we need to chase down,' Valko said.

'Boss.'

Davidson spun and Valko didn't need a mindlink to tell that the man's thoughts were whining about being sent to the American ruins. At least he'd had the sense not to make an open complaint. Perhaps there was some hope for him after all.

Part II

Quod intus conficimus veritatem exteram mutabit

What we achieve inwardly will change outer reality.

— Lucius Mestrius Plutarchus —

Chapter 6

Valko found himself once more summoned to Odegebayo's office. Having two meetings with the Old Man, in as many days, was unheard of. There was no wait; he was ushered straight in.

'Ah, Valko. Come in. Sit down. I've received your report. Very interesting. I appreciate the way you dealt with that wei-zhuce. My concerns about you losing your edge were obviously unfounded. Now, tell me how far along your investigation is.'

'Weiyuan, we can clearly link the murder of Dr Fisher with that of the young woman found dead in Berlin Plenum in the drudge's quarters,' Valko said. 'Her name was Vinnetti — she was a whitecoat working in Dr Fisher's Lab. The modus operandi of her death was the same. An energised filament extruded into her brain and a small device — War-era tech called a flashburner — was used in an attempt to destroy evidence. There is no security footage from the scene of her murder, but it must be the same killer.'

Odegebayo gave him a stern look. 'Have you apprehended the drudge to whom the quarters were registered?'

'No, Weiyuan. He cannot be located. Tracking last detected his beacon at Outpost Theta outside the New York burn-zone. The information I received from linking with Koewatha allowed me to see his memory of the Fisher murder. He was clearly there…'

The Old Man steepled his fingers, 'Yes, I've reviewed the recorded image flow. What I lacked were the emotional responses. You described his terror in the report.'

'Yes, I'm certain that Koewatha was merely an observer and not linked to the murderer. They were clearly not known to each other. I am certain that he was being truthful.' Valko met the Old Man with a steady gaze, using all his mental discipline to keep out thoughts of Koewatha's true fate.

'That doesn't surprise me. From what I could see, the perpetrator of this terrible act was sophisticated and professional. Someone unlikely to have dealings with a wei-zhuce, then leave them alive. That leaves the question of why he left a potential witness alive. Confidence in his disguise, perhaps?'

'Her disguise, Weiyuan. I was able to see that the murderer is a woman.'

Odegebayo arched an eyebrow. 'Very astute of you — a detail I missed. That rules out the drudge as a suspect. What was his name, Actor?'

'Darius Actur. I agree, but he may be in possession of useful information or he may be another victim. Either way, there is a potential evidence trail.'

Odegebayo stroked his beard as he said, 'I presume that you have checked the records of beacon traffic in the area of the murder?'

'Yes, Weiyuan. One of my kensakan was tasked with that: Davidson.' Even as he said it, Valko felt like he was making an admission of wrongdoing.

'Oh yes, Davidson.' Odegebayo's tone spoke volumes and even his well-practiced smile began to look forced. 'Did he find anything?'

'No, there was no beacon present at either crime scene around the time of the murders, except for the victims', of course. I've dispatched Davidson to Outpost Theta to try to locate Actur.' Odegebayo relaxed again, no doubt from the realisation that Valko was deploying Davidson in a suitable manner rather than trusting him with any real responsibility.

'What about the other whitecoats on Fisher's staff? You're satisfied that all of their alibis hold water?'

'Yes, Weiyuan.'

'Good. You have things well in hand. Now, what I'm about to tell you goes no further and does not enter any of your reports. Do you understand?'

Valko nodded, taken aback.

'The Conclave had an emergency session yesterday, where I informed the others of the murder of Dr Fisher. He was due to deliver a report to us at the time of his murder. The timing cannot have been a coincidence. For some time now, the Conclave has been overseeing his latest project.'

'Sorry to interrupt, Weiyuan, but I thought that scientific research fell within the purview of the Temple?'

Odegebayo gave no sign of irritation at the interruption,

but Valko knew that he was pushing his luck.

'That's correct in normal circumstances. Eugene Fisher has been granted remarkable leeway, as was his father. You'll understand that — given the importance of the Fisher family to us all and the contributions of Fisher's grandfather in particular — it was appropriate to make allowances. You are not to share this information with any representative of the Temple, do you understand? On pain of immediate execution.'

'I understand,' Valko said, holding his breath while Odegebayo stopped, gathering his thoughts.

'You are thinking, why tell me this, yes?'

Valko nodded.

'Fisher's research was, shall we say, not entirely in accordance with Temple doctrine. He was attempting to find a way to achieve faster than light travel: to provide us with a means of travelling to other planets more conducive to human life than the Mother has become.'

Valko gawked at Odegebayo. His surprise came not from the fantastical nature of the research but had a visceral source. From birth, the Enclosed grew up surrounded by the belief that humanity was a macro-virus, a destructive plague that needed to be controlled. The Temple of the Wounded Mother claimed that it acted on behalf of the planet Herself, to curb the actions of her wayward children. The highest honour that anyone in the Plena could earn was Martyrdom — the duty to live outside, tending the wounds in the earth and trying to bring some life back to the Mother. The Temple would regard any research aimed at spreading the human plague as the gravest of heresies.

While a Moderator was nominally a secular agent of the Centra Autorita, they were all required to submit to more intense Temple indoctrination than the average Enclosed was, though the rate of success was only a small margin above the baseline. It had never taken a particular hold on Valko — his cynicism had won out — but he wondered at the degree to which Odegebayo and the other Conclave members had strayed from the fundamental values that indoctrination had burned into all of them. What the Conclave had done was not a crime in a secular sense, but if the Temple found out there would be serious consequences.

'Yes, Valko. It was not his only field of research, but you can see how it might have been the one that provided a motive for someone with professional skills to be sent to kill him and Vinnetti. She was, by the way, his closest assistant, regarded by many as his protégé.'

'I don't understand. If the Temple knew, surely they would have taken some action against the Conclave?' Valko said, feeling uncomfortable that Davidson's guess about a possible perpetrator had fit what Odegebayo was now telling him.

'The politics are far more complicated than that. We don't know that the Temple as a whole has discovered what we were doing. It may be a single high-level Hand or a lone zealot. It may have been someone on Fisher's team more susceptible to indoctrination than the rest. If the Temple did know, they would risk much by taking overt action against the Conclave. They need us as we have needed them. They might, however, take covert action against individual members of the Conclave.'

'Hence the urgency of my investigation,' Valko said

'Precisely.'

The Old Man was sweating. Valko reflected on how this man — so callous with other people's lives — was so desperate for fear of losing his own.

'I have no jurisdiction over the Temple, as you know, Weiyuan. How can I investigate without alerting them? If they are not involved and remain ignorant, wouldn't any investigation risk them finding out what the Conclave has been doing?'

'Yes. Perhaps you do understand. One day, maybe, you will find yourself called to the role of Pravnik, Valko. Solve this situation and you will be one step closer to that.'

How typical of Odegebayo to assume that Valko's motivations were the same as his own. Being a Moderator — the best Moderator — was the beginning and the end of his own aspirations.

'I understand, Weiyuan. I will have my sergeant make subtle enquiries at the Temple. His son is being considered for full indoctrination, so he is likely to have a greater degree of access, without raising suspicion.'

'Excellent. One more thing, I note the contents of the autopsy report. You should ask our pet whitecoat what level of expertise would be required for someone to know which area of the brain to vaporise. I suspect that anyone without a high level of training would choose total destruction of the head. That the killer focused on merely removing the memory centres of the brain, and didn't simply try to maximise collateral damage, suggests someone who thinks with precision. You might say, surgical precision.'

Valko held back a comment. If he'd understood what Orla had told him in the past, then memories spread through the brain and didn't reside in one single place. Interrupting Odegebayo again would be a bad idea, however, so he listened instead.

The Old Man continued. 'Check with Orla whether I am right. While you're at it, get her to give you a physical, I want to be sure that you are truly back to your old self and not harbouring some residual damage from your earlier foolishness.'

It was the closest to genuine concern for another's well-being that Valko had ever seen in Odegebayo, though his paternal act never quite convinced — what he was really saying was: I haven't forgotten your mistake. There remained one last issue — here was the moment for asking about the access records.

'Weiyuan, with respect, there is one more question I have before I go,' Valko said.

The Old Man scowled. It was a fraction of a twitch of his eyebrows, in truth, but enough of a danger sign. 'Go on, Tantei Gangleri.'

'Forgive me for raising such a minor issue but I noticed that Pravnik Hampton was also overseeing the investigation. Should I prepare a separate report for her as well?' He chose not to mention the edits to the case file that she must have made. It would be dangerous, perhaps fatal, to so much as appear to be questioning a Pravnik's motivations. Then again, even they were not above the law.

Odegebayo's face was emotionless. No grandfatherly warmth. No wrathful god of the ancients. Flat eyes bored into Valko's, 'Proceed as normal, Tantei Gangleri.'

The Old Man's attention shifted back to his work, as sure a dismissal as any other. Valko slipped out of the room — a mouse escaping the cat's notice.

ᚠᚠᚠ

Satoshi let out a marrow-deep sigh as he returned to the

small rooms he shared with his assigned mate. Five years after revival, and well into his integration into the life of an Enclosed, the Centra Autorita had selected Iona as the ideal genetic match for him. She was, to some eyes, beautiful. To him, she was pretty. There was and never had been any spark. When he looked into her eyes, he saw nothing but his own reflection staring back at him, diminished. Iona was strong and intelligent — focused; she knew exactly what she wanted. She had bought into the belief system prevalent in the Plena completely — the Temple occupied her mind as much as the Centra Autorita dictated her actions. Perhaps that was the root of the problem.

Satoshi knew he'd been a tool of the Superstates. They'd used him. His war record showed enough for him to know that. But while waking into the future had, at first, left him alienated, the loss of his memories had set him free from the horrors of a war he could no longer remember. Reflex made him touch the side of his head where an old scar was barely visible under his close-cropped hair. The headshot might have helped some too, he thought wryly.

Though he didn't remember why, he knew that he could never accept the rules and beliefs of this closed in world. Ever since waking to them, he'd bounced from one horror to another. People were not expendable. At times, there seemed like no way out. It didn't matter. He would always strive for more. Iona, though, she was a true believer.

There was also the age gap. He was well over one hundred years old, though the face he saw in the mirror every morning when he shaved looked early thirties, despite the scars. Iona was a genuine twenty-eight. Given the huge gaps in his memories that didn't make a great difference — he'd had only twenty-three years of memories when they'd met. If anything, it was like she was an older woman.

Sure, there was a difference to the way he thought — his mind had been conditioned to react by his experiences in a way independent of memory — but the real distinction was that they came from different times. He still remembered echoes of the world before Enclosure — she had never seen the open sky.

The door slid back with a scrape and the noise of his son playing reached him. It was strange that his feelings could be so different for the boy but that was human nature. He worried, sometimes. Iona did not show any mother's love for their son but only an expectation of what he could achieve — what he could achieve for her. For a moment, there was no sign of Iona. Then he saw her sitting, watching Sadiq playing, and the look on her face was one of pure joy. Oshi felt ashamed of himself. He always thought the worst of Iona. She did love the boy.

Then Iona caught his reflection in one of the metal surfaces in the room. He saw her expression resume its usual mien of control and, as she turned to face him, the slight upturn in the corner of her mouth communicated nothing but contempt.

'Satoshi, I thought you were in Berlin?' *How could she know that? I don't remember telling her where I was going — has she been checking up on me?*

'I've just got back. What's going on?'

'Sadiq's been accepted into the Temple's Martyr to the Mother Youth Division.' There was pride in her voice and Oshi knew it was genuine, but he felt a chill down his spine when he caught the glint of ambition in her eyes.

Being careful to choose his words to avoid anything treasonous or blasphemous, he said, 'I don't think he's ready. Seven is too young.' There was a flash of anger in her blue eyes but he pressed on. 'He needs a chance to be a child, to learn who he is before he chooses a path in life.'

'What better path for him than to mix with other children who will go on to guide the Temple and the Conclave? You'd rather he ends up a whitecoat or else some drudge? Or do you want him to pick over corpses? Like you?'

'No, I just want him to be and do what he wants. Why is that so hard to understand? Life's not predictable.'

How could he make her understand, her childhood had been so different from his own. The world had been different then, still called Earth and not just the Mother.

'You mustn't let any of the Hands of the Mother hear you speaking like that. It would undo all of my hard work.' Iona fixed him with yet another of her glares, her tone like that she adopted with Sadiq when he was misbehaving, as young children do — as they should.

'Why do you want our son on the path of the Martyr? Don't misunderstand, I admire the selflessness, it takes a certain kind of courage to be willing to sacrifice your life to restoring the outside world. But how can you want our son to take the risk? No Martyr ever dies easy; it's either radiation poisoning or getting taken apart by nanodestroyers or going too far out and dying of starvation or thirst. That's the way you're pushing him!' Satoshi's voice had risen and he could feel his face heat with blood.

Only Iona could produce this loss of control in him. Far from being cowed by his anger, it only spurred Iona's own. Her wrath was the opposite of his, though. Ice far colder than his fire could burn hot.

'Don't be a fool. The one way for him to advance to become a higher member of the Temple is by walking the Martyr's path. He needs the training. Of course, he won't actually have to be one of the ones who leaves the Plenum. Only the purest of candidates are allowed that blessing. With a father like you, he has no chance of being selected for that privilege,' she said with such venom that it cut right through Satoshi.

He could feel the need to break something come over him but the violent impulse made his stomach churn. The thought came to him unbidden, *I've seen such violence.* He needed to escape somewhere, to run through the forms of his kata. Only they let him slip away to that empty state of mushin. Only by focusing on the void could he deal with it all.

Iona turned away from Satoshi.

'Why don't you go and waste more hours with your kata? Or is it another woman you're spending all your time with?' She said over her shoulder, face averted.

'I don't spend that much time away!' He said.

The kata soothed him, they stilled his mind so that an hour could blur by. She made it sound like he was gone for most of an evening. Another woman. Thoughts of Orla bubbled up and he fought them down. *I'm not that man!* He told himself.

Satoshi opened his mouth to explain, but Iona had already gone back to whatever task she had started before sitting down to watch their son. He had looked up watching them when his father had shouted. After a glance at his mother's back, Sadiq studied his father and smiled a small, sad smile. He understood the dynamic between his parents and knew that Satoshi never lost his temper save with Iona. Not once had he been anything but kind, loving and gentle to his son. His son knew him. Even as he began to go to Sadiq, Satoshi's hub chimed.

†††

Valko began making his way to the medcentre. He sent a short text only message to Satoshi.

«The Pravnik is concerned that there may be low-level Temple involvement, perhaps a lone zealot. Use your contacts through Sadiq's training to test the water. Give nothing away.»

He could rely on Oshi, so he checked on Davidson and was pleased to see that his beacon showed as having left the Plenum. Given the average speed of transpods, the slovenly kensakan should arrive at Outpost Theta within the hour.

The ever-present tides of people swept Valko along. For the first time, he felt a sense of communion with his fellows — all of them moving together like part of the same organism. The reek of different body odours and the scent of illicit perfume assaulted his nose; he could smell an undercurrent of tabac, zigzag and the suggestion of buzzpop. It reminded him of the Hotbed and the woman, Jean. With the memory, a lassitude came over him and he fell into a pleasant reverie lulled by the press of bodies and their almost tidal rhythm. The daydream died as he found himself washed up at the F-shaft leading to the level below. Valko descended, the tingle of static from the shaft bringing him fully out of his daze, and again allowed himself to drift along through the g-moss choked interior of the Plenum. He managed to steer his way to the medcentre and left the crush of people. It was at once a relief and at the same time a loss, like being drawn from the warm embrace of love.

The medcentre where Orla was based was in one of the older structures of Arcas Plenum. It had been a built a short time before the War and had none of the gravitas of the surviving structures of other Plena. Old Berlin structures that would fit in the Plenum and not compromise it endured, albeit covered in g-moss. Some of these ran through many levels of the Plenum and a half square mile of the old city centre had been enclosed.

His home, Arcas Plenum, was different. It had been the first of a planned series of purpose-built cities that would operate on a multilevel system. Pedestrians could move between structures above ground level and be able to cross from one side of the city to the other without ever touching the ground level. The perfection of the architect's vision resonated with Valko — but like all perfect visions, the reality fell short. The buildings had all been pristine structures of silver and white made of self-cleaning, self-repairing materials but sometimes, Valko wondered how much of the grim future the patron of the project, Erasmus Fisher, had foreseen. The number of the city's subterranean levels hinted at his fear of imminent catastrophe.

The UNWG's flagship project — saddled with the moniker Test Site One — had been designed to ease the population problems of the world. A metropolis that could house the population of a medium-sized capital city, with a footprint of less than half the usual size. Its design had made Enclosure far easier — so much so, that it seemed to have been its purpose from the start. Even so, the desperate flood of refugees from other overcrowded Plena and those fleeing the devastation outside had filled the enclosed city centre to more than four times the population it was designed to hold.

Now, Arcas Plenum looked similar to the others — if more beautiful in its logical layout and Spartan architecture — it had the ubiquitous g-moss and g-ivy and the opaque exterior shield. The clever planning of the city, with ideas of crowd fluid mechanics, had given false hope that the overcrowding problems of the other Plena would not be as noticeable. Such ideas worked in disparate ways at different scales of overcrowding. No previous city planner, architect or psychologist had envisaged the density of crowding of the Plena. The need for travel between them to share expertise and skills didn't help. Perhaps, Arcas was easier to navigate, or maybe that was an illusion. Unlike Berlin Plenum, for example, you couldn't always travel to different levels within the original buildings. It was something to do with preventing overcrowding within the buildings themselves. Of course, now it made the crush outside even worse.

Valko entered the building. One of the hospitals within the city when the UNWG first built its new capital, the medcentre radiated a sense of being sterile and clinical. The Centra Autorita had long since deactivated the smart materials of the building, for fear of what might happen if the nanobuilders — key to their functioning — became corrupted. G-moss, grown for the medcentres, covered every surface, soaking up contaminants and sterilising the air. Valko made his way to Orla's lab. No one checked him on his way; everyone here recognised the Moderator, and gave him a wide berth.

Orla's lab was situated on the second floor of the building, away from the recovery rooms and closer to the medical prep areas, to stop patients wandering into the area. He passed through the security monitors and entered the lab. It was divided into three sections and was far more spacious than was usual. Unlike his so-called office, Orla's remit required she have enough space that she could actually do her work in it. She appeared to be doing so now, sitting at a desk behind an old-style projection terminal — an affectation that he had never questioned.

Nostalgia for the past remained among some of the Enclosed, whitecoats in particular. The program of indoctrination by the Temple tended to partial success — unless you pursued it and sought to become a full member. Orla had not, hence her appreciation of the Old world.

She looked up at him and smiled. It made Valko feel uncomfortable — he had never been nice to her and yet she showed every sign of appreciating his presence.

'Tantei Gangleri, good to see you. Is this a social visit?' Her smile became wry. In five years of working together, Valko had never paid her, or anyone else, a social call.

'No, doctor,' he said, giving her the traditional title she so appreciated.

Most whitecoats didn't hold the title and even most medtechs would not merit it. Orla was better qualified than most; it puzzled him why she was working for the Moderators, rather than as part of a research team like the late Eugene Fisher's.

'The Pravnik ordered me to see you for a check-up on my implant. He also had some questions about the autopsy reports.' Valko Gangleri, straight to business as always.

'The Pravnik?' She stressed the word 'the'. 'You mean Old Man Odegebayo?' Her cheerfulness faded as she spoke his name.

'Yes. Forgive me,' Valko said. 'I forget that you assist several departments. He wanted to know what level of medical expertise would have been required to know precisely which parts of the brain to, what did you call it?'

'Cauterise. It was perhaps the wrong word. Whoever

murdered those two people did so by burning out those sections of their brains a post-mortem mindlink could read. They didn't bother to destroy all the parts of the brain that might store memories — merely those we could access.'

'I see. The question then is why bother with that sort of precision? If you simply wanted to prevent a post mortem mindlink, total destruction of the brain would be easier. Odegebayo's theory was that the person who did this had such expertise that she didn't think in such a basic way. I tend to agree with him.'

'That is… possible. The weapon used was a superheated microfilament. Larger than monofilament wire and thus more useful. Very dangerous.' Orla absently brushed a stray strand of hair from in front of her eyes.

'I'm not sure I understand. I thought that monofilament wire was the sharpest cutting tool,' Valko said, sitting down on the edge of the old desk.

'Yes, but it's really only useful for precise surgical procedures and with some technological applications,' Orla said. 'I have a monofilament scalpel. It's so delicate that I can't use it directly. I have to use a prosthesis to remove involuntary movements and reduce the pressure I'd apply by a factor of about a hundred. You couldn't use it as a weapon in this way.'

'I see. So why a microfilament?'

'They're much larger than a monofilament and yet still so sharp that they can easily cut through unprotected flesh and bone. It's also possible to superheat them with a relatively low level of charge. The best way of thinking of them is as a long chain of nanodestroyers, locked in place,' Valko repressed a shudder at the mention of the nanotech. 'Once the tip is fired into the target, it burrows in, bringing the rest of the wire with it — finds the target area and triggers the charge, just at the tip or the whole length. White hot wire, only a few molecules thick. Retract. Reuse. They make an excellent tool for what the murderer wanted to do. Hard to get hold of, though.' Orla paused, looked down at something on her desk then looked up at Valko once more. 'You said she? So you know that you're looking for a woman?'

'Yes, I'm certain of it,' Valko said. 'Who would be able to use a microfilament?'

'Well, it could be used by anyone able to program it. Your

killer didn't need to actively direct the filament. Once triggered, it'd be fired through skin and bone compressed to the density of needle's tip. Then after it had penetrated the skull and fully extruded, it would've been programmed to do precisely what it did. The medical expertise would come at the programming stage.'

'So whoever did it would not need to be a medical expert if someone else programmed the weapon?' Valko scratched his cheek, noticing with irritation the stubble that was shadowing his rangy features.

'Yes, but anyone with some basic understanding of anatomy and access to a datapad could, in theory, program the microfilament. It was designed to be a simple tool with the precision to excise a single ruptured capilliary. To use it without that level of precision — well, it's almost child's play.'

'That means we are left with the question of why think with that level of precision in the first place?' He suppressed a sigh; medical expertise had been a useful way of limiting a potential pool of suspects — every whitecoat's specialisation was a matter of record.

'It suggests to me someone who was very focused on the particular goal of destroying the accessible memories of the victims. Someone who tends towards an obsessive, narrow focus on whatever they are doing.'

'Like a Zealot.'

Orla raised an eyebrow. 'No, I wasn't thinking of anyone in the Temple. The obsessiveness of Zealots would tend towards the passionate. They would've been more dramatic. I've seen a couple of victims of purging by Zealots in the past — it wasn't pretty.' Orla seemed troubled and picked up a stylus from the desk, which she began tapping against her palm, absentminded.

'What about a professional assassin?'

'You are the expert on the criminal mind, Valko. I don't know. I haven't encountered an assassination in all the time I've been here. What do you think?'

Valko was unused to this collaborative brainstorming. It was contrary to his normal deductive process, but he was... what? Enjoying it.

'I think that a professional would have focused on being

more efficient. Would have used a weapon that was less, shall we say, unique. I would expect a heavy implement used to strike the head repeatedly, or a specific necrotoxin for the more subtle killer. Someone more reckless might have used unfettered nanodestroyers — although they would have been hard to come by. An amateur or inexperienced pro might have used a projectile. An idiot would use a blade. Whoever it was, they must have known the limitations of the mindlink but we don't exactly advertise how it works.'

'Yes, I understand. Most citizens — ' Valko couldn't help the look on his face at her use of the archaic term; Orla ignored the look. 'Most citizens believe that you Moderators can pick the thoughts out of their heads and talk to the dead. They don't really understand the mindlink process at all.'

'Therefore, our suspect is someone with an understanding of Moderators,' he said. 'Sufficient medical knowledge to realise a way to prevent us from acting; not a professional and unlikely to be a Zealot. Someone who is obsessive in their attention to detail enough to lose sight of the more efficient methods available.'

'That, or they were focused on destroying the information in the brains of their victims and murdering them was just an unavoidable side-effect,' Orla said.

'Yes, justification. It almost always comes back to some need for justification. Thank you, Orla. Very helpful.'

'Really? It sounds more like I've damaged your theories,' she said.

'Not at all. Instead of looking at an outsider, I need to be thinking of someone on the inside. Perhaps a researcher on Fisher's team after all. Tell me. Could Vinnetti's injury have been self-inflicted?' Valko asked — even though his own observations had been that no one could have inserted a needle at that angle, the monofilament might make it possible.

'Once the microfilament was set then, yes. Yes, it could have been. She would have been dead or at least unconscious immediately after extrusion but the filament would have finished its programmed task. It works on a trigger...' she clicked her fingers '...then that's that.'

'I don't think that it's very likely, but if it is a possibility, it's one that I need to rule out. Someone cleared up afterwards but didn't do a good job.'

The undetonated flashburner — could Vinnetti have set it herself? He was grasping. Actur was the key to all of this. He had to find him.

'Do you really think it could be suicide?' Orla asked.

He couldn't explain it to himself. Not even once had there been a time when he had relied on a so-called hunch. It had always been a meticulous process of finding evidence and testing theories. If a theory lacked supporting evidence, he put it to the back of the list but only ever discarded it when disproved. He knew some of the kensakan and even the other Moderators played hunches, but they turned out wrong more times than right. This time — for the first time — he felt a strong feeling, an instinct, that Vinnetti was not a suicide. Something didn't feel right about the circumstances of her death — why had she been in Actur's quarters.

'No, doctor. I have several theories and I'm trying to eliminate them one by one. If suicide can't be disproved then it remains a valid theory,' he said. 'Which means that she is still a potential suspect for the murder of Fisher.'

'Forgive me for saying this, but that is very, uh, scientific of you. I thought the scientific method was frowned upon, outside of the whitecoats?' Orla asked.

'It's logic. Deductive reasoning. Not science.' He knew, even as he said it, that it was sophistry. No matter how you played with semantics, logic and science were bound together.

'I see. Sorry. So, even though the weapon had been removed from the scene, you still think suicide's a possibility?'

'Why the interest, doctor?' He asked, curious but not adopting his usual attitude of suspecting anyone with an interest — this was Orla after all.

'I'm sorry, but Iduna Vinnetti. She went through her early training at the same time as me. We didn't really know each other but I recognised her name: she was always top of the class, I never could catch up. And we're the same age. I can't help but feel connected to her. Like, it could have been me if things had been a little different.' Orla's eyes were shining, with tears not quite formed.

The old, cold flatness asserted itself. 'Don't allow your emotions to interfere with your judgement, doctor. If your objectivity is compromised, we should transfer the medical part of the investigation to someone else.'

Orla reacted as if he had slapped her in the face.

'Yes, Tantei. Was there anything else?' She asked, her cheeks reddening.

Valko fought an upwelling of emotion, though he couldn't put a name to the feeling. 'I'm sorry. I know I can be inflexible and cold at times.' Why had he said that?

'I understand. What you have to see, what you have to do requires a certain state of mind. I suppose you can't let that go or it all comes tumbling down. Don't worry about it, Valko.' She seemed mollified and her use of his name released the tension he'd felt building in himself. 'You need your implant checked, is that right?'

'Yes. To make sure I am up to the job.' He couldn't keep a trace of bitterness from his tone.

'Lie back on the couch, I'll do a quick scan,' she said.

Valko settled down on the couch while Orla bustled around setting up the scanning equipment. He noticed that she was humming to herself as she worked and felt lulled by memories thought long forgotten.

The scan cycle took a few seconds. Orla clicked her tongue against the roof of her mouth as the results displayed on the old style monitor and spent some time adjusting settings on the device.

'Any headaches or dizziness?' She asked.

'No, not since I left the medcentre two days ago,' Valko said and sat up. Had she found something wrong?

'There's still some mild swelling, particularly around the implanted synthorganics. Nothing serious,' Orla said.

'I thought swelling to the brain was dangerous,' Valko said, a thread of cold winding its way down his spine.

'It depends on the degree. This scan is extremely accurate — the degree of swelling wouldn't be visible to the naked eye. Some degree of reaction is inevitable after suffering neural shock but you're perfectly healthy. The synthorganics, of course, function somewhat differently from the other areas of your brain. The swelling there is greater but that's part of its protective reaction. Similar to the way your natural body reacts but without any of the usual negatives that come with inflammation. We'll check again in a few days. Just to be on the safe side.'

Valko got up and readied himself to leave.

'One more thing doctor, before I forget. The DNA used for initial identification of Fisher showed signs of rapid decay. Was that also the case with Vinnetti?'

She turned to her screen again.

'Yes. Sorry it's not something I'd picked up on. OK, both corpses do show some unexpected deterioration of the DNA and RNA sequences too.'

'Could it be a side effect of the weapon?'

'You mean the microfilament or the explosive?'

'Either.'

'No, I mean, I don't see how. The explosive seems to have left some mildly elevated radiation levels but nothing that would explain this kind of breakdown of DNA and RNA. Let me just…' Orla tapped away at her terminal, tongue wedged in the corner of her mouth.

'That's it!' She said. 'Simple. It's an effect that's been observed in patients who've undergone recent retrogening or who've had a transplant of cloned material. So, both Fisher and Vinnetti had either been the recipients of cloned organs or, more likely, they'd undergone some retrogening in the past six months or so.'

'It's detectable for that long?'

'Yes, it can take up to seven years before retrogening becomes undetectable. Even then some tissues remain that aren't replaced. The treatments can cause a degree of DNA and RNA plasticity. That's the probable cause of the finding.'

'Not a cloned organ transplant?'

'They usually settle down much faster and any such procedure would have to be within the current medical records — there's no evidence of that. Though Dr Fisher's are quite limited.'

'Can you check to see whether either of them had undergone retrogening?'

'No sign in what I can access from here. These records only go back three years, the rest will be archived. Do you think this is important? I can put in a request.'

Valko rubbed the bridge of his nose — *this is just a distraction.*

'How long will that take?'

'Couple of days max, if I can put your reg number on the request. Longer otherwise, you know how slow the Administration are…'

'Fine. Do it,' Valko said.

His head was pounding now and he moved towards the door.

Orla smiled at him. 'You might want to take another dose of NOTT when you get a chance. It helps to regulate your implant and should aid your recovery. Take care of yourself, Valko.'

Again, she was using his first name. He scowled but didn't feel anger. 'Yes, thank you, doctor.' Turning sharply, he left before she could say any more.

Chapter 7

The tides of humanity filling the Plenum's central areas showed no signs of slackening as Valko made his way to his quarters — in the upper mid-sections, near enough to the elite without being part of them. He entered the cramped space: one main room and one smaller one with all the necessities for life and little in the way of luxury. He'd left the previous owner's décor as is; it was easy on the eye — for the most part, anyway — with a reddish tint on the g-moss that gave... a touch of warmth to the main room.

The combined sleeping and bathing chamber had g-moss in a cool greenish turquoise. It wasn't that leaving things the way they were reflected Valko's approval of the décor — it just didn't distract him, so he found no need to change it. Now, entering the familiar main room for the first time in days, he felt its cosiness. Why had he never noticed it before? He shook off the question and set about sourcing some food from the reprocessor.

He needed time to reflect and he needed sleep, only not yet. From the main room, he could gaze out at the core spire of the Plenum as it reached through the many interconnected levels. Looking in another direction, he could see the outer edges of the Plenum protective barrier, choked with vines of g-ivy and smothered in g-moss. In between were the clustered buildings, walkways and plazas, all filled with the buzz of humanity: packed tighter than insects in a hive.

There were times when he — lost in thoughts about a case — would stand at his window staring out for hours. It was as if the view helped him process his thoughts and he found it more relaxing than the sleep his mind retreated from but his body craved. His state of semi-trance carried no risk of dreams but it did need an exercise of willpower to avoid certain fragments of memories. Some were his own, but others were the echoes of mindlinks with suspects and — worst of all — victims. It was not always easy to separate them and, in dreams, he could find himself living childhood memories of someone long deceased, or even flashbacks to their murder.

Whenever he dreamt someone else's memories, the

emotional content was that he brought to it himself: whether happy memory or terrifying and painful ordeal, it always felt hollow.

Staring out at the structures and the surging crowds far below, he let his thoughts wander over recent events. The investigation was proceeding but bitter experience had taught him how leads could dry up and a case that promised resolution would dead end. There would be pressure to find a culprit — even if it were not the real murderer — for no other reason than to avoid the political fallout between the Centra Autorita and the Temple. They would select a convenient scapegoat if he couldn't solve the crime.

That said, Odegebayo wanted to get to the truth or something near the truth. The Old Man was not renowned for his patience, though: he had better get results before much longer.

Motive had to be a big factor in identifying a suspect. A clear motive was not necessary to work out who a murderer was, but he'd always found it a useful part of the process of investigation to consider. He couldn't rule out a sexual motive as a remote possibility, but no one who'd known either victim had suggested any intimate relationship between them. Indeed, Fisher presented as a man obsessed with his work. While Vinnetti... well, she was listed as homosexual and had been so for almost a decade. Which she might have faked. After all, the status benefits of homosexuality were all but the same as for celibacy.

Over the years, many breeders had tried to fake a different sex drive — or none at all — but they tended to get found out early on. The special unit within the kensakan, which — in addition to the elimination of sexual undesirables like paedophiles — tested the Enclosed to eliminate false claims to the elite status of homosexuality or celibacy, was efficient, as far as kensakan could be. Their tests weren't infallible but were supposed to be over ninety-nine percent accurate.

Put the person in a simulation with an attractive member of the opposite sex and check for arousal using a headset monitor to scan brain activity. Then, if that was clear, do the same with one of the same sex. If there was no arousal or arousal only at the lowest levels, then the coveted status of celibate was awarded — albeit annual checks would be made. If there was arousal only with members of the same sex then homosexual status was granted on the Register of the Enclosed. Anyone who showed signs of arousal over a certain low level with a member of the opposite sex was labelled a breeder — even if they were more aroused by members of their own gender.

Either elite status would allow an Enclosed to enter the top echelons of the Temple and apply for Martyr status, though the latter always had to prove celibacy before their Martyrdom. Some would prove celibacy by showing that no sexual activity of any kind had taken place in ten years or — and this was an extreme but common route for the religious — neuter themselves. Although the Centra Autorita was less anti-breeder, it still favoured those less likely to increase the population.

Sterilisation after the birth of one child had been trialled, but this only succeeded in preventing male breeders from entering long-term relationships and put off many women from having children at all, which was contrary to the Centra Autorita's aims. It didn't want the extinction of the human race, just a reduction in the population of the Plena to manageable levels. Instead, attempts were made to select bondmates for identified breeders with acceptable characteristics in the hope that future generations could be improved. There had been a period where sterilisation of less desirable breeders had been compulsory — like in Davidson's case — but the practice had been found to be counterproductive. Now, selection appeared haphazard and most breeders were left to get on with their own liaisons. There was still a limit on the number of births but, with the reliance on central control of food sources through the processors and the ease of effective contraceptive medication delivered in the food and water, fertility was low.

No, in all the circumstances, he tended to accept that Vinnetti was what she claimed to be. Although, it was possible that she had engaged in relations with Fisher to advance her position. Strange, though: Fisher had a limited registration file. It declared little more than birth Plenum — here in Arcas — , age and elite level status. The other information must be there at the forbidden level that he, and maybe even Odegebayo, was denied access to. Given the importance of the Fisher family in the history of the Plena, perhaps it was unsurprising that they had special safeguards.

If Fisher was a breeder it might affect his status, yet, being who he was, he had merited top-level elite status, regardless. Unlike the average citizen, his contributions — and those of his father and grandfather — had been so great that he could get away with almost any environmental infringement without triggering a reduction in his rating. Far better to keep such things out of his record, though.

Maybe that meant that Fisher was a breeder, perhaps a prolific one. Vinnetti had been young and attractive. It was possible that there had been something between them. Maybe it was unwilling on her side, so she had killed him and then, realising what she had done, killed herself? Why go to Actur's quarters? He couldn't credit that she had been having relations with both Actur and Fisher.

Although it was well known that sexuality was not immutable, hence the annual checks on anyone with enhanced status who had not been neutered, shifts tended to occur in people who were already indicated as having some flexibility in their preferences. His own status, tested on entry to the Moderators, had returned an unambiguous breeder result, albeit with a couple of percent likelihood of a switch. If unchanged it would bar him from rising to Pravnik, but that suited him fine. Vinnetti was almost the opposite of him, her test scores suggesting a mere three percent likelihood of her switching to breeder status.

The jealous lover angle was still a possibility but a remote one. With no evidence to rule it out, he would continue to pursue it as a line of enquiry, but it could not be the focus of his efforts now. He didn't have enough time to approach this with his usual meticulous eye for detail and felt compelled, if not to make an intuitive leap, then to prioritise based on probability.

What were those other possibilities? Random murder, of two people with a particular modus operandi? It was feasible — barely. There had been, and always would be, serial killers. The Centra Autorita did not regard them as being much of a problem so long as they avoided killing useful members of the Enclosed.

He remembered a case that the late Bezant had been in charge of, where the identity of the killer had been obvious for months but he had been allowed to kill over a dozen further victims — all low-level drudges — before his predations had started to affect efficiency and he had been recycled. It had frustrated Valko at the time. Not for the wasted lives, though that began to bother him now. No, at the time it was what he had seen as the corruption of the method of uncovering the truth. They'd known who the killer was but delayed due process. That was against the code of the Moderator: to identify criminals and punish them with pitiless haste. Ruthless Bezant certainly had been, but he had not been swift nor had he been efficient. That kind of corruption was anathema to Valko.

What militated against the random murderer theory was the proximity in time and the clear links between victims. With the particular M.O. of the murderer, there would have been previous, less proficient murders on record; a serial killer testing out her technique. Nothing in the records of any Plenum showed a similar method.

Perhaps, the killer had been one of the other hundred or so researchers. A jealous colleague, maybe. It made sense for one but not for both. Vinnetti may have been Fisher's preferred underling but she was not in a position where she would have taken over his station: she was far too inexperienced. Removing her would see, at best, an assistant get one step higher. The benefit for a jealous colleague — and indeed the source of their envy — only made sense if they were of near equal standing to one or other victim. In which case, the only reason to murder the other was to remove a potential witness. Since the two had been in different Plena — Fisher in Arcas and Vinnetti in Berlin — if either had been a witness to the other's murder they would have had the time and opportunity to contact the kensakan before their own demise. There were other problems with the jealous colleague theory: the link with Actur's quarters and the specific M.O. The theory had to be low on the list of possibilities.

Which left two options: some zealot killing those linked with a scientific project, which threatened all that a fully indoctrinated Enclosed would hold dear, or a professional hit on behalf of the Temple. Either could point to a colleague acting out of a religious motivation. By religious, he could only consider adherents to the creed of the Temple of the Wounded Mother. Other religions had existed in the past but the pogroms after Enclosure had swept these away. People had rejected belief systems that posited a benign deity or that suggested that the Mother was a creation for their benefit. The incipient kensakan had hunted down those who clung to the false beliefs of the past and given them an extreme, often fatal, indoctrination. Even the secular Centra Autorita had approved of the removal of competing religions but whether this was to secure its alliance with the Temple or for its own reasons had never become clear.

That said, none of the other religions that might still exist, hiding within the Plena, espoused as great an objection to science and thus whitecoats as the Temple did itself. The tight control of whitecoats, and particularly on any engaged in research, ensured a focus on furthering the goals of the Temple: they sidelined anything beneficial to humanity, favouring research that could speed the work of the Martyrs in healing the Mother's Wounds.

Fisher's project, aimed at spreading human life beyond the Mother and outside the solar system, would be against all that any true adherent or fully indoctrinated Enclosed believed. He, himself, felt the tug of his long ago indoctrination telling him that it was a monstrous crime.

Targeting two members of a team working on a method of faster than light travel suggested that it was not a mere attack against a couple of whitecoats by — what was the term Davidson had used? Oh, yes, 'religious vacjobs'. No, it meant that whoever had murdered them would have to know of the project, in outline at least. It would explain the destruction of the parts of the brain to prevent any download of memories via mindlink and it would explain the destruction of Fisher's briefcase and its contents. Had one of his colleagues sold him out?

If this theory were right then it would also mean that the murderer knew the specifics of a Moderator's abilities: the use they could make of a dead brain if they reached it fast enough. While it was not a total secret, the Centra Autorita frowned on dissemination of information about their abilities. His heart throbbed against the cage of his chest as he thought on how much he had allowed Jean to understand the mindlink, skirting an infidelity with his Moderator's Oath.

Overall, he reasoned that this was the best theory. Fisher and Vinnetti both murdered because of the project they were working on. Whatever stage it was at, it would provoke a strong reaction, but more so if they had been near a breakthrough. Perhaps, Jean would be able to help? Was he seeking an excuse to see her? The two possible motives for a colleague to have committed the murders, could, he supposed, make her a suspect. Thinking of her in this way felt wrong, but he put aside feeling — it had no place in an investigation.

Satoshi had compiled a list of statements from each of the whitecoats at Fisher's lab and details of their alibis. Most were a simple matter to confirm with beacon records. He pulled up the list and searched for Jean's profile. She'd given a simple enough alibi — neither so basic as to be lacking nor so involved as to raise suspicion. *Just what a pro would do.* A feeling of tremulous heat threaded through him — as he sought the beacon confirmation — and crashed back down to nothing. Her beacon had sporadic traces, but it was nowhere near either murder scene at the material times.

He turned his thoughts back to running different scenarios, but a traitor concern slipped through: *What if she gave them up to the Temple?* He dismissed it, Jean had struck him as a typical, if intriguing, whitecoat. The idea that they would sell out one of their own was farcical — there'd be no benefit, they all lived among the elite already. And it wasn't like someone from the Temple could have just infiltrated Fisher's team — from the look of their records, each of them had proven themselves committed to science over the faith. The idea that one of them would abandon that to be embraced by the Temple made as little sense to him as the corollary. A Temple adherent wouldn't be able to stomach the affront to their beliefs that would be necessary to join a team of researchers as specialised as Fisher's were.

The level of knowledge and the skill of the murder, with its single-minded focus on destroying any possible research data, suggested that it was not a lone zealot. He recalled his discussion with Orla — a zealot would have made more of a show of the killing and been far less surgical. They might also have accepted responsibility, believing that what they had done was a noble thing. Also, they might have been less discriminate in whom they killed.

Any one of the hundred or more whitecoats who worked with Fisher on any of his projects could have been targeted, yet no one else had been attacked. He didn't have the resources to protect them all but he worried for Jean — an upwelling of the need to defend her at odds with all he knew of himself. If the killer were a zealot, unlikely as he thought that was, she might be in danger. His rational mind dismissed this. She had been able to wander into a Hotbed and no one had attacked her. If anyone were considering killing her, they would have had plenty of opportunities to do so by now. If anything, he needed to stop thinking about her like this. The thought that he could ignore her potential as a suspect, at least as far as providing information to the murderer if it was a Temple agent, risked compromising his objectivity. She'd never given him a satisfactory reason for her attendance at the Hotbed, after all. But his gut told him she wasn't involved — no scrap that, it was a part of his body a little lower down.

Valko returned his attention to case theories, no use second-guessing himself. More likely a professional killer working for the Temple than a zealot, whether alone or as a group. If it were the Temple as a whole, there would have been more fuss created — maybe even a widespread conflict. It smacked of the clandestine action of a single powerful figure within the Temple — learning of the research and choosing an efficient way of removing the threat to their beliefs without seeking to cause any kind of civil war — hot or cold — between the Temple and the Centra Autorita. If this theory was right — and it was the best theory he had right now — then there were a minimum of two suspects. The killer and the one who sent her.

Last, he considered the leftfield possibilities. Agents from Mars? Improbable in the extreme. Although the colony there would not appreciate the Centra Autorita being able to extend its powers, they would have no way of knowing what Fisher had been doing. The distances were so vast that travel between the planets would take months. He wasn't aware of the Centra Autorita still having space shuttles that could attempt the journey and, as far as was known, Mars lacked the resources to send a vessel to the Mother.

Closer to home, there were the Remnants: those who had survived outside the Plena against all the odds and did not ascribe to the beliefs of the Enclosed. Most were either cancer ridden or in other ways deformed from the radiation, toxins and diseases that they would have encountered. What reason could the able-bodied Remnants have to take any interest in Fisher or his research? Anyway, wouldn't Koewatha have recognised one of his own? It would explain why the wei-zhuce had been allowed to live, but that was too tenuous a link. Valko ruled them out as a reasonable possibility.

Then there was the access records and the edits to his reports: Pravnik Hampton must be above suspicion. And yet, he couldn't shake off a feeling that — despite claims to the contrary — there were political wrangles between the Pravniks, which must also include the other Weiyuan in the Conclave. It made some sense that she might have accessed his reports to remove the references to stolen research. If the Temple reviewed the file, as he was sure it would do, her tampering would not be obvious and they might overlook the break in procedure of a second Pravnik overseeing an investigation. They might even put it down to the importance of the victim. What they wouldn't now see was any suggestion that the murder related to the nature of Fisher's research.

Why wouldn't Odegebayo have known about her efforts to protect them from that possibility? He had taken the news of her access in his usual calm way, as if it was no news at all, but that revealed much. The Old Man was willing to show mild surprise — it suited his act of being a normal human being — but when that surprise was so complete as to knock him out of the act, dissipate the grandfather shroud for a moment, it must mean that he was deeply troubled.

Valko recalled the emotional sense he had got from Odegebayo at the moment he had raised the matter: absolute absence of emotion. That shouldn't have bothered him — it was one way in which they were alike — but now it made him cringe at how far from the norm the Old Man's psyche was.

If the Old Man hadn't known, did Hampton's interference point to some deeper involvement? She couldn't be behind the murders, not with the level of indoctrination the Pravniks underwent every year. Yet, Odegebayo's theory that the murders had been committed by Temple agents of one sort or another, didn't fit with Hampton's actions. If the Temple had killed Fisher over his research, why cover up its presence? Ergo, the two Pravniks had not discussed Hampton's precautions: confirmation that the response to the news — the absence of feeling projected by the Old Man — meant that Hampton had been acting without his knowledge. Valko couldn't see how this fit in, since the complexities of the politics dealt with the aftermath of the murder and they provided no motive for its commission. It was something he would need to take into account from now on. Failure to consider a political angle might not affect his investigation, but it could leave him open to other dangers.

That left the unthought-of and unexpected. By its nature, he couldn't put any theory in this box but left it open in his mind. Experience had taught him that there were times when the unanticipated would happen in an investigation and were he to commit to any one theory, he would risk missing a vital clue. So the trick was to keep an open mind but stick with the most logical plan: pursue Actur and have Satoshi continue his gentle probing of the Temple. He'd set Chang to look into the jealous colleague angle — it was always possible that someone had wanted to steal credit or had felt overlooked. Even one of his kensakan should be able to handle that.

Satisfied he had covered every angle, Valko walked to his bunk, peeled off his uniform and lay down, pulling the bunk's thin thermal regulating foil sheet over himself. Within moments he was asleep: the dreams stampeded over him, dragging him through the fevers of an addict and the squalid life of Joey Koewatha. His mind settled on the single fragmented image he had seen in Iduna Vinnetti's lifeless brain. It flickered in and out of his dream. Sometimes her face reflected in the droplet of water, sometimes his own. To wake up screaming would have been a release but the dreams were not so kind. He lay, stifled in their grip until the alarm woke him. Its piercing shriek was his daily relief.

✝✝✝

The droning of the Sutras washed over Satoshi as he entered the Temple, the voice of the member of the faithful chosen for the honour catching with emotion, 'And so did fire rain down upon Her face, for her children had betrayed her.'

'Inane rubbish,' Satoshi thought to himself as he donned the heavy metal chain that all penitents were required to wear. It was so heavy it forced the head to bow after a brief time and caused considerable discomfort. They contrived an aspect of contrition in all those who entered, reminding them of the weight of sin shared by all members of the human virus. To Satoshi, the weight of the

heaviest chain there was irritation and little more. On any other occasion, he would comply with the rule but then take pleasure in keeping his head bolt upright, challenging Hands and Templars with his proud gaze.

This time was different. He was under orders to be subtle: antagonising the Hands wouldn't get him the information they needed. It was a struggle to put aside his anger at the Temple — it wanted his son. But that was a matter for another time. Breathing deep down into his belly to lower his consciousness so that he sat outside his own emotions, beyond the commentary of his inner voice, Satoshi adopted a look of pain: head bowed and shuffling like the other supplicants. The sutras droned on and on in the background.

He made his way through the crowded entrance hall to one of the smaller side rooms where a Hand gave sermons to the repentant. Like all organised religions, some material sacrifice was customary, but, unlike those dead institutions, the Temple demanded no filthy lucre. Instead, it sought payment in pain and a commitment to the future mortification of flesh or spirit — and Iona wanted this for their son?

The fundamental tenet of the Temple was that every human owed a debt to the Mother that they could not repay until She was healed. So the Hand would task the faithful with punishing themselves in some way. A day without water, two without food. Work a double shift but do not have it count against one's quota. That must follow the direct, physical pain delivered by the Hand — a quick jab with a shockstick that sent agony burning through every nerve. It was not a relief from the burden of sin but a way of understanding the Mother's pain, if only for an instant. He held back another snort.

Satoshi braced himself. He would have to go through the whole process, but if he gave a credible performance, he might find a request for a private meeting with the Hand granted.

Soon he found himself with a group of about thirty others crammed into the small room and listening to the usual spiel about their worthlessness and all the other nonsense.

The Hand began the daily admonishment, the same drivel as the sutras, 'No Man, no Woman may walk unrepentant on Her face. All share the burden of Sin. With our own Blood must we wash her Wounds. With our Flesh and our Bones must we nourish Her. Only in Martyrdom are we set free yet only the Unpolluted among Us may thus be redeemed.'

Satoshi pretended to pay rapt attention, making all the appropriate groans and wails as required. When his time came, he bore the shockstick's burning jolt in silence and leant into it — like a rabid zealot trying to steal a few moments more communion with the Mother. The Hand gave him a penance of deprivation, either food or water. When the service was complete, the small crowd began to filter out of the room, while the Hand waited for the next group to chastise.

Satoshi saw his moment. He approached the Hand and dropped to one knee.

He said in as agitated a tone as he could, 'Faithful servant of the Mother, I deserve so much more punishment. Nothing can forgive our sin but I beg you: task me with chastising the enemies of the Mother — those filthy whitecoats who still threaten her sanctity.'

Satoshi had vague memories of acting in a school play when he was younger. It had been an attempt at a traditional Noh play that had proved far too ambitious, but he'd retained some of that acting skill — he hoped.

The Hand, after a startled moment, leant forward and touched Satoshi's head. 'Your passion to right the wrongs done to the Mother are commendable, young man. But focus that rage, not against those who have turned the evils of science into a means of seeking Her restoration. We are all deserving targets of that rage, but perhaps, in time, you will be favoured with a clearer path. We must hurry to heal Her wounds but do not let your passion burn so bright — for the bright flame may burn too fast. The slow, controlled flame may serve to sear away more of our sins. Do not let your passion be consumed and burnt out all in a rush but hoard it so you may embrace the long years of suffering to come.'

The Hand eyed Satoshi, appraising him, then made a stern gesture towards the exit.

Satoshi left without another word and made his way out of the Temple, walking as if he carried Atlas's burden on his shoulders. Once he was clear of the vicinity of the Temple, he relaxed and gave a long slow whistle. With luck, he would now be marked as a potential zealot. They might check his record but that was no concern: his son was being considered for the program that could lead to Martyrdom, and kensakan, though servants of the Centra Autorita through the Justeco Centro, were nonetheless tasked with responsibilities to the Temple as well. He'd worked the odd Envirocrime case and that too would stand him in good stead.

There was a fair chance that they would go to such efforts; it would be obvious to all that he was a veteran. His record would attract the sort of person who might have ordered the deaths of Fisher and Vinnetti — someone who was looking for another professional killer.

Satoshi felt a surge of certainty that the Temple was responsible: everything about their twisted philosophies showed contempt for human life. Ordering a murder would be no great step for one of the Hands or the higher ups.

†††

Davidson sat at the small, cramped desk he shared in the Justeco Centro, feeling like a schmuck. Not a goddamn thing had been said about his speedy apprehension of that stinking, worthless piece of shit, Koewatha. His only reward was a pointless and uncomfortable trip to Outpost Theta and back. Waste of his goddamn time. Satoshi and Gangleri both deserved a long slow bath in one of the recyclers as far as he was concerned. Bastards, the pair of them. He'd taken a major risk — what was that phrase he liked, oh yeah: he'd gone out on a limb, to get the information out of Slim Jan before that 'pop whore's gaping asshole Gangleri could get in and ruin their operation. Nothing from Jan either. Maybe it was time he reminded the bloated prick who had the power in their little arrangement.

He was beginning another cycle of ranting and swearing to himself, when the decrepit monitor in front of him gave a ping. Darius Actur's beacon had sprung to life and was transmitting a steady signal, at the standard rate of one pulse per second. The carrier wave registered at the expected one hundred and seventy-five kilohertz. He had a lock on the source of the signal and sent an interrogatory to the beacon. It synchronised with the main system, switching to a more rapid rate of communication, and confirmed location, altitude and status of Darius Actur: alive but with suppressed vital signs. At first, he seemed to be motionless, but as Davidson watched, the beacon's coordinates shifted a decimal point. So the guy was moving slower than walking?

All beacons had some degree of alarm system that the Centra Autorita could use to warn the Enclosed of dangers such as the Plenum's outer shell being compromised. Even though Actur was outside of any Plenum or Outpost, the alarm system should work. Davidson triggered it but there was no reaction, Actur stayed moving at that same slow pace. What was more, his vitals didn't alter for a moment. Maybe he'd been drugged? Maybe the movement he was detecting was the guy pacing around a cell? Davidson hoped not. It would make recovery that much more hazardous if the suspect was in the custody of one of the Remnant groups operating in North America. With Lady Luck on his side, he wouldn't be the one sent to retrieve Actur. Then again, that bitch hated him.

Davidson weighed up the potential risks of reporting his find to his superiors and those motherfuckers rewarding him with a trip to the wilds of North America — so soon after his return from the blasted continent — versus the possibility that his success here might, finally, garner him the recognition he so richly deserved. Greed won out over fear. Besides, fucking Gangleri would want the glory of being the one to scrag Actur. He composed himself and allowed a respectful frame of mind to take over — hard though that was. Once he felt sure that he wouldn't be leaking his true feelings for Satoshi or Gangleri he donned his headset and made his report.

†††

A headache pounded behind Valko's eyes. Pain suppressors and his own mental control did nothing to alleviate it. The dreams of the previous night had been so intense that he felt they were more real than the waking world. A weight in his chest, as if his heart was heavy, dragged at him when he recalled the broken lives he'd seen. There'd followed a dream about Jean, a replay of their meeting at the Hotbed, but subverted. She'd been the 'pophead and he'd been Koewatha — negotiating a trade. Waking in the middle of the dream, he'd felt dirty. And he knew the reason why. He was letting his attraction to her cloud his judgement. First thing he'd do when this damn headache receded would be to get her into an interview room. She'd not explained why she'd come to the Hotbed, not enough to satisfy him. Time to stop thinking with his balls and start being a Moderator again.

Then he received a message from Davidson and Jean fell back to the bottom of his list. Actur had been found. Fighting to control himself — excitement tumbling head over heels with the sorrow he couldn't shake off — Valko washed, using the same greywater as yesterday. He dressed while reviewing his options: he could send Davidson with Chang and maybe Rennard to retrieve the missing man or Satoshi instead of Davidson or he could go himself. He couldn't focus. What had Orla said? That his implant was slightly swollen... This felt worse than that.

He messaged her and, making his mind up about what to do as he went, hurried into the medcentre where she worked. Orla repeated the process with the scanner, clucking and fussing about him with genuine concern.

The scan revealed that his implant had grown 0.01% since the last scan.

'Why now?' He asked.

'The change appears to have started shortly after that neural shock you suffered,' she said. 'One of the functions of NOTT is supposed to be a stabilisation of your implant but it clearly isn't working properly. Maybe we need to adjust your dosage. You say that you've been feeling strange?'

'No, Orla. I've been having strange feelings. Over-emotional. A loss of clarity. It's distracting me from my duty.'

Orla laid a gentle hand on his arm as she adjusted a setting on the scanner. For the first time, Valko took full note of her tenderness — her compassion was palpable and he squirmed in the sensation of it. She'd been tolerable before, her efficiency and professionalism satisfied him, even if her tendency to be over-familiar had irritated him as much as the same traits in Oshi did. Now, as she ministered to him with a genuine smile and a soft voice, he realised the power of her sympathy, the importance of its sincerity. Her instincts — her ability to see into the hearts of others — brought awareness beyond his own natural calculations. Only with the foxfire of NOTT inside him, would he see clear as her empathy. Thoughts pressed on him. What insight might she have into him? He groaned.

'Are you in pain?'

Valko sat up. 'No, doctor,' he said and regained his focus. 'Can you treat the swelling?' Small details of her face became stark, his perceptions of her coalescing to the minuscule.

'I'm sorry it's beyond me,' she said. 'I'll have to refer you to the senior whitecoat in charge of implanting your synthorganics.'

'It'll have to wait a while,' he said.

Orla was checking her monitor, looking who to refer Valko to for treatment.

'Oh. Oh dear. It was Dr Fisher himself,' she said. 'Look, I'm sure that one of his staff will be able to help you. It must have been something they've dealt with before. After all, Moderators have had these implants virtually since Enclosure. Look, I'll flag your case for immediate attention. Until then, standard procedure with implant malfunctions is to give you a fresh batch of NOTT, just to make sure the one's you have haven't degraded. I don't think that's your problem but it can't hurt.'

She handed him a new pack of capsules and he switched them with his old ones. Orla took the bag over to the recycler and dumped it in.

'Maybe it was just a bad batch, you never know,' she said.

Valko stayed silent. He buttoned up his uniform and headed to the door.

'Tantei Gangleri?' She said, her tone light.

He turned towards her, noticing again how she shone with her heart fire. His mouth was dry.

'What is it Orla?'

'I'm sure you'll be alright. But if you need to talk to someone, you can always link with me.'

Her eyes were shining and there was a soft smile on her face. It came to Valko then — she cares for me. The realisation stunned him. There was a split second where he wanted to reach out to her — to the embrace of his lost mother that he saw reflected in her — but then that inner wall, which had protected him from these feelings, began to slide down again. It was slower and less solid. He writhed inside, trying to keep it from slamming down, but he couldn't overcome his fundamental nature.

'Thank you, I will consider it,' he said, then turned away

and left before she could say another word.

†††

Valko requisitioned a small transpod — capable of making the journey to Actur's location and back but little more. It was an almost unheard of waste of resources: an entire transpod for the use of three people. Valko had expected to travel to the nearby Outpost Theta, then be forced to travel to the location over land. A journey of some sixty or so miles to the west of the Outpost, itself on the edges of the New York burn-zone. With the saturation of burn-zones throughout United America, it could have taken them days by slow moving ground crawler — if one were available. More likely than not, the Outpost would have provided them with some limited supplies and left them to make their way on foot. They would've had to wind a careful path between burn-zones to avoid the risk of straying into an area infested with nanodestroyers or one that had been hit not by a flashburner in the first wave of strikes but a primitive nuclear warhead as the Lunar War had tailed off. With a transpod at their disposal, they could reach Actur and be back to Arcas Plenum in under twenty hours.

Satoshi had reported about his attempts to present himself as a potential zealot for the Temple. It was an interesting ploy by the sergeant: he'd tried to be cunning for a change. Whether it worked or not would depend on how desperate any particular Hand might be. The plan — while having some limited potential for the long term — would not produce results within the time frame they needed. That said, Valko understood that Satoshi had done it, in part, out of a sense of friendship the man felt for him rather than for duty's sake. Valko had listened to the report and picked up on the distress that emanated from Satoshi when he spoke of his son. Not being a father himself, Valko had still found himself trying to empathise. The prospect of a person you cared about more than anything else in life volunteering for an exile, which would end in painful death after years of struggling against the odds, was nightmarish.

Valko's thoughts turned to the dangers of the operation — they were equipped for the risk of a hard extraction: hardened envirosuits would protect them, for a short time at least, against nanotechnological, biological, chemical or nuclear threats. And the suits would provide a degree of resistance to primitive ballistic weapons or blades and such. If Actur were in the hands of a group of Remnants then they could count on a low level of offensive technology relative to their own. Unless they were unlucky. Remnant raiding parties sometimes came equipped with pre-Enclosure tech — scavenged from the deep, underground ruins of military installations that had survived a flashburner strike or from a private illegal weapons cache outside any area of direct bombardment. If a Remnant group held Actur and they were equipped with even one energy weapon — say a low yield hand maser — then the envirosuits would be next to worthless.

There was a risk in taking this action, but the three of them — Satoshi, Chang and him — were experienced enough to be able to assess any situation before committing themselves. They'd not forgotten armaments: each had a riot issue, high capacity frag gun stowed in the rear compartment of the transpod. Every shot of a frag gun could be set to tear a single target apart or else act like a wide-angle shotgun spread, killing or maiming multiple targets. Justeco Centra sanctioned use of the weapons was rare but the last time there had been a Plenum riot, some twenty years prior, the records showed that twelve kensakan had slaughtered over a thousand rioters within minutes. The weapons would give them the edge against any threat short of an armoured naukara, the meat-machine slaves of the SuperStates that still haunted the blighted badlands. He recalled the grisly vid footage of the creatures he'd seen in training: glad that he'd never seen one with his own eyes and that there had been no reports of any in the area around Outpost Theta.

Valko leant back in his seat. It felt wrong to be able to relax on a transpod. The sense of space, afforded by being three in an area that sometimes as many as fifty people would jam into, was luxurious. All that he and his two subordinates needed to do now was wait as the transpod's automated pilot flew them to their destination.

He'd left Davidson behind monitoring their progress and the quality of the beacon signal. The kensakan had finally shown himself to be of use. Perhaps, Valko had misjudged him.

There was little conversation on board during the flight. Chang looked too scared of Valko — no doubt, expecting disapproval of anything he said that did not bear on their mission. Satoshi looked preoccupied — probably thinking about his son. Valko, his usual cool reflection lost, felt desperate for conversation. He was unused to the feeling so, not knowing how to make small talk, he found himself stuck waiting for some mission-related conversation to start to fill the silence. All he could do to stave off boredom — when had he ever felt bored with an investigation to occupy him? — was stare out of a small, dingy window at the landscape below.

They'd completed the longest part of the flight: overflying all of the old Eurussian territories and coming at North America from the West, instead of taking the far shorter and more direct route over the Atlantic. No sense risking the airspace over the ruins of the Atlantis project, which still generated dangerous storm fronts, even now. They reached the west coast of North America and skirted the Washington burn-zone. The ground below showed clear signs of the devastation: the uniform beige of soil with all life scoured from it. Areas where a high-powered flashburner had created great ripples in the Mother's skin flitted by below. Ridges and valleys rippled where once had been flat farmland or open forest. It was as bad as the worst parts of Eurussia. Perhaps, worse: United America had held out the longest in the Lunar War. It had endured more of the Moon's fury than anywhere else had, before the success of the last, desperate gambit to plant fusion bombs within the two lunar colonies.

For someone born after the cataclysmic events, like Valko had been, it was difficult to fully understand the terrible consequences of the War. He'd learned about it as a boy and heard enough sermons during indoctrination to know what had been lost, but the worst of the horrors were behind them now. Trying to imagine the periods of nuclear winter and the so-called nuclear summer, which followed was hard — he had no frame of reference.

Those who'd lived through the time were long dead but he knew the atmospheric upheavals — extreme cold and extreme heat — had been short enough that they hadn't killed off all the vegetation. No, North America was still capable of supporting a wide diversity of life in Colorado and a few other States — he could see evidence below them at times. His skoler days had been full of lessons on the hubris of unrestrained tech use: the extent of nanotechnology that had been present throughout United America was held out as the prime example. To stay ahead of the competition, the Superstate had allowed nanotechnology to suffuse every element of its society.

After the annexation of South America by the North, Congress had made the decision to allow aerosol dispersion of nanodefenders. It was lauded as the greatest victory for American freedom: protection from whatever the other Superstates could throw at them. Right up until the defensive technology — the airborne nanites that would create a continent covering immune system to guard against nanotechnological or other attacks — turned against them.

No one had believed the ease with which the scientists based on the Moon had hijacked the nanodefenders and turned them into nanodestroyers. History recorded it as revenge, by a few remaining scientists, for the fusion bombing of Armstrong and Aldrin. They caused the death of over ninety-five percent of the population of United America: a higher casualty rate than anywhere else on the globe. Survivors had been limited to those areas where low temperatures, or some other environmental factor, had prevented the spread of nanodefenders. These then further divided: those who managed to escape to the Plena, which the rest of the world had hastily erected, and the Remnants. Eking out a miserable existence on the edges of areas of painful death, desperation drove them to acts that made the Enclosed dread them. Mother's Tears, he hoped they didn't run into any of the savages.

There were Remnants all over the globe in greater or lesser numbers, but the Americans were the most feared. When the last bombs had fallen — used not by an enemy but in a desperate attempt to destroy the areas of greatest nanodestroyer infestation — much of United America lay in ruins. But there remained vast stockpiles of technology — resources left untouched when the first wave had wiped out the people who could have used them. The American Remnants were far more skilled than other Remnant groups at retrieval of technology from these areas. The lack of Plena on the continent had also led to a greater degree of isolationism and more desperation. Where a meeting with a Eurussian Remnant group might not always end in bloodshed, with the Remnants in United America, one way or another, there would have to be a slaughter.

Looking out of the small windows in the transpod, Valko felt a heaviness in his chest as he contemplated the landscape below. They overflew the astounding natural beauty of the mountains: a rampant symbol of United America's former glory, morning sun rising behind them and casting burning spears over the virgin snow. Cresting the peaks, the transpod descended on the other side — down, down until they ghosted over the corpse of the heartlands, which lacked even the fetid microbial life to animate the cadaver. Absent rot, the land lay lifeless, like some mummified king fallen from grace, hollowed and shrouded in a mantle of radioactive dust.

Dawn's light — that ever-mendacious bringer of hope — could not sunder the damnable truth: only the blood of generations could redeem this poor earth. Yet, not enough vitality remained flowing through the veins of humanity to meet the ultimate challenge that Death had laid before them. Never before had such thoughts entered Valko's mind or tortured his soul. Now, a solitary, despairing tear marked his face.

They were within ten miles of their destination when it happened. One moment, the transpod had begun descent to low altitude to locate a suitable place to touchdown. The next it was rocked by an explosion. Alarms screamed with agonising intensity, as fiery they fell.

Chapter 8

Davidson picked his nose as he watched the flight of the transpod on his monitor. He was bored. This was turning out to be routine after all. Three hours earlier, after reporting his finding to Valko, he had received a direct summons to the Justeco Centro by a Pravnik. He'd gone, shitting himself and expecting it to be Odegebayo — what with the Old Man's interest in the case. Instead, it was Pravnik Hampton, the youngest appointee to the rank at forty. She'd told him to report in full about the entirety of the investigation and listened in silence as Davidson wrung out his brain recalling every insignificant detail. He neglected one thing. The ITF restriction that Valko had activated. Part of him wanted to fuck Gangleri over but he'd waited too long to report it and now it risked looking like he was complicit.

When he'd finished, Pravnik Hampton picked up a large cup of coffeine and sat drinking it, watching Davidson over the rim of her mug without saying anything. Her expression was neutral but her eyes never left his. Davidson began to sweat. Did she already know? Had this been a loyalty test of some sort? He began to rethink whether he should tell her about what Gangleri had done, but then she spoke. Her voice was dry and cracked, yet it was a strong voice that carried with it both professional confidence and sexual superiority.

'Jack, you left out your dealings with Jannick Del, also known as Slim Jan.'

'Uh, ah, well you see…' He said.

'Yes, I do see,' she said. 'You know that the Justeco Centro turns a blind eye to most activity by kensakan, so long as it doesn't cross certain lines, interfere with an investigation or lead to inefficiency. It's one of the perks of your job that you get to exercise a little power — that you can enjoy a little corruption. But you! You've entered into a business arrangement with a fence and smuggler. You've allowed serious offences to be discontinued because the perpetrator gave you sexual favours. And from the looks of you, there must be some serious chemical assistance being used to allow you to pass the kensakan physical.'

Davidson hung his head. What was the point in denying any of this? She knew the truth and, for a Pravnik to be taking the time to have this conversation, there was no doubt in her mind about his guilt. He was fucked and he knew it.

Hampton had paused, allowing her words to sink in. She smiled with satisfaction at Davidson's silence.

'The penalty for what you have done is more than exile to an Outpost or removal from the kensakan. No, if any of the other Pravniks knew, they'd execute you. Pravnik Odegebayo has oversight of the investigation in which you're currently involved, doesn't he?' She asked.

'Yes, ma'am,' Davidson said, trying to regain some dignity by finally behaving like a professional.

'I don't need to tell you what his reaction would be, now do I?'

'No, ma'am.'

'Good. We understand each other. I hold your life in my hands. Now, you will do precisely what I tell you, won't you?'

Davidson met her gaze, hope filling him, 'Yes, ma'am. Anything you say, ma'am. Thank you, ma'am.'

Hampton laughed; it was a rich sound of genuine amusement. 'You're an amusing little worm, aren't you, Jack? Well, if you even think about double crossing me, then you'll wish that Odegebayo had gotten his hands on you. Now, tell me everything about Tantei Gangleri's dealings with this person of interest,' she looked over at a datapad, 'Xiang Rhea, a whitecoat on Dr Fisher's staff.'

'Who? I mean, sorry Ma'am, I don't know who that is.'

She pinned him with her gaze again, then inclined her head a fraction, 'Alright, Jack. Never mind. Here is what you're to do…'

Davidson recalled the conversation with a shudder. Then he snapped out of it — long-range tracking no longer showed the transpod at the expected altitude. He quickly flicked through the various radar stations that he was synced with, but the transpod didn't show up even on Outpost Theta's medium range units. Scrolling back through the tracking records, he saw what had happened. One minute the transpod was there, the next it had disappeared off the scope. He checked transmission logs but there'd been no radio contact on any frequency. Then he checked the beacon signals, getting a faint reading. The transpod had been downed. Remnants or someone else — Hampton, maybe? She was ruthless enough to do it.

Davidson did what he'd been told to in the event of something unusual happening — this sure as shit qualified. Opening a secure hub link to Pravnik Hampton, he left her a message telling her what'd happened. Then he sat back and waited. There was not much that he could do from here, but he knew that sooner or later he would need to do something.

† † †

Valko squinted in the bright light: the yawning hole in the canopy still smouldered despite the automatic fire suppressors.

The computer declared that the transpod had suffered, 'Sudden catastrophic failure.'

The explosion seemed to have been on the outside of the 'pod. Could it have been an impact? Valko could only recall the sound — a swell of agony in his ears and everything dropping away. The onboard systems couldn't verify the cause. All the pilot computer could suggest were a number of possible mechanical failures — none of which explained the smoking hole in the rear compartment.

Satoshi was already on his feet. He'd been better protected from the crash by his altered physique. Chang was another matter: his head was a mass of bloody pulp. It had been caved in by striking the edge of one of the structural supports within the transpod. Valko groaned and sat up.

'Oshi, Chang's dead, isn't he?' He asked, feeling his vision blurring — not with tears, surely — and his stomach twisting in knots that sought escape.

'Yes, sir,' Satoshi said. 'Nothing I could do for him. Looks like it was quick though — probably happened before he knew anything about it. We can't do anything for him but we need to get out of here — fast.'

They'd come down in the middle of a burn-zone; there were no active nanodestroyers in the air — or they'd have already died screaming. Radiation might be another matter.

'Best get into our envirosuits. Never know out here,' Satoshi said, as he unpacked the light armoured suits with their rebreathers and adaptive camouflage. 'Not as reliable as War-era stealth cloaks… but if we were shot down, they may make it harder for anyone pursuing us.'

'What about the frag guns?' Valko asked.

Satoshi shifted his weight to his left foot. 'They were stowed in the weapons locker in the rear compartment.' He pointed to the hole in the canopy. 'The locker's gone, the frag guns and explosives with them. Guess we're lucky they got sucked out before they could detonate or we'd not have survived.'

Valko looked over at Chang and grunted. Then asked, 'How far are we away from the coordinates?'

'That calculation is currently beyond this unit's capabilities. Please, try again later,' the pilot said, in the same faux-cheerful tone that it would've used to tell them they'd reached their destination.

'We can get a positional fix when we've gotten clear. Better move quickly — if someone shot us down, they'll be coming to the wreckage. We don't want to be here when they do… You alright?' Satoshi asked.

Valko scowled at his subordinate's concern but this time it was more out of habit than from any real resentment. 'I'm fine. You're right. Let's move,' he said.

Part of him wanted to stay to make their attackers pay for the death of one of his men.

'There will be a reckoning, Chang — I promise you,' Valko said, as he pulled the dead kensakan's jacket up to cover the ruined head. 'Can we get anyone on radio? We're out of reach for hub comms I take it?'

'Yes, sir,' Satoshi said. 'I tried but all I can manage is to get the pilot computer to transmit an automated distress signal. That should alert Davidson that we survived being downed, then all he needs to do is sync with our beacons to track us.'

'Fine. Then let's get out of here,' Valko said.

He picked up the smallest of the four envirosuits that they had brought with them. Satoshi selected two, one to fit his bulk, the other for Actur. If they found him alive, he'd need its protection.

They suited up and tried to exit the 'pod. The door had seized but, working together, they managed to prise it open by using a strut from one of the passenger benches that had broken loose in the crash. Strained by the exertion, Valko paused, holding his hand over his eyes as white light flashed through his skull — the pain was staggering. When it receded, he opened his eyes. With a lurch of disorientation, he realised he was looking out through Satoshi's eyes — as if by a hub link, only he could hear his sergeant's thoughts. The man was preoccupied with opening the door and hadn't noticed that Valko must have been standing rigid, locked in fugue.

Satoshi was thinking how easy it would have been to open the door if he could use his synthorganics. A shiver slithered through his nerves — craving for the power the implants gave him. In that moment, he was glad they required activation by the Centra Autorita's medtechs. Thinking about medtechs brought Orla to Satoshi's mind and a warm fug of desire replaced his previous yearning. His cheeks warmed and he glanced at Valko, convinced that the Moderator could pick his thoughts out of his head. The man looked pained — one hand over his face.

The connection broke and Valko was back in himself. He lowered his hand from his face; Satoshi was just looking away from him. Had that happened? Valko ran a hand over his stubbly head feeling for any sign of injury — there was none, just the familiar transverse lines of old scars. If he'd hit his head it wasn't very hard — such anomalous implant effects were uncommon but not completely unheard of. Still, this wasn't the first weird experience and — what with the mild swelling of his implant — he'd have to insist on the whitecoats from the late Eugene Fisher's team giving him a thorough examination. When the investigation was over.

Valko pressed on. His ribs ached, he must have injured them in the crash. They didn't feel broken and the pain wasn't sharp enough to trigger his auto-hypnotic pain suppression — though the head pain should've been but still hadn't. The ache was enough to distract him, making it an effort to breathe and slowing him. His irritation grew.

Outside the transpod, the damage to it became obvious. 'Look at the way fuselage's scorched,' Satoshi said. 'The damage doesn't look as bad from out here.' He pointed up at where the two largest of the craft's four EHD modules were located — both looked intact. 'The point of impact's precise, right below the high altitude impellers. Knocked out their power supply.'

'So?' Valko said, rubbing his eyes.

'Well, it looks like a low-tech, low-yield missile hit us; anything more sophisticated or powerful would have done more than just down the transpod — it'd would've blown us apart.'

Valko started turning over the problem in his mind as they clambered up a rocky hillside.

'How could a low-tech missile have been so accurate?' He asked. 'Luck?'

'No such thing,' Satoshi said. 'To be that precise suggests to me it was limited by design: a weapon selected to bring us down rather than destroy us.'

'That would imply a pretty sophisticated opponent.'

'Yeah. Not good news.'

'On the other hand, the weapons locker blew outwards, so maybe it wasn't a missile at all but a bomb?'

'I see where you're going...' Satoshi said. 'I don't like the implications, sir.'

'Think about it. If it'd gone off before we'd begun our descent, we'd have dropped like a rock from 10,000 feet.'

Satoshi scowled, 'The 'pod wouldn't have survived a crash from high altitude and neither would any of us.'

'But the blow out could have been from the loss of cabin pressure,' Valko said. 'I mean, if there'd been a bomb in the locker then we'd all have been killed.'

'Unless the bomb was placed outside?'

'No, the transpod was a last minute requisition, only the Justeco Centro and through it, the Centra Autorita itself could have known,' Valko said. Satoshi raised an eyebrow, but didn't say anything. More for his own benefit than Satoshi's, Valko added, 'It couldn't have been a bomb.' *Then why do I sound so uncertain?*

Satoshi waved a hand at the surround area, 'Who could be out here to have shot us down? With respect, sir, we should act as if we *were* shot down, but I'm not convinced.'

They lapsed into silence — Satoshi ranging ahead and Valko moving as fast as he could with every breath a struggle.

Every Enclosed had heard tales of survivors living in the burn-zones, but even the Remnants wouldn't be desperate, reckless or stupid enough to risk entering for more than a kilometre or so. Nowhere but the ruins of cities were worth that risk. It might be a clear, safe burn-zone or it might seem that way and all of a sudden turn out to be a death trap. Besides, there was nothing left out here: it had been the only way to stop the rampage of the unfettered nanodestroyers. The extreme temperatures of high yield flashburners and — when they ran out — old-world fusion bombs, combated the uncontrolled nanites when nothing else could.

Ever since the Moon Terrorists had turned them against the world, the technology had been proscribed. Microscopic machines were too dangerous: subject to the whims of whoever had the best hacking software, in much the same way as the old naukara. What worried Valko was that most nanodestroyers left in the environment remained on the intruder deterrent setting. Anyone — like them — who was not identifiable as a member of the Superstate with control of an area, or at least as an agent of the UNWG, would be deterred from their trespass by being stripped apart molecule by molecule. Although he'd been taught that the only unfettered nanites which remained were infertile, every Enclosed feared the return of ones that could self-replicate.

If there hadn't been a paradigm shift away from the deadly machines, his implant might have been the product of nanotechnology. It had, after all, been the prevalent medical tech before Enclosure. Synthorganics had bridged the gap in medicine though it had been in its infancy — barely tested. In some way, the parallel organic and synthetic cellular systems had shown themselves to be superior: they couldn't be hacked because the synthetic cells worked like their organic counterpart — obeying an enhanced DNA code not some computer program. Without the medical nanites used in the implantation of the Veteran's synthorganics, the technology was hack proof. Valko was confident using the mindlink, knowing he couldn't be subverted — now, if his implant had used nanotech...

As for Satoshi — how vital the nature of his implants was to the sergeant's reliability. Valko imagined, with a shudder, relying on a naukara instead. How easy they'd been for the scientists to hack during the War, turning them against their handlers. Sure, they were tougher — in a purely combative sense — but synthorganics were more stable, adaptable and ultimately more sophisticated — everything from respiration to reproduction duplicated and enhanced. It was the difference between making soldiers and making slaves to the machine.

Valko watched Satoshi climbing the ridge ahead of them; he was loyal, capable and most importantly possessed of a will of his own. Valko's mind conjured a different image — the machine man, stomping up the slope, no thoughts save the directive to follow its master's commands — and maybe the silent, agonised scream of the scraps of human flesh underneath. Then the disturbing thought came to Valko: Satoshi was not so safe as he seemed, not so reliable. Despite the benign technology of the synthorganics — the synthetic duplicate protected the organic cell and preserved it from DNA damage and mitochondrial decay — there was a hidden danger.

The synthetic cell did the same job as the organic — with greater efficiency and with some added functionality, like Satoshi's synthorganic muscle fibre, which didn't replace the natural fibres but worked in synergy with them. But medical nanotech had been involved in seeding the synthorganic cells, at least the kind his sergeant had. Everyone knew the stories of what had happened — the imperfect hack of the Veterans. So they hadn't become puppets but the Lunar Terrorists had created within them a trap: Lunar War Syndrome. All the whitecoats in all the Plena hadn't been able to undo the psychological damage after scouring the nanotech from the Veterans.

Satoshi seemed to be lucky, a stable Veteran, and many of his artificial cells had been deactivated by a complex system of auto-hypnotic suggestion and suppressor implants, themselves synthorganic. Yet it didn't cure the problem, just controlled it — reducing the danger if he went on a rampage. There remained some risk; he could still use his organic musculature, which had itself been retrogened beyond human norms. Worse, it was said that the synthorganics could be brought online by the Syndrome, in spite of the safeguards.

If Satoshi's Lunar War Syndrome were triggered and that activated his synthorganic muscle tissue, he'd be ten times stronger. Helped by synthorganic-reinforced bones and similar fortification of skin and connective tissue, he'd become beyond lethal.

Valko shook his head, to clear the thought — it had been

fifteen years and there'd never been any sign of his sergeant degenerating. Valko had known him for over half that time — the only concern he'd ever had about Satoshi was the extent of the man's bleeding heart. On top of that, no less than Eugene Fisher had cleared him. No, the giant sergeant was the best possible backup for a Moderator — Valko knew he was lucky to have him.

Even deactivated, Satoshi was a tough son of a bitch, Valko thought with a smile — dismissing how wrong his emotional response felt: its deviation from his norms. He'd seen the Sergeant slashed with a blade by a suspect as they tried to seize him for interrogation. The blade was so sharp that when Valko had examined it later, he'd cut his thumb on its edge. The slash had been to Satoshi's face and the big man had deflected it on his forearm. Valko had seen where the blade had struck the skin of his forearm: instead of cut tissue, there was an angry red line, as if he'd scratched a fingernail across the skin without enough force to draw blood. It was rumoured that a Lunar War Vet could withstand an old-world shotgun blast to the torso with only minor injuries. Valko regarded this as an exaggeration but he had to concede that Satoshi was well protected against any primitive weapons — like the kind of weapon Remnants often scrounged. Still, synthorganic tissue was vulnerable to nanodestroyers, like everything else, albeit it'd take a lot longer for Satoshi to succumb.

Valko stumbled to one knee in the compacted dust that covered the smooth obsidian of the ripples of the ridges and valleys. In his distraction, he'd failed to notice that they'd reached the ridgeline — it wasn't like him to lose himself in irrelevant reflections when being focused on the needs of the moment was more important. Perhaps, he'd banged his head in the crash and not realised it? A concussion would explain the feeling of dislocation he was experiencing, almost as if he were walking in a dream. He pulled himself back to reality:

Satoshi had bounded up ahead and was checking their surroundings. He had an auto sextant out and was leaving it to calculate their position while he scanned the horizon for threats. The primitive navigation system was the best they had, now there were no more satellites to be relied upon. They'd all — or almost all — crashed down to Earth during the War. Either they'd been weaponised by the Allied Lunar Colonies and rained down as kinetic bombs or lack of maintenance in the chaotic decades that followed had caused their fall.

What had driven those bastards to betray the planet that had birthed them? Valko couldn't understand it. He had a vague memory of overhearing a conversation as a child — maybe between his parents — talking about Mars and wondering whether she would help Earth. Valko knew that Mars had been, and remained, teetering on the edge of self-sufficiency. The occasional info broadcasts in his hub mentioned sporadic contact with the Mars colony and the efforts made to re-establish trade to get at the resources diverted there from the asteroid mines. An equal number of broadcasts were harangues from the Temple of the Wounded Mother — preaching that the colonists must return to the cradle to show their repentance and atone for the sins of humanity. Telling them that Mars was a false home and that they were symptomatic of the human disease's tendency to spread wasn't going to warm relations with the distant colony or lead to any trade.

They crested another ridgeline as the sun began to stain the blasted land rust red. As before, there was no sign of any pursuer but Satoshi insisted they follow the same procedure: checking they were safe before mounting the ridge and dropping below it again as fast as they could. Contrary to all Valko had believed possible, there were signs of lichens growing on the larger boulders. Life was trying to find a way but, without human help, it was doubtful that it would ever amount to more than this. The achievement of the Martyrs — bringing green back to the Mother's disfigured face — was more of a miracle when set against the scale of the devastation.

The sun sank below the horizon and, as the light faded, the clear night sky filled with stars. This far away from any outpost, there was no light pollution whatsoever and the endless depths pressed down on them. At first, Valko was captivated by the uncountable stars but then he felt diminished by them. Like everything was meaningless on the human scale. It was hard to feel that he mattered — that anything he might do was worth a damn. Then he recalled the strange sensation he'd felt when he'd suffered neural shock. He stared back at the stars and realised that what mattered was perspective. From here, even the stars were insignificant: they didn't matter more than he did. Perspective made them smaller than him. Why did he feel so comfortable with such arrogance?

⛧

Satoshi was enjoying himself. The crash and the fear of pursuit made him feel almost as vital as when his implants were active. He breathed the cooling air and relished its harshness. The envirosuit's onboard systems had confirmed that they were not in a nanodestroyer hot zone, nor was there residual radiation or other contaminants in the air or ground. The wider area looked like it had been hit by a flashburner, which would explain the lack of radiation, or maybe it had just been scorched and scoured by the atmospheric changes that had come in the War's aftermath. Either way it was safe.

One day, the Martyrs would make it here and the land would flourish. He imagined the barren ground as green valleys with modified trees and grasses. Maybe he'd live to see it, maybe not. For now, though he could appreciate the raw beauty of the land. He took in the stars above them, noting the constellations and finding that he knew their names and how to use them for navigation. Another fragment of knowledge, out of place in his mind and disconnected from any memory that might explain how and why he knew what he knew. The stars themselves didn't bother him. To Satoshi the heavens were nothing to be bothered by, no more than another part of the scenery. Beautiful but just background.

Even while he was considering their surroundings and imagining the land's regeneration, his guard didn't drop. His eyes, sharper than any natural human's, roved the landscape for hazards: natural or artificial. He kept a tight control of the tingle of anxiety that wriggled deep inside him. It warned him to take care and kept his edge well-honed but he didn't let it dominate him. It was a tool, the fear, nothing more.

Their hubs continued to detect Actur's beacon, showing a strong signal — now stationary, with no sign of the creeping tick of coordinates he'd read in Davidson's report. The roughness of the terrain complicated Satoshi's efforts to keep them on the right heading, and Valko's injury didn't help either. His Moderator was struggling up the crumbling slopes with a vacant expression on his face. Satoshi hoped it was a side effect of the auto-hypnotic pain suppression training all kensakan and Moderators underwent and not something more serious. Even so, they were making good time.

He stopped and waited for Valko to catch up.

'If we can walk for another hour or two,' Satoshi said. 'We'll stand a chance of throwing off any possible pursuers.'

Valko looked at him and nodded — the rasping of his breath audible even past the respirator.

They carried on, their pace slowing as Valko flagged behind. The light from the stars and the cracked face of the Moon was enough to see by, but no tracker would be able to follow their trail without daylight. Satoshi stopped again and while he waited for Valko to catch up, checked the horizon behind them for any lightening of the sky that might indicate pursuit in ground vehicles — none was visible.

The terrain remained unchanging and hard. Every dislodged rock made Satoshi hold his breath as he waited for the sound of discovery, but if someone had shot them down, they were either more interested in the wreckage of their transpod or else was an inadequate tracker.

The silence between him and Valko was comfortable. Neither remarked on their situation. To Satoshi, their course was clear but the prickle at the back of his neck whenever a pebble rattled downhill warned him of how far their voices might carry. Maybe sound would alert a pursuer or attract some other lurking danger — Remnants on the prowl. Putting his worries aside, Satoshi smiled as he looked at Valko: Moderator and Sergeant moving together, efficient — for the first time a genuine team.

When the Moon had reached its zenith, Satoshi called a halt. He half-expected Valko to admonish him for his presumption but all he got was a wan and weary smile. They settled near an outcrop of rock to get some shelter and engaged the night mode on their envirosuits, which inflated to provide for more comfortable sleeping by increasing insulation, now that they wouldn't be generating body heat from their exertions.

The evening meal was a single cold ration bar and a high-energy isotonic drink — the fluid generated from the sweat they'd produced during the last couple of hours. With no discussion of keeping watch, Valko — looking exhausted — fell into a deep sleep. Satoshi, knowing that he could, but not really remembering why, relied on his ability to wake at the slightest unusual sound. After a few minutes double-checking the security of their position, he likewise allowed sleep to wash over him.

†††

Valko found himself looking down at them both. They were huddled among the rocks, camouflaged from aerial view. Strange to be looking down on himself like this — he could still feel the lassitude of his body but the greater part of him was free. He remembered the stars: billions of them, countless trillions, all calling to him. His focus shifted skywards — he began racing upwards, out amongst those bright points of light. In an instant, he'd flashed to a nearby star. It grew in his vision bright enough to be blinding, yet it didn't take away his sight. There was heat but it was an awareness of mind, not a physical sensation. Nothing could touch him here.

The scale was wrong: he approached the star — a roiling, blazing sphere larger than the Sun — close enough to touch it, yet it seemed no bigger than he was. Concentrating he reached out to it: not with a hand, for he no longer had any hands. Then he was holding the star. His consciousness created the image of holding a glowing ball of light in his hand, but he knew it was an artefact of his need to understand this in the body's terms.

Scale shifted again and the star was no bigger than a grain of sand. He looked around himself without eyes to see but still he perceived the vastness of the galaxy spread out beneath him. There were billions more galaxies all around him, the impossible distances between them nothing but a thought apart. Feeling godlike — for there was no better way to describe this sensation — he looked down upon them.

With a thought, he raced in amongst the dancing motes of stars but his perspective changed again. The swirling galaxies were each now little more than pinpricks of light making up clusters and superclusters. Despite their minuscule size, he could perceive each and every star that made the whole, even while seeing everything on the grander scale.

Another shift and the universe — all that eyes could see and all that lurked in the dark — was arrayed beneath him. He was down there: amongst and part of it all. He was down there: sleeping under an outcropping. He was down there: yet he was here as well. Above. Beyond. Within. Outside.

A flare of radiance, burning with cold darkness, stole his attention, drawing him across fields of pain and valleys of joy to somewhere Other. The sharp spinal cords of Titans impaled him, as they birthed out of Oceans of Blood. Beatific beings tore him free and sated all his earthly desires. From behind them all, gazed eyes that promised terrors of pleasure — if he would but look away. Yet there was a flicker of hope. A child's smile, a baby's gurgle, a mother's whisper, out there in the void. He strained every fragment of his being to perceive it. With a final lurch, it came into focus within him. Not one shard of being: many. Billions, trillions. The numbers were meaningless, an ephemeral figure so close to infinity he could not distinguish it, yet each fragment was distinct — laid open to his perception. In that swift eternity, he stood dislocated at the pinnacle of all things in the empty depths of existence.

He understood.

Then it was lost and he rolled over in his sleep, slipping into dreams unremembered.

𝍩

Davidson stared at a scope showing tracking data from both the crash site and Valko and Satoshi's beacons. Not Chang's. He'd sent a ping to it since it hadn't been transmitting, already knowing what that meant. Sure enough, the beacon uploaded its monitoring data on Chang: he was dead. Davidson had leant back in his chair — stunned by the loss — his tainted tongue stilled.

Chang had been, not a friend, but one of his guys. A quiet man, who was always intimidated by their Moderator and his overgrown sergeant, Chang had still made things feel like a team. He'd say nothing — doing his job — then out of nowhere crack a joke. Deadpan. At first, Davidson had been irritated by the habit, never sure if it was a joke, serious or if he was being mocked. Over time, he'd understood and lost count of the times he'd roared with laughter at one of Chang's one-liners. Now, that was gone forever.

Still no word from Hampton. Sweat was running free down Davidson's spine. The longer he waited to take action — like trying to organise a rescue mission from Outpost Theta — the harder this was going to be to explain.

Chapter 9

The morning air was cold and bright. It would heat up soon enough but for the moment, its crispness was refreshing. Condensation had formed on the envirosuits, all of it sucked into the smart fabric and processed to restock internal reservoirs. If this kept on, they'd have plenty of potable water. Rations might run out though and there was nothing out here to eat. Nothing but dirt and rocks. Valko had half expected to see some sign of pursuit, yet there was nothing but the eerie stillness and the sound of his and Satoshi's breathing, made stentorian by the envirosuits' filters.

He watched Satoshi check Actur's beacon trace.

'Any change?'

'No, sir.' Satoshi said, but he looked puzzled. 'It's still transmitting — the signal's consistent and strong, but it's not moving anymore.'

'What about vital signs?' Valko asked.

'That's the problem — the signal is strong but it's stopped responding to interrogatories.'

Valko pulled back his hood, and rubbed his eyes before settling the respirator back in position.

'I can't think of any reason it'd do that unless the beacon couldn't receive our signal. If he'd rigged some kind of antenna to amplify his signal, it would work both ways.'

'We'll find out soon enough, sir,' Satoshi said. 'We're closing in on his position. I reckon we'll make it by nightfall. Maybe midday, if we can maintain our pace.'

'Alright, sergeant.'

Valko rose, stiff everywhere he shouldn't be. He felt different today, the dream still lingering with him and refusing his efforts to shake it off. It had felt so real, so different from his other dreams, the kaleidoscope memories of dead minds — where had it come from? Part of his training in using his implant had been in understanding his dream states: it was vital that he have the tools to separate dreams born of his own subconscious, from dreams formed from fragments of the minds of those he linked with. If he couldn't separate those things in the waking world, he'd have poured himself down the well of insanity within a year.

The various auto-hypnotic triggers that had helped fashion his mental resilience had given him the means to cope with the frequent nightmares that trailed him. None of those states of mind helped with the dream he'd had. It puzzled him. His training said that his own genuine dreams were a form of psychological housekeeping. Problems perceived by the subconscious that he needed to work through. Dreams weren't omens — some sort of foretelling of future events — but they were important and could sometimes have meaning. He hadn't the faintest idea what the cause of this dream was or its meaning.

They trekked on, making fine progress and seeing no sign of pursuit. By midday, the sun was startling in its brightness. Valko's eyes — the eyes of an Enclosed — ached in the shine. Heat beat down on them and the fractured landscape so hard that, even with the envirosuits, they needed to take regular breaks to avoid Valko suffering from heat exhaustion.

Even Satoshi was beginning to flag. He was carrying all their supplies and the spare envirosuit yet he would frequently break off from their route to mount a rise and check their surroundings for any sign of life — pursuer or otherwise.

A strong wind began, blowing from the south-west and carrying fine dust with it. Clouds swirled overhead, devouring the sun as they thickened and darkened. Dust in the air became denser, mirroring the heavy air in the sky above them. The ceaseless burr of particles against the hoods of their envirosuits gave way to the suits' own warning pings. The dust carried with it the sneak thief of life: radiation clicking upwards from the baseline of twenty to thirty microroentgens per hour, to three, then four roentgens. Nothing their suits couldn't handle but then the storm began bringing dust from farther away — hot dust. Not only with the slow separation of spirit from body, that too many rads would bring, but also the flesh tearing death of nanodestroyers. The wind had become Death's steed: on it rode humanity's suicide machines, now registering at one part per billion.

'We've got to find cover,' Satoshi shouted over the howl of the wind. Valko could do little more than nod as he battled against fatigue.

If the counter reached two hundred parts per billion the suits would no longer protect them and Valko knew his death would be assured, maybe even Satoshi's. If the storm brought a denser concentration, their last moments would become more spectacular: less of a quick illness and more of a flensing.

'Actur's beacon is within a few hundred metres,' Satoshi shouted. 'It's our only hope.'

'If he's in a structure,' Valko said, it was low, not meant for Satoshi but he saw the giant's grimace and knew his sergeant had heard.

'If we stay out here, huddling behind the ridges won't save us,' Satoshi shouted.

Finally, the autosextant and their hubs put them at the source of the beacon signal. They appeared to be standing on top of it. The landscape all around them was the same, depressions and black-knife ridges creating wave after wave of small valleys. It was the tell-tale pattern of an area hit by a flashburner, now swirling with lethal dust.

The envirosuits switched over to their internal air supplies, sealing them off from outside. Valko could hear nothing over the dust-laden wind and his own breath, amplified by being contained, as it rasped in short, panicked gasps.

After a bit of poking around amongst rock formations, they uncovered an old, pitted pressure door, which, when they examined it, turned out to be the entrance to an underground bunker. As if responding to their salvation, the storm front moved on and the winds dropped away, seeking other victims.

The bunker was old — Pre-War tech, built in expectation for a showdown between the Superstates. Dust crusted the plug door but there were clear signs that it'd seen recent use. Not so often as to dislodge the dirt built up on its outer surface but enough to leave channels on the floor where the door had shifted previous dust and a clear line around the door's seals. There was an old-world keypad to one side of it. The keys were coated in dried blood, the stains beginning to flake off in the arid conditions.

Satoshi stepped forward and raised a cautionary hand. 'It might be trapped, Val. Be careful.'

The sergeant's use of his name in such a familiar way, for once, didn't annoy Valko. He felt different today, as if last night's dream had included a low dose of NOTT that wouldn't go away.

He did a quick visual inspection of the terminal; the bloodstains were no more than a smear and showed no discernible pattern that might have given away the code. Valko held one of the envirosuit's insulated metallic probes — designed to detect heavy metal contaminants in water — near to the keypad. There was no arc of electricity, so he tried pressing a key with the tip of the probe. The small display on the keypad lit up, demanding an eighteen-digit passcode.

'Oshi, take a look at this, would you?' Valko asked, without any of the usual command in his tone.

Satoshi examined the keypad and grunted. 'No way to connect our hubs to it, so we can't have them hack it. Fancy guessing the passcode?'

'Don't be ridiculous,' Valko said, a hint of his usual self returning. 'Give me your sidearm. No, not the tranqgun, your veteran's pistol.'

'It's an omni-pistol. Have you used one before, sir?' Satoshi asked, handing the bulky handgun over.

'No. But it has an energy beam setting, doesn't it?'

'Yes, but it won't have enough power to cut through the door.'

'It's not the door I'm going to cut through,' Valko said.

He familiarised himself with the weapon and set it for a mid-yield energy beam that would burn through metal with only a mild explosive capacity.

'Better double-check your goggles; the beam uses a variable strength laser to reduce the radiation generated by the particle beam. If that laser refracts back at you, it'll blind you,' Satoshi said.

Irritation clicked back into the place from which the dream had dislodged it but Valko did not respond. Taking careful aim at a section of bunker wall beside the heavy pressure door, Valko waited for the pistol to confirm its capacitor had charged and that it had locked on the targeted section of wall. When it gave a soft ping, he squeezed the trigger. There was a flash of light and the smell of superheated metal as the laser beam struck the wall. A short particle beam pulsed along the laser's path and the metal cover on the wall burst open. Inside, cables and wires were visible — scorched and with their plastic covers melted.

'Uh, I think you've just fried it,' Satoshi asked, making no effort to hide the look of disbelief on his face. 'How are we going to get in now?'

Valko said nothing as he poked around amongst the wires, clearing them to one side. Then he stood back and gestured to Satoshi to take a look.

'Have faith, Sergeant. There's the manual door release.'

Satoshi looked into the smoking hole before grunting, grabbing the lever and straining against it so hard it looked like he might tear it free from its housing. With an abrupt screech, the release moved and the door seal cracked open with a faint hiss. The air that came out smelled processed but not stale.

Satoshi reached up and ran his fingers along the crack until he found a point where he could get purchase and, with a grunt of effort, he pulled the door open.

'Pre-War tech. They were paranoid — but clearly not enough,' Satoshi said. 'The designers probably intended this for protection from a nuclear strike not as a bunker to hold against an invading army. How'd you know?'

'It's in the kensakan training manual, section fifty-two: Raids on Remnant Strongholds. You should read it sometime,' Valko said, no trace of a smile on his face.

Satoshi squinted at him for a moment, then chuckled. 'I must have forgotten that bit.'

'A symptom of your age, perhaps Sergeant?' Valko allowed his amusement to show — this was... refreshing.

'Something like that, Val.'

Their levity faded — if anyone had been inside they'd have been alerted to the forced entry. Valko listened but no sound came from within and lights began to flicker on when the door was half-open. Satoshi took the lead, his tranqgun in hand and set to lethal, while Valko held the omni-pistol at the ready. Now was the time he really began to miss the security of the frag guns they'd lost in the crash.

They entered a short passageway. The floor was covered in a fine layer of dust for the first few feet and through the middle of that there was the track like something man sized had dragged through it. A line of smeared blood — fresher looking than the curling fragments on the keypad — ran the length of the corridor. Each step they took triggered lights to come on ahead of them, illuminating more of the trail of blood — sometimes thicker, sometimes thinner. The air remained still and no sounds came from ahead.

All too soon, they reached the end of the passage. Valko took up position at one corner of the door and peered into the cavernous room. It was dominated by a central lab area filled with large cylinders containing fluids and tissue samples. There were several powerful looking computers arranged around the lab and reams of hardcopies strewn around work surfaces. Three of the work surfaces had terminals projecting their screens into the hazy air — it looked so like Orla's setup that Valko almost expected to see her step out to greet them.

At the base of one of the desks with an active terminal — this one given over to a dense wall of text — he could see a pair of feet sticking out. The smears of blood led to those feet.

Satoshi raised a hand and signalled that he'd take point. He moved forwards, out into the open — gun trained on the body with Valko covering the rest of the room. They alternated position, one covering the other, until they both stood over the man lying on the floor, curled in the foetal position around a puddle of blood. The gelatinous membrane of a respirator covered his face though the membrane that should have covered the closed eyes had been cut away, leaving a ragged edge. The respirator's gills still fluttered a soft rhythm. Not a corpse then.

The man was dressed in a brown wearall, soaked with a dark stain of blood over the abdomen and streaked with other smudges. Beneath the fresher stains from his own leaking vitae, there were older marks of grease and lubricants — the vital fluids of the machines he'd worked with.

'Actur?' Satoshi said, without looking at Valko — eyes still sweeping the room, gun held level, following his gaze.

'It's got to be. We'll see soon enough when we can get a look at his face. Beacon trace says it's him, but I'll wait until I get a hub sync.'

'I'll sweep the rest of the area.'

'You do that.'

Satoshi prowled off over to where another short passageway led off at the back of the lab. He disappeared down it, not making a sound.

Valko looked down at the body below him. He was no medtech, but the pulsing membrane of the respirator was sending a simple enough message. Its semi-translucent flesh was blushed red. That meant only one thing. He didn't have much time.

His hub pinged with the result of the full beacon sync. This was Darius Actur. Vital signs had been depressed for days — since Vinnetti's death. Had she done this to him? Valko carefully undid the wearall to see a blood soaked wad of cloth that it had been holding pressed to the belly. Valko retrieved his envirosuit's medikit and found its wound sealant. He pulled back the sopping red cloth. There was a blackened and blistered hole burned through Actur's stomach — wide enough for a finger to pass. It looked to be a through and through. The sealant would do all of jack for such a wound. Blood was seeping out, not pulsing, but the amount that Actur had lost was the problem. They had nothing that could stop all the bloodloss from a wound like this and nothing to replace the life that was being lost a drop at a time.

Satoshi strode back over to him, his previous stealth abandoned.

'All clear. There's a compact living area with supplies and equipment for air and water processing. Someone could have easily seen out the War in here. What about him?' Satoshi nodded at Actur.

Valko sighed and stood, wiping the blood off his hands. 'Not much we can do for him. Without the transpod, there's no way we can get him to a medcentre in time.'

'So... that's it?'

'No. Worst case, I can link with him post-mortem and dredge his recent memories. We should at least be able to see what happened to Vinnetti. If he did it, or if it was our female assassin.'

'You think he interrupted her in the act?'

'Maybe, but she wasn't bothered by Koewatha, was she? Let's not speculate. We'll know soon enough.'

Actur's eyelids flickered and opened, slowly. Valko leant over him and Satoshi towered behind him. The injured man's eyes seemed vague and unfocused, then they fixed past Valko. A look of horror gripped the face under the membrane and lips moved in words stolen by its encompassing mass. The man pressed backwards into the desk, cowering under it. Actur's bloodied hands scrabbled up at his face, tearing the g-creature away. Without it, he rasped a wheezing breath and tried to speak.

'Ben... ben...' His voice was little more than a gurgle. His eyes lost their focus and rolled upwards as he body collapsed downwards, almost in on itself.

Valko's hub gave bleeped an alert and Actur's lifesigns displayed a trio of flatlines.

'Who in the Mother's Name is Ben?' Valko asked.

Satoshi shook his head, 'He seemed terrified, Val. Not what I'd expect from a murderer, but if he's just a witness then why would he be so scared of us?'

'I don't know, Oshi. He was almost out of his mind — that's not going to make memory retrieval easy. I'll have to let him cool off or the emotion will overwhelm me. What's puzzling me is, how did he know to come here? This man is — was — no simple drudge.'

Both men stood wordless. The occasional bubbling sound from the cylinders in the lab and a short whirr from one or other of the computers broke the silence. The age of the place, combined with the impression that it had been vacated by some mystery occupant not long before Actur's arrival, lent it an eerie feel. Valko couldn't help the ribbon of fear twisting through him as he stood over the dead body of a man who had spent his last moment overcome with dread. From the look on Satoshi's face, his sergeant felt the same.

'Sir, look,' Satoshi said. 'I think he was trying to leave a message on the terminal.'

At the bottom of the text, which floated in air above the desk, was a new line that contained just four letters. B-E-N-E. The terminal's input was smeared with blood.

Valko looked around the desktop and at the rest of the text on the screen, 'None of it's jumping out at me. It must mean something but all I can see is just whitecoat babble.'

He stepped back into the main lab area, negotiating the metal railings that surrounded it. Some of the experiments were incomplete and several of the displays flickered with streams of data, as they continued some long running program. Nothing that he saw seemed to relate to faster than light travel; from the little he understood of what he found this was pure biological research. There was no other reference to 'Ben' or 'BENE' and he could see no sign that Actur had touched anything else there.

Satoshi stayed by Actur's corpse, still covering the area with his gun.

'He was expecting someone else to be here,' he said. 'Was he working with some renegade whitecoat?'

Valko didn't answer. His sergeant was close to something, something dangerous. If this was part of the Conclave's project, he had to be careful not to reveal too much. He put the omni-pistol in the thigh pocket of the envirosuit, set his hub on a tabletop and ordered it to analyse the data on the nearest display. Then he began to rifle through the hardcopies. Time dragged as he looked for some clue as to the identity of the bunker's former occupier.

'Whoever he was expecting to find must have been here recently,' He said. 'Within the last few days I think.'

'No, it's been almost two months,' a soft and all too familiar female voice said from behind Satoshi. Both men whirled to face the newcomer.

'Jean, what in the Mother's name are you doing here?' Valko asked.

She stood framed by the entryway; dressed in matt-black, code-covered body armour that absorbed the light and hazed the air. Valko felt his stomach twist. He recognised this woman. Yes, it was Jean but it was also someone else. Someone who'd terrified Joey Koewatha. Fisher's murderer. The revelation hit him so hard he couldn't find any words. She spoke first.

'I think that should be my question, don't you? Here I find you in *my* home and with blood on your hands.'

'As far as I can see, the blood is on your hands, Jean. If you've come to finish the job, you're too late. Actur is already dead.'

'Dead? Yes, I am too late. But if you think I killed him, you're a fool.'

'A fool? Yes, a fool for not seeing through you sooner.

You shot us down, trapped us here. It's a big mistake, Jean. If that's even your name.' He felt the shock fading and a crawling at the back of his head, a tingle that was growing as his whole body started to feel hot.

'Shot you down? No, Valko. I want you alive — if I'd shot you down, you wouldn't be here. They don't want you talking to me.'

'Why should I believe you? You're a murderer. Blaming some nebulous group isn't going to change my mind, Jean. You've manipulated me, but I can see why — it's all about this,' Valko said, casting his arm around to encompass the lab and his voice rising with his temper. 'If this is your home then I can see why you killed Fisher — you're trying to steal his research.'

'His research?' She shouted, almost spitting the words out.

'What I don't understand is why you murdered a young woman and this man. But I'll find out soon enough. Sergeant Tomari, seize this woman.'

Satoshi started forwards, moving slowly and keeping his gun trained on Jean.

'I'm not your enemy, Valko. Think!'

He ignored her. This wouldn't be the first time he'd heard conspiracy theories from suspects.

'Under my authority as a Moderator, you are sub aresto. You will be interviewed and your guilt will be determined. You will then face sanction for your crimes,' Valko said — lost temper now retreating behind his merciless inner voice.

Jean sighed, her previous anger evaporating replaced with what? Resignation?

'You force my hand,' she said. 'Such a pity Valko. If you had played along, I could have delayed this. Let things run their course. It might have been painful at the end but maybe you would've had another year or two of life.' Her regret sounded genuine, the sense of it flowing into him through the open door of his implant. 'Some of my former colleagues would no doubt love to speak to you. To find out what you have seen, what you will go on to see. Maybe your death would have been your transcendence, a service to humanity, but now, you force my hand.' The woman who'd called herself Jean smiled at him, but it was a thin smile that carried no triumph, more... sorrow? She turned to face Satoshi as he neared her and raised her right hand, palm outwards.

She said, 'Benedict Arnold,' in a loud clear voice.

The change was immediate.

Even as Valko was asking himself, *'Who the hell is Benedict Arnold? Ben... BENE...'* Satoshi was shifting position. His features changed as the cords on his neck stood out and his teeth gritted. His eyes lost their usual warmth, becoming fixed pinholes.

Jean looked at Valko with sympathy in her eyes but said to Satoshi, 'Restrain him and bring him to me. If he resists, use force as necessary but don't kill him and don't harm his head. I will be in the shuttle outside.'

Satoshi continued to stare at her; then his face twisted, his eyes widening so much that they seemed to be trying to escape his head and his mouth hanging open, lips drawn back from his teeth. He began to advance on her.

Jean shouted, 'Benedict Arnold!' at Satoshi again: he picked up pace.

She didn't hesitate further but spun and raced through the door behind her. Satoshi bounded over the low metal barrier that separated the lab area from the entrance and pounded down the corridor after Jean. Valko lost sight of both of them. He was shaking. What the hell was happening with Satoshi?

There was a metallic screech, followed by the sound of metal being struck with great force, resounding within the bunker. Then came a guttural cry of absolute rage, and abrupt silence.

Without warning, Satoshi slunk back into sight. He moved like a predator stalking prey it knows it has cornered. All sanity — all trace of man — had vanished from the loose face. Drool poured from the corners of his mouth as he advanced on Valko — hands held wide in the aspect of beast.

┼┼┼

Davidson nearly leapt out of his seat when out of nowhere his hub connected to Pravnik Hampton's. Ever cool, he covered his surprise well.

«*What can I do for you, Pravnik?*» He asked, trying to avoid sounding obsequious.

«*Any change?*» She sent.

«*No, ma'am. They've reached the signal location and they've been static there for maybe a quarter hour. Actur's last beacon update showed a fatality,*» he sent.

«*That is of no concern. Radar showing any contacts in the area?*»

«*No, ma'am.*» He stopped himself from asking, 'Why? Are we expecting some', knowing he was one misstep away from dead.

«*Interesting. You will purge the beacon and radar records from the point of the crash. You will say nothing of this to anyone, but I will give you a report to give to the Old Man. Is that clear?*»

«*Yes, ma'am, but what about…*»

«*Do as you're told, Jack. I don't need to remind you of your alternatives, do I?*»

«*No, ma'am. I'll do as you say.*»

«*Good.*» She signed off.

Davidson let out a long sigh. He wanted to swear, but fear that Hampton might still be able to monitor held his tongue. Christ but she was a stone cold bitch. What she wanted of him was very much like killing Gangleri and Satoshi. While he disliked them — hell sometimes he fucking hated them — this was wrong. What were his options though? It was him or them.

He struggled with himself but, soon enough, his hands reached out and adjusted the scope, almost with a will of their own. The scope flickered and the three beacon traces disappeared. Davidson switched the scope off and saw his own reflection glaring back at him in the darkened screen. Staring into his own eyes — how dead they looked — he beheld a stranger.

Even escaping into one of the vids he so enjoyed was denied him. He tried but he soon encountered a scene where the hero was talking to the villain of the piece — good cop talking to dirty cop. Caught in the aware time, between the births of the lies he sheltered under, Jack Davidson didn't know who he'd wanted to emulate his whole life.

'Fuck, fuck, fuck, fuck, FUCK!' Head held in hands, he uttered the word as a mantra.

†††

'Oshi, what is this? It's me. Val. Stop. Don't make me tranq you!'

Valko backed away, bringing his tranqgun up to bear. Satoshi didn't slow — he just gave a low, animal growl. Valko shot him. One, two, three, four. All centre mass. Each tranq shot was enough to take down even the largest human in an instant. Satoshi didn't even register the hits.

Valko backed behind a lab bench, trying to get its thick metal bulk between him and his friend. Satoshi grabbed one edge of it and wrenched the bench free of where it was bolted to the floor. He heaved it aside, without apparent effort, and closed on Valko. The Moderator stumbled backwards, if he was caught it'd take Satoshi less than a second to kill him. His sergeant's synthorganics were active — he could twist Valko's head off as easily as click his fingers.

Valko grabbed at the omni-pistol in the right hip pocket of the envirosuit. He came close to dropping it in his panic but his Moderator's training came into play: he cradled the butt of the pistol in his left hand to stabilise it. Raising the heavy sidearm, he aimed at Satoshi's head and heard the weapon bleep as it registered a lock. Satoshi began to surge forwards at Valko. At the last moment, Valko raised the pistol high and shot into the ceiling. He couldn't kill his friend: he owed Satoshi his life. Besides, if what Jean had said was true, he had little time left anyway. And Satoshi had a son.

The pistol — set for a lethal beam — scythed through the ceiling supports and sent an explosive pulse after the initial laser burst. In an eruption of debris, the ceiling collapsed. Heavy crossbeams crashed down on Satoshi as his feet left the air at the start of his leap. He disappeared in a cloud of dust and, for a moment, Valko feared he had killed his friend after all.

Wreckage began to shift, grating and groaning. It should be impossible, but Satoshi was still moving. Unharmed — albeit covered with dust so he looked like some painted barbarian — a heavy crossbeam had pinned him so that he was bent forwards with only his head and upper shoulders visible. From what Valko could see, Satoshi's legs were pinned between the lab bench and another beam. Despite this mechanical disadvantage, the superman was beginning to shift the incredible weight of the debris off himself. He was still coming and, judging by the blank expression on his face, was still trying to kill Valko. Satoshi began to shout, but it was incoherent. He was lost in fury — a berserker.

Valko knew he had to reach Satoshi. There was one way he could think of, but his hub was out of reach. Maybe there was a fatal chance, he didn't even know if it would work on someone gone killcrazy but he was dead if he didn't try.

Taking a vial of NOTT out, he broke the seal on it; his eye noted the serial number by habit even as his hands shook not with craving — with fear. PSXE323α — it struck him as so odd for a moment that his investigator's instinct started considering its meaning, even as he struggled to open his wrist valve. He'd never noticed a serial number with anything other than standard letters and numbers before. His dispassionate side dismissed it as a trivial detail, even as the rest of him trembled and his guts twisted.

The valve in his wrist wouldn't open — the transpod crash must have damaged it. Try as he might the damn thing remained closed, all while the debris was shifting and soon he'd be dead at his friend's hands.

He needed to get the NOTT into his blood fast. Swallowing it wouldn't be enough… but maybe inhaling it would be? Valko raised the open vial and forced every last breath of air from his chest before snorting the contents of the vial — drawing it into his lungs as hard as he could. He hacked, trying to cough — an insect tickle in his chest denying him breath — as he began to feel detachment take over.

Convinced that it was working, Valko seized Satoshi's ravening head tight, exerting all his strength to hold it steady against his friend's thrashing. A hot tear traced fire down Valko's face, and the clawing of his breath thrashed free. Forcing his churning emotions aside, he drove the cold-fire splinter of his mind forward — out of his own skull and into Satoshi's.

The raving stopped. Satoshi's arms slackened against the rubble restraining him. Then — as one — they screamed.

Part III

Mutatio est universum; vita est quod fingit mens.

The universe is change; our life is what our thoughts make it.

-MARCUS AURELIUS-

Chapter 10

'Flashburner – get down!' came the cry from the corporal. Oshi threw himself flat and rolled his stealth cloak over him. In the low gravity, the shimmering cloth flowed like water given fixed shape. The flashburner detonated, sending a sheet of hyper-intense light and short-lived radiation down the corridor.

There was an instant of searing agony — Oshi realised a small part of his left arm, just below the elbow, was exposed. Despite the pain suppressants in his armour — and the heightened pain tolerance from the retrogening he'd undergone as part of project Warulv — Satoshi could not hold back a scream of pain. The agony was paralysing. Worse, it signalled a significant breach in his armour.

His thoughts finally began to clear as mental reflexes engaged and he entered an alpha state — the benefits of the auto-hypnotic induction he'd undergone. His enhanced mind-body connection allowed him to shut down the signal from his synthorganic nerves in his right arm, cutting off the scream from his natural nerves at the same time.

He took a ragged breath. Agony in his arm from a flashburner could only mean that part of his body, and part of his armour, had burnt away. He'd also received a dose of radiation but that was the least of his worries. With a compromised suit, he was vulnerable to nanodestroyers in the air, poison gasses or vacuum.

The flashburner lacked a fission bomb's EMP but there'd been enough of an electromagnetic discharge to disable his suit's on board electronic warfare suite. The overlapping magnetic fields that it generated to repel nanodestroyers were inactive. Combined with the suit breach, he might as well have been wearing nothing but his skin.

Oshi sat up and saw that the rest of his squad had fared better. Their stealth cloaks had protected them — the optically neutral material had flowed the energy of the flashburner around to its opposite side. It had scorched the ground beneath them, then repeated the process — transferring the light, heat and radiation back and forwards a million times or more before all the energy was dissipated. An unexpected benefit of the stealth technology which had saved his, and his squad's lives. The side effect was obvious: the cloaks — once having all the appearance of water — were now a yellow brownish colour and no longer seemed to flow. Useless now, they were discarded, though as each cloak fell, the soldiers whispered thanks to the man who had brought the technology to UNWG — the charismatic Erasmus Fisher, a hero to all of Earth.

Oshi took in his surroundings, and, seeing no threat, focused his attention on his suit. There was a small rent in the armour near his elbow. The armour was blistered around that point and missing within it, as was the flesh beneath. Oshi noticed, in a detached way, that he could see bone within the wound where part of his forearm had been vaporised. He activated his suit's automed unit and it flushed thousands of nanites into his system, where they began fighting infection and repairing his wound.

It was a risk but a necessary one. Although everyone knew that these moonbug terrorists could hack cybernetics — as the naukara sent against them had discovered — no one knew about their skills with nanotech. There was no way of knowing if flooding his system would increase his danger given the presence of the machines already dormant inside his skull. But he was dead without the nanites.

Riding the adrenaline wave, he rushed to apply a small package of grey putty to the break in his armour. More nanites — these ones of the nanobuilder class — within the putty reorganised the hyper-steel solution they were suspended in, into the microlattices of a new layer of armour plate, bonding it in place at the molecular level. That done, they spread out on the outer surface of the surrounding armour, forming a temporary defensive layer against hostile nanotech.

Oshi allowed feeling to return to his arm. There was pain, but he could manage it — the automed's nanotech had tweaked his pain receptors around the injury site. The dose of radiation he'd received — even in such a small percentage of his flesh — could have been lethal but he trusted in the automed's ability to contain the radioactive particles in his body and transport them away, without allowing any permanent damage.

The sounds of ballistic weapons fire chattered. The

solitary enemy Scientist, whose lab complex they were storming, had engaged five of Oshi's fellow specialists in a firefight. They had him pinned down but the Scientist's hyper-magnetic shield was deflecting their shots away from his body. The resulting ricochets caused him to flinch and keep his head down, even though they were no threat to him. He popped up and fired his weapon.

Oshi blinked rapidly as a line of white fire burned across the room. The purple afterimage on his retina occluded his vision but he could see enough to tell that Corporal Udin had been hit. The fusion beam had bored a foot wide hole right through his chest — tongues of flame leapt up around the edges of the wound.

'Suppressing fire!' Oshi shouted over his suit comms.

He pulled his hypersteel blade from its sheath at his back and hurled himself forwards, vaulting over the makeshift barricade made by the scientist. The rest of his squad had opened up, causing the man to flinch back just as he'd once again brought up the array of his fusion gun to fire, the multiple tines and antennae protruding from its muzzle beginning to fluoresce.

Oshi yelled, mirroring the qi-ai of his Peichin ancestors — those ancient warriors of Okinawa — as he charged the stunned man. Taking advantage of the momentary distraction his war cry had afforded him, he brought the hypersteel blade of his long knife slashing in a vicious diagonal arc across the man's neck — allowing the natural funnel between head and shoulder to guide his strike.

The blade met the stiff resistance of the scientist's vacsuit — its toughened surface designed to withstand micrometeorite strikes. Such was the ferocity of the blow — driven as it was by all Oshi's retrogened and synthorganic enhanced strength — that the blade sheared through the suit. It cleaved through flesh, vertebrae and spinal cord before lodging in the denser material of the suit's chest piece.

Blood sprayed out — crimson droplets that floated to the ground in the low gravity. Oshi realised that the man in front of him was dead, held up only by the blade stuck in him. He wrenched it free and kicked the corpse away from him — the body fell in a lazy arc to the floor. Only then, did he notice the low thrumming coming from the scientist's weapon — its shot was still charging. For the second time in as many minutes, Oshi hurled himself aside, over the makeshift barricade. The world turned white.

He couldn't see. Behind him he felt the reassuring hardness of a wall. Focusing on his other senses, Oshi felt panic rise. He could hear the hiss of escaping atmosphere and a gurgling wet sound of someone asphyxiating. Then there was a tapping noise. It sounded like it was coming from the airlock. *Tap. Tap. Tap.*

†††

Valko opened his eyes and focused on Satoshi's face. Sanity had returned.

'Val, I mean Sir, where am I?' Satoshi dark grey eyes had returned to their normal dimensions, the pupils no longer constricted.

'It's alright, Oshi. You'll be fine — it's over for now. I was able to reach you,' Valko said.

He still clasped his friend's head but the tenderness caused him embarrassment and he let his hands drop to his sides.

'Where is she?' Satoshi asked.

'Gone. She did something to you. Called you a name I think. It made you go Amok,' Valko sighed. 'She seemed to think you were going to do whatever she told you but, instead, you went killcrazy. She ran. I assume to the shuttle she said she had waiting. She must've managed to get away from you, so you came back.'

'What did I do?' There was a pleading look in Satoshi's eyes.

'It's alright, my friend,' Valko said. 'You weren't yourself. She tricked us. She was the assassin all along. Somehow, she tried to use some kind of... I don't know. Maybe some kind of protocol within your neural conditioning to turn on your Lunar War Syndrome. It didn't seem to work the way she expected.'

Valko paused as the thought registered of what that meant for him, if every Veteran had undergone the process. Every Moderator, every kensakan who'd been trained in auto-hypnosis — so similar in its way to Satoshi's neural conditioning — could be a threat. Unless it was the synthorganics themselves? No, there was no one controlling his mind… was there?

'How do you know about my neural conditioning?' Satoshi asked. 'Even I didn't know I'd had it until…'

'I shared your flashback, Oshi. I could see the conditioning as a barrier between that memory and your mind. I had to punch through it to reach you.' Valko couldn't meet the other's gaze — didn't he know that Moderators underwent training that was nearly the same?

'How can you have done that without a hardwire? I don't understand.' Incredulity clouded Satoshi's face.

'It's new to me as well. A lot has happened to me of late, none of which I understand. Now's not the time to discuss it! When I shot the ceiling brace and it fell on you, I think I compromised the structure's integrity,' Valko said, pointing at the ceiling.

'Go, leave me. I nearly killed you,' Satoshi said.

'Oshi, don't get all noble and self-sacrificing on me. It wasn't your fault. What kind of friend would I be if I left you like this?'

'Val, really, what's happened to you? You're different.'

'Yeah, maybe, but I don't know how long it will last for. I feel like…'

The structure overhead gave an ominous groan, which subsided as if it were a tired sigh.

Satoshi inhaled sharply, 'It's pressing down on me.'

'What can I do?' Valko said, adrenalin suddenly flooding his body as his heart jolted to an erratic high, his thoughts blurring. Panic! Why was he panicking? He never panicked.

'Whatever you did when you shared my flashback switched off my synthorganics. There's no way I can lift this beam off myself,' Satoshi said through gritted teeth.

'I can try turning them on again,' Valko said.

'Too dangerous, what if I try to kill you?'

'Good point.' Valko checked the omni-pistol. It was down to ten percent charge. 'Charge cell is nearly out. I don't know — maybe there's enough to cut through.'

Another groan came from the structure overhead.

'Try it,' Satoshi said, wheezing and the strain evident on

his face.

Valko took careful aim with the omni-pistol. He set it to tight beam and turned it up one step to the maximal lethal setting. Holding the trigger down he scythed a beam across the strut that was pinning Satoshi. The steel of the beam melted and ran in channels down the edge of the strut. Some dripped to the floor close to Satoshi but none touched him. The strut began to sag but the energy beam had not cut all the way through.

'Try again,' Satoshi gasped as the strut bent across his upper back.

Valko raised the pistol and squeezed the trigger. A weak beam flickered out but died before making it a quarter of the way through the existing cut in the metal. The omni-pistol gave a feeble beep and shut down.

Valko's panic surged: the return of human feeling was unwelcome. He couldn't concentrate on what he needed to do.

'What do I do?' he asked, trying and failing to keep the uncertainty from his voice.

He knew that Satoshi had never seen him be anything other than clear-headed and certain — except, perhaps, for when he was plugged into another's mind. Satoshi should've been taken aback by the change in his superior's tone but Valko could see that having an unknown and increasing weight on his broad shoulders was creating a more pressing distraction for the sergeant.

'It's getting... too heavy... to hold,' Satoshi said, jaw clenched tight and his face purpling with the effort.

Valko made a decision. Gripping Satoshi's head, he once again sent his mind spearing forwards.

'No...' Satoshi gasped.

✟✟✟

The only illumination came from the stars and the crescent Moon, where — until six months ago — the cities of Armstrong and Aldrin had been visible on the occluded half as two shining beacons, made from ten thousand pinpricks of light. For now, the Moon looked as it had done for most of history but, when it was full, the terrible scars on its surface showed themselves. Unavoidable reminders of the conflict: the wages of War, marked in perpetuity.

Oshi gripped his flechette rifle. He was wearing a light suit of synthetic sharkskin and had just emerged from the sea. Salt water ran in rivulets down the suit, leaving beads of water to dry in the warm night breeze. He didn't remove his rebreather — fearing a gas attack and not trusting to his altered lungs alone.

The Panasian Alliance forces shouldn't be expecting an infiltration from the sea. Their heavily modified naukara were incapable of functioning in the water and ITF intel was that the United America, African Congress and Eurussian naukara were no better able to cope. They were too heavy and any breach in waterproofing risked a short circuit, but the enemy wouldn't be expecting a non-naukara strike force. After all, unaugmented troops wouldn't last a minute against a fully amped naukara — no matter how good their equipment or training.

Oshi smiled and rolled his neck, his taut vertebrae crackling and popping. This was a test of his abilities — one he knew he was equal to. There was a savage ferocity within him, familiar but also out of place — too intense. It must be the synth hormones beginning to flow, driving up his aggression and his will to fight. His predator's instincts caused him to roll to the side and come up flechette rifle trained, as a shadow — black on black out of the night — materialised at the water's edge.

'All clear, Sarge. We're undetected,' Cooper subvocalised and transmitted over the secure line of sight laser comms.

Oshi released his breath but didn't answer. He gestured for Cooper to move up to the edge of the nearest building. There were just the two of them: it would be enough. Oshi stalked forward, silent. He sprang to the low roof and crept along, making no more noise than the mellow seabreeze. Catlike, Cooper bounded up to join him.

Their target was near the centre of the camp: an officer — non-augmented, which meant high ranking. ITF Command had intercepted a transmission that suggested he'd recently recovered intel on the whereabouts of some of the surviving Moon dissidents and would soon dispatch it by secure courier to the Panasian Junta.

All sides were hunting the renegades for the technology they held. Although the fusion bombs detonated six months previous had destroyed the lunar colony, a significant number of the scientists and their families had escaped beforehand.

Below, a patrol of two naukara marched along the camp's perimeter. They would have been near silent to unaugmented human ears, but, to Oshi's hearing, they sounded like a pair of tin men in desperate need of an oil can. He drew a bead on one, knowing that Cooper was covering the second. They watched the targets continue on their sweep — in ignorance of their proximity to silent death.

Oshi saw the target building: a small auto-prefab bristling with satellite dishes and antenna. There appeared to be a clear path between buildings. He could see another patrol, still some way off in the night, moving contra wise to the first. Image intensifier nightvision was too easy to fool, so the naukara would rely on thermal infrared for their lowlight vision. They wouldn't see Oshi and Cooper coming: in addition to assisting in movement through the water, his sharkskin suit was thermally neutral, storing his body heat in a high efficiency heat sink for up to an hour at a time before needing to vent the excess thermal energy or replace the heat sink's cartridge.

The naukara wouldn't see him any sooner than a normal human would, yet he could see them clearly, as if it were an overcast day — albeit colours were absent, the world rendered in greys. Synthorganics provided more efficient rods and cones in his eyes but didn't alter their fundamental function, though that would surely come in the near future.

Signalling to Cooper to maintain position and assume sniper duties, soundless, Oshi dropped to the ground and, crouched over, dashed between the buildings. His speed was astounding as the synthorganic muscles in his legs engaged, driving him forward faster than the long extinct cheetah could have run on the African plains and with less noise. He made it to the target building and approached with caution.

'No movement,' Cooper said, over the laser comm.

Oshi remained silent. He contracted his flechette rifle — shortening the barrel and folding the stock to make a useful close quarter's carbine. In this setting, the vicious weapon would function more like an automatic shotgun: one that sprayed shards of synthetic diamond at extreme velocities. In his other hand, he readied the hypersteel blade he'd retrieved from the wreckage of the laboratory in Armstrong those fateful months before. It still bore signs of the fusion gun explosion, but its hardened edge was as sharp as ever and the striation of markings along the blade gave it a unique look. It was almost like it were pattern welded or folded to produce a hamon. Oshi found it pleasing that a tool of death should be rendered beautiful.

Oshi slunk around the base of the building. The prefab walls were made of an electromoulded thermoplastic: excellent for use in rapid deployments and proof against environmental extremes; it could withstand a fair degree of force. Creeping along, he realised he'd have to enter either by the door or by a window. The opaque windows were moulded parts of the thermoplastic structure. Whether the opacity was two way or not, Oshi couldn't tell, so he took no chances. He reached the door and paused — lowering his consciousness, he entered the alpha state that helped him activate the synthorganic enhancements to his senses. He focused on his hearing: from inside there came the faint hum of electronics — a datalink? — and past that, the beat of a single human heart. The target.

Oshi glanced up at Cooper and received a nod in reply: good to go. With a surge, Oshi burst through the door, gun levelled, ready to pounce on the unaugmented human. It was a mistake: the hum of electronics came from a naukara, the heartbeat from the same. A bodyguard.

Without hesitation, the augmented guard swung at him. Its right arm was a metre-long, whirring blade; the left held a short-barrelled gun. Oshi made a choice — parry the blade with his rifle, instead of firing and dying with his opponent. The blade chewed into the rifle, rendering it useless, but it gave Oshi enough time to leap forward within the arc of the naukara's swing. Its gun discharged — a quick, volatile flash of superheated particles, missing Oshi's head by a finger's width before burning a hole in the ceiling. By then, he was inside the naukara's guard, pressing his left forearm into its blade arm, above the blade but below the elbow.

In a blur of motion, he reached his right arm under his left and pivoted on the balls of his feet, switching to the outside of the man-machine's arm. Without hesitating — now he was in the dominant position — he delivered a vicious elbow strike to its faceplate. The blow didn't even slow the naukara. It dropped its gun and grabbed at Oshi. Following through from the elbow smash, Oshi stabbed his knife down into the thick cabling at his opponent's neck — severing one of the cables and stopping the whirr of the arm blade. The naukara twisted round hard, batting him aside.

The force of the blow was tremendous: sending Oshi crashing backwards despite his enhanced physique. The injured cyborg leapt forward, seizing Oshi by one arm and bringing up the blade arm to stab him. The mechanical hand gripping his arm had ruinous strength, and from its fingers razor sharp talons slid out, through Oshi's suit and into his arm.

There was no time to acknowledge the pain — the blade arm punched forward to end his life. Oshi remembered the lessons of his youth — the training in his family's martial system he'd kept secret from all his drillmasters. He twisted his feet in a swift body change, moving a fraction round to his left — the blade scraped past him. At the same time, he made an outward circle with his right hand — the arm seized by the naukara — and thrust forward at the apex of the circle: reversing the grip so that he now held his attacker's forearm. The pain as the claws tore out of his forearm was exquisite but he let it flow through him unhindered; his mind, clear of thought, didn't acknowledge the hurt.

On the outside of his opponent's arm again, he used it as a lever to push the naukara off balance, then brought his knee hard into his opponent's groin. There was no augmentation there, just light armour that crunched inwards under the force of the blow. The groan of pain sounded all too human but it cut off as the naukara's implants desensitised the pain receptors.

The distraction was enough for Oshi to get into a close and dominating position, now on his opponent's left side. He smashed a left elbow strike into the naukara's faceplate again, shattering the hardened plastic, then rotated at his hips driving his right elbow hard into the occipital region at the back of the man's head.

The blow — a lethal technique between unaugmented humans — would've had little effect on the heavily altered man but for Oshi's synthorganic musculature and reinforced bone. There was a satisfying crack as the black carapace surrounding the back of the skull splintered.

Not waiting for his enemy's response, Oshi arm-barred him across the throat with his left, uninjured forearm. This strike — not a static pressure as his drillmasters had taught, but a powerful bi-directional blow, force going forwards and outwards — collapsed the windpipe, reinforced though it was. The naukara crashed to the floor flailing with its enhanced limbs, each still a lethal weapon.

Oshi darted back and snatched up the fallen gun — a novice's mistake. Too late he realised it was handprint coded and fell to the ground jerking as electricity burned through his body. It would have killed a normal man but Oshi was only stunned for a few moments — just long enough for the downed naukara to scramble over to him and seize him by the throat; its own breath coming in ragged, strained gasps.

Oshi grabbed the arms that were bearing down on him. Pinned on the floor as he was, none of his more sophisticated techniques for escaping a stranglehold would work. Instead, he improvised, pistoning his knees up into the torso of his assailant, as the enhanced musculature in his neck strained to resist the crushing force the creature applied to it. He didn't grab the arms but reached up with both hands, fingers to either side of his opponents head, and drove his thumbs through the eyes — one augmented, one not. Still, the naukara's grip didn't relax.

Oshi's vision began to dim. The arms — machine not flesh — must be controlled, not by the human brain of his opponent but by the microchip in its head. In a panic, he seized the arms and applied every fibre of his muscles — both retrogened and synthorganic — to prising them off his throat. He felt the grip begin to drag free then the pressure released in a rush. It took him a moment to realise why. Cooper stood over him, his own combat blade buried in the back of the naukara's head.

Cooper did a quick visual check of Oshi. He gawped at his sergeant.

'Sarge, how the hell are you alive?'

Oshi groaned and sat up. 'I'm wondering that myself, Coop. Where is that officer? See what you can find in here while I get myself going.'

Oshi stood slowly, flexing his arms and massaging his injured neck. He felt the flush of blood pumping through the damaged tissue — his boosted physique working hard to speed the healing process.

Looking around, he saw clear signs that the occupant of the prefab had been engaged in strategic planning. There was a large flexi-map on a desk, showing live updates as assets in the field and surviving stealth satellites transmitted their intel. A number of encrypted datapads lay strewn around and a high capacity comm system was set to standby. Cooper returned, a blank look on his face.

'Sarge, there's no sign of where he went, but maybe his bodyguard knows?'

'He's dead, Coop,' Oshi said.

'I know Sarge, but his cerebral implants can be hacked.'

'Sure, if either of us had the gear or the knowhow. And that data is only useful until they discover our infiltration. I don't plan to be around when that happens. You?' Oshi leaned on the desk with both hands, trying to think of a plan of action.

'Ah, no. I see your point, Sarge.'

Cooper cleared his throat then took up position by one of the windows to check their immediate area.

Oshi straightened, 'Still, you may have an idea. The bodyguard had to have some way of knowing where his charge was when he wasn't with him. Which raises the question. Why wasn't he with him now?'

'Because he didn't want a record of what he was doing?'

'That's got to be it. It's not like a naukara's loyalty is open to question — unless you hack them. No, it's because he doesn't want his superiors knowing what he's up to.'

'Two possibilities then, Sarge. He's betraying his own side...'

'Or he's committing war crimes,' Oshi said.

'Sarge, why would the Panasians care?' Cooper asked.

'Come on, Coop, you know how it is. Deniability. Share prices. Breach of treaty. Before you know it this relatively cold war would get as hot if not hotter than the Lunar War. Remember, every one of the Superstates — United America, the African Congress, Eurussia and Panasia — wants to be the heroes. The good guys. None of them are.'

'Are we?' Cooper asked, frowning.

'Does it matter? We've got a job to do. Leave the

questions to the bleeding-heart politicians on the UNWG Council. Let them claim authority over the Superstates and the corporations and see whether their high morals survive the squabble for power. Grunts like us are good for one thing. Got it?'

'Yes, Sarge.'

'So... war crimes. Prisoners? See if you can find a comm unit in that.'

Oshi waved in the direction of the dead naukara and started to check the map. It showed a small representation of the armed camp, which he zoomed into — the tell-tale layout of a detention block was instantly recognisable. He turned to Cooper.

'Any luck?'

'No dice, Sarge.'

Cooper's hands were covered in blood and other more gelatinous material — he'd been probing around inside the cleaved open skull of the naukara, extracting implants and microfibre cables. He wiped them off on the corpse's clothing and sprang back to his feet.

'Then let's try the detention block.' Oshi said, walking to the doorway and peering out.

Neither of the patrols was nearby, so he gestured to Cooper before ducking out of the door. They stalked from cover to shadow to cover. Soon the detention block came into sight. It was of similar construction to the other prefabs but with no visible windows and a heavy-duty security door. The warning glow that indicated a nanowire fence surrounded it: each invisible strand contained a string of nanites that, if broken, might do nothing more than deliver a paralytic or they could flense an intruder in seconds.

Two Panasian soldiers flanked the door. They were naukara: enhanced optics glittering in the darkness and bulky bodies covered in grey striped reactive camouflage armour. No doubt, like the patrols, they were just relying on infrared to sweep the night for intruders. Once more, the wisdom of using the synth sharkskin suits to infiltrate by sea struck home for Oshi.

He signalled to Cooper to take up position with his flechette rifle — again set for sniping — and target the left-hand guard. Satoshi knew his corporal, an ITF spec forces veteran, would be setting the flechette rifle's muzzle to fire two simultaneous splinters — one trajectory aimed for the guards head and the other for its heart: the classic double-tap. Naukara or not, without a brain or heart it'd no longer pose a threat... so long as there wasn't a deadman's explosive wired into it.

Cooper indicated his readiness to Oshi with a simple hand sign — thumbs up. This close to the guards the use of line of sight laser comms was to great a risk — the noise of the sub-vocalisation might be audible. UNWG forces had records of the scanning patterns used by each of the Superstates, intelligence that'd cost a lot of effort and lives to secure. It had revealed that the Superstates all used a standardised range of frequencies for line of sight laser comms. A shift outside this part of the spectrum, would allow the UNWG's laser comms to be as invisible to the augmented eye as to the organic one.

Oshi, lacking a functional flechette rifle, relied instead on his heavy pistol. There'd been limited progress designing a so-called *'omni-pistol'*, to give ITF agents the flexibility to deal with multiple scenarios. The weapon would include a directed energy beam — akin to a pulsed laser but frequency adjusted to reduce the risk of blindness — recoil balanced hyper-velocity, explosive projectiles and a high capacity electroshock arc — for scrambling cyborgs or robot sentries. There was an argument over whether it should have tranq gun functionality for delivering nerve toxins or incapacitating drugs but that risked making the already unwieldy pistol completely impractical. The most advanced concept was its capacity to fire slugs of nanodestroyers, which could tear apart any target not coated in nanodefenders within a matter of minutes — ideal against heavy armour that might otherwise resist the pistol's considerable armaments.

Oshi's weapon was only one of the prototypes of the omni-pistol design — given to him for field-testing several missions earlier. It had remained in his possession when he'd found it to be an excellent sidearm, though almost too bulky. In time, it would surely get the planned refinements but, for now, his version was limited to a particle beam — radiation-restricted by using a laser to create a short-lived vacuum along the beam path — and a high velocity, high explosive, penetrating sabot shell.

The pistol packed a lot of punch for a handgun but, by necessity, had limited ammunition: six shells for the ballistic setting and power for five shots of the particle beam. Limited or not, it would be enough to take out his target. There was no way that he'd risk getting into melee with another one of these naukara — even with the benefit of surprise.

Circling the building until he was out of sight and possible hearing range of the guards, Oshi vaulted over the nanowire fence. It was a dangerous leap and one that would have been impossible for an unaltered human — impossible for a naukara as well. The weight and power restrictions, which came with their augmentations, meant that too much functionality would have to be devoted to achieving the leap for the cyborg to remain a combat threat. Synthorganics had no such limitations.

With another soundless leap, Oshi gained the roof of the building. He placed his feet with silent care as he inched forward to the edge of the building, right over the heads of the guards and lined up on the top of the head of the right hand one. Both of them stiffened but that moment of alert was the trigger for both Oshi and Cooper to fire.

The prototype omni-pistol blasted the top of the naukara's head with the particle beam and then spat out a projectile. The top of the guard's helmet vaporised and a split second later the shell drilled into its head, detonating once it had penetrated the skull. The small explosion was muted but the effect was as spectacular as it was stomach churning.

Cooper's target dropped without any such display. A perfect fist sized hole through the centre of its head and a similar wound through its chest. It didn't matter what redundant functions the naukara might have, it was dead by the time its body hit the floor.

Cooper activated laser comms and asked, 'What gave you away?'

Oshi was still surprised that the guards had detected his presence. He'd not heard his own movements, only the beating of his heart.

The disturbing answer came to him. 'They heard my heart beating…'

No matter that he, Cooper, and the other Lunar Vets possessed abilities beyond the human norm, the capabilities of the naukara made Oshi uneasy. The technology for naukara was advancing as fast as the capabilities granted by synthorganics.

Oshi's feelings of superiority were fading, his sense of invincibility already broken by the vicious hand-to-hand combat of mere minutes earlier.

Cooper's naukara was still twitching, its augmented hand moving towards the dropped rifle mere inches from it. Astounded at its resilience, Oshi drew his knife and, stepping on the hand, reached down to cut a pair of power cables running alongside the naukara's spine. There was a brief spark from the cables then the hand was stilled. Being careful to hold the longarm by its stock, Oshi retrieved the naukara's rifle and checked the handgrip. It showed no sign of security — standard issue then. Tentative, he took hold of the handgrip — and breathed a sigh of relief.

He re-sighted the rifle to suit himself and, turning, saw Cooper surveying the surrounding area. Without a word, the corporal grabbed the nearest body and hefted it over his shoulder — his flechette rifle configured for storage and stowed in its holster along his thigh. Cooper jogged to a small cluster of containers — their markings denoting that they contained heavy water for the base's portable reactors — and hid the body behind them. It wouldn't prevent discovery if there were any kind of organised search but any chance of delaying discovery was an advantage.

Oshi stood sentry while Cooper disposed of the second guard in the same way. There was no way to conceal the blood soaking into the ground but, in the dark, it wouldn't attract immediate attention. Unless the naukara had some kind of olfactory enhancement tuned to detect blood, which was, he supposed, possible.

Cooper withdrew his rifle again and configured it for short-range usage. Taking the lead, with Oshi following close behind — the naukara's longarm charged and ready — Cooper eased open the prefab's door. It was unlocked and swung open without a sound. They advanced into the dim interior, covering the corners as they entered.

There was no illumination, not even the red low power lighting Oshi'd expected. The interior consisted of a corridor with rows of cells on both sides and an empty guard station at the end furthest from the entrance. One of the cells had an open door. Advancing down the corridor, Oshi could see that there was no sign of any occupants in the cells. When they reached the open cell, there was the reek of a used latrine and signs that the small bunk had been slept on. There'd been a prisoner but he or she must have been moved.

They reached the guard station and saw that someone had tampered with the monitoring system. Instead of showing the cell door open, it was showing as closed and there was a shadowy figure curled up on the bunk. The correct time was displayed but the recording had clearly been looped. The overview of the corridor didn't show their presence at the guard station either. Oshi gestured at another screen. It appeared to show a vacant interrogation chamber filled with various devices for *humane* extraction of information. All were inactive and the camera was on a low light setting.

Cooper, staying silent, pointed down at the floor behind the guard station. There was a hatch recessed into it. Motioning for Cooper to cover the hatch, Oshi set his longarm down and carefully opened the hatch. It lifted up and swung to one side without protest, he could just make out a ladder leading down a single level. Lights were on below, but only glowing emergency red — giving minimal light spillage.

Oshi motioned for Cooper to descend the ladder, while he picked up the particle rifle to cover his corporal, again sighting down it at any potential threat. When Cooper signalled that he'd cleared the base of the ladder, Oshi slid down after him.

They both paused: the sound of muffled sobs echoed down the narrow corridor. The short red-lit passageway lead to a door outlined by white light visible around its edges — the sounds were coming from within. Oshi and Cooper exchanged glances. They approached the door with care but the occupants sounded like they were too distracted to hear them. Oshi raised his left hand, three fingers up and lowered them, one by one. When he made a fist, they burst through the door together, guns immediately tracking targets.

Both men, hardened veterans, stopped as they took in the scene before them. The interrogation room was a sterile looking environment. There was no need for using torture these days. Secure restraints, what seemed like a pharmacopoeia's worth of drugs and direct neural stimulation were the *humane* approaches for forcing most prisoners to answer any question put to them — physical torments had gone out of fashion.

So the horror of seeing an interrogation room turned into a torture chamber made the seasoned warriors pause. Their shock came from the sight of a young woman, only just out of her teens, in the restraints in a contorted position, gagged and stripped naked. Their target, the Panasian officer, was leaning over her, and making short precise motions with his right arm as she whimpered. Blood had trickled down the chair was slowly pooling at its base.

Oshi focused on her face, fixating on the tears running down from her eyes as they made tracks in the dirt on her cheeks. Cooper reacted first, leaping forwards and driving a fist into the jaw of the officer as he began to turn to face the intruders. When he fell away from the girl — reaching for the holster attached to his belt — Cooper delivered a hard and sickening kick directly to the man's genitals. The result was immediate, satisfying, if less than he deserved, and the sick bastard collapsed to the floor groaning. Cooper retrieved the gun and began securing their prisoner's hands.

'Under my authority as an ITF agent and by the powers granted to me by the UNWG you are under arrest for War Crimes. You have no rights unless they are awarded to you. Please give me any excuse, you piece of shit.' Cooper tightened the restraints and jerked the man upright. 'Now, you're going to tell us where the geneticist you've been tracking is or else you'll be standing trial as a eunuch.'

Saying this Cooper pulled a short, serrated blade — usually used to cut wire fences or cables rather than as a weapon — and positioned it between the man's legs.

While Cooper was having this little chat, Oshi hurried over to the girl. Her skin had been flensed away in strips on her abdomen. Thin slivers of flesh peeled off her. Working on automatic, not allowing himself to think about what had been happening here, he took out his medikit and sprayed wound sealant over the deep cuts. Then, not bothering to undo the restraints, he flexed his synthorganic muscles and broke them open.

He found the girls clothes — little more than rags — and gave them to her, all the while telling her that she would be all right, that she was safe and that they would protect her. He turned away to allow her to dress and interposed himself between her and the officer — her tormentor — watching with grim approval as Cooper enthusiastically extracted the information. Their target was stuttering out what he knew with no sign of dissembling — he freely admitted the torture, claiming it was the only thing that worked on those moonbug freaks. So that was where he'd been getting his intel — torturing it out of this innocent young woman.

'I don't think this piece of shit deserves a trial Sarge. Do you?' Cooper began inspecting the edge of the short knife, its teeth catching the light and glittering with promise.

'No, he doesn't, Corporal. But we have orders to bring him in alive, if possible. You take him. I've got the girl. We'll exfiltrate according to plan.'

Oshi gathered the now dressed but still sobbing woman into his arms and carried her out of the room, as a father would carry his wounded child.

Cooper followed, after roughly gagging the officer and hoisting him over one broad shoulder. They hustled along the corridor and out of the detention block.

'So far so good, Sarge. They haven't found the bodies,' Cooper said as he swept the area.

There was no sign of a patrol near them so they began to move, shadow-to-shadow, back to the water's edge.

A few metres short of the beach, the patrol found them. The clicking of a laser blast was the first sign Oshi had; the pain of the finger-sized hole the beam had made when it hit him from behind came a second later. It'd burned through his left shoulder then carried on creating a similar sized hole in the girl's head that rested there. Oshi staggered forward and couldn't help dropping the now limp corpse of the girl he'd held so gently. Before he could recover, he saw Cooper hurl their prisoner to the ground and bring up his weapon, returning fire.

Oshi reached down and grabbed the prisoner by the scruff of his neck with his left hand, even as he brought the rifle he'd slung over his shoulder into his right hand — ready to fire it one handed. Despite his injury, he was combat capable: he dropped one of their attackers. He hoped it was the bastard who had shot him and the girl. Cooper had taken down two assailants when another charged him. It was a big naukara, similar to the one Oshi had fought in the officer's quarters. One arm unsheathed a metre long whirring blade. The naukara thrust forwards and drove its blade straight through Cooper's sternum. The blow was so hard that Cooper's feet left the ground before the augmented man threw him backwards.

Oshi brought his rifle round and fired, just as the red lightning of a particle beam grazed him on the right side of his head, dumping a large dose of radiation into him. It wasn't enough to kill him straightaway, but Oshi had to fight to hold onto consciousness as the thermal shock hit him. He fell back, into the water, seeing that his own shot had blown the naukara apart. Before oblivion overtook him, Oshi jerked his left hand, still holding tight to the officer's neck. There was a wet, satisfying crack as the vertebrae broke — the last sound Oshi heard as he passed out.

†††

Something in the memory struck a false note in the symphony of their mental communion. Valko seized it, a knot of twisted mind-matter — within lay the truth of what he'd just witnessed through his friend's eyes, but now was not the time to untangle it. He traced the tangled ends, finding where memory was bound to ligature, the puppet's string that was choking Satoshi's free will. Valko focused his mind, his whole being, into a blade to slice through that cord. It pinged away as if under great tension, and he found himself cast away, their entwined consciousness slipping from him.

Valko hurtled between scintillating planes of light that stretched to infinity above and below him, with nothing to either side. He felt the same feeling of growth, like in his dream but different this time: more intense and painful. He sped onwards, his viewpoint beginning to spiral, faster and faster until, at the other end he encountered... something. It devoured him and, as the agony of his consumption reached its zenith, Valko realised he'd been devoured by himself.

He stared into emptiness with eyes no longer there. He had no form, yet he could still perceive all that was around him. It was like having eyes that saw in all directions, though at first there was nothing to see. He concentrated and formed the Universe around him, the face of the Earth distant below and at the same time all around him. There he was — his body, at least — a small speck on the world below.

All in a rush, he was aware that his perceptions were growing ever greater: the scope of his existence continued to expand. He was too large for the body below, too large for the World, even the Universe to contain him. The being that was at once Valko and yet more felt a sensation of rushing outwards, even as it ceased the need to rely on physical sensations as a metaphor for experience. It perceived the Universe and many more like it. All around were other consciousnesses, other Minds, close and far away and as vast as his — its — own. They knew each other: all of them intimate but with many unfolding and hidden places, yet to unfurl. Conjoined yet separate; a part of something greater — something intangible and beyond reach — and able to see everything but that greater thing: the final piece of existence to seek.

Some glided around the infinite space between the stars and within the stars and between universes — inside them and outside them — through echoing eternity. Others remained motionless: observing, thinking, seeking within. Still Others joined with multiple consciousnesses: their coupling in no way sexual but producing the joy of shared thought and knowledge — each contact granting another perspective to their vast intelligences.

Valko — the Mind acknowledged that it had known itself by that name even as it acknowledged how meaningless a name was — perceived trillions of other consciousnesses. All were focused down into bodies. Some on Earth, some on Mars, some further afield and inhuman. Some focused themselves into animals and plants instead. Each Mind was at once unable to compress themselves into such small frames and yet, at the same time, was absorbed in what they were doing to the exclusion of all other stimuli.

The Valko Mind reached back and found the body it had been focused in, a short time before — there it was at an incredible distance but well within reach. The apogee of Consciousness was within his reach: the source of the transmission that was... he. But identity had returned. He'd found himself and once more became the signal — beamed back, his awareness at its perigee. There he found only pain and his, now limited, mind shied away from its awakening. The World eluded him.

Chapter 11

Mere seconds had passed, when Satoshi opened his eyes again. Still trapped under the ceiling braces, but now his synthorganics were operational and under his control. More than that: he remembered. His life — not bit by bit, but everything had flowed back into him as if he'd never forgotten it. It had come to him as he relived the infiltration of the enemy camp: the death of the young woman and Cooper. His guilt and impotent rage at the injustice hit him as a physical force, releasing something in him. A fury of such pure focus that it'd broken through the barrier which had contained him.

The flood of synthhormones released as his reaction to whatever the woman Jean had tried to do to him, burned within him but they were slackening off as he asserted control. He wasn't in combat and he didn't need to be driven into a fearless rage — couldn't afford to give into its seduction.

Bracing, he began to shift the heavy metal beams off himself. Then he noticed Valko sprawled on the floor at his feet. Blood trickled from the Moderator's nose. His eyes, part open, were rolled back in his head, showing only their whites. Valko's body shifted on the floor as spasms wracked it. With a growl, Satoshi threw all of his strength into shifting the debris pinning him. Shrugging it away, he rushed over to Valko and cradled his head.

'Val, it worked. Wake up.' There was no response. 'Val. Val. Valko. Shit, please wake up.'

Satoshi lowered Valko's head to the floor then sprang up and ran to the entrance hallway. If he could get to that woman's shuttle maybe he could capture it — surely, it'd have some medical supplies. Hurling the door open to the entrance corridor open, he raced to where the heavy bunker door was still closed. He pounded on the automated release button but all that produced was a grinding noise. The bunker's plug door wouldn't open on automatic, so he set to the manual release wheel. It spun with ease, and the massive bolts retracted with an audible reverberation throughout the bunker. He pushed the pressure door, expecting it to swing open — easy and noiseless like before. It didn't: there was a hiss of air as the door's pressure seal was broken but that was it. Satoshi set his shoulders to the door and exerted all his considerable strength, natural and artificial, to force the door. Nothing.

He got mad at it — let the synthhormones drive him to a near frenzy — but it still wouldn't budge. In a desperate choking rage, he ended up beating his fists into the metal, until even the toughened skin on his knuckles split and bled but it made no difference. They were trapped down here.

Satoshi kept a keen sense of the passage of time. He feared for Valko; his friend was showing no signs of coming round and he didn't have a clue what the problem was. Satoshi ran through all the medical training he'd received — both as a Moderator's Sergeant and from his training as an agent of the United Nations World Government's International Task Force. He could've dealt with ballistic injuries, stab wounds, or particle beam burns — had done on numerous occasions — but he didn't have the first idea what was wrong with Valko.

Satoshi searched the lab and attached habitation facility. Someone had been living here until recently, that was clear. Was it the woman... what had Valko called her? Oh yes, Jean.

He found nothing to use: there was no terminal attached to an outside network; no satellite uplink; no radio; not even an old-world telephone. It was as if the previous occupant had chosen to cut herself off from the world. Perhaps, she'd wanted to avoid any distraction from her work but Satoshi suspected it was more to do with avoiding giving her position away.

How had Actur known to come here? He must have been working with her. It would link the murders and fit with the theory that it was one murderer for both. If she'd killed Vinnetti as well as Fisher, didn't that mean she'd caused the injury that had killed Actur? But then why would he come here, to the lair of the person who'd killed him only to write a message?

Jean must have used him to spring a trap. It didn't explain his injuries unless she'd known he'd come here. Why would she have chosen this place to spring her trap? Why give up her secure base? Why not just deal with them when she had shot their transpod down? It could only have been her, couldn't it?

Satoshi recalled the signal that had brought them here —

the random ping from Darius Actur's beacon implant. It must have been amplified for the Centra Autorita to pick it up. Part of him idly wondered what might have been different if they'd sent Davidson in their stead, but anyone who knew enough about Valko to want to trap him would understand the man's thoroughness, his need to control an investigation and his lack of trust in his subordinates.

This had been their best lead on Fisher, Vinnetti and now Actur's murderer. It had paid off: Jean — whether that was an alias or her real name — was the same person as the shadowy figure Valko had seen in the memory of Joey Koewatha. The image he'd saved for the record had been hazy when Satoshi had reviewed it, but it was clear enough to be sure — Valko's reaction told him that.

His thoughts returned to Darius Actur. For his beacon to be strong enough to send the signal that had drawn them here it must have been amplified, at least temporarily. It would explain why the signal had appeared after such a long time dormant. Actur, getting here by some means, triggering a signal boost. To alert them? To alert Jean? It didn't matter right now. If he could find whatever had amplified the signal, if it was in the bunker, then maybe he could use it to contact Arcas Plenum.

He hurried over to Valko, he'd need the Moderator's hub since his own remained crushed under the debris that had pinned him. There was still no sign of improvement in the unconscious man, but Satoshi made him as comfortable as he could — lifting him and carrying the still twitching form to the sleeping cell.

After he'd settled Valko in the bunk there, he retrieved the hub from the Moderator's envirosuit. It was still functional though without access to EATS it had switched to power-save mode. He donned it and relaxed a little — it was still showing a clear trace on Actur's beacon. Sweeping it about just made him frustrated by the lack of precision on the device. It could locate Actur's beacon, but so what, right? What he wanted was the signal booster. But no matter what he did, Satoshi couldn't get the hub to search for a carrier signal between the beacon and the transceiver he knew must be around.

Satoshi's frustration began gnawing at the cage he'd put round his anger — the repeated message made no sense. No matter where he went in the bunker — the habitation section, the laboratory or the entrance corridor — the locator just lead back to Darius Actur.

Maybe the signal had come from Actur's transport, but if Jean was prime suspect in his murder, she must have done something to whatever was relaying the signal. She'd trapped them here with no hope of rescue. The destruction of their transpod a short way away had been meant to strand them, to give them no way of escape if they figured things out before she pounced. What could she want with Valko?

The way she'd tried to use him against his Moderator began to prey on Satoshi — what had gone wrong? She'd thought to control him as if he were an automaton programmed to obey her, yet — even with his memories returned to him — he knew nothing about such programming. He remembered undergoing auto-hypnotic training but he could not recall all of it because of its nature — Valko had shown him that it had contained a deeper level of neural conditioning, but what was that for?

Had it just been to block his memories? What was so dangerous about them? His last memories before his decade's long sleep must hold the answer. He ran through them: being shot just after Cooper was killed and being picked up floating out at sea. The Panasian forces had left him to be pulled out to sea by a strong current — they must've thought he was dead, but perhaps they'd not been able to see him once he was in the water. His synthetic sharkskin's thermal sink may just have saved his life.

There'd been a trip to a medcentre, called a hospital back then, and treatment — a dim and hazy memory. Some point after that the pulse had been triggered which rendered him and the other Veteran's comatose, but he couldn't recall it. Even with his memories returned, there were vast gaps where he must have been unconscious and even more memories that were hazy or disordered.

Having his memories return hadn't been a flood of images and recollections; it'd been a fog in his mind burning away, letting him see what had been there all along. But a lifetime of memories was a lot to process. He could no more hold them in his mind — entire and complete — than anyone could.

ttt

Satoshi topped off his flask from the water reclamator and took it over to Valko. He held the unconscious man's mouth open and dripped water in.

Two days had passed in a blur, as Satoshi had striven to open the bunker. It was futile — Jean must have done something to the door from the outside. Thankfully, the systems within the bunker still had power. There was air recycling, plenty of potable water and he soon located freeze-dried rations, which were, in his opinion, a major improvement in flavour over the foul slop the processors in the Plena produced. Now able to remember good food, he could appreciate just how awful his diet had been for the last fifteen years.

After hours of trying, he'd gained access to the computer systems in the lab — those that had survived his berserkergang — breaking past the streaming data walls of the experiments and accessing the data behind. Old ITF training had proven its worth, though the sophistication of the programming gave him limited control. The research meant nothing to him but he'd found reams of intercepts bearing Plenum data architecture and material of even greater antiquity.

He'd sat through a recording of the last United American President, Esperanza Rosario, giving her final Address to the Nation before the bombs fell, with the aching sense of his own dislocation in time, *'My fellow Americans. Our worst fears have come true. They have unleashed the Plague to end all plagues upon us. They have turned our technology, our protection against us. There is only one way to stop this. I hope that enough of you survive the coming cataclysm to forgive me, to forgive us for failing you. May I suggest that you pray to God, in whatever way you keep him and hold your family close. I promise you this: our vengeance is already begun. God bless America, God save us all.'*

From the date stamp it was clear that her speech had come less than a month after he'd been rendered comatose by his injury in the raid on the Panasian camp, but though he'd never heard the words before, they evoked the time — his time. A place forever lost to him.

Rosario's speech had sounded off in his ears, her English almost closer to the language of the Remnants than the Anglo-Esperanto of the Plena. When he talked now, it was with words drawn from a dozen languages, shaken together in the closed environments that had kept most of humanity secure. Trapped.

Part of him longed for the old divides — the freedom to be different. Rosario had understood the need for the people of the world to be whom they chose to be. She'd known that difference could be strength — a richness in humanity rather than an inevitable cause of division. Freedom begetting freedom. He wondered how her idealism would have reacted to the conformist nightmare of the Plena.

Thinking about her brought back memories of the ITF briefing he'd been given: she'd been a candidate for first UNWG president — joint favourite with Erasmus Fisher himself. Both described as critical individuals. Here in this computer system there were links to his past beyond his reawakened memories. Hidden truths. He yearned to dig through them, to fill in those gaps but it would have to wait. Survival — his and Valko's — came first and foremost.

There were some intercepts of a different nature, a higher order of information storage, which chimed with his recollections of tracking fugitive Scientists from the Allied Lunar Colonies. After grappling with the arcane software, in vain hopes of sending a message, Satoshi thought he'd begun to get somewhere when suddenly the screen in front of him began showing warning signs that he'd triggered some virtual security system.

If his ITF training wasn't too outdated, then the warnings could only have related to an external network. The screen had gone black, taking with it the secrets of the past and his hope of rescue. His short career as a hacker ended with his fist smashing through the monitor.

Although they were at no immediate risk of dying, the idea of being entombed drove him to fits of rage. With the return of his memories came some degree of mental and emotional instability — he knew it. He'd try to remain rational but sometimes it became close to impossible. Roiling in the grip of Lunar War Syndrome, close to full on killcrazy, all he could do was keep a check on his behaviour. He spent time meditating and finding solace in the familiarity of the old movements of kata taught to him by his grandfather. Moving through the positions and techniques of the family martial system, cleared his mind and helped him to regain some measure of equilibrium but, when the frustration grew too much, the sole release came from pounding on the sealed entrance door until his fists ached.

Valko was another matter: he'd ceased fitting — if that's what it had been — but lay unconscious. Sometimes he appeared to be dreaming but nothing Satoshi did could wake him. He accepted water dripped into his mouth in small quantities and had even swallowed some nutrient powder that Satoshi had mixed with the water. It made no difference: he stayed comatose.

༄

'Come in Jack,' Odegebayo said, in the usual feigned good humour.

Davidson obliged, his heart thundering in his chest. Did the Old Man know? It would be typical of the twisted old fuck to bring him in here — all smiles and first names — before selling him down the river.

'Don't stand there sweating, take a seat. What did you do, run to my office?' The Old Man said with a warm chuckle. Not a care in the world.

Davidson sat, his legs starting to give way beneath him. He held his hands to either side of his legs, out of sight so the Pravnik couldn't see them shaking.

'No, Weiyuan, I was stuck in a crowded transpod, that's all.'

'Yes, they're uncomfortable. One day we'll have more space. Did you know that the population is down nearly one and a half percent? That's real progress.'

The conversational tone was meant to be disarming, but Davidson wasn't lulled by it.

'No, I didn't. That's peachy.'

He forced himself to relax and speak as if he was confident in his position as a kensakan — secure, not hanging by his balls over the Fire.

'Peachy?' Another chuckle. 'Jack, you certainly have a way with words. I suppose you're right. It is 'peachy'. Now, to business.' The smile snapped off his face so fast it could have been elasticated. 'What can you tell me about Tantei Gangleri's mission? I've been waiting for his report for two days now.'

'Weiyuan... it's a mystery. The Moderator's transpod reached its destination but then it stopped transmitting. I haven't been able to get a read on any of their beacons and the suspect's is no longer transmitting either.'

Any attempt to maintain a hint of his usual sass fled, and even his grammar tightened up. What was it about Pravniks that gave them this power over him? Oh yeah — they could order his death on a whim.

'Why wasn't I informed? If they were attacked it might be linked to the perpetrator of these monstrous crimes.'

Odegebayo's face, seamed with wrinkles, now scrunched up tight, his scowl lending him a fearsome aspect, like some vengeful, ancient god.

Without warning, Davidson could feel his bladder: full, with his control giving out. One wrong word and he'd soon see the inside of a recycler. With a frantic gasp of breath, he trotted out the script Hampton had given him and — feeling the jaws of desperation worrying at him — he'd tried to learn.

'Weiyuan, if they'd been attacked then we'd have received a status update from their beacons. Even in the event of a fatal crash, or something of that nature, the destruction of a beacon triggers a final signal pulse that would notify us. No, the only thing it can be is that they have entered some underground facility and the signal is no longer getting through. Their beacons are still transmitting; we simply can't receive the signal.'

He ran out of breath and stopped, dragging air into his lungs. Before he could continue, the Pravnik sat back in his chair and once more adopted his supple smile.

'You'll inform me the moment anything changes, won't you Jack?' He said, again all friendly old grandfather.

'Of course, Weiyuan.'

Trying not to dash out of the room, Davidson left. He fled the Justeco Centro and lost himself in a crowd. Only when anonymous among the press of thousands of others, did he feel safe enough to message Hampton.

«*He bought it,*» Davidson sent.

༒

Satoshi sat in one of the lab's reclining chairs, or rather, he lolled. Something was wrong with the internal air recycler — a side effect of whatever had sealed them in here. At the beginning of their imprisonment, all the bunker's systems had seemed to work but, by the end of the second day, he'd noticed the temperatures rising and the air tasting stale. Now, evening on the third day — if the hub's clock could be relied upon — the air had a definite taint to it. Not a build-up of carbon dioxide as he had first thought. No, there was a chemical in the air that had formed a thundercloud that boomed inside his skull. He thought he could see a haze of vapour or smoke forming just below the ceiling — a haze that was drifting lower; a sneaking killer that knew its prey was cornered.

He was no techspert to be able to fix the damaged machinery and no whitecoat to be able to work out what the chemical was and find some solution. He was just a soldier, just a kensakan. He could survive situations which neither of the specialists that he needed now would have had a hope of living through. He *had* survived such situations, time after time. It didn't matter: they were going to die in here and he could do nothing about it.

Crazy ideas about hooking up the omni-pistol's charge cell to the internal power had led to him nearly electrocuting himself when the systems turned out to be incompatible. He'd worried he'd done permanent damage to the gun but it was useless to him anyway. The ballistic settings couldn't penetrate the thick bunker walls. Even the armour piercing setting would only scratch the surface and, as for the explosive shells, they would do more harm than good — start a fire or collapse the unstable ceiling.

He hadn't given up, but he was out of ideas and even his enhanced physique was tiring — he'd not slept more than a few hours. His body stayed strong but his brain needed rest, so he sat reclining in the chair while he quieted his thoughts. The warm, stiffening air embraced him; he began to drift off to sleep.

The whole structure shuddered and began to hum with a steady, but intensifying, vibration. Satoshi was on his feet in an instant, his dented but functional tranqgun in one hand, omni-pistol in the other. Scanning around the room, all he could see was a steady stream of dust falling from the ceiling.

He covered Valko, who remained comatose, with his own body. Then it started: there was an intense high-pitched whine coming from the bunker's entrance, followed by an abrupt popping sound. Even muffled by the thick walls and surrounding rock it could only be one thing: explosives.

'Val! Val, wake up. I think we're being rescued.'

Satoshi didn't bother trying to contain his elation. When he'd realised that he couldn't find whatever had boosted the signal from Actur's beacon, he'd begun to think that this had been a set up. No one from the Plena would be coming for them. Now, that paranoid despair gave way to wild hope.

His ears popped as the outer door breached and the air pressure began to equalise. The smell of melting metal flooded the room — they must have brought a high-end cutting laser. Making sure that Valko was in a safe position, where no debris might fall on him, Satoshi rushed to the entrance. Had Davidson come through for them? He owed that man an apology.

His guess was right, someone was using a laser torch to cut through the door, the beam focused so it was not emitting into the corridor. The final cut came, accompanied by a metallic crunching sound as the door, no longer supported, settled into the cuts. It was pulled backwards with great speed and two figures, a third following close behind, strode into the corridor.

Satoshi opened his mouth to greet them but, as the swirl of dust that accompanied them cleared, instinct drove him scrabbling backwards. Each figure was tall, taller than he was. There was no sign of a face, just a blank eyeless mask where a face should be. The figures whirred softly as they moved, their limbs covered in a thick off-white armour. Though they were not encased in the usual black carapace, these were familiar beings. More machines than men, three heavily armed and armoured naukara advanced on him.

Satoshi turned and sprinted back to the lab, vaulting the metal barrier without a thought. There had to be something he could do. Looking back, he saw the leading pair of naukara take position on either side of the doorway, while the third continued to advance. Their weapons were raised and being brought to bear on him: large particle cannons from the look of them, which would vaporise him in an instant if they hit. Worse, they were probably unrestricted, so that even if they missed the ionising radiation would be lethal. Death would just tarry a bit before it took him.

The third naukara, now in the lead, carried no weapon. It

needed none. At the end of its thick mechanical arms there were no simulated hands; large claws — that looked like they could rend a man to pieces with ease — protruded.

Satoshi readied himself to fight, though it was hopeless. These naukara were the same model as those that had gone to the Moon ahead of his team, back when they were still just called cyborg soldiers. They were the deadliest shock troops that the Superstates had ever developed. Each a recruit — whether willing or unwilling — who'd undergone such extensive surgery and modification with mechanical devices that they could no longer be called human. What shreds of flesh remained were prisoners inside a cage of metal that — though it allowed for human ingenuity and lateral thinking — brooked no disobedience to its directives. There would be no reasoning with these things.

Synthorganics and retrogening made Satoshi the equal of ten or more unmodified men. His skills in hand-to-hand combat, learned from his grandfather, enhanced his worth as a warrior to the level of the superhuman. No hero of the ages — not Achilles, not Musashi — could have stood against him for more than an instant, yet he was overmatched.

Against one naukara of this type — using wits, skill and low cunning — he might just triumph. Three, with two covering him with particle beams while the other tried to tear him to pieces, would be a story with one ending. But if he were going to die, he'd do it fighting, not cowering.

Remembering the turbo penetrator shells still loaded into his omni-pistol, he grinned a savage grin. If he could get close enough to fire it point blank into the head of one of those things, he could take one of them with him into the abyss of death. He chose to disregard his own death in favour of killing his enemy, a sentiment to make his distant ancestors, of both East and West, proud. Satoshi gave a deep bellow, a war cry to turn a normal man's bowels to water, and charged.

╫

Davidson vomited noisily. He'd been trying to hold it back for the last ten minutes but couldn't any longer. A stinking mess spattered onto the floor beside his bunk. The woman next to him — a pathetic 'pophead he'd picked up for a minor violation earlier that day — groaned and elbowed him but didn't appear to wake.

His head was swimming. He'd been drunk before but never quite like this. Something had come over him and he'd not been able to stop. He'd got hold of some illicit booze easily enough then picked up the evening's entertainment nearby. It wasn't enough; it hadn't satisfied his need.

Levering himself to his feet, he went to the small washroom where he pissed yellow fire before cleaning the vomit from his face. He'd make his guest see to the mess by the bunk before he sent her on her way. Staring at the reflection in the tarnished metal mirror he saw eyes rimmed red and a stubble-lined jaw. He'd aged about ten years.

A knock came at his door and his heart jumped. Was this the executioner or only another errand for Hampton? The knock came again and his befuddled wits focused on it. It wasn't the confident pounding of someone come to carry out a sentence on him or even to summon him to a Pravnik. No, it was more of the furtive, nervous sort of rat-a-tat-tat that told of a visitor who was uncomfortable with being here.

'I'm coming!' he yelled, pulling on his uniform, still stinking of spilled hooch.

When he swung the door open, he saw a woman whose beauty was so intense it knocked some measure of sobriety back into him. Davidson straightened up and tried to hold his gut in, while smoothing out his uniform.

'What can I do you for, miss?' He asked, voice croaky from a throat still thick with phlegm.

'Are you Jack?' She asked.

'Yeah... Look, lady, you're not, er, catching me at my best here. Can you tell me what it is you're wanting?'

'You work with my bondmate, I think. You work with Satoshi, right?' She said, biting her bottom lip.

Davidson couldn't help but notice its perfect swell. Images of what he wanted to do with her mouth began to fill his sewer-like mind. Then what she said penetrated the booze haze.

'What? Satoshi? Yeah, yeah, he's my sergeant. So what?' His tone should've become more respectful, but Satoshi wasn't an issue anymore, was he?

'Do you know where he is? He's been gone for days and I'm worried. I mean, our son is worried about him. Please… can you help me?'

Something about her desire to hide her own concern for Satoshi got to Davidson. Here was someone who cared for that prick but was trying to hide it. He didn't know why she would but it was one more reason to hate the bastard. Still, he may have had the luck to have a woman like this, but that luck had run out now, hadn't it?

'Look, lady, what did you say your name was?' he asked, wincing at a particularly brutal pulse of headache, before finding some relief in staring at the woman's chest.

'Iona. Please can you tell me anything that would put my son's mind at ease?'

'Listen Iona, it's like this: Satoshi and the Boss went on a trip to an outpost in North America. We've been trying to track them, but they're out of range for now. We didn't get an alarm from their beacons, so you've got nothing to worry about. It's not like they're chasing down some dangerous crim anyhow, they're looking to talk to a witness — that's all. And that's the way it is.'

'Oh. But they've been gone so long. Oshi has never been away this long before.'

'Here's what I'll do for you. Soon as I hear something I'll come over to yours and fill you in? How would you like that?' Davidson licked his lips and continued to eye her up and down, tumescent fantasies forming.

'Yes… thank you. I'll leave you to your business.'

Iona backed away then turned and left. Davidson watched her go for a long minute, then he went back inside. Stepping over the pool of vomit, he shook off his uniform and moved over the semi-conscious 'pophead. She whimpered while he grunted away — the image of Iona burning in his mind as he exorcised his lust.

†††

A quiet, calm voice said, 'Stop.'

It held such simple confidence that Satoshi could not help but listen. A man of normal proportions — diminutive next to the hulking naukara — stepped into view. He had skin so dark it almost shone and a handsome face. A form-fitting bodysuit, in the same off-white colours of the naukara, revealed a chiselled physique. His eyes shone from his face but it was the expression on those handsome features that most assured Satoshi. He had a broad, almost goofy smile showing pristine teeth. His voice when he spoke was a fraction higher than Satoshi would have expected from his appearance but not in any way ridiculous. The accent was one that took Satoshi back years: he'd met someone from the country called England, when there'd still been such a place. The accent was almost the same — not the clipped tones of Received Pronunciation but the natural twang of a city dweller.

'It's alright, mate. We're here to help you, got your message. I wasn't sure you'd be in the mood to chat, hence the boys here.' At this the man made a casual gesture indicating the naukara, they apparently took this as an order to stand down and the weapons were lowered. 'Don't you want to come with us, get out of here? Get some grub and maybe a cuppa?'

'I don't know what you're offering but we do need to get out of here. My friend is hurt, he needs a medtech,' Satoshi said and unclenched his fists, fighting his own reluctance.

'It's alright. We know, we've been monitoring you since you hacked our systems. Thought you were someone else at first, an old friend. Anyway, Rupert here,' he said, laying one hand on the massive metallic shoulder of the naukara with the claws 'will carry him to our ride. We'll get this sorted, don't worry.'

Satoshi tensed again as the armoured figure called Rupert towered over Valko's unconscious form, but the terrible claws, when unfurled, proved not to end in sharp talons made to rend but cushioned discs to reduce the pressure of their grip. They wrapped around Valko and lifted him supporting his head and spine. The naukara cradled him as if he was an infant and Satoshi felt the tension drain out of him.

He asked in a low voice, 'Who are you?'

The man, who had been facing away as he surveyed the lab with interest, turned to him and said, 'What's that?'

Satoshi cleared his throat, finding himself hoarse. 'Who are you?'

'That my friend will take quite a bit of explaining. Now, let's discuss it when we're on our merry way.'

With that, he reached up and put a hand on Satoshi's

shoulder, leading him past the sentries, out into daylight.

Some sort of vessel hovered over the bunker's entrance. It was immense, yet difficult to focus on, as if fogged by a permanent heat haze. Satoshi had little time to look at it before he found himself escorted up a ramp and on board. He was soon strapped into a comfortable, almost over-padded seat that conformed to his body. Harnesses wrapped round him and then, with a slight vibration, he felt a sensation of rising upwards — like a dust mote in sunlight.

There was an abrupt burst of immense pressure, driving him into the seat. He fought it as he sank deeper and deeper into the padding. It flowed around him and he felt a prick on his forearm, followed by a deep relaxation despite the mounting pressure. Something locked down over his face and a sweet liquid flooded his lungs, then he knew nothing but blackness.

Chapter 12

The stars had wheeled and grown once more into immensity. There'd followed a period of blackness. How long it lasted, Valko knew not. No sound, no vision, no feeling came from his body at all.

Then he felt his hands: heavy, warm and numb. Their weight on his lap made him notice the rest of his body and he drew in seven slow breaths.

Valko opened his eyes. The world drifted back into focus, yet part of his mind, his being — maybe even his soul — felt like it was still transitioning back. His essence was being poured back into the glass, his body nothing but a receptacle for his vital self. For a moment, he felt a pang as he sensed that there was more of his being than could fit into the vessel of his body.

'Welcome back.' A voice, deep, cultured and soothing intruded on his inner musings.

'What?' Valko snapped.

The intrusion into his moment of personal transcendence provoked those most primal parts of him, still his own and not part of the replaced tissue in his brain.

'Ah, dear boy, a cup of tea may soothe your choler. Join me'

His vision returned, Valko examined the speaker: a balding man who appeared to be in his late sixties. His face — kindly, seamed with wrinkles and part obscured by oversize glasses — was lit to one side by the flickering light of a fire. It came from within a small stone fireplace, with actual logs made of wood burning with a real open flame.

Valko was incredulous — breaches of environmental protection codes 108-J through 111-D. Offences demanding summary execution. He lurched to his feet and reached for his sidearm. It was missing and his garb was different. He found that — like the speaker — he was dressed in strange fabrics. They were rough and scratchy against the skin of his legs, but appeared to be a grey woven fabric. Underneath a jacket of the same material he wore a light shirt, again with a strange texture.

The speaker had brown patches on the elbows of his

jacket, leather perhaps. Valko had seized some of the material during his time working black market and smuggling cases, but he had never seen it so casually worn. The old man was sitting in a chair, deep and comfortable looking, covered with more leather; the quantity of the rare material being used was shocking. It had been dyed green and had row upon row of indents in the leather at repeated intervals, with leather buttons at the bottom of each indent. The man held a curved wooden item, similar to a 'pop addict's diffuser pipe but shorter and with a glowing coal of matter burning in its bowl. A sweet aroma pervaded.

Another use of an open flame. Another serious violation. The icy core of Valko Gangleri came to the fore with a rush, as the grip of Temple indoctrination seized him, knocking aside all his recent sympathies.

'You are in clear violation of the laws protecting the Mother and the safety of the Plena. You will state your name and then submit to custody,' Valko said.

The man chuckled, a warm, unexpected sound, which Valko could barely recognise, except in the most distant echoes of his memory.

'Were we within a Plenum, you would be right,' he said and exhaled a plume of smoke.

Valko was unfazed, he knew that he had left Arcas Plenum, his memory was not affected but he did not know how he had reached this strange room, which had shelves stacked with actual print books. Ownership of real paper, another offence.

'My authority encompasses the whole planet. My duty in protecting the Mother extends to all of Her face.'

Another chuckle blossomed, kind and warm. 'Were we on the surface or, indeed, in the bowels of the Earth, you would be right. No, no, no, we are somewhere else entirely. You are, I'm embarrassed to say, in my power completely — but worry not. I have no plans of a diabolical sort for you. In fact, I rather hoped we could enjoy a civilized conversation and a pot of tea. Tea always goes better with a slice of fruitcake or a biscuit I find. If you'd prefer scones, I will have the kitchen prepare them.'

Wrong-footed, Valko sat back down on the couch he'd risen from, the influence of his indoctrination relenting, and his emotions whirling back as his old, familiar, jagged steel edge yielded. Numb, he accepted the proffered cup and saucer from his erstwhile captor, mind racing.

The last remnants of NOTT had fled his system, yet he had to acknowledge the difference in his feelings: the recent changes in him had crystallised. Gone was the dominance of indoctrination but so was his pure rationality — that comfortable space in his mind where events could be dissected, separate from the intrusion of emotion and empathy. Valko felt the human warmth of the man sitting opposite and was touched by the eccentric and paternal attitude that radiated from him.

A small motion near the fire drew his attention. There was a container of some kind, a basket he decided, resting in front of the fireplace. In it, a creature — an actual living animal — had shifted position. The animal was white furred and mottled with patches of black fur, one patch over one of its eyes. Its sharp features were softened by an expression of contentment as it straightened its front legs and pushed its head out nearer to the heat of the fire. Triangular ears, less furred than the rest of it, were turning pink in the heat and from it emanated a rhythmic thrumming, like a softly running engine. A real, live cat? Wonder began to fill him but it was interrupted.

'I'm sorry, I've been dreadfully rude. I know your name but have yet to introduce myself. I am known — here anyway — as the Philosopher but that moniker is somewhat cumbersome so you can simply call me Phil. If you like, that is.'

'What am I doing here? I was in a bunker...' Valko asked. 'Where's Satoshi?'

'Your hulking friend? He is here — unharmed of course — and as for what you are doing here, let me start by telling you where you are. You are in my study within a complex of buildings we call the College. It is part of a much larger and more imposing structure with various nomenclature, Apollo Station being the one most likely to be familiar to you. In short, you are amongst those of us who survived the Lunar War on the side of the angels. Oh, I'm sorry, I forget my manners again. You no doubt believe in the righteousness of the other side.'

'You're telling me that you're one of the whitecoats that started the War? That destroyed the ecosphere and devastated the Mother? None of those traitors survived. What kind of trick is this?' Valko shouted, finding himself angry and craving the lost coolness of logic.

'I can see we have gotten off on the wrong foot. This is no trick, I assure you. I was not — am not — a whitecoat, as you put it. My interest in science was limited to the extent to which it coincided with my philosophical and theological investigations. Yes, I was and still am part of Lunar Colony. *We* did not betray anyone nor did we devastate the Earth. You have been lied to, all your young life, which is, however, beside the point.'

'So you say. Why am I here?' His anger hadn't abated but Valko couldn't keep uncertainty from his voice.

'The deepest of questions — though no doubt you mean it in a more prosaic sense. You are here because you needed our help and, in return, we hope for yours.' The Philosopher puffed on his pipe until he produced a cloud of sweet smelling smoke.

Valko raised a hand to his head, the surreal nature of the situation keeping him from clear thought. 'If you are who you say you are, what help can I possibly give you?' He asked.

'Ah, the key question. Our interests are academic. I don't mean that they are unimportant, rather that we are focused, as we always have been, on advancing knowledge. I would be happy merely to discuss the implications of your, shall we call them, visions.'

'How do you know about them?'

'Your brainwaves are unusual in the extreme. Emanating from the implanted brain tissue which one of my former colleagues designed. She meant it to explore some of my theories but, somehow, it has been placed in your head.'

The man paused to draw some of the smoke and sip his tea. Valko could but sit, jaw loose and feeling like his mouth wanted to hang open.

He scarcely managed to grunt, 'What?'

The Philosopher continued, 'You are, as all in the Plena are, the victim of a monstrous deception, but it is not at my hands. I hope that you will listen to me.'

'What choice do I have, since I'm in your power?'

Valko couldn't keep the mordant tone from his voice. He was in the hands of enemies; they'd want to cut him open just like the whitecoats in the Plena would if they thought it could help the Mother.

'Please believe that, in due course, I will ensure you can

return to any point on the Earth you wish — if you wish — at liberty and totally unharmed. You are not a prisoner, but I have questions for you which I simply must ask. I will put no pressure on you, but you may be the proof of all my theories. Forgive my enthusiasm but I feel somewhat... entitled, for you see, bringing you here saved your life.'

'What do you mean?' Valko asked as his analytical mind began to reassert itself, its steel now tempered with emotions.

The Philosopher sat forward, eyes bright behind his large glasses. 'You had been poisoned by a drug overdose of your so-called NOTT.'

'What? How's that possible? Trimethyltryptamine is nontoxic, even in very large doses,' Valko said.

'You do not need Trimethyltryptamine to use your implanted brain tissue, it is, after all, produced internally by your implant. No the drug you have been taking served a different purpose.'

'What?' Valko said. His head was filled with turning questions and doubts as he sought to grasp the implications of what he was being told.

'Allow me to explain. We've analysed NOTT, the substance which you have been taking all these years, and it is something else entirely. A cocktail of addictive drugs to suppress your implant's normal function with only a small quantity of tryptamine to prompt the implant's special functions. Given what we found in your blood stream you are truly lucky to be alive. Our conclusion is that it was a convenient deception to make you, and the other Moderators, think you were reliant upon an external compound for your insights. All the substance really did was regulate a genetic switch within the synthorganic structures of your implant. Oh, and give withdrawal symptoms which closed the switch once more. The switch, and of course your reliance on the substance linked to it, is a crude addition to your implant.'

'How can you possibly know that?'

Valko felt another surge of anger. Whether he was being lied to now or had been deceived for far longer, he hated being taken for a fool.

The Philosopher, leaned back in his chair and set his pipe aside, folding his hands in his lap. He stared hard at Valko, but said nothing. His eyes, magnified to disturbing size by the glasses, did not waver for an instant. Smoke stopped curling up from the pipe.

Taking seven breaths, Valko calmed down. 'I'm sorry,' he said.

'Quite alright, dear boy. You're understandably upset.' With the tension between them broken, the pipe was taken up once more. 'Bugger — my pipe. Excuse me a moment.' The old man tamped down the pipe with his thumb and rekindled the flame with a match taken from a small box at his side. After a few puffs, he returned his attention to Valko. 'Let us continue. Our doctor has quite an experience with implants such as yours. She learned from their creator after all, not to mention her hands-on experience, you might say. Come, let me show you.'

They left the study, with its sleeping cat and cosy surroundings, and walked down carpeted hallways. Soon the décor gave way to a more sterile and cold environment. Within this there were numerous unmarked corridors but the Philosopher didn't hesitate at any junction.

As they walked Valko felt the need to break the silence. 'What is your name?'

'I beg your pardon?' The man squinted up at him.

'Your real name. What is it?'

'I have forsaken it, as have we all. We have chosen to set aside the arrogance of seeking to have our names live on with our discoveries. Instead, each breakthrough is a tribute only to humanity and not to any individual.'

They carried on in silence and soon reached a room containing a multitude of transparent vessels. Within these there were large quantities of tissue — some that appeared organic and some part machine. An oversized brain, complete in a jar and overlaid with a network of flickering cables, dominated one corner. Whitish, fibrous cables came from all of the tissues leading to the bottom of each jar.

'These are extensions of mine and my colleagues' brains,' the Philosopher said. 'I am linked to a number of these brain tissues. Most of us have chosen to retain our normal human brains within our own skulls, albeit with extra capacity provided by linkages to external tissues. Extra brain power, if you like.'

The Philosopher had taken on the tone of one delivering a

lecture; he clearly enjoyed the role of a teacher.

'Some of my colleagues have gone further and have moved parts or the entirety of their brains out of their bodies to secure locations like this. Some have designed completely synthorganic brains for themselves'

The Philosopher gestured to the oversized brain.

'This is Ari's — you will note it is more than twice the size of a normal human brain, synthorganic and capable of thought far faster than a natural human brain. His original brain is kept elsewhere, since his head is mostly filled with synthorganic tissue used to relay his thought processes and feed sensory input to the stored natural brain. To prevent any developing insanity or delusion within it, you see. Far too complicated for me, but he claims it makes his research possible'.

'His research?' Valko was struggling to take it all in.

'Ah, I'm glad you asked. Ari was working on the same problem which your young Dr Fisher was investigating. Quite interesting — they seem to have come at the issue of faster than light travel from opposite angles. Ari the purely theoretical — a level of mathematics which is so far above either your or my rudimentary arithmetical skills that we are like sparrows being asked to do differential calculus. Fisher seems to have stumbled upon a practical experiment, which may prove Ari's theories without Fisher having to grasp the maths himself.' There was an unmistakable smug flavour to his tone.

'Faster than light travel?' Valko asked.

His investigative mode clicked into play — were these scientists responsible for Fisher's murder? If they saw him as a competitor or else were seeking to steal his research it would give them a strong motive.

Valko raised an eyebrow and said, 'You're remarkably well informed on Fisher's research.'

'Yes, we maintain anonymous links with some interested parties in the Plena and your communications are hardly difficult for us to hack. How do you think we found you so quickly? We respond to any cry from help from our former associates, but your large colleague had only skimmed the surface of our network. Not to mention, how we learned of your particular condition.'

Valko remained silent, he'd found that it was often the most effective tool for encouraging a suspect to reveal more information.

'Why FTL?' The Philosopher leant back in his chair, drawing on his pipe, almost talking to himself. 'Simply put, the expense in terms of materials in building vessels large enough to carry a decent sized crew and powerful enough to reach a meaningful percentage of the speed of light is prohibitive — we cannot truly begin to settle other systems without a reliable and fast means of travel to them. All that messing about with time dilation would be such a drag, you see. We are currently limited to speeds barely over one percent of lightspeed, but with the right resources could no doubt build something capable of carrying enough fuel to accelerate to ten times that speed and maybe more, if we can find a way around the fuel problem. Still too slow though.'

'Other systems?' Valko asked. 'Are you talking about colonising other worlds?'

This was the kind of heresy that would lead to a full on Temple scourging. An uncomfortable thought occurred to Valko — this was the kind of heresy that Odegebayo had admitted the Conclave had been engaged in, what made them any different?

'Humanity is not as your religion causes you to believe. I'm sorry I assume you follow the beliefs which you have been indoctrinated to?' The Philosopher's quirked an eyebrow at him.

Valko nodded, not wanting to reveal that his commitment to the Temple's precepts was not a matter of belief but indoctrination, and they were as law in the Plena. Accepting that he didn't believe was, perhaps, easier now that his recent experiences had made it difficult to see people as a virus. Before, he'd experienced little difficulty in doing so — save for when NOTT was coursing through his system.

'We hold to the ideal that humanity is not a macro-virus. Not a plague on the Earth, rather we are her sons and daughters and, like any parent, were she consciously able to do so, she would wish us well. She would encourage us to leave the nest and fly off into our future.'

'So, you deny the tenets of the Temple of the Wounded Mother? You wouldn't be the first disavower, nor the last. But what has that got to do with Fisher's research?'

'Ah, yes. Forgive my tendency to wander tangentially. One day, humanity will recover from this fear caused by the damage done to our world by the War. We are making efforts to repair the damage — though it was not caused by us. We, as a species, have a chance to learn our lesson, and a harsh lesson it has been. Yet it means that we can go forward into the Deep — wander between the stars — with respect for what we find. We do not need to lose our respect for ourselves. What you have seen here is our attempt to further understanding. What you have experienced is an unexpected offshoot of our research.'

'What do you mean?' An uncomfortable feeling was creeping up Valko's neck.

'If I'm right, the changes in your implant and associated brain tissue have lead you to have certain... experiences?' The old man tilted his head to one side.

Valko realised he was being prompted for a response. 'What do you know about it?'

'Oh, it's an educated guess. You see, we have some remaining tissue from the early experiments, which lead to the creation of your implant — all an effort to see past the limitations of our physical perceptions. To raise the level of our consciousnesses as well as of our intellects.' The Philosopher indicated a smaller clear tube, which contained a strange, pinecone shaped piece of flesh about the size of Valko's thumb. 'This is a prototype, if you like, of the implant in your head. It is far closer to natural tissue and thus produces a lesser effect. We've each tried the experience but it is somewhat... unsatisfying.'

'What experience?' Valko asked and found his defensiveness receding, replaced by curiosity.

'There's the problem. There is little consistency. We've all experienced common elements to the visions but never quite the same. Most of the others had written off the experiment as nothing more than hallucinations until now. After all, the effect can be produced using various narcotics — has been for millennia, in fact.'

'So you're saying that everything I'm experiencing is just an hallucination?'

'No, no. That's not it at all. I have studied every scrap of information, on every esoteric and mundane philosophy I could find. I know that there have been people who have believed that this realm of the senses is but a dream or, if not illusory, then but a small part of a greater journey.'

'Are the visions real?'

'What is real?' The old man was fiddling with his pipe, unlit but still in his hands. 'Will you tell me what you have seen?'

Valko considered it for a long moment. 'I will. But you said that you needed my help. Before I tell you anything, you will tell me what else you want from me.'

The Philosopher nodded. 'A fair exchange. We want you to carry through your investigation, with your eyes open.'

'That's it?'

'It means you need to hear our side of things, but yes that's it.'

His suspicious nature suppressed, Valko found a certain relief in the thought of sharing his recent visions. 'Alright, I'll tell you what I've seen — what I remember of it.'

'Let us return to the comfort of my study.'

The Philosopher led him back to the cosy room and Valko, sitting back on the comfortable couch, began to unburden himself.

†††

Hampton clicked her tongue against the roof of her mouth. 'Jack, what's this I hear about you talking to Satoshi's bondmate?'

Davidson shifted his feet. His face still stung from the hasty shave he'd had before answering the latest summons to the Pravnik's office.

'She came to me, ma'am. I told her everything was fine and that I'd let her know as soon as I heard anything. I was trying to put her off the scent.'

'Hmm, well whatever you said to her, it sent her straight to another one of the kensakan on your team. He's been poking his nose into the tracking systems. He'd better not find anything.'

Hampton's voice made Davidson wince, it dragged across his nerves more harshly than the old cutthroat razor he'd shaved with.

'That's got to be Rennard. Look, there's nothing for him

to find. I wiped all records of a crash or the death of Chang. We're all good.'

Hampton sat forward in her utilitarian chair and her dark eyes narrowed. 'We are most certainly not "all good". No cover up is ever complete enough to remove the risk of something being revealed by direct scrutiny. We will need to accelerate things.'

'Accelerate things? I, er… what do you mean, ma'am?'

'You'll find out soon enough, Jack. Now, I want you to find this Rennard and give him something else to think about.'

Hampton sat back and crossed her legs. Despite the level of fear coursing through him, Davidson couldn't help but eye their supple, muscular length. He found himself fantasising about them being wrapped around him, then — even as his groin experienced a sudden rush of blood — his brain caught up with what she was saying.

'You want me to kill him? Jeez, I'm not sure I can do it, ma'am.'

'No, you idiot. That would only draw attention: the Old Man's attention. No, find some task in another Plenum. An investigation to send him on. Then pay this woman, Satoshi's bondmate, a visit. Tell her that there will be a further kensakan dispatched to provide backup — if they do not check in within another twenty-four hours.'

'What if that doesn't shut her up?'

Hampton sighed. 'Persuade her, Jack. I'm sure you can manage. Besides, what more can she expect than that we would send backup?'

'OK. Wait, are you sending someone out there after them?'

'Yes, Jack. You. Better hope we resolve things before time's up, otherwise you'll need to go out there and find their remains.'

Davidson swallowed. This was getting worse and worse, 'Yes, ma'am.'

☩

The Philosopher listened, puffing away on his pipe, until

Valko was finished. He leant forward, his eyes bright.

'Fascinating. Your visions have gone beyond anything we have experienced here. Despite our synthorganics we, like the rest of humanity, can all still die a physical death. For many thousands of years we, as a species, have sought an answer to whether that meant a cessation of being. If your visions are true, maybe you can answer the question?'

'But how can they be real? How can it be possible?'

This all sounded mad and he began to fear that maybe he was going insane. The old man smiled an apology.

'I can only say what I posit. I must leave it to others to explain with...' His tone became sardonic '...scientific rigour. What I think is that, whenever your implant is activated now — in its tumorous state — it accesses a different energy shell of the experiential...'

'What? Tumorous? What the hell are you taking about?' Valko's shock flashed through him like a hot wave.

'Oh, my goodness gracious. I am so terribly sorry, dear boy. Curse my clumsy tongue,' the Philosopher said, his expression suggesting chagrin.

'I find it hard to believe you'd slip up and say something you didn't mean me to know,' Valko said.

He found himself getting irritated at the other's pretence at being a doddery, old man. A cold realisation crept over Valko.

'What tumour?' He asked.

The anomalous readings when Orla had tried to refer him to the late Fisher's team to check his implant; Jean's reference to things running their course and her insinuation that his time was short — of course, they meant something like this.

'It appears your implant — the synthorganic matrix interlocked with your natural brain tissue — has developed a tumour.'

'Matrix? Interlocked? That can't be right, I was told that the implant had only replaced some parts of my brain. Can't it be removed and replaced?' A slick beast named dread began to claw at Valko from inside, seeking escape.

'No, no, that would never do. The brain is a lot like the musculature. The more it is used the stronger it becomes. The nerves form better connections and such. From what I understand, synthorganics work in such a way in which the more they are used, the more closely they grow into surrounding tissue — accelerating synaptic pathways or nerve fibres and strengthening bone and muscle tissue. The implant is not a lump of meat but a reactive system which will grow into surrounding tissue, and its location within your brain, the pineal gland and surrounding tissue…' The old man sucked in a deep breath. 'Very difficult.'

'But this must happen a lot; there must be someone who knows how to treat it? If you can survive moving your own brains into jars, then you must be able to save me.'

Valko's breath became laboured as emotions began to overwhelm him. There was no solace in any auto-hypnotic triggers; there was no trace of the structured system of psychological defences in his mind. He sat down hard in a chair by one of the workstations arranged around the room.

The Philosopher spoke softly, 'Yes, we can do incredible things, but the problem is stopping your implant taking over your brain. We have no experience with this. I have synthorganics throughout my entire body, believe it or not. They are safe but unlike you, of course, mine spread slowly after an injection of synthorganic precursor cells. You have had more of… well to put it bluntly: the butcher's approach.'

Valko felt the beginnings of nausea. He knew what'd been done to him but facing it in such graphic terms was difficult. To learn that it couldn't be undone, when it might kill him, was worse.

The Philosopher reacted to his discomfiture by rocking to his feet and coming over to place a gnarled hand on Valko's shoulder.

'Please understand, this has never — to our knowledge — happened before. The implant's creator might be able to help you but she left us many years ago. You may be able to persuade Jean to help you.'

'Jean? What does have to do with my implant?'

'She developed the technology — before she left us. Some of her research ended up in the hands of Fisher or rather I mean his grandson and the results ended up in your head.'

'She's a murderer,' Valko said, the thought that someone he was hunting for ending a life might have created a technology as lifesaving as synthorganics, had no place in his conception of the world.

'So Satoshi said. Jean was always rather prone to extreme emotions, where her work was concerned. No doubt because of her reasons for starting her research in the first place. Yet, I thought Satoshi said that Fisher junior had been killed over his FTL research? I find it difficult to believe that she acted without good reason — though she was always rather hot-blooded.'

Valko digested this. His thoughts were all over the place. Whatever else was going on, he had a job to do and maybe he could get closer to finishing it if he could find out about her. He felt so confused: part of him angry, almost hating Jean; the other part still felt that inexplicable and intoxicating attraction to her. Overshadowing everything else was what was happening to him. It didn't seem real, but he imagined he could feel the cold waxen hand of death creeping over him.

With an effort of pure will, Valko took control of himself. 'If there is nothing that you can do to help me, then why should I listen to a word you say?'

The Philosopher withdrew his aged hand but an expression of sympathy remained on the weathered face. 'I understand completely. Perhaps, what we can do is help you to understand what you are going through and give you the truth of what has been happening all these years. You'd want the truth wouldn't you?'

'Of course I want the truth,' Valko said, knowing at his core that the truth was what had driven him all his life. 'Why should I believe that you could give it to me?'

'Quite. I see your point. Actually, I must say I have to concede that I couldn't provide you with the absolute truth — I'm not sure that there is such a thing. Rather, let me do the best I can: which is to tell you, in as unbiased a way as I can, what lead us to this state of affairs. Maybe then, you will understand our motives and trust us.'

With that, the Philosopher began the long account of the history of the Lunar Colonies, the short lived Lunar War, the years of pursuit that followed and the collapse of the Superstates. Everything he said left Valko reeling.

Satoshi relaxed. He liked it here — it felt... familiar. His hosts had provided him with clean clothes: a flawless kimono in muted tones of green and brown. They'd also given him the best food he'd tasted since leaving his grandparents' home all those long years ago. True, he hadn't seen Valko but he had been given constant reports. Once in a while, the man who'd brought him here appeared and talked to him — telling him things but also asking him about his memories of the old world. Music and sports were his particular interests. Some of what they discussed brought back childhood memories.

It was a pleasant way to spend his time, though he was aware that, thrown in amongst the reminiscences, were subtle probes for information. His host was clever: never coming at any issue directly but always alluding to matters that must have been his real interest. The way that he interspersed small, yet superficially significant, snippets of information about himself and the others with him was no doubt meant to instil a feeling of trust.

That wasn't all. Satoshi reflected on how he'd been allowed to wander around, though he'd been warned that some areas were dangerous without supervision. His host, understanding that this would provoke his natural curiosity, tried to quell it by showing Satoshi many of the closed rooms by camera footage. It was hard not to respect his host's right to some secrets but his duty to Valko would not be set aside. More than curiosity, it made him yearn to escape the watchful camera eyes and seek out their hosts' — or captors' — true purpose.

The man — he'd called himself Ari but then explained that it wasn't his birth name — was strange. At first, he pretended to be interested in mundane things but then he'd say something that revealed an intense intellect and a wide knowledge base. His accent remained steady but the words he used shifted. Sometimes he spoke in a long-dead argot — not difficult to understand but requiring careful listening — at others it was in a clear but straightforward manner, which would fit in among the whitecoats of the Plena.

He'd pressed Ari for information, trying to get an idea of their location, but the best he'd been told was that, if the time came to return to any of the Plena, it would take them a few hours. No, Ari had been more precise than that. He'd said six and a half hours and done so with a great degree of pride, like it was a significant achievement.

Satoshi began his kata. In many ways, they had been the only true link to himself through all the years he'd been trapped in ignorance of his past. With the return of memories while trapped in the bunker he'd turned yet again to the kata, needing their calm. The patterns were so ingrained in him that they'd never be lost — in that there was a certainty he could cling to.

Before, he'd remembered his childhood but only now did he realise how much of that had been locked away. While he went through the familiar movements — feeling them click into place with memories they'd been severed from — he found a state of meditative peace. All these years in ignorance he'd felt the compulsion to go to his training place — a deserted space under his habitation block's feed-pipe to the recyclers. There'd been a cramped room that stank of the run off, but the smell always faded away as he lost himself for hours in the movements and the calm of the void. Now, memories drifted to the surface of his mind but did not take hold.

There was so much to understand. All the time, memories were jumping to the forefront of his mind, demanding attention. Some gave him a clearer picture of what had happened to him, but not a complete one. It was frustrating, yet he knew that if he were patient, the secrets of his past would reveal themselves to him. More important, the exercises — with their tendency to create a state of *mushin*, no mind — had helped him gain a firmer control over the effects of his Lunar War Syndrome. Before, it had only ever lurked as a vague threat in the depths of his psyche. Now, it was a demon he waged a constant war against. If he let it win, killcrazy would take him — Amok Disorder was such a mild term for the bloodbath he'd leave behind him.

He returned his focus to the movements, aware that he'd made a mistake. Not pausing to consider the error — as a novice might have done and further disrupt the flow — he finished the kata and then began it again, correcting what was wrong. This time, it flowed and his mind found tranquillity — that part of him that was no more than a slavering beast held at bay.

'If all of this is true, I can't keep it to myself,' Valko said. 'If we're not only living a lie in the Plena because they've taught us that you were to blame but also a deeper lie told by the Temple — that we are no better than viruses — I have to reveal the truth.'

The core of him rebelled against such emotive altruism, but it was swept aside by unaccustomed, gushing enthusiasm.

'I never imagined you as a candidate for a messiah complex, Mr Gangleri.' The Philosopher grinned at him.

'That's not what I mean. Only, what's the point of knowing the truth...'

The old man interjected, 'If you do...'

'Yes, if I do know the truth, what's the point of leaving everyone else in ignorance?'

'How fascinating. Considering your name, I mean.'

'What do you mean?' Valko asked.

He was, once more, distracted by the Philosopher's cat, who'd climbed out of her basket, stretched indolently and was looking around the room.

'Well, you probably know the origins of your surname, don't you?' The old man reached down and scratched the cat's head between her ears.

'Not really, it's an old Italian name from before the dissolution of nations and the creation of Eurussia,' Valko said, puzzled and irritated at the tangent, yet his eyes still locked on the small animal — the first he had ever seen.

'Who told you that? Gangleri is not Italian. Maybe if it were Ganglieri, I could understand the mistake. No, no. It is Old Norse. One of the names of the god Odin.' The lecturer's tone had returned to the Philosopher's voice.

'So what?' The cat walked over to Valko and inspected him. He sensed in it some echo of the vast consciousnesses he had dreamed.

'So what... Young people!' The Philosopher said. 'Don't wallow in your ignorance. Your name meant Wanderer. Appropriate, don't you think?'

'Yes, yes but what has that got to do with my question about telling others the truth?' Valko said, wearying of the intellectual.

His irritation seemed not to bother his other watcher, and the cat sprang up on to the couch beside him, rubbing her head against his left hand. With her touch his irritation faded — *why get so worked up over all of this?* — he found himself thinking

'Well, don't you see? Odin was a psychopomp.' The Philosopher drew again on his pipe.

'Fantastic, a mad killer god,' Valko said, watching in apprehension and fascination as the cat climbed up the back of the couch, to lie behind his head.

The Philosopher snorted in derision, 'They teach you nothing these days. That so-called Temple of the Wounded Mother has no deep thinkers within it — no theologians. A psychopomp is a guide for the dead or, rather, the literal translation means guide of souls. You may have heard the legend of Charon, the boatman? Or the Greek god Hermes who the Romans called Mercury? Or of Yama the Death God? Or of the Valkyries, who took the brave who died in battle? No?

The Valkyries served Odin, ensuring he had the choice half of the slain while the goddess Freyja took the other half.'

'Why the hell would I know, or need to know, any of that? And what's that have to do with my question?' Valko couldn't keep his exasperation from his voice.

'You mustn't be so obtuse. If you, given the name of a spirit guide to the dead, have developed — albeit through artificial means — the ability to guide others on the hmm, on the spiritual plane, doesn't that say something about predestination?'

'Predestination? I chose to join the Moderator program, it wasn't predestined,' Valko said.

'Yet you — who have had what the ancients regarded as the seat of the soul, the pineal gland, removed and replaced by the artificial — you are experiencing more clearly than anyone else in history the great mysteries which have tested humanity since our awakening to sentience. Doesn't that signal something to you?'

'About what?' Valko asked, his patience running dry.

The Philosopher puffed on his pipe, and then said, 'About a meaning for everything. Maybe, even, about whether there is some sort of plan: a design drafted by a divine consciousness?'

'What the hell are you talking about?'

The old man sat forward, unhooking the stem of his pipe

from his mouth, and said, eyes bright, 'My boy, you might be able to answer the question of whether there is a god.'

The cat purred into Valko's ear.

⁂

Davidson found Rennard hunched over a terminal, one connected to the main monitoring station for beacons and transpod communications. It was the terminal right next to the one he'd used himself. His fellow kensakan was focused on the screen with intensity — sweat glistening on his bald head.

Davidson walked right up behind him, without being noticed, and roared, 'Moz, what the hell are you doing?'

Rennard reacted with such a start that Davidson strained to contain his laughter. This moron wasn't going to find anything, and if he did he wouldn't know what to do with it anyway. From out of nowhere, the sick feeling of his guilt punched hard in Davidson's chest — he batted it away.

'Oh, er, Jack. Look, I was checking to see if there was any news on the Moderator and our Sergeant,' Rennard said.

'Yeah, well, there's none. I got something I need you to look at. Can't be letting other investigations slide while we wait for the Boss to get back. You'd better brush up on your Swahili — I need you to go to Abuja Plenum. We've got another death. Not like these — but it's important. You've got to do the preliminaries until a Moderator can look at it.'

'But Jack, I thought…'

'Don't "but Jack" me. Look dumbass, this is a real opportunity for you. Might even get your sergeant stripes — if you don't fuck it up. You should be saying, "gee thanks Jack for giving me such a chance".'

'Yeah sure, Jack. Sorry. What're you going to be doing?'

'Nosey today, aren't you? Don't worry about me. I'm supposed to sort out what's happened to the Boss. If we don't hear from them by tomorrow, yours truly's going to have to hitch a transpod to Outpost Theta and ride a shank's mare out to where they're no doubt making life difficult for some other poor bastard.'

'Shank's mare?' Rennard said.

'Shit, Moz. Haven't you ever watched any old vids? It's American talk for "walk", back when they used to call it the Wild West. Dead West would be more like it, these days. Shit. You guys amaze me. Next you'll be telling me you've never seen any cop vids.'

'No, Jack. I haven't. I stick to the approved list. All that stuff, well you know, Temple doesn't like it.'

'Never took you for a fully indoctrinated, Moz. You getting religious on me?'

'No, Jack. I'm no zealot, but we've got to respect the Mother. Those people who made the vids and wrote the books and the people they were about — they had no respect for Her. They're why we're all in here and not out breathing clean air. I've got no time for them. Surprised you do.'

'Moz, you and I are going to fall out if you keep talking like this. Now, shut the fuck up and get moving.'

'Ok Jack. Ok. Don't get mad.' Rennard picked up his datapad on which he'd been making notes and headed towards the door. 'Hey Jack. Where is Abuja Plenum, anyway?'

'In the old African Nations territory, dumbass.' *Fuck me sideways, Rennard's stupid.* 'There are what, like thirty-seven Plena in the world and you've never heard of it? Get the fuck out of here.'

†††

Valko lay on his bed in the comfortable and cosy room. His thoughts were churning. Most of what he'd learned sounded patently insane, so, after the Philosopher's disturbing revelations, Valko had demanded proof — none had been forthcoming. These scientists were hoping for something more from him than they were saying — his Moderator's instincts had kicked in. He could almost smell, what? Desperation?

Some urgent need drove them. Was it their existing obsessions or something else? Guessing would do little to help him; it might close his mind to facts that were right in front of him. His cool analytical mind warred with unleashed emotions.

A NOTT driven empathy could be controlled — barely. Now his empathy and his emotions were more intense than he'd ever known — like a constant NOTT overdose. At the same time, after his system had been flushed of the quasi-narcotic, it was easier to deal with his feelings — they were more a part of him. Still, it was a faint hope that his experience with the psychoactive drug in the context of investigations had inured him to the worst of his emotional imbalances — they were getting stranger.

Gathering his thoughts yet again, he was more and more certain that the scientists wanted something specific from him. If he didn't agree to give them that something, there'd be consequences — perhaps, he'd have to remain here permanently. But then what would he be to them? A laboratory experiment? Right up until the time his tumour killed him or he faded into insanity.

Caught between fury and fear, he tried to still his mind; something Oshi had once told him about the martial arts came to him. The need to — what was it? Lower one's consciousness. He tried: focusing on the sensation that his mind was located somewhere above and behind his eyes, he took seven deep breaths and allowed his shoulders to settle. His point of focus moved so that he visualised his mind sinking so that it was below the level of his eyes.

Almost at once, it brought a feeling of detachment — not cold analysis, but freedom from both his racing thoughts and his churning emotions. No mind. No emotion. Relief from the chaos inside him was temporary but it made him think that there was a way out of this, if he could keep his cool.

It was unlikely that Jean would be able to cure him; she'd given no impression that it was what she wanted. What she had wanted was him as her prisoner, but why? If she had designed his implant and it'd been stolen from her, she must want to know what it was doing. To see the end result of the experiment when the controls put in place by Centra Autorita were disabled. So he might be of value to her alive. It gave him hope, but it was hope tarnished with the knowledge that his fate might lie in the hands of a murderer. A murderer whom he was duty bound to bring to justice — even if that justice were delivered summarily, outside the Plena.

†††

After he'd slept they took him to Satoshi. Their reunion was warm but it was interrupted when the Philosopher brought a handsome, dark-skinned man in with him. Satoshi stepped aside and nodded to the man.

'This… is Ari. Satoshi, I think you have had the chance to get to know him rather well but Valko here needs the chance too.' The Philosopher ushered Ari forward.

'Don't exaggerate things. I'm a simple mathematician. Good to meet you,' he said, offering his hand to Valko.

'So you're the mysterious Ari?' Valko said, not taking the hand — a gesture that had long ago lost its meaning within the Plena.

Ari lowered his hand, for a moment seeming knocked off his stride but it was fleeting. 'No, there's nothing mysterious about me. You probably guessed I'm not exactly like Phil here. He was a posh boy back in the day. Where was it you went to school, Phil, one of those public schools, wasn't it?'

The Philosopher shifted his feet, appearing nonplussed at this. 'Those things don't have any meaning now.'

'Course they do, bruv. Who we are is about where we came from, innit?' Ari made his slight accent more pronounced, thick even.

'I suppose you can take the boy out of Hackney…' the Philosopher said, with a sigh.

'Too right. Now, onto business.' Ari folded his arms. 'You've got some questions and we all feel that Phil here is being a bit too — sorry to say this — long-winded. You need a straight talker and he tends to be indirect.' The older man harrumphed at this; Ari looked over at him and said, 'Sorry, but it's true. You get all excited about your theories. We all respect you, but you know this needs to be handled a bit more, you know, directly.'

'And you're the man to tell me how it is are you, Ari?' Valko asked.

'Yeah, that's me. I'll give it to you straight up: we didn't start the War. We didn't want to fight anyone, but we didn't want our inventions or our theories being used as weapons either. One of us didn't agree: he was important, someone who helped connect all our different fields of study. Something of a unifier, but too much of a politician.' Ari said, with disgust. 'He thought he could manipulate the Superstates, turn them round. Maybe make the UN World Government a serious thing, instead of a paper tiger. You feel me so far?'

Valko nodded, just about understanding what he was being asked.

'Well this man, he betrayed us. Took all our secrets to United America. They were the heaviest hitter back then, the African Congress close behind, with Eurussia and Panasia following. Our boy, he double-crossed United America, though, let all those lovely secrets fall into the hands of the other Superstates. By then, our fate had already been decided.

You probably know this part. They sent cybered lads, like Rupert and his mates, up to capture us. They were convinced we had more to tell them. Anyway, we reprogrammed their tin soldiers. Some we sent back as a warning — leave us alone. Some stayed with us. Poor sods don't have any free will, so we thought better have them here. We'd treat them right and maybe one day be able to fix what they had done to them.'

'Why am I getting this history lesson again? He...' Valko pointed at the Philosopher, '...has already told me most of this. Even if I believe you, what use is it?'

'Slow down, this is important, alright. If you understand then you'll know what you need to do. Anyway, we thought we were safe, didn't know that the traitor had taken synthorganics. It was something that Jean was working on — quietly. When your mate here...' He indicated Satoshi '...and his crew came up we weren't ready. Some of them planted fusion bombs and boom!' Ari made an expansive gesture with his hands. 'All gone.'

'How did any of you survive then?' Valko asked.

'Well, not all of us were on the surface. Those of us who survived weren't in Armstrong or Aldrin. It was mostly our families and some very specific experiments. The real work was already happening here, on Apollo station.'

'So, they killed your families and you, what, bombed the Mother in revenge? Killed billions to get back at them?' Valko almost spat the words, his anger burned so intensely.

'No, mate. Easy, easy. We didn't do anything to the world. We all had family there too. Sure, some of us wanted revenge hence what was done to Satoshi and his mates. But some of us didn't agree — you can't treat people as puppets — and we'd been working to become better people. To be better, so we could help the World be better, you know.'

Valko sat down his legs feeling weak. The man was radiating sincerity. Valko's implant revealed Ari to be someone who really believed what he was saying was true.

'So who destroyed the world?' He asked

'You know already. They destroyed themselves. UNWG became your Centra Autorita. We were the convenient scapegoats — our rebellion was just a pretext to hunt us down for what we knew. What with all the chaos of the Plena being erected, it was easy to lie — to make sure the people did what they were told. It was all manipulation. All to cover up the fact that those who were then leading the UNWG's efforts in setting up Enclosure were the ones who'd sparked the whole damn mess in the first place.'

'Who? Dammit, tell me who.'

'You know who. The biggest hero of the Plena was our original administrative head. Dr Erasmus Fisher.'

'You expect me to believe that the man who saved all of us, who made Enclosure possible, was really responsible for the destruction that made it necessary?' Valko was back on his feet and shouting — his hard-won control gone.

'Steady on, mate. Yes. He played his part.' Ari said, both hands up in a placating gesture.

'Val, I think he's right,' Satoshi said.

'What? Oshi, how can you believe this nonsense?'

'I don't know all of it, but I remember Fisher. He was there when they were treating me, after the raid on the Panasian camp. I saw him, just before I was put under. Next time I wake up, it's his grandson leaning over me, telling me it's been eighty years and every memory from before was lost to me. But I remember now. No one person, or even a small group, could have triggered the release of the nanodestroyers. Or made the Superstates use flashburners on themselves. These scientists were scattered — we were hunting them and Fisher was leading us, telling us who to go after.' Satoshi stood. 'Believe me when I tell you, Val, this is the truth. Come on. Use your skills; you can pick the lie out of someone's head.'

'If this is true and you need me to believe it, then one of you must let me mindlink.'

'Dear boy, allow me. I have nothing to hide,' the Philosopher said.

'You sure, Phil?' Ari asked.

'Yes, Ari. Your head would be too full of numbers, Hilbert spaces and other mumbo-jumbo for anyone to make sense of anyway. Valko, if you wait we will get your hub for you. I'm sure we can synthesise some NOTT if you feel it is necessary, but you do understand that it's a placebo?'

'I don't need any of it anymore,' Valko said.

The Philosopher raised one eyebrow but sat down. Satoshi pulled one of the heavy chairs in front of him. Valko sat down and both men leaned forward.

'I'm ready,' the old academic said.

Valko reached up with both hands and held the other man's head — noting as he did so that the skin, though it looked old, was firm like a young man's. He reached out with his mind and found the connection: an electric shock through his fingertips.

He was there. Floating in the vast space of the Philosopher's mind.

«*Seek whatever you want, but please, leave an old man some dignity*»

Valko acknowledged this with a flicker of thought, as he delved into the man's memories. The mind he was entering was vast and cavernous; he'd never connected with anyone who had the mental architecture he was encountering here. There were well over a hundred years' worth of memories and they were arranged in sequence. It was like the mind of the Philosopher had been sorted by an overzealous librarian. All memories were catalogued and filed — a vast archive of his life. There were other parts to the colossal structure of the mind: an area of seeming chaos, which spilled over into his perception. It was like a billion bright ideas, each bound to every other by a thread.

«*My creative process. I like to wormhole from one idea to the next — all things are linked, you see*»

«*You're aware of me?*»

«*Oh yes. Don't worry, I will stop interfering*»

Valko had delved into memories before but never with a conscious mind allowing him this degree of communion. He remembered the difficulty he'd had in accessing the 'pop addict's recent memories when he linked with her in the Hotbed. That memory brought back thoughts of Jean — he suppressed them with his anger and hurt at her betrayal. Then the thought crawled up from the recesses of his being, what is she to me and I to her that I call it betrayal?

In the memories before him, Valko saw the Philosopher's early life unfold. He skimmed over it but noted the man's real name and saw that he'd been born long before the War. He charted the studies of his subject and saw how he excelled in confounding his teachers, in a place where everyone spoke with the same clipped and precise accent that the Philosopher himself did. Then followed something called University, where he rose to become a leading figure. He met a young man from somewhere called London. A genius, some said, who'd come from a humble background. Mother a bus driver, father a policeman. The young Ari. He saw that man's real name and understood something of his importance to the Philosopher. The young man who would become Ari excelled at mathematics and physics, becoming a brilliant figure, first in the University and then on the world stage.

Valko followed the threads. He saw how the Philosopher and Ari had become friends, each finding balance in the other. Then the Allied Lunar Colonies were founded and both were invited in — Ari as the wunderkind of the scientific world; the Philosopher as the soul of the project. All arranged by Erasmus Fisher, himself a respected renaissance man of the scientific community.

The newly formed colony had flourished and, being an enclave of the brightest and best, had produced remarkable results. Then he saw her. In the Philosopher's mind, he called her Gene not Jean, but it was the same person — she looked like an older version of the woman he'd last seen in the bunker.

Valko saw her aged a little more than he knew her but now he comprehended her brilliance in the field of biology, specifically genetics. She had produced the prototype synthorganics and suddenly she and most of the other scientists looked younger. Only Fisher and the Philosopher retained their outward appearance of age, though the process had stopped.

The betrayal by the Superstates sponsoring the project all rushed into view — all the politicians began to demand the fruits of the research. The Scientists reached consensus: there would be no sharing of dangerous technology. Fisher disappeared with copies of all their current research. Despair filled the colony to be replaced by a renewed commitment to carry on their research.

Valko watched the memory of Fisher contacting them, demanding any further developments. He saw their principled refusal and the naukara sent to take by force what they would not give. The brilliant minds had reprogrammed the machine men with little effort. It seemed the War would end in a stalemate, but synthorganic soldiers like Satoshi appeared. He shared the horror of watching Armstrong and Aldrin devastated with fusion bombs.

Through memories stained red by grief and rage, Valko saw Apollo station being moved well out of orbit, using the new engines that had been developed based on Ari's theories. An concept, proposed long before when their chief would have been dubbed the Visionary, blossomed. They changed their names, each adopting a name taken from some aspect of their specialty. The Philosopher. The Arithmetician. The Geneticist. All of them, a community now no more than twenty strong, made a commitment to divorce themselves from their own personal and trivial concerns and instead focus on the future of the whole human race.

Valko felt the alarm, the bewilderment the Philosopher had felt when the nanodefenders started malfunctioning. He relived the pain of watching the exodus of some, Gene included, and hearing the subsequent reports of them being hunted. The Philosopher's sorrow at watching Earth being blasted by some of the very weapons his people — his family — had created on the Moon for peaceful purposes. A sorrow replaced by hope when Fisher used the advanced nanotechnology he'd stolen from them to begin Enclosure.

Years blurred past, the small community continuing their research into the tissue samples that Gene had left behind. Valko shared the Philosopher's sudden understanding that she had been pursuing his idea of expanded consciousness, parallel to intellectual advancement and his stunned realisation that she was close to achieving her aim.

Afterwards followed long years of seeking lost colleagues, lost friends and of looking for a way to heal the damage done to the world. Valko heard the furious arguments and broken sobs of the scientists as they realised they had become scapegoats for all the pain the Earth had suffered.

Valko pulled back, flitting over the memories as they streamed past him. He saw himself as separate again and doing so, he perceived that the Philosopher, at least, did believe that he, Valko, was accessing some higher level of being. The hope that filled the man washed away Valko's anger at him.

With a gasp, he pulled his hands back from the wrinkled face. Tears streamed down from both of their eyes.

'Now you understand us,' the Philosopher whispered.

Valko wiped his eyes and breathed deeply seven times, before speaking, 'Yes, I do. That's why I can't stay.'

'What?' The old — no ancient — man's eyes widened with shock. 'I thought if you knew what we were trying to achieve…'

Valko stayed him with a hand, 'Yes, I agree that it's important, but most of the human race is back on the Mother. I'm part of that world, not this one. Your old world is gone — send me back to mine.'

'What are you going to do?' Ari asked.

'My job. I'm going to catch a murderer and find the person who killed my man Chang. Then I'm going to find the truth behind all of this.'

'I have shown you it,' the Philosopher said.

'No, you've shown me your perspective. And you don't know who actually tried to kill me. Who killed my kensakan. That's not good enough. When I know the truth of what happened I'll deal with it, then tell everyone — all the Enclosed. After all, I've nothing left to lose now, have I?'

††††

The wind blew dust swirling around him and obscuring his vision. Only normal inert dust — for now, at least. Davidson hunkered down behind the rocks at the top of the ridgeline and cleaned the dirt from his binoculars before he tried to get a better view of the wreckage below him. It was the transpod all right. There was no sign of movement within but he waited and watched. It looked like it'd suffered some sort of explosion — the damaged area of the fuselage was scorched and blackened.

Had Hampton arranged this? He'd no idea what her game was or why she'd want Gangleri and Satoshi dead. Poor Chang. He'd been — what was it called? Collateral damage.

There was no beacon reading from either Satoshi or Valko. He'd thought that what he'd done to cover up the accident in the records, might have affected the datapad he was using but he'd picked up Chang's beacon easily enough. It was still giving a low energy trace. With no living body to provide power for it, the device would run on backup for a month or two before going silent.

There was no sign of anyone else. He knew what he had to do. Covering the wreckage with his rifle, in case scavengers had been attracted to it, he edged down the slope. Loose rocks rattled down ahead of him.

Right near the bottom of the slope, he slipped and crashed down with a curse. Lying there, on his back, the enormity of what he was doing hit home. He didn't know whether to laugh or cry. Then sheer panic took over as he seized the container he'd been carrying, slung over one shoulder. If it was broken, he was a dead man.

'Holy shit!' He shouted, seeing a dent in the metal.

He'd landed with the container, a red, metal cylinder with a complex electronic lid, underneath him. Despite the dent in it, the dial on the lid continued to show that there was a complete seal — he might still survive this.

Taking care not to have a further slip, Davidson scrabbled to his feet and — dignity somewhat restored — he crept over to the wreckage. Who was he kidding, caution was a pointless exercise after the fall. Unless his antics had caused a waiting foe to drop their weapons with laughter, then they'd have had plenty of time to take him out while he lay on his back. Still, he couldn't force himself to relax.

Nerves jangling, he entered the transpod through the door that'd been left, forced open. Dust and grit had already begun to accumulate inside — a side effect of strong winds with no vegetation to stop it from carrying great quantities of dust into every corner. There was a creaking sound as the wreckage settled when his added weight shifted its balance. Davidson held his breath but there was no other noise, save the mournful whistle of the wind and the pounding of his own heart.

Making his way to the cockpit, he noted that the automatic systems had entered power save mode. He didn't restart them — no sense in leaving any additional record of his tampering, in case this plan didn't work.

'Mother's fucking Tears — Chang!' Davidson said, seeing the corpse.

There was an odour but it was nowhere near as strong as he'd been expecting. A side effect of the dry air, perhaps. Unpleasant though, enough to make his stomach start to turn. The body, its face covered with the dead man's uniform jacket, was sprawled as if just lazing in the chair.

For an instant, he had an overwhelming urge to remove the jacket and see what was underneath. His hand reached out and he grasped the fabric before he stopped himself. They hadn't been friends but he'd liked Chang and didn't want to remember him as he would be. Whatever lurked under that jacket wasn't his colleague anymore.

With a shudder, Davidson went back about his business: retrieving the craft's computer core and substituting it for the one Hampton had provided him with. Then he went back to the entrance and placed the canister he'd brought on the floor. The dial on top still showed green, so he input a command into it. The lid would open in about an hour: plenty of time for him to be well away.

Inside were about a billion short duration, sterile nanodestroyers. They'd devour the transpod over the next ten to twelve hours but couldn't reproduce themselves. No, that wasn't right. They *shouldn't* reproduce themselves, but with nanotech there were no guarantees. Little would be left of the wreckage, he doubted even the fake computer core would survive but it was unpredictable. The damage would be enough to obscure all other signs that it had been anything other than a crash into a burn zone still hot with nanodestroyers.

Wherever Gangleri and Satoshi were, was another matter. They were a potential loose end that could ruin all of this but there were no tracks to lead him to them. He'd have to hope that Hampton's confidence in their terminal fate was not misplaced.

Satisfied that everything was set, Davidson scuttled off as fast as he could manage, back to the ground crawler he'd been forced to borrow from Outpost Theta. With any luck, he'd be safely inside the Outpost before dark.

┼┼┼

They tried several times to persuade him to stay longer: the Philosopher in the hopes that he could witness another vision and this time monitor it. Ari saying only that he wanted to make 'it' up to Satoshi. He'd say no more.

Valko remained resolute; they needed to leave and find Jean. Satoshi, ever the loyal friend, sided with him — though whether it was from friendship or because he agreed, Valko wasn't sure. Perhaps, it didn't matter. The scientists, true to their word, prepped a vessel to return them to the Mother.

It'd take a few hours to ready and less than seven to make the journey. They couldn't take him to a Plenum or even too near Outpost Theta but returning a short way out might enable them to locate a Martyr's Preserve and, from there, get back in a few hours.

While preparations continued apace, Valko shared a cup of tea in the room with all the books — they'd told him it was called a library — with both Phil and Ari, the Philosopher and the Arithmetician. The Philosopher's cat was nowhere to be seen. Valko quizzed Ari on his particular choice of name and was amused to see the man get defensive.

'It's what I always enjoyed most in mathematics,' he'd said.

Their conversation remained light at first but Valko could tell that both men wanted to ask him more about what he'd seen. They wanted to persuade him to change his mind, but to their credit, they didn't harass him.

'If you seek out Gene, beware of her,' the Philosopher said. 'Given what you have told me of these murders, she has changed much since we knew her so well, but bear this in mind: we found you, in part, because we received a signal indicating where you were. I doubt it came from anyone else but her.' The Philosopher stopped, sipping his tea and taking a bite from a slice of dark fruit cake.

'He's right but you know if anyone can help you with that implant, it'd be her,' Ari said. 'Watch yourself though, mate. If she's become as ruthless as it sounds, she might promise you a cure only to snag you.'

Ari's advice was welcome, but Valko had thought of the possibility already. Then again, she'd not offered any hope in their brief conversation in the Pre-War bunker.

'Ari, tell me about this faster than light research. It might help me understand why Jean would kill for it,' Valko said.

'Listen, I doubt that she's interested in that.' Ari said. 'Maybe she was trying to cover things up. What you need to understand is that, despite Phil's enthusiasm, I don't believe that faster than light travel is possible.'

'Then why are you wasting all that time?' Valko asked.

'Well it's a problem — one of the greatest. See, the young Dr Fisher, he was looking at the same problem from a different angle.' Ari placed unusual stress on the word young.

'How do you know what he was doing?' Valko asked.

'Twenty questions, is it?'

'I think I've only asked you three,' Valko said.

'No, it's an old saying… oh, I feel you. Very funny.' Ari grinned.

Valko allowed himself a smile. He wasn't sure what was funny but better to go along with it.

'Yeah OK, so Fisher junior…' again an unusual stress on the word junior, '…was doing some experiments. They gave out a lot of strange radiation because of what he was working on. Something he called tachyonic conversion. Once we picked up the signals, we kept an eye on it. Had some inside help from a sympathiser. Never did get their name but they uploaded lots of his research to us.'

Could it have been Jean? It had to have been — Valko recoiled from the idea that there might have been several spies in Eugene Fisher's lab.

'Anyway, I was looking at the theoretical side of things. Mathematically, I'd found a way that you could, in theory, convert normal matter into tachyonic matter — that is if tachyons can actually exist. None of that messing around with altering the quantum vacuum or pissing about with inertia.

It looked like it was relatively simple to, how to describe this? Look there's these particles that do certain things. Some are linked to electromagnetism, some to gravity. We think that some relate to time but that's a bit of a wild theory. Anyway what's important is: why do the particles have the effect that they do?'

'I've got no idea,' Valko said, wishing he'd not started this discussion — Ari was even worse that the Philosopher.

'Well we've got a theory — and so far all the equations line up — that these particles have a code. It's like they were programmed. Certain sub atomic quanta tells them what to be, what to do and how strongly they should do it. So what the theory says is you can tell matter to be tachyonic instead of non-tachyonic.

They don't need to be accelerated, you change their fundamental nature so that their energy is no longer expressed as mass but as an electromagnetic wave. They propagate at faster than the speed of light — they become a form that's natural state is superphotonic.'

'Ok, so faster than light travel is possible. Why would Jean want to kill for it?' Valko asked.

'Theoretically possible. If — the big old if — tachyons exist at all. I doubt Jean was interested, unless it was to stop the Centra Autorita from having that kind of power. Yeah, no one wants that Temple thing of yours spreading across the universe. Anyway it's all useless, even if it could work.'

'Why do you say that?'

'Well there's this thing called causality.'

The Philosopher groaned. 'Not this nonsensical rubbish again, Ari.'

Ari gave him a withering look. 'Phil here doesn't understand it. It isn't supposed to make normal logical sense, Phil.'

'That's because it's fallacious and you pure scientists buy into it because you haven't the courage to cast aside all the ridiculous assumptions that lead to the stupid idea.'

'Look, is this my story or yours?'

'Carry on.'

'Cheers. Now, Val, what you have to understand is that if something could become tachyonic three things would happen. First, it'd zip off at very high speed. Second, it'd become very difficult to detect. Third, it'd stop interacting with normal matter

— in most ways.

All the matter that becomes tachyonic wouldn't stay together even if you tell it to remain cohesive and travel to the same place because all the forces that bind matter together only move at the speed of light — they can't interact with each other at light speed.

That'd only get worse if you could travel faster than light. Once matter was tachyonic you couldn't capture the damn stuff to convert it back and things that move at the speed of light become light-like, so behave as wave functions and all that. Tachyons — well, who knows? Bloody useless mate. Can't undo the transformation. Causality at work protecting us from time travel, paradoxes, end of the universe type stuff.'

'Oh pish,' the Philosopher said.

'Anyway what Fisher junior…' Again the stress on the word junior caught Valko's attention, it was slight, unconscious — or was it? This Arithmetician had a mind as arcane and complex as the Philosopher, who knew what subtleties he was capable of? Thoughts raced while Valko continued to listen to the droning scientist, '…had done — apparently — was find a way to turn far-out theory into reality. Tachyonic conversion — in practice. We don't think he'd actually finished the experiment so he was probably struggling to realise it was worthless for travel. But maybe he'd begun to see its other potential uses.'

'Like what?' Valko sat forward, interested in the sudden change of Ari's tone from the know-it-all to the conspiratorial.

'It's like the curse of FTL theories: the ones that might work tend to lead to the destruction of your destination, like that Alcubierre drive, or more localised risk. Think about it: you can convert ordinary matter into tachyons that *can't* be recovered. It could be a devastating weapon with no way of shielding yourself from it.'

'Maybe that's why she killed him,' Valko said and realised he was trying to find a good excuse for Jean.

'Maybe. Though I don't believe that he could have made it work — so she'd have acted too soon. What's it matter anyway? If you know she did it to him and that Vinnetti woman you mentioned?' The Arithmetician clicked his fingers, as if to say it was all done.

'Yes, but motive is useful in making sure a theory holds

water,' Valko said, savouring his greater expertise in at least one field. 'What will you do next?' He asked, without thinking of the consequences of his question.

'Well, talking to you I've had an idea. A way to prove to Phil here that causality is real. I'll use it to predict the outcome of a simple experiment — one I don't think anyone's tried before.'

'A simple experiment no one's tried before...' The Philosopher said, sarcasm creeping into his tone.

Valko was wondering where this was going. He watched as the Philosopher began gearing himself up for the argument. They were like... bondmates.

Ari droned on explaining his experiment in language more incomprehensible than Remnant argot. Phil nodded away as if he understood everything.

'...it'll generate a binary signal sending the message — a grovelling apology from me to you.'

'Genuine, I'm sure,' the Philosopher said, arching one eyebrow.

'Ah, but my bet is that you will never receive the message. I predict it will not be possible to reliably alter the particle's spin — or some kind of interference will be generated obscuring the measurement of that spin. Thus, Causality will be upheld by preventing the data transfer.'

'And if you're wrong?' The Philosopher asked, scowling.

'If I'm wrong, I'll have to listen to you saying I told you so until my synthorganic ears wear out.'

Ari winked at Valko who smiled, hoping it didn't look too forced. It was another reason to leave. Stuck with these two for much longer he would go truly insane — if he wasn't already.

╫

Valko settled into the acceleration couch. He'd been warned what to expect by Satoshi and, after querying the process with Ari, had been satisfied with its necessity. The vessel they were using operated with an engine called a quantum impeller. He didn't grasp a tenth of the explanation that he'd been given but gathered it had something to do with space time being forced through the device in some way, causing massive, if short lived acceleration.

There he'd been, expecting some sort of large, atomic rocket. Ari had declared that the craft was capable of one point one percent of the speed of light and that its acceleration was fearsome. Valko hadn't understood what he'd meant and had needed a visual demonstration.

Ari had taken a few fresh tomatoes from the station's gardens and had stuffed it into a container before inserting that container into one of the experimental devices in the labs on board. It all seemed like a waste of time and resources, but Ari insisted on proving his point with almost childlike glee. He'd been using some kind of accelerator to test out a theory about reducing the effect of acceleration, which he called g-force. Even though his experiments had not lead to any breakthroughs, Ari had told him that the accelerator they'd built was a fantastically useful tool.

He could accelerate a small cylinder up to a hundredth of the speed of light and he did precisely that to the unfortunate tomatoes. The acceleration was akin to what Valko would experience. Suffice to say, the results were demonstrated by the decision to have tomato soup for the last meal before departure. Ari had assured him that the acceleration couches would protect their occupants from the forces, albeit even they had a limit.

Impressed with the possibility of being turned into red, human puree, Valko didn't complain when he was submerged into the couch. It was a lot easier to enter it, knowing that when he woke up some six-point-six hours later, he'd be back on the Mother.

There was a countdown — something of a tradition according to the scientists — and then the vessel shot out of Apollo Station's docking bay. Satoshi and Valko were the only people on board, save for the naukara — Rupert and Tristan.

Ari's incongruous choice of names for them had come from some of the Philosopher's old school friends, whom he described as having even fewer braincells than the poor naukara. The names made the fearsome metal giants seem more human, and Satoshi confided in Valko that he was beginning to feel regret for the total disregard he'd had for the lives of enemy cyborgs.

He talked, in his low rumble of a voice, about how he'd never spared a thought for them, in the way he had the men and women soldiers he'd been forced to kill in battle. He said that he felt guilt but it was tempered by the knowledge that, for most of them, it would have been the best chance for release from the torment of their condition. Valko had stayed quiet — listening and holding back tears.

He'd tried to talk to Rupert but received no response. When he questioned Ari about it, he'd been granted a limited access code which would at least allow conversation. He needn't have bothered. It was almost impossible to get anything more than a status report out of the hulking creature. He kept trying to think of it as a man but he realised with sorrow that it was only partly true. Valko had challenged Ari on why they kept the naukara around in what must be a living hell.

'Yeah, we thought about ending it but there's more to them than you know. We gave them a choice: death or waiting until we can fix them some day. The ones you see are the ones that chose to wait. Look mate, it's horrible, but we really do think we can help them, it'll just take time. It's not like we haven't fiddled around with brains before.'

Further musing was cut off by the final envelopment of the acceleration couches. While the drug induced slumber began to take him, Valko had a mental image of the vessel streaking away in a burst of sudden acceleration, pushing the limits of its drive, with g-force so great that even the naukara were cocooned in protective devices. As he fell into the womblike embrace and warm darkness of the couch, Valko knew that, in the time it would take a transpod to fly halfway round the globe, they'd have returned to Earth's atmosphere and be setting down twenty miles out from Outpost Theta. His last thought was one name — Jean.

Chapter 13

The acceleration couches receded and Valko blinked at the bright light. Sparkles of pain blossomed inside his skull and his ribs felt bound in a steel cage. The injury from the earlier crash had been treated while he'd been comatose and he'd not even noticed it during his sojourn on Apollo Station but now it was making itself known.

Satoshi was the first out of his couch. He looked none the worse for wear — the benefits of extensive physical augmentation with synthorganics and retrogening, Valko thought sourly.

'Thanks for the ride, boys,' Satoshi said to the naukara, both of whom turned their blank metallic masks in his direction but otherwise gave no response.

The outer hatch popped and Satoshi bounded down it; Valko followed, his body stiff. Trying to look back at the vessel was no help for Valko's headache — the exterior skin shimmered and shifted making his eyes fight to focus on it. He turned away and began to make for the nearest ridgeline.

They were back in the mutilated landscape of North America, twilight closing in and a dirty rain, turbid with chemicals, pattering off their envirosuits. Far from the centre of any burn-zone, at least. He could spot signs of lichen on the rocks in the dimming light: life fighting its way back from the brink, with unthinking tenacity.

'Oshi, can you see any sign of a Martyr's settlement?' He asked, the sergeant already at the crest of the ridge.

'There's a couple of light sources about a mile away. We could get there before full dark, if you're willing.'

'The sooner we get to the Outpost the better. We need to locate Jean.'

Valko wheezed as he joined Satoshi; his breathing was difficult with the soreness in his ribs. There was a low vibration and they both turned to watch the vessel that had brought them back rise on a column of shimmering air. It was hard to see where the air ended and the vessel began. Before his eyes could adjust, the craft shot into the sky and vanished from sight, leaving a vortex of swirling rain in its wake.

'Will you ever return to them, Val?' Satoshi asked, sounding almost wistful.

'I don't know. Probably not. I don't think I have enough time to do everything I need to as it is,' Valko said, his face grim. 'But they're good people, I think. Maybe they'll have a part to play in fixing all that's wrong here.'

'You believed them?' Satoshi asked.

'Yes… they were telling us what they believed to be true. I think what I was brought up to believe isn't true but I don't know. I can't fully shake off the Temple indoctrination. I can't stop feeling that we're unworthy of this world, but I think I can see that we're not some plague on it. Come on, old friend, we've a long way to go and you may need to carry me before the end.'

'Are you alright?' Satoshi's voice was filled with concern, his previous ebullience evaporating.

'Yes, Oshi — it's only my ribs. Nothing wrong up here a good night's sleep won't cure,' Valko said, touching a hand to his head.

They walked off into the gloaming, a chill wind beginning to blow around them. The light source ahead reminded Valko of the familiar glow of low thermal output lighting used in the Plena, not the flickering of a fire that might indicate they were approaching a Remnant camp. Out here, there was little chance that they were approaching anything other than a Martyr's preserve.

The landscape remained harsh and barren but it lacked the deep, petrified ripples that indicated the use of a flashburner. Here, the land was merely broken. Something brushed against his right boot. Bending, he saw that he'd walked through some scrubby grass; though it was robbed of most of its colour in the dark, he could tell it was the green of wakened life. A sure sign of a Martyr's work.

Valko felt a little nervous, a prickling up the back of his neck even — he'd never met a Martyr before. Would they live up to their reputation as paragons of the virtues espoused by the Temple? Self-sacrificing and caring nothing for their personal wellbeing, each Martyr placed their duty to the Mother above all other considerations. Not one had ever come to his attention as a suspect. Even when he'd been investigating smuggling into the

Plena, there'd never been Martyr involvement in the crime.

Given his newfound insight into the realities of the world, post-Enclosure, Valko wondered whether he'd think the Martyrs tragic in their naivety or still heroic.

†††

The ground crawler continued its slow trundle back to Outpost Theta. Night was beginning to close in and Davidson was pissed off. The journey had taken far longer than he'd expected. At one point, he'd found himself coaxing the old vehicle up a steep rise only to realise that the timer on the nanodestroyer container had finished. He'd panicked — was he still in range of a stray gust of wind and an excruciating death? — and had sat sweating for several minutes, the only sound the grinding of the crawler's gears as it inched its way upwards.

Death had not blown his way and he'd eventually relaxed back into the boredom of the slow crawl back to the Outpost. It would have been quicker to get out and fucking walk, but, of course, doing so would be riskier. In the end, his inherent laziness had prevented him from even considering the hike when he could get away with sitting in the old vehicle he'd requisitioned.

With the controls to automatic for several hours, he spent time catching up on an old vid he'd saved to his datapad. The black market emulator — he'd squeezed it out of a Hotbed dream seller — produced a fuzzy image and jerky sound, but it was a story he'd watched countless times before and it comforted him. For maybe the fiftieth time, he was swept up in the investigation of a group of unorthodox police officers attempting to trap a cunning gang of narc dealers. Shit, he'd always loved this vid. There was one, an Irish cop, he really liked. So many times, he'd wished he had that guy's easy charm and way with the ladies.

It all derailed: the damn automatic controls were shot and after two hours, he'd realised that he'd taken a circuitous route set to avoid obstacles that weren't even there anymore. Cursing Davidson had taken over on manual again and was now bored out of his sordid little mind.

Boredom that he shook off when the radio crackled to life.

'Jack, can you hear me?' Hampton's precise tones cracked out, near deafening in the crawler's cabin.

He dialled down the gain on the radio then answered 'Yes ma'am. You're coming through clear. What can I do you for?'

'I take it you're on your way back?' She said.

'Yes, ma'am. With bells on.'

'Jack, you'd better not have been drinking. Snap out of whatever childish daydream you're having and focus. Does your datapad have signal?'

The smile wiped off his face, Davidson pulled out the datapad and checked.

'Yes, ma'am. Receiving your transmission on it as well: fives.'

'Good. Switch it to beacon tracking mode.'

'Sure thing, ma'am. Are you going to tell me why?'

'It seems your Moderator and his Sergeant are on their way to the Outpost,' she said.

'What? What the fuck do you mean they're on their way to the Outpost? I thought they were fucking dead!' He couldn't help raising his voice as panic set it: they were deep in the shit now.

'Calm down, Jack — remember who you're talking to. Now, they're not there yet. Perhaps, there's time for a little… reunion,' Hampton said.

'You want me to grab them? Fat chance I'm going to get the drop on Satoshi.'

'No, you idiot,' Hampton said. 'If you can't do it at range, then you meet them and make it seem like your rescue attempt is genuine. We'll have to find a way of resolving things, before they can report to the Old Man. If you do get a chance, you know what to do?'

'Listen, ma'am, we've talked about this. I'm no murderer,' Davidson said, though he was beginning to doubt those words. Would Chang say different — that covering up for a killer was as bad as being one?

'Don't be a fool, Jack. If it's you or them you'll do what you have to. I'm telling you: it's you or them. Understand?' Her voice snapped at him, the gain on the radio jumping upwards once more.

'Yes, ma'am,' He said, cowed by her anger.

†††

Valko and Satoshi approached the small cluster of buildings as night fell. The light from within the largest of the structures still glowed its steady cold light out of the windows — their smart plastic doing little to add cosiness to its harsh glare. Each structure conformed to the basic modular design the Plena used for temporary structures but there were signs of considerable wear.

An occasional clatter came from within and the sound of a male voice talking too low for Valko to hear. Satoshi listened for a moment, then raised his hand with one finger held up. One occupant — so who was he talking to?

Deciding that the best way to get assistance was the straightforward and honest approach, Valko pulled off his hood and walked towards the door to knock on it. He was about a couple of metres away from it, when an alarm sounded and strong spotlights dazzled in his face.

A moment later, he heard the sound of a gun cocking and a stern voice said, 'There're no easy pickings here for you, friend. Only a face full of steel'

Valko held up both his hands, rain coursing down his face, hoping that Satoshi didn't choose this moment to be rash.

'I'm a Moderator from the Plena hunting a criminal. I ask for your aid, Holy One.' He hoped he'd kept enough sincerity in his tone.

'Moderator are you? Then tell your hulking companion to step out into the light, where I can see him,' the voice said.

'Oshi, do as he says.'

Valko's eyes had adjusted to the bright lights enough for him to make out the shape of a man holding a large frag gun pointed straight at him. A twitch of the man's trigger finger and he'd be… tomato soup.

Satoshi stepped to the edge of the illumination — keeping his movements smooth and slow — and extended both hands into it showing that they were empty. After a short pause, he took a careful step forward.

'That's far enough!' The man never took his eyes from

Valko's. 'Now, lie down with your hands clasped behind your head, while I talk to the Moderator here.'

Satoshi did as he was told, prostrating himself on the wet earth. Valko felt a flash of frustration flow over him from Satoshi — his sergeant was seething.

'Now, Moderator, tell me your name.'

'Valko Gangleri, Tantei Plena Orbum, V R seven, six, one, nine break gamma. I report to Pravnik Odegebayo. This man is my Sergeant Satoshi Tomari. We are in pursuit of a murderer who killed Dr Eugene Fisher and an assistant of his.'

A slow trickle of sweat had stared to weave its way down the side of his face — Mother's Tears, he hoped it wouldn't be taken as a sign that he was lying.

'And you've come all the way out here to find him, this murderer?' The frag gun wavered for a moment. 'You don't look like Remnants. I suppose you'd better come in, but try anything and you'll meet my friend here again. Understand?'

'Yes, thank you. We won't give you any trouble.' Valko exhaled, his tension draining away as he regained his equilibrium.

'You already have, I've burned my damn supper now because of you.'

The man, Valko could see him now as he walked out of the glare of the lights, was grizzled in the way of someone who'd spent long hard years at the mercy of the elements. He still carried himself upright and with pride, despite the grey in his beard and an obvious pain in his hip.

'We're sorry,' Valko said, as Satoshi stood and dusted himself off. The scowl on the big man's face did not look sorry in the slightest, but he kept silent.

'It's alright. Living out here makes me less than trusting, but I can see that you are from the Plena. Come in out of the rain and I'll try to bring life back into the food I've cremated.'

The man's voice was soft and clear, not the rasp that might have fitted his face. He had a slight accent to it that reminded Valko of old recordings of United American broadcasts.

'Holy One,' Valko said, following the man inside the small hut.

'Don't "Holy One" me, young man. Martyrs are holy because they're supposed to give their lives to the cause. I'm still here, after more than twenty years. Guess that means I'm not as holy as my late brethren now, don't you think?'

'I, uh, don't know what to think, uh, Holy, er. What should I call you then?' Valko asked.

'I used to be known as Shen. Names don't mean as much when you're all on your own. Pass me that pot there — the one with the herbs in it. Yes, that's the one.'

Valko had half expected to hear Shen say herbs without the 'h', the way that the United Americans had. It might have been a sign that he'd gone native after extensive contact with the Remnants, who still spoke in the old language of their land, corrupted only a little by time and circumstance. Shen's accent was curious but not such a clear indicator: it was slight. Some contact with the Remnants was to be expected and, given how little other human contact Shen would have had, was explanation enough for a shift in his accent over the years. Had his fundamental way of pronouncing words changed, it would have been a cause for concern.

The smell of the cooking food was enticing. It hadn't been cremated, instead, the overcooking had deepened its flavour. When served in simple bioplastic bowls, the food — which turned out to be a root stew with other vegetables Valko had never seen before — was delicious. Even after the meals he'd eaten on Apollo station, this food was something special. It conjured images of a different way of life, of living with the land. Food grown more nourishing for the spirit than the, almost clinical, gardens on the space station could produce — as if the act of digging in the dirt was communion with the Mother.

Valko, not used to excess, found himself feeling stuffed; the satisfied groan from Satoshi told a similar tale of gluttony.

'Nothing like home cooking, is there?' Shen asked. He was filling up a second bowl with more of the flavoursome stew. 'It might seem a tough life out here, and it is, but there are plenty of compensations.'

'The side of Martyrdom they don't teach in the Temple,' Satoshi said, his lips quirking.

'Perhaps, if they did, it'd be easier for people to dedicate themselves to achieving holiness,' Valko said, falling back into the comfortable familiarity of the Temple's doctrine after so much recent soul-searching.

Shen almost choked on a mouthful of the food, though whether it was from laughter or disgust, Valko couldn't tell.

After Satoshi pounded the martyr on the back and received a disgruntled dismissal from him, Shen said, 'There's more to this world and being in touch with the Mother than you'll ever learn in the Temple. This life teaches you some different lessons. Either that or you wind up dead within a month.'

'What do you mean?' Valko asked.

'Well, first you have to learn to co-exist with the Remnants. Not too closely mind, but not immediately shoot them on sight. Then you have to realise that you're not going to achieve anything by dying for a patch of irradiated soil. So you find somewhere that's not too bad. Take it slow. Make sure there's no tendency for fallout or the wind whipping up a dust storm and blowing in some nanodestroyers. That's when you make a planting. Small at first, saving your precious seeds and not using too much of the g-bacteria for restoring the soil. Then when you've got some life back into the ground, that's when you expand. Never too fast.'

'Why not?' Valko asked.

'Because if you waste all your seeds and bacteria you've got no way of growing more. Supply runs might keep you alive for a short while, but those bastards will quickly cut you off if they realise you're relying on them because you've wasted your resources. Hell, the only thing to do then, is go Remnant or starve.'

'The Temple cuts off your supplies? Are you sure? We're all taught that you're to be treated with the greatest respect and always aided if you ask,' Valko said.

Satoshi snorted in derision, his views on the Temple had never changed.

'I've seen it, Valko. Most of us are sent out in small groups, supposed to work within a certain distance of each other for support and to give each of us a better chance of survival. Sometimes, people stay close but that's rare. When you're fresh out here — all those sermons about sacrifice and the pollutant that is humanity still echoing in your ears — it's hard to choose to be around other people at all.' His voice took on the tone of one chosen for the daily recitation in the Temple, *'And know, as you walk in valleys that echo with the Mother's pain, bear with you your righteous fury at humanity. For in your passion you will know her suffering and so renew the sacred compact that you so callously sundered.'* Shen shook his head. 'That's what they send you out hearing, believing so you feel it in your bones but it soon changes. Anyway where was I?'

'You were just explaining that you'd seen it happen,' Satoshi said.

'Yes, that's right, I was. Yes, there's sometimes those who can't take it. Reality sets in too quick, or not fast enough, and they either go crazy with despair or else throw themselves into the fight with too much fervour. In my group, there was one like that. He kept on and on, chanting all the sutras and stayed far out from the rest of us. Then we'd start seeing the supply drops to his Project. They were coming frequently, right up until they stopped.

After a week, when the rest of us had met up to check on each other and he'd not shown, we went to see him. He'd used all his supplies trying to bring back this toxic stretch of land. Even the g-bacteria couldn't handle it. He'd restocked on seeds and bacteria five times, never food for himself. Been starving for days and near incoherent from dehydration. Anyway, they must've figured out he was wasting the seeds and cut him off.'

'What happened to him?' Valko asked.

'We tried to take care of him but he ran away from us. We found him crouching over the same patch of ground, clawing at it with his bare hands. He wouldn't be helped. You can guess the rest, I'm sure.' Shen sighed and straightened up. 'Now, what can I do to help you on your way?'

'We need shelter for the night, then maybe you can tell us the best way to Outpost Theta without encountering any Remnant activity,' Valko said.

'Alright, Outpost Theta. You know, I remember when that was first built. That was why so many of us were sent here then: they thought we'd create a buffer against the Remnants, at least, that's what I think now. Anyway, shelter and directions and maybe a hot breakfast too, if you're lucky.'

Shen stood and showed them to a storage area. There was a pile of packaging material for protecting crops in winter, which he told them would make tolerable beds.

'I'm sorry but I'm not used to visitors, save those that I keep at the end of a frag gun during their stay.'

'This will do fine, Holy… I mean Shen,' Valko said.

They soon settled in for the night after making a couple of makeshift beds from the material and some supply crates dated over ten years previous — Shen really had survived off the land for as long as he claimed.

†††

Davidson neared the small cluster of buildings. It didn't look like a Remnant dwelling but more like something produced with Plenum tech.

'Shit,' he whispered to himself, as if half expecting to be heard.

Unless this place was abandoned, there was one possibility that made any sense: Valko and Satoshi were sheltering with a Martyr. Davidson used a scope to examine the buildings. If they were deserted, it must have been recent, given the apparent age of the structures. They were too well preserved to have been left unoccupied for long. Besides, in this dark there was little chance that those bastards would have stumbled across the place by accident. They must have been drawn there by the light, which he'd first noticed more than a mile away.

This was going to make things complicated. Maybe, he could pick off one of the bastards when they left; he'd make it Satoshi. Then disappear and track Gangleri's signal until he was well away from this place, out where it would be easier to deal with the arrogant prick.

Davidson's stomach churned at the thought of the double murder he was contemplating. Could he do it? Even if his life depended on it? It'd been one thing to wish them ill and be satisfied at the likelihood of their deaths but killing his two superiors? When he'd found Chang's corpse, the reality of what had happened and what he found himself involved in had begun to sink in. Now — faced with a do or die situation — that reality was showing its teeth.

He'd driven the ground crawler partway up a ridge, noticing that the signal he was pursuing had been heading deeper into a zone of low radiation and — even more reassuring — zero nano traces. Using the crawler's upper scope to peek over the brow of the hill, he'd seen the small cluster of buildings.

Now, he lay on his belly with his rifle resting on a short stand. So maybe he was no sniper and had never performed better than average at the firing range, but he could do this, if he just concentrated. In conditions outside a Plenum it'd be harder shooting at any target over short range — what was it the instructors said about windage and the rate at which a projectile might drop as it sped to its target? He couldn't remember, hadn't paid attention, to be honest. It was simple anyway, a slug left a gun and travelled in a dead straight line to wherever he aimed it — that's how it worked within the Plena. Tranqguns had high accuracy at the short ranges needed — a rifle was meant for shooting outside, so it would just be the same. His first shot would blow the head off whomever he targeted; he didn't need any of that pre-Enclosure tech that would have done all the targeting for him. No, the rifle had a retractable scope that would allow a competent shooter, like him, a fair degree of accuracy. Such a shooter, whether a true sniper or not, wouldn't need to test fire the gun, bother cleaning it or muck about adjusting the sights to their own preferences and the anticipated range and prevailing weather conditions. Pre-Enclosure tech would have done it all on automatic and included guided ammunition, but he didn't need it. None of these things applied to Jack Davidson — he just needed to point and shoot.

He waited, left eyelid twitching away, expecting his quarry to leave with the sunrise. Gangleri had always been a stickler for a full working day for both himself and his subordinates. Satoshi probably hadn't even needed to sleep. *Freak*. An extra ration of coffeine had keyed Davidson up and kept him alert. The stuff was making him twitchy — it tweaked his nerves and added a definite shake to his hands.

There was a low creak from the main building and its door swung open; it was caught by the wind and banged against the wall.

'This is it, Jack,' he said to himself. 'You a man or a mouse?' Stupid fucking question, he was a man, goddammit.

Satoshi exited followed by Valko, an old man a step or two behind. They moved out from the building and stopped. The old man began pointing off into the distance. He was standing about three metres closer to the open door than Valko, who had

Satoshi to his left. Davidson aimed at Satoshi, not thinking about centre mass but going for the impressive headshot, like the gunmen in the vids might do.

Big breath — squeeze the trigger. He looked up straightaway to see the result of his shot: a combination of nausea and triumph warred within him — the head had exploded and the body fell to the floor. It was only then that he saw that he'd missed Satoshi, missed Valko and killed the old man.

Davidson watched, his balls trying to shrink back up inside him, as Satoshi reacted to the shot, throwing himself down and dragging Valko with him. Davidson could see him scan around, looking over at the ridge as if close to guessing where the shot had come from but waiting, probably hoping the shooter would give himself away. But locating a single unexpected shot from range and with a strong wind was beyond even that freak. There sure as shit wasn't going to be a second shot.

Davidson rolled onto his back.

'What have I done?' He sobbed to himself.

He'd killed a Martyr — fuck, oh fuck. He half expected the ground to open up and devour him, so great was his sin. Then self-preservation set in — Satoshi was a veteran and would be coming for him. Davidson knew that there was no way that he could take the freak on up close. Keeping low below the ridgeline Davidson, scurried to the crawler and disengaged the brakes allowing the vehicle to roll away downhill before gunning the engine and hoping Satoshi couldn't hear it.

††††

When no further shot came, they stood up slowly, Satoshi doing a quick visual search, hunting for signs of a sniper. His senses were straining for any giveaway, but whoever had fired the shot must have slipped away. When they'd been lying on the ground, he'd felt a distant rumble — maybe a vehicle of some sort? Whatever it had been, there was no sign now within his sight or hearing.

'Poor old Shen must have fallen foul of the Remnants after all,' Valko said. There was an openness in his face, that Satoshi couldn't remember seeing before.

'I'm not so sure, Val. Why not wait until we left then eliminate him? Maybe this was a warning to us.'

'From who, Oshi? No one could know we were out here.'

'Unless they could track our beacons,' Satoshi said. 'It wouldn't take much to locate the signal even if it couldn't be decrypted.'

'Ah, you don't think it's the same person or group that shot down the transpod?' Valko asked.

His tone had become familiar — so much so that even in a moment like this, Satoshi couldn't help but feel the difference in Valko. He'd finally become the person Satoshi had always hoped lay buried in him — the fossil of a real human locked in permafrost. But at what cost?

'I suppose so,' Satoshi said. 'Though they keep missing us. And I'm pretty sure we were blown up and not shot down.'

'It'd fit what she told me,' Valko said. 'She said she wanted me alive.'

'Yeah, but if it was a bomb, maybe she or someone working with her would have had the skill to just knock us out of the air. Give us no choice but to follow through to the bunker.'

'Maybe, Oshi. Maybe.'

'So this. Could it be Jean, finally deciding that you're too much trouble to keep alive?'

'Thanks for that.'

'Sorry, Val. You know what I mean. She must have already hacked Plenum security — she could find us out here with our beacons.'

'But why would she kill Shen, except by accident?' Valko asked. 'Everything we know about her points to a reason for her actions, albeit with a tendency to react emotionally. Besides, she seemed a bit more competent than this — if she was trying to kill me, I don't think she'd have missed. I don't see how Shen could have provoked that reaction from her and I don't see what she could stand to gain from his death.' Valko looked over at the corpse of Shen. 'I suppose he truly is a Holy Martyr now. Come on, whoever did this may have gone but we'd best not stay around long enough for them to come back.'

'What about his project? All those years of hard work?' Satoshi asked, affected by the old man's death more than he was willing to show. Not all true adherents to the Temple's creed were bad, he'd learned too late.

'We'll report it when we return. Perhaps they'll send another Martyr to take over,' Valko said. 'Whatever else, he brought life back to lifelessness and it'll continue in one way or another without him. Help me with him.'

'What are we going to do?' Satoshi asked.

'I think a shallow grave is the best we can give him, and it would accord with his beliefs, giving back to the Mother even in death.'

They found some tools and dug a shallow grave before placing Shen within. There was no need to fear scavenging animals — Satoshi doubted that any could be found within a hundred miles, but regardless, time was against them with an unseen opponent dogging their steps.

†††

'You did WHAT?' Hampton screeched.

'I was aiming for Satoshi. I've never shot anyone before, not for real. It happened. Must be something wrong with the damn rifle.'

'Listen to me very carefully, Jack. Tell no one else about this or there will be no saving you from the most agonising death imaginable. I will keep your dirty little secret but you WILL KILL GANGLERI!' The transmission cut off.

Davidson sat there sweating in his seat. He didn't know why he'd told her — he must be out of his goddamn mind — but panic had overtaken his mouth and it had spilled out. Now, what was he supposed to do?

A ping from the beacon locator attracted his attention. Gangleri and Satoshi had moved off and were making good time towards the Outpost. Despite his grumbling about the speed of the crawler, it could still move faster. If he could get ahead of them, maybe he could meet them coming the other way — make it look like a rescue. Mind made up, he gunned the engine and moved off on an intercept course.

Chapter 14

Valko stretched and pulled off the hood of his envirosuit, running a hand along the scars on his head. The source of all his trouble. Right now, though, he had more immediate problems. Satoshi bustled about setting up a makeshift camp. They'd run out of options.

After half a day of hiking through the broken landscape, they'd come close to stumbling into a nanodestroyer burn-zone. At the last minute, their envirosuits had triggered a warning and they'd sprinted away before the concentration of micro machines could increase to dangerous levels. Valko could still feel tension curled around his shoulders, its weight a snake waiting to strangle him. Now, they had the dilemma of which way to circle around the area. Without better detectors, they'd be stuck having to guess a safe direction and then hope to the continued efficacy of their envirosuits.

It'd started an argument about what to do. Tired, hungry and suffering with his ribs — Valko was in no mood for a challenge to his authority. So he'd ordered Satoshi to get on with the camp, while he thought of a solution. Only none was coming.

There was a crackle of fire, Satoshi had managed to collect enough dried roots and dead vegetation to cook some of the rations that they'd been given by Shen. Valko gave up all pretence of problem solving and slumped down by the pitiful campfire. Satoshi handed him a bowl — some reheated vegetable mush. Each mouthful brought the old martyr to mind and Valko imagined exacting revenge on his murderer. He didn't need to look at Satoshi's grim expression to know his Sergeant was sharing his thoughts of retribution — the stink of anger was coming off him in waves. There was little chance they could ever identify the perpetrator and if it'd been Remnants there was no chance at all. Still it couldn't have been Jean, she…

Satoshi stiffened, before rolling to his feet in a half crouch, omni-pistol drawn.

'What is it?' Valko whispered.

'I can hear an engine, sounds like it's getting closer to us.'

Valko drew his tranqgun — though what use it would do against a vehicle, he didn't know. He strained his ears and realised he could also hear the rumble of an engine, getting louder. After an anxious minute, the vehicle came into view: it was a battered, archaic ground crawler coming towards them from the general direction of the Outpost.

It must have circled the burn-zone but Valko could see that it'd been in encounters with nanodestroyers in the past. Sections of its hull plating were abraded in a pattern familiar to any who'd seen the work of the nanites. From its markings, the vehicle was clearly from Outpost Theta and, before it came to a stop in front of them, he recognised the pouchy, screwed up face of Jack Davidson peering out through the scratched and pitted windscreen.

Davidson exited the vehicle, holding a rifle and searching the horizon for threats. He looked almost... competent.

Turning to Valko, he said, 'Glad to see you made it, Boss. We were all worried when you disappeared — no radio contact. You alright?'

'Jack, it's such a relief to see you,' Valko said, actually meaning it.

He couldn't help but feel some amusement at the expression on the man's face at hearing such warm words. It felt good not to be so predictable anymore.

'Well done, Jack,' Satoshi said, though he was plainly more pleased to see the ground crawler than the man.

'Look, you'd better get on board so we can get out of here. The weather monitoring station at the Outpost is reporting an approaching dust storm. There's a hot zone not too far away from here and we don't want to be here if the storm blows those little machine bastards this way.' Davidson gestured to the open door of the ground crawler.

'Jack, are you alright?' Valko asked. There was a high level of tension in the man evident to Valko almost as a static charge surrounding Davidson.

'Yes, Boss. I'm just want to get out of here and back to the Outpost.'

They entered the cramped confines of the crawler and Davidson settled himself into the driver's chair. He leant his rifle to one side and started off. The crawler's engine coughed and spluttered; Davidson gave it more power and the crawler leapt away. It wasn't enough acceleration to provide more than a lurch but that was all it took to make the rifle fall to the floor of the cabin with a clatter. Davidson scrabbled for it but Satoshi reached over and picked it up.

'Davidson, you *baka*. Didn't you learn not to leave a loaded weapon leaning against things? If it had gone off the ricochet could've hit one of us,' Satoshi said.

Davidson was looking in terror at the rifle in Satoshi's hands. Valko wondered what was causing the strange reaction, sure that it couldn't be to the simple, and rather gentle, admonishment.

'It won't happen again, Sarge. Sorry.'

Davidson reached out and took the rifle from Satoshi with hands that trembled, before securing it beside him again. The strange behaviour wasn't lost on Satoshi either and he raised an eyebrow at Valko.

The shrilling of the crawler's alarm warning blared out before either could speak — they were approaching an area of nanodestroyer saturation. Davidson hurried to alter course and, once safely away, settled into the job of driving them back to the Outpost, his earlier panic seemed forgotten.

The three rode in silence for the couple of uneventful hours it took the crawler to roll through the broken landscape. Valko mused about his strange experiences and thought about Jean. A confusing mix of images arose in his mind whenever he contemplated her. Interrogating her often shifted to romancing her.

It was a struggle to get perspective. As his thoughts shifted this way and that, Valko found himself studying Satoshi. It was a simple thing, unforced, to feel the surface concerns running through his friend's mind — no, said his old ego, reasserting itself for an unexpected moment: not friend, subordinate. This was not quite like the mind-to-mind contact of an interview but more like… an echo. Satoshi was thinking about Sadiq and worrying about what Iona might have done in his absence: with the boy and the Temple. He was imagining his son growing up to become someone like Shen and the thought was filling him with sadness.

The insight faded, and Valko closed his eyes, letting the

tension that had coiled round him ease off. He didn't bother turning his seer's gaze on Davidson, the man — so long a minor irritant to him — had now slipped into a different role in Valko's mind. The harmless, well-meaning — if somewhat incompetent — underling.

┼┼┼

Davidson had far more immediate concerns. In between berating himself for allowing his weapon to fall into Satoshi's hands — then the rush of watery churning in his bowels as he thought that the veteran would recognise it as the weapon that had shot at him — his weasel mind was conjuring scenarios where he could get away with killing these two. All of his ideas were fanciful and, as the landscape began to show signs of green life — a sure sign of the approach to the Outpost — his calm began to crack.

Hampton now had the justification to order his immediate execution and the only awkward question would be: what was he doing outside the Plena in the first place? The explanation that he'd been sent to recover his superiors, then had chosen to attempt their murder, might raise a few eyebrows but he didn't think that it'd lead to an investigation that could threaten her. On the other hand, if he tried to pop Gangleri and failed, or didn't deal with Satoshi, his life expectancy would be as short. What about confiding in them, instead of trying to kill them? They'd want to know that Hampton was gunning for them, wouldn't they? How would he explain killing the old man, who'd obviously been a Martyr? If he admitted that much to Gangleri, he knew he was a dead man — no matter any other explanation he might give. Could he conceal it from them yet still get their help? What could he tell them anyway?

If he told them everything else he'd done, they'd kill him. He didn't even know why Hampton wanted Gangleri dead: he didn't have a clue as to her motivations. Then the solution popped into his head. It was so blindingly obvious, he had to stop himself from slapping his forehead. He'd do what he had to: kill them if he got a real chance. But, if the chance came to point the Moderator and his freak sergeant at Hampton — subtly mind you — he'd take it instead. Serve that ice-cold bitch right for screwing with Jack Davidson. His certainty held for the space of a few pounding heartbeats then — like every confident, joyous moment in his life — it was subsumed back into the turmoil of churning doubt at his core.

†††

Within a further two hours, Outpost Theta reared into sight. Valko gazed at the structure as they approached: so different in form from the Plena.

He checked himself; looking at the structures had been his concession to curiosity the first dozen times he'd flown between the Plena. Crowded transpods had few windows, if any, yet he'd fought to get a view. Then it'd all become mundane.

'Looks so much better than the Plena, doesn't it?' Satoshi said, looking up at the silvered needlepoint that almost pierced the clouds.

'You know I'm not so sure,' Valko said. 'I mean they all look different from each other — almost organic.'

'Yeah, but Arcas aside, they all look like some kind of toxic fungus.'

Valko laughed. 'Would you rather live in an Outpost, Oshi? I can put in a transfer for you if you'd like…'

'Er, no thanks, Val. They're not exactly safe are they?'

'They're not so bad compared to being outside.'

'That's temporary though. I wouldn't want to bring up Sadiq in one of these.'

Satoshi fell silent and Valko left him to think about his son. *Must be nice having children.* Where the hell had that come from?

Fleeing the dangerous thoughts of parenthood, Valko looked again at the Outpost. Until now, feelings of curiosity had fallen away. Like everything else, he'd ceased to give a damn about life beyond the needs of the job. Until now.

The satisfaction of curiosity for curiosity's sake — not just in service of his overwhelming need for the truth — was a pleasure he'd long forgotten. That old serpent of his mind — the snake coiled around his heart that had kept it choked, unable to truly feel — still hissed at his preoccupation but it was just a small part of him now, not the greater part as for so long before.

So he looked with fresh eyes on the towering majesty of the Outpost. Nearly finished, it had its silvered exterior coating — electrostatically charged to repel low-level saturations of nanodestroyers — covering its lower three quarters. Without the final mirror coating, Outpost Theta's top third looked as if it had been blackened by the touch of flame. Without the almost living skin of the Plena, which could heal punctures or breaks, the Outposts required thousands of maintenance hours. But the differences ended when you dug beneath the skin. The internal organs of each Plena were like the Outposts: a far more primitive set of systems.

Set against the way the Plena had sprouted around old world city centres, this construction was slow. The loss of the Plena technology — matter stripped apart at the molecular level and repurposed into hyper-resilient structures in mere days — was costing more than just time and resources. Blood had been spilt and lives lost by the thousand for every one of these splinters driven into the land.

It all came back to the Temple. The cost of building each outpost lowered the quality of life of every human on the planet but, by having a foothold in areas that were a great distance from the nearest Plena, they could spread their efforts to heal the Mother's wounds and find new areas for Martyrs to find their Holy Martyrdom. Once he would have thought nothing of the cost in lives, in suffering, that the Temple's singlemindedness entailed. Now, he found it hard to comprehend how anyone could condemn so many to agonising deaths or deny so many children life's necessities just to resurrect a few square kilometres of ground.

He sighed. Like Satoshi, he wasn't relishing the thought of spending time in an Outpost. The difference was that for him fear of the places had been programmed into him since childhood. After trekking through the barrens of North America on foot, it should feel trivial. Yet, knowing he'd soon be in a structure barely able to keep out the threats of radiation, airborne toxins and the swift winged death of nanodestroyers kept nagging at him. It felt like he was surrendering his own luck, his own fate, to take on the fate of the Outpost. Sharing in its story, when so many Outposts had been lost without warning over the decades since Enclosure.

The crawler started to pick up speed, encountering fewer and fewer obstacles, as it entered the cleared space around the Outpost, which now reared above them so that it was hard to believe its tip didn't truly pierce the sky. They drove into an opening in the side of the shiny metallic spire and Valko felt a mixture of relief and distress at once more being Enclosed.

He'd heard of many Plena dwellers who'd suffered uranophobia from being beneath the limitless sky — feeling that an angry deity frowned down on them with malign intent. Echoes of past beliefs surfaced from time to time. The Temple would crush the occasional throwback — a group practising teachings of a God outside the Mother. But the fear persisted. For him, there'd been no such dread: only the pleasure of feeling his vision, so long constrained, stretched by distant vistas.

Within minutes, they entered the communications centre within the Outpost and Valko requested a link to Pravnik Odegebayo. He psyched himself up for the inevitable close probing he'd endure from the Old Man — he could keep the most unusual aspects of his recent experiences secret, he had to.

It wasn't that he'd lie, but he would fail to mention the extraordinary trip to Apollo station and his own inner journeying. They had nothing to do with the case and he didn't want Odegebayo to doubt either his sanity or his loyalty. Besides, if he mentioned anything about having a terminal condition related to his implant, the Old Man would take him off the case in an instant. If he were really unlucky, he'd find himself sedated and surrounded by whitecoats desperate to run tests on him — tests he probably wouldn't survive or maybe wouldn't want to survive.

Instead of the expected hub link, the communications clicked on to a nearby monitor. To add to his surprise, it wasn't Pravnik Odegebayo on the screen.

'Pravnik Hampton. Forgive me, ma'am, for interrupting you… I was trying to contact Pravnik Odegebayo,' He said, trying to cover his surprise.

'Tantei Gangleri, so good to see you hale and hearty. We had begun to fear that your special talents were lost to us. I'm sorry to say that Pravnik Odegebayo is currently indisposed. I will be overseeing your investigation from this point forwards. You may give me your report.'

Despite her pleasant mien, Valko knew that Hampton was

at least as ruthless as Odegebayo and, unlike him, she was an unknown quantity. He began to deliver his report, informing her of their crash and the high likelihood that they'd been shot down — he kept his suspicions that they may not have been shot down so much as blown up to himself — the encounter at the pre-War bunker and his subsequent period of unconsciousness. He left out Satoshi's savage episode and any mention of the intervention by the Apollo scientists.

'Remarkable, Valko. How were you able to escape from the bunker?' Hampton's voice suggested genuine curiosity. She gave nothing else away.

'There was a high capacity cutting torch located in the bunker's storeroom. We were able to recharge it with Sergeant Tomari's omni-pistol energy cell. We were fortunate: the device only suffered terminal failure as we finished the final cut.'

Where had that come from? The ease of the lie — and the return to his formal tone — amazed him. Thankfully, Satoshi was standing beside him, just outside of the view of the monitor so the lie wouldn't need to be repeated for his friend to know what to say if questioned.

'Remarkable,' Hampton said again, this time making it sound almost as if she were using one of Davidson's choice phrases: bullshit. 'Do you have any further leads on your suspect? Any known associations?' The inflection of her voice had tightened by degrees and now held him vicelike.

'None that are clear at this time, ma'am. But I'll start by interrogating the other whitecoats who worked in Dr Fisher's laboratory. They may know something.

Ma'am, with respect, I think it is important for you to inform Pravnik Odegebayo that the motivation for the murders seems to have nothing to do with any action of a zealot. It may help ease his mind.'

'Yes, thank you, Valko. I will pass on your message to him, when he can receive it that is.'

Hampton reacted as if she grasped the import of his message, but Valko wondered whether it was a ploy in the hopes that, by feigning knowledge, she could coax him to reveal more. Either way, he would remain silent, unless otherwise ordered.

Hampton broke the link and only then did Valko see that Davidson was, like Satoshi, making an effort to listen in, while remaining out of sight of the monitor.

'Jack, can you arrange immediate transport for us back to Arcas Plenum?' Valko asked.

'Yes, Boss. Right away. The transpod I came on hasn't left yet, I'm sure we can get on board before it does.'

'Excellent. We need to get moving.' Davidson hurried off and Valko turned to face Satoshi. 'Oshi, we need to work out what the hell is going on here. Why is the Old Man indisposed? I don't like this sudden change. There's more going on than only Jean's crimes.'

'I think you're right, Val. We've got to be careful. If there's been a shift in power within the Centra Autorita, we may be walking into a very dangerous situation. The question is, is it Odegebayo who's making a move or Hampton?'

'You're right,' Valko said. 'But we need to focus on locating Jean. Once we have her in custody, we can think about what to do next, what to do with what we've learned.'

Valko stopped for a moment — his obsession with the woman was growing. It was far more than the hunt for a criminal, it was as if something had wormed down deep inside him and curled around his heart, where it spawned the emotions of another, a man not Valko but now living within him. This was different from the other changes wrought by his implant, the running on ice of his artificial soul gone haywire. This new sensation gnawed at him like a parasite, tainting all his motives.

†††

They set about readying themselves for the return trip. Paranoia made Valko order a restock of their envirosuit supplies and they took the opportunity to re-arm themselves. Satoshi selected a ballistic rifle for himself, the match of the one Davidson was carrying. Valko settled for a tranqgun. It should be a fast journey once they boarded the transpod but, in the meantime, Valko put on his headset and familiarised himself with reports from his kensakan, logged while he'd been lost. He noted, with some surprise, a high degree of diligence on Davidson's part in attempting to track them. The records suggested that he'd spent over ten hours a day on the process; Odegebayo must have ordered him to focus his efforts on their retrieval. Whatever had happened to the Old Man had taken place after Davidson had left to search for them.

The next item was a report from Rennard: he'd travelled to one of the main continental African Plena — Abuja Plenum. Moz Rennard had applied an unorthodox investigative approach by Valko's reckoning. He'd played a hunch, but it'd worked out and he'd solved an investigation that, in normal circumstances should've required a Moderator's input. Wonders would never cease. Even more surprising was that the records showed that he'd been looking into their disappearance in his free time before he'd been re-tasked. It didn't show who'd ordered the placement, which seemed a bit strange — Odegebayo's office would ordinarily note if he'd ordered a reassignment in the absence of a kensakan's supervising Sergeant.

Further introspection was interrupted by an urgent contact ping on the headset-hub. The source of the contact was hidden, which was more than a little unusual. He hesitated for a moment, before accepting the link.

«*Valko, you're alive! I was afraid you'd been killed.*»

It didn't seem possible but it was Jean, her words backed by a clear sense of genuine relief flowing through the link.

«*Jean? What do you want?*» He asked, mind reeling that she could contact him in this way and that she would dare to.

«*I'm sorry, Valko. I wanted to come back to the bunker to help you but I ran into some trouble. By the time I got free and came back with help, I found the door was cut and you and Satoshi were gone. I guess you must have triggered an SOS to my old colleagues. Next thing I know, you're back in the Outpost.*»

How the hell could she know we're here? Then Valko reconsidered, he and Satoshi had been lead into a trap by following Darius Actur. The signal had been boosted at the right time to send them chasing after him, leading them to the bunker just in time for Jean to swoop in. If she could accomplish that, she could track their beacons with ease. The question was, why claim otherwise? She was still radiating genuine concern and palpable pleasure at contacting him. Had she found a way to fake her emotions over the link? There didn't seem to be the delay he'd get from a Pravnik's link.

«*Listen to me,*» she sent. «*You mustn't go back to Arcas Plenum.*

Not yet. Things are happening there and I think you'll be walking into another trap.»

The nerve of the woman.

«*What should I do then Jean, trust you again?*» He asked, surprised at the bitterness in his tone that would be obvious to her even without a Moderator's implant.

«*I'm sorry I deceived you — lied about who I was. It was necessary. Look, I know I've given you no reason to trust me but I'm the only one who can help you. We're on the same side. Please, listen to me.*»

Her tone was pleading and waves of sincerity flowed behind her words. He detected something else, she was near terrified and it felt as if it was for him. Such a subtle degree of emotional content was hard to read over a standard link — hard enough with a direct mindlink — but he was sure that she was concerned for him, not for herself. His tone softened as the thread wound round his heart tightened.

«*Alright, Jean. Why don't you come to Outpost Theta and we can discuss this. I may be able to help you with the murder charge, if you can show that you had serious justification.*»

«*Murder? You think it was murder? Oh Valko, there's so much you don't understand.*»

«*Then explain it to me. Come here and talk me through it.*» Stimulated by her obvious concern for him, his own feelings towards her — nascent as they were — still thrilled through him. Behind them, easy to dismiss, came an echoing thought crying out in warning.

«*I can't come to you, Valko. You must understand it's what he'd want.*» Who was he? «*You'll have to meet me. It can't be near the Outpost for the same reasons but I can tell you an area to come to.*»

«*Next, you'll be telling me to come alone.*» He sneered, feeling foolish for beginning to believe in her.

«*No, of course not. You're not safe alone, not now. If Satoshi is no longer, oh, how to put it? If he's himself again, then bring him and someone else you trust. You'll need to be armed. I'll meet you in the lobby of the Empire State Building.*» The name was familiar, but for a moment he struggled with why — history had never been of interest to him. «*I promise I'll tell you everything if you'll trust me.*»

The coordinates for the structure came through the link to him.

«You want me to enter the New York burn-zone?» He asked, his incredulity rearing even as waves of emotion flooded through the mindlink — a stifling shroud over his doubts.

«Yes, there's a safe route, if you approach Manhattan over the water from the south. Valko, I've got to go, he's nearly tracked me. Remember, bring only someone you can trust.»

She broke the connection. There was no trace of the origin of the contact and no return contact details. He checked the hub's records of the link: it showed no evidence of a link having been made, only a string of digits giving him coordinates for the ruins she'd mentioned. Jean's grasp of technology, like that of the occupants of Apollo station, was far beyond his own.

†††

Against his better judgement, Valko decided that he had to take a chance on Jean. He'd spent a long time wondering whether it was just his testicles doing the talking but no, there was at least a strand of truth in what she'd been saying to him. It wasn't only the emotional undercurrent he'd read in her — emotions that seemed to push their way into him they were so strong — but also what she had said about the dangers of events taking place in Arcas Plenum. It triggered a feeling of unease within him, whenever he considered his contact with Hampton and the supposed absence of Odegebayo.

The Old Man had always seemed bulletproof. Medicine might not be today what it had been at its height eighty years ago but enough was still remembered that most natural diseases and conditions could be treated with retrogening. It was unlikely in the extreme that Odegebayo could have encountered toxins or nanodestroyers without the whole Plenum succumbing — something that hadn't happened since Sydney Plenum, back in the first year after Enclosure.

No, Odegebayo was destined to die of old age or misadventure. The former was still a fair way off, at least twenty years. Which left misadventure. It was beginning to add up. Something was going dangerously awry and he needed to return, in a position of strength. For that, he had to know what the hell was going on and Jean was his only current lead. Besides, they had unfinished business — of one sort and another — and there remained the faint hope that she could provide a cure for his condition.

Valko gave Satoshi the good news, expecting a long argument urging more caution but, to his surprise, the reaction he got was one of excitement, as if they were on a grand adventure. The return of old memories made Satoshi worry less — a more adventurous, less responsible part of his sergeant had reawakened. It had been with a guilty look that Satoshi had agreed to contact Iona and try to get information from her. She didn't answer, which was, Valko was beginning to realise, typical.

Given his recent efforts on their behalf, Valko had little trouble in deciding that Davidson should accompany them. That, and the fact that there was no one else to hand.

'Of course, Boss. Shouldn't we get backup first? We don't want to get caught with our asses hanging in the breeze if she's playing us.' He'd said, which Valko had interpreted to mean that Davidson thought this was a bad idea.

He was probably right but he'd only put up a feeble effort to persuade Valko to return to the Arcas Plenum first, seeming almost relieved when his arguments failed.

They retrieved the crawler before it was re-tasked and Valko requisitioned a set of pontoons to allow the amphibious crossing of the mouth of the Hudson River. Now, the standard warning on exiting the Outpost scrolled across the vehicle's HUD, a stark reminder of the danger Valko was leading them into, 'WARNING: you are now leaving a secure zone. Protective gear is advised at all times. Radioactive dust clouds have been detected within 12 km. Nanodestroyer contamination risk level: 07.49%.'

It'd been eerie accessing maps overlaid with names of landmarks which no longer existed and places where humans no longer went. The old records still showed a bustling metropolis; only some maps had been updated to reveal the truth of the landscape: blasted and barren. Where there'd been no reliable reconnaissance, old records remained unaltered — without satellites to provide an overview the true shape of the land was hidden.

On the old map of New York City Valko'd used to plan their route, the Empire State Building appeared amid a bustling city centre. He'd found recorded imagery from the street level, buried in the records, but it was the view from above that interested him most. A moment captured by satellites over eighty years before. The level of detail was astounding: he'd zoomed in to such an extent he could see figures on the 86th floor observation deck. There was a little girl pointing out at the view to a man beside her. A moment of innocent excitement at what must have been a fantastic view. He knew that if he could see out from that same observation deck now, all he'd see would be scorched ruins. An upwelling of sorrow for the loss of all that had gone before struck him for the first time in his life. Then followed a swift anger. If the Centra Autorita had been the UNWG and was responsible for the devastation, then he needed to do something to reveal the truth. He'd zoomed in to see the girl's upturned face as she looked at her father, nothing but joy in her expression. Tears had coursed down Valko's face.

†††

They rolled along old broken roads, pitted and cracked. Near to the Outpost there'd been signs of plant life breaking through the road surface but it stopped almost half a mile along. Now, they were driving along the cracked remains of Route 95, fast enough to kick up dust behind the crawler. The HUD displayed an overlay of old satellite data showing their route through built up areas and along a congested busy road. To one side, ghost vid images of the world as it had been displayed — a leftover from a past when every road could be travelled virtually. Now, it revealed how much had been lost.

At least we don't have to worry about the traffic, Valko thought.

The vehicle's engine was straining at its maximum speed and the miles were ticking by but time dragged as they sat in silence. Davidson was at the controls, focused on their course. Satoshi had his eyes closed and was lolling in his chair, asleep. Occasionally, his right hand would twitch, closing then opening and he'd mumble something. Valko envied him. He doubted that he'd dream if he closed his eyes. His nagging headache — as if there was too much pressure behind his eyes — wouldn't let him relax. Part of him feared it was the implant growing faster and putting pressure on the rest of his brain, but reason said that it was just tension. If he drifted off to sleep, would he find his mind expanding beyond its normal limits? Closing his eyes — lulled by the hum of the engine and the rocking of the cabin — he drifted off to sleep. For once, blessed rest was all that waited for him on the other side of consciousness.

┼┼┼

    Davidson glanced over his shoulder and saw them both sleeping: Valko curled up in his seat, Satoshi more sprawled in his. This was it, his perfect chance, but he couldn't leave the controls while the crawler was still moving. His last attempt to use the automated guidance system had proved its unreliability to him and the treacherous terrain to either side of the road made the risk of setting the crawler to automatic too great. At times, deep cracks in the old blacktop grew wide and filled with water that shimmered with pollutants; at others rents in the earth left ragged walls rearing out of the pitted asphalt. The on-board computer suffered too many glitches to be trusted not to plunge down the cracks or smash head on into obstacles. He could just picture it: standing over Satoshi; rifle aimed at the freak's head, ready to do it... Crash — the crawler smashing into something; Satoshi waking up and shoving the rifle somewhere the Sun don't shine.

    Better to stop, do it right. Hands shaking, Davidson began to ease off on the throttle. The humming sound in the cabin diminished to the barely audible. Satoshi began to stir. Davidson pushed the throttle back to maximum, and with an incoherent mumble, Satoshi drifted deeper into sleep once more.

    No, this wouldn't work either. He'd decided on the best solution and he'd see it through, as soon as they returned from this dumb fucking chase. A foul, hot rain began to fall — contaminated air returning poisons to the earth. Davidson turned his attention back to the road. A vague prickle at the back of his neck reminded him of the beacon buried there. It felt like Hampton had one sharp fingernail just tracing back and forth across his skin. He shuddered.

    After a couple more hours of travel, they left what remained of Route 95 at the New Jersey Turnpike and careened along the south bank of the Raritan River. They'd been cruising along but now their rate of progress dropped off. Ruined buildings were visible looming out of the haze of rainfall: most little more than rubble but some retaining large parts of their structures. They made straight for the mouth of the river, where the water was deep enough to float across instead of risking getting snagged on debris lying on the river's bottom.

Coming up from the south, onto Perth Amboy, the environment did indeed seem to be clear of significant contamination — though the crawler's systems reported evidence of bio toxins and radiation at the edges of its detection range. On the other side of what the old maps identified as Staten Island, black clouds hung over the carcass of New York. The Mother's Tears were still falling from the overburdened sky and washing down the rubble-strewn streets, carrying the dust of once noble edifices through rivulets that wended their way, roundabout, to the sea.

⸭

Valko eyed the ruined structure with disappointment. The old concrete was pockmarked and scorched. Cracks ran through it and steel rods poked out — twisted out of position as if some benighted beast had burst from the building's heart, leaving ribs splayed out from its mutilated husk. He'd half expected to see the magnificent structure as he'd seen it in the records. Towering and mighty, even amongst the taller, more advanced structures surrounding it. In its destruction, it retained more of its former majesty than the derelicts around it; those spires which had dwarfed it were now little more than piles of broken and melted smart plastics. They'd either liquefied or shattered, in the high-energy blast of the flashburner.

Perhaps, the surrounding structures had provided some shielding effect for the Empire State Building. It was less than half its previous height now, but still recognisable. In fact, it was once again the tallest manmade structure in New York, and second only to Outpost Theta in all of North America. A good landmark to choose for the meeting: when they'd been crossing the cursed water of the Hudson, using the crawler's pontoons to provide buoyancy, it had soon come into view and provided a clear point to aim for, rising from the wreckage of Manhattan.

Now, looking up at the ruined structure Valko felt keyed up, senses burning; he didn't need to check the others to know they felt likewise. But there was no sign of anyone else around. The poisoned rain had given way to a cloudless sky — the air crisp with cold, the impartial sun looking askance at the tortured body of the once proud city, as it lay sprawled below.

'Has she set another trap for us?' Satoshi asked.

'I'm not sure that she set the last one, Oshi,' Valko said. 'You won't remember, but she was shocked when you turned on her. Someone else must have done something to you — twisted whatever conditioning she thought you'd received.'

Satoshi was silent for a moment. His face remained impassive but Valko could see past that — see the troubled thoughts racing away behind the grey eyes. It was tempting to probe, to tease out the truth of what lay buried in his friend's mind — was it Lunar War Syndrome scrabbling away like a rabid dog in a corner of that mind, or some construct of another's making? Maybe there was no difference. Maybe Satoshi knew, but couldn't admit as much to Valko — so he'd wait for Satoshi to deal with it — wait, but not too long. Davidson stared at them both for a moment, a quizzical look on his face, but didn't interrupt.

'Well, if she hasn't set a trap, then maybe someone else has. Where exactly are you supposed to meet her?' Satoshi asked.

'She said the Empire State building. That's what these ruins used to be but there's no sign of her.'

'Hey Boss, maybe the broad meant actually inside the ruins?' Davidson said.

'Broad? Jack, can you stop the funny talk for once. It's like talking to an old vid. But maybe you're right. Now that I think about it, she suggested we meet in the lobby — lobby...?'

'It's the main hall, Boss,' Davidson said.

'Oh, she meant foyer, right? Thanks, Jack. Why don't you stay here with the crawler and keep an eye out for hostiles. You any good with that?' Valko gestured towards the rifle.

'Ah, not really, Boss. I've not really had a chance to try, you know. Crawler's got some defences anyway.' The grubby man licked his lips.

'OK, Jack. I understand. Not much use for longarms in the Plena, after all. Try to give us a warning if you see anyone coming, but don't take any risks.'

Valko favoured Davidson with a smile.

'Sure, Boss. You take care in there.' Davidson looked disconcerted but turned and re-entered the crawler.

Satoshi and Valko climbed over the rubble of the ruins and managed to find a stable entrance — a staircase that had been broken open. Foetid water dripped from the ceilings and the basement level and foundations had been flooded. The stink of the rancid water permeated everything, and — despite the scouring of life from the city — mildew had survived.

To Valko, born and raised as an Enclosed, for such a large building — impressive even by Plenum standards — to lack any g-moss seemed exotic. He'd never been in such a place, and he could see from Satoshi's face that it was bringing back old memories from the sergeant's distant past. The presence of some life in the form of the mildew had a different effect on each man. Satoshi looked depressed but Valko felt buoyed up by it — it was a sign that life could reassert itself, even without humanity's assistance.

Many places on the planet were blasted plains, with traces of only the hardiest microbes and spores, most lying dormant; nanodestroyers killed all traces of active life even at the microscopic level. Here, surrounded by devastation, mildew spores had found a foothold; whether because the surrounding ruins acted as barriers to windborne nanodestroyers or because the burn-zone had cleared, allowing the ingress of the spores, he could only guess.

If the New York burn-zone had cleared, it would make the skeletal shell of the city a rich resource for Outpost Theta to exploit. If it were simply that the wind had been diverted, then they were in constant danger while they were here — all it would take would be a stronger gust to bring a lethal concentration of nanodestroyers.

'So, why don't we wait here for her to turn up?' Satoshi asked as they eyed the dark corridor leading into the ruined structure.

'Because she may be waiting for us inside. Look Oshi, I don't want her to get away. For now I believe her, but if she's lying we need to bring her in, or kill her.' He felt sick at the thought of it, when deep down he knew he should just see it as doing his job.

'OK, Val. This is a bad place to be caught in an ambush. If she is lying, if she's trying to trap us again… I mean it wouldn't take a lot to bring the building down.'

'Oshi, I can't say why, but every time I doubt her I get a burst of feeling telling me I can trust her. It feels like… like it's coming from outside myself — it's got to be from my implant.'

'I understand.' Satoshi sighed. 'You're trusting your gut. Something I never thought I'd see you do. Come on. I'm with you.'

They crept down the ruined corridor — Satoshi in the lead. Each step was nerve-wracking, waiting for the floor to give way or the ceiling to cave in — all the while senses straining for the sound of a waiting ambusher. Every room they came to needed to be checked — the tension each time there was a closed door that had to be tried was almost unbearable — but there was never any sign of occupation and it felt like they were on a fool's errand.

Eventually, they reached a room that could only be the lobby: long and high ceilinged. Its ceiling was high enough as to be difficult to make out in the murk — the only light was coming through what must have once been the main entrance. There was a latticework of twisted metal that looked like it might have once held glass and below that, space for wide doors. They'd entered from the wrong side of the building. *Typical.*

'So she's not here waiting for us, do you really think she's coming?' Satoshi asked. 'Or is this going to turn into another trap?' The big man's eyes roved over their surroundings.

'I don't know. Why make us come all this way if she's not going to come? I suppose something could have happened to her.' Valko was feeling foolish. 'I wish we'd scouted round the outside first.'

Satoshi looked at him and shrugged, not even appearing to sweat inside his envirosuit despite the tension. Valko walked towards the end of the lobby, where some great mural was visible under the grime. Chunks of it had fallen out but he could just make out the shape of the building as it had been long ago — proud and conveying a nobility of spirit that said tomorrow would be a better day. That sentiment had fallen apart: as much as the mural had, as much as the building itself had. He stopped — but the foundations remained.

His presence was insignificant to this still vast, structure. It had been built to last through the generations and its survival, even in this ruined form, was a tribute to that desire: to craft an enduring monument to humanity's drive for progress. He gazed back down the lobby towards the entrance, out beyond into the corpse of the city — only then did he see them.

Multiple black armoured figures were converging on the tower, scuttling over the ruins like beetles — instantly recognisable as naukara.

'Oshi, there's a horde of naukara incoming!' He shouted.

Satoshi ran to his side, the rifle he'd commandeered from the Outpost already wedged into his shoulder.

'I see them. There's somewhere between ten and fifteen. We'd better get out of here.'

'Too late,' Valko said, pointing towards the crawler as it drove into view.

Davidson had begun to move the vehicle round the building and was making a feeble effort to activate its defences. They were limited — the crawler hadn't been designed for combat. The best he could do was slow a couple of the naukara down with blasts of shrapnel, which, while they might have shredded someone unarmoured, did little but scratch the black plating of the naukara's carapaces and knock them backwards.

'Go on, Jack. Get out of here!' Valko said over the radio

There was no way that he or Satoshi could get to the vehicle past the naukara — some of the black armoured shapes were already heading towards the entrance to the ruined building.

There was no reply from Davidson but he steered the crawler sharply to the left, coming close to tipping over on the uneven ground. In doing so, he brought the front round into a naukara who'd been trying to reach the cockpit from the outside. The unfortunate machineman was crushed by the heavy vehicle, his mechanical parts cracking open and the soft remains of flesh inside spilling out in their misery. Yet it made little difference. The side of the vehicle was soon torn open and two hulking figures scuttled inside. The crawler rumbled along for a few more metres before running into a section of melted building. The hulking black figures emerged, one of them carrying a limp form over its huge shoulder.

Satoshi lined up his shot with lethal precision — fired, striking the naukara's right eyelense. It penetrated: the man-machine toppled as its head was blown open. Satoshi tried again but its companion — scooping Davidson's body up — raised an arm girded in thick plates of armour as a shield in front of its face. Satoshi's shot, when it came, pinged away.

'We'll never make it trying to take them on, Val. Sorry.'

'It's alright. We knew this was a risk. I'm sorry that I trusted her, sorry I lead you into this trap. What do we do?'

Rank ceased to matter where combat experience was key — Valko wouldn't have survived half of the firefights Satoshi had been involved in — he relinquished command of the situation without much regret.

'Up the stairs. It's a delaying tactic, but they'll have to search each floor. We'll just keep pushing for the top — give us a chance to think of something,' Satoshi said.

He began moving, firing off shot after shot — few making any difference. They dashed up the stairs, Valko staggering by the fourth floor, while Satoshi moved implacably, not even breathing hard as he bounded ahead. He stopped, turned back, grabbed the front of Valko's envirosuit and hoisted him over one shoulder. The giant sprinted up the stairs, taking them three at a time and at a pace that the athletes of the previous century would have envied, even on the flat. Steps groaned and creaked under them and dust rained down, but Satoshi didn't slow. Not until they reached the top — the thirty-sixth floor. It was the last to have a ceiling, and that had fallen down in several places. The stairs ended halfway to the thirty-seventh floor. There was no easy way up and — from the looks of the collapsing ceiling — that was a good thing.

'This is as high as we go,' Satoshi said as he put Valko down.

Valko looked around and walked out from the staircase. Every step was tentative and as he moved, he noticed with alarm that the structure around him groaned and shifted. Debris fell from the ceiling above but, after a terrified moment of stillness, he was able to move again.

'Oshi, we're in as much danger from the structure as the damn naukara.'

'I wish that were true. Listen!'

Valko heard the stomping of mechanized feet coming from below. The naukara were taking the steps almost as fast as Satoshi had. The sounds of their ascent boomed out only a few floors below them — stealth was not a naukara strength.

'What do we do? They're coming straight up here!' Valko asked.

'Try to hide in the rubble. It's the only thing I can think of. If they have to scatter and search individually I might — might — be able to take them down, one at a time.' Satoshi checked his rifle. 'Seven rounds left and two reloads. For what good it'll do us, I'd need to hit the eyelenses for any hope of getting them. Hand-to-hand's my best chance.'

'You really think so?'

'Yeah. These look like an earlier model. They're not like the ones on Apollo station, I wouldn't last long against them. These. Well, we'll soon see.' Satoshi gave Valko a firm push away from himself. 'Get going, Val. We need to separate. Try to get to the floor above if you can, they'll be too heavy to follow you up. Good luck!'

'You too,' Valko said then hurried off, looking for a way out.

The ruined building at least had plenty of space on this level to hide in. Then the reality hit. If the naukara had individual beacon trackers it wouldn't matter. Why hadn't he thought of it earlier? They knew where he and Satoshi were and there was no hiding it... or was there?

'Oshi, you need to remove your beacon!' He shouted.

Concealing himself behind some rubble, he pulled out one of the envirosuits utility blades from its boot sheath. Valko probed around the back of his neck until he found the small bump where the beacon was located. It would hurt like hell but there was no other choice. Reaching back — the knife in his right hand and the fingers of his left acting as a guide — he tried to cut into the skin around the beacon. The pain was so much worse than he'd expected — his auto-hypnotic pain suppression had been stripped from him by the implant's malfunction, leaving every raw sensation. He persevered, cutting his fingers in the process. Hands now slick with his own blood, he probed around with the knife — wincing as the blade scraped bone.

Heavy footsteps thudded into the floor of the thirty-sixth

level — the knife's tip slid under the edge of the beacon. With a gasp of pain, Valko prised the small disc of metal out from the back of his neck and cursed as it slipped from his wet fingers. It bounced and rolled into a gap in the rubble. Dropping the knife, he shoved his right hand down into the gap, feeling the approach of black clad death as the heavy footsteps neared his position. The remorseless thing would find him but if he ran, he'd be shot. There was one chance.

There — his fingers touched the disc of the beacon. It was warm, unlike the surrounding debris, and sent a mild tingle into his fingers even as his touch caused it to slip away from him. An arm in black carapace came into view, mechanical claws at its end flexing open and closed in anticipation of the kill. Then he had it. Held by one thin edge between his index and his middle fingers. He drew his hand out and gripped the beacon in his hand for an instant before throwing it. It flew away from him, skittered and bounced along the floor and then dropped down a crack. The naukara stepped into full view and swivelled away — tracking the beacon and turning its back to Valko.

He held his breath while it stomped past his pitiful hiding place: all its focus on the electronic pulse of the beacon. The device would already be transmitting an alert to indicate it was no longer detecting his life signs. Would that show up on their tracking or only its location? He wasn't going to hang around to find out.

Valko kept low and crept along, desperately seeking a better hiding place. He rounded a pile of debris; there was Satoshi. The massive man had compressed himself into a small gap in some broken masonry. There was blood streaming from the back of his neck. Good, he'd also removed his beacon. Valko was about to try to go to him, when he saw what Satoshi was looking at. Another naukara. This one armed with a large particle beam rifle and no other obvious weapon.

It was fixed on its destination, still tracking Satoshi's beacon. It raised the rifle and fired — a bright reddish blaze of light followed that blew a rubble pile ten metres in front of the naukara into incandescence. Dust billowed as the rubble disintegrated and Valko's envirosuit clicked as it detected the release of radiation caused by the firing of the weapon — designed for use in a vacuum — in an atmosphere.

Satoshi chose that moment of flashing radiation and flying debris to move. He sprang upon the naukara and — discarding his own rifle — wrapped his left arm around the creature's neck while he drove a short utility blade into the cabling at the rear of its head with his right hand. A shower of sparks erupted from the cabling and bright blood spurted. Satoshi carried the stroke through and into the human brain beneath the technology, bringing final quietue to the trapped scrap of flesh that had once been man or woman.

Satoshi seized the particle rifle from the thing's dead grip, wrenching it from the vice of the mechanical hands. He spun, aiming at Valko and, for a moment, the look in his eyes was that same berserker fury he'd suffered in the pre-War bunker. Valko raised his hands in front of him, half expecting to be shot.

Red lightning streaked from the barrel of the rifle; a burst of heat scorched Valko's left cheek, even through his helmet, and an explosion blossomed behind him. Bits of black metal and smart plastic flew in all directions and a shard of armour embedded itself in his shoulder, cutting clean through the envirosuit. Warning icons flickered to life in the corner of his vision, alerting him to the breach in the suit's integrity and the wave of ionising radiation that had accompanied the particle beam pulse.

Valko spun and saw the smoking remains of another naukara — the one he'd avoided by such a narrow margin a short while before.

'Are there any others?' He asked.

His answer came not from Satoshi but from the dark figure that rose up right behind his sergeant. Valko was about to cry a warning but it was too late. The naukara slammed down with one armoured fist, knocking the rifle from Satoshi's grip, even as it brought its own snub-nosed frag gun to bear on him. With a slight twist of his feet, Satoshi shifted his body to the left, flowing to the side of the frag gun. He struck the muzzle with one palm while striking contra wise with the other hand at the stock. The gun went spinning away out of the naukara's grip. Satoshi was on the outside of the naukara's right arm, controlling the arm and staying where the armoured behemoth couldn't strike him across its own body with its left arm.

Every move the naukara made with its right arm, Satoshi

redirected with a firm left hand pressing on its upper arm, just above the elbow. All the while, he moved around, changing position as the naukara tried to come to bear with him. That wasn't all — as he moved Satoshi delivered a series of vicious short whipping kicks to exposed areas around the creature's groin and legs. He alternated that with strikes to the throat, face, and ribs with his free hand, probing for weaknesses. His footing became precarious as they moved onto some of the rubble and, for a moment, Valko feared that his friend had lost the advantage.

He needn't have worried: Satoshi drove a heavy knee strike up into the man's sternum, hard enough to crack the carapace there; delivered a crushing elbow smash to the windpipe with his right arm before pivoting and using that momentum to send his left elbow driving into the naukara's occipital bone. It toppled to the ground and Satoshi pulled his omni-pistol in one fluid movement, jamming it to the base of the naukara's skull and pulling the trigger three times in quick succession. He stopped and squinted up at the awestruck Valko.

'Are we alone up here?' Satoshi asked.

'Oshi, that was incredible!' Valko said, spluttering with amazement. 'I thought you were dead... but you dropped that thing like it was easy.'

'Hardly, Val, but strength and resilience don't count as much against skill,' Satoshi said. 'I grew up being taught how to fight in the old tradition of my family. This poor bastard probably didn't know anything except the system they taught in basic training — more sport than combat. It's not like he was commando trained. Those guys knew how to fight.'

'One of these days, Oshi, I want you to teach me. Right now, we've got to get out of here and try to do something for Jack.'

How Davidson had stopped being merely an underling... An almost undetectable voice, now deep down inside him told Valko he was being a fool. Giddy with the rush of near death, his emotions ran roughshod over the quiet, calculated warning.

The sounds coming from below had changed. Valko could hear the rattle and report of rapid-fire ballistic weapons, answered by the blinding flashes of multi-hued light and high speed clicking that denoted the discharges of laser weapons and the red lightning, crack of particle beams.

'Mother's Tears, what's going on down there?' Valko said.

They hurried over to a break in the outer wall and peered down. The naukara were surrounded by a much larger force, yet they were holding their own. The new group were ragtag and disorganised — Remnants. Despite their appearance, and the disparity of arms, they were keeping the naukara pinned down.

It was their one chance of victory — in close quarters the fight would be one sided. Every time one of the warriors in black carapaces tried to close with a group of the ragged men and women, one of a pair of Remnant warriors — the first armed with a rocket launcher the other with a tripod mounted anti-armour laser — would emerge from cover and explode the naukara into chunks of electronics and gobbets of meat. For every single naukara that fell, two or three of the Remnant forces were blown apart, vaporised or cooked where they stood. Still more fell back clutching their faces as they were laser blinded — too late finding out the flaws in their scavenged goggles through the agony of retinas burned away.

Out of nowhere, a lithe figure — clad in matt black cloth which made the eye want to slide off of it — appeared in the midst of the fighting. The naukara paid it no attention — as if their machine eyes couldn't see it — while the figure stood amongst them and input something on a device in its left hand. The naukara stopped. They raised their weapons upright to their shoulders and marched into a tight column, where they stood at attention, immobile.

There were whoops and victory cries from the Remnant forces. Valko strained to make out the shouts of 'Yee Haw!' and 'Yippee Ki-Yay!' from several of the dishevelled group.

'Is that Jean?' Satoshi asked, pointing at the shadowy figure.

'Yes. It's her,' Valko said.

She was speaking with the leader of the Remnant group — a man who looked familiar — and gesturing towards the ruins of the Empire State building and was having some sort of argument with him.

'We'd better get down there,' Valko said.

'You're right. Here take this,' Satoshi said, handing Valko the frag gun and collecting the energy rifle he'd used earlier. He cradled it to his chest in a professional manner.

'I'm fine with a pistol but I've never actually had to use a frag gun before,' Valko said.

'It's easy. Just like in training. Point it at whatever you want dead and pull the trigger.'

Valko couldn't tell if Satoshi was serious or not, but his sergeant had already begun to move. He must've meant it was that simple.

Hands shaking and stomach churning as the adrenaline began to wear off, Valko stayed leaning against the wall — distracting himself by gazing through the break in it. He became lost for a time in the sweeping view of the ruined city. There were no other structures remaining at a similar height but he could see the occasional building that remained over twenty stories high: melted spikes of slag but some would have interiors that could be accessed. Who knew what they might contain, what lost knowledge? Would it be prosaic or would some hold secrets of the Old World, thought lost after Enclosure? It wasn't for him to find out.

His frustration building as the shakes and queasiness subsided, Valko kicked a loose section of concrete rubble, fist sized, and watched it fly out into the air to make a steep arc down towards the ground. His eyes followed its trajectory and he found himself looking at the slim dark figure. Jean. A jumble of emotions he had no names for broiled in his chest but his mind felt empty.

Going down the more than six hundred steps to street level was much better than the indignity of being carried up on Satoshi's shoulder. Still, by the time they reached the ground, Valko's legs burned with the effort; Satoshi bounded ahead full of energy.

'Careful, Val. If they decide to turn nasty, we've got nowhere to go except back up those stairs.'

'A fate worse than death,' Valko said.

Satoshi barked a short laugh before he paused a second, appraising Valko.

'You really have changed. Is this who you were all along? I always hoped so.'

'I don't know. I don't know. Sometimes, I think that this me is the lie and how I was before was the true me. I'm not sure it matters now. Not unless there's a way of changing what's happened — what's happening — to me.'

'I'm sorry, Val. Last thing you need right now. Look, stay in cover, I'll move forward and see what they have to say.'

'No, you're the better marksman and you've given me the close quarter's gun. I'll go out there, you stay back and keep a bead on them.'

'Yes, sir,' Satoshi said, snapping into sergeant mode with a salute, but there was a smile on his lips.

†††

Valko drew seven breaths — hoping to slow his furiously beating heart — and stepped out from cover, walking out through the gaping doorway of the broken down building. In a heartbeat, the handful of survivors of the fight focused their guns on him, but lowered them just as quick when they saw he wasn't a naukara.

The shadow-clad figure approached and called out, 'Valko, it's Jean. You're safe now.'

Her voice betrayed no hint of falsehood but it was too little to say for sure. He walked towards her, frag gun held in both hands, pointing downwards but ready to swing up at a moment's notice.

'Jean, who are your friends?' He asked.

'We be the High Mesa ken. You be the Gangleri?' The familiar looking man said, stepping forwards and making an expansive gesture.

'Yes, I'm Gangleri. Who are you?'

'I handle Denwar Koewatha, you be known to me. You be blessing to the Koewathas. We not losing we payback.'

The American Remnant leader was trying to tone down the thickness of his argot, yet what stood out for Valko was how close his speech was to that of Joey Koewatha, a Remnant from the Eurussian region, over three thousand miles away.

'Koewatha? How's that possible? I met a Koewatha at Arcas Plenum, how could you know about that?'

'We owns the longspeak like you do. Ken good brother cousins from whole face of world. Koewatha's not forget we other — have grab to shift all places — payback of one, payback of all. You closed men, can't keep we out. None you done for we like you done, not ever.'

Denwar, his face streaked with dirt and burned brown by the sun, grinned at Valko out from under a mop of messy red hair.

'Jean, what the hell are we doing here? Why did you send me to that ruined building?' Valko asked, turning his attention to the woman — heart pounding in his chest as he drew closer to her, thrilling to a different rhythm.

'Best way to stop them following you, I needed bait for the trap. I figured you'd go up — the top of the ruins was far enough out of the way to keep you safe. Now you know, it's not me that you have to worry about,' she said.

'Yet you control the naukara,' Valko said.

'Now, I do. It takes time to hack their systems, their security has improved a lot since the War. Anyway, if I wanted to harm you, why would I stop them?'

'Fair point. Look, can we discuss this somewhere less, er, exposed?' He asked, feeling uncomfortable under the appraising eyes of the Remnants.

'Mass-mass, man. We show's ya place, then we scrams. Payback done busted square, right?'

The Remnant leader held out one dirty hand and spat in his palm. Valko, recognising the gesture — but not sure from where — imitated him and took the other man's firm grip.

Denwar stepped back and let out a high yipping cry that turned to a deep ululation. The rest of his group faded back into the ruins, taking their dead and injured with them. He turned and began to walk, surefooted, through the debris and rubble.

Jean gestured to Valko to follow. 'Satoshi can join us now,' she called.

Valko nodded and saw Satoshi step out from the ruins of the Empire State building. He jogged over to them, his eyes wary and a dark scowl on his face as he regarded Jean.

'I don't understand, Jean. Why were these Remnants here? They can't really have heard from a clan member in Europa can they?'

'What you did spread through the Remnant comm-net.

When I heard about it, I knew that I could leverage Denwar. Their society is far more complex than anyone in the Plena realises,' she said.

'What's your part in it?'

'I'll explain, but let's just say they owe me.'

A sensation of pressure, a denial of curiosity, blanketed Valko once more. He cast about for some other focus, trying to bring himself back to the moment.

'What about them?' Valko asked, indicating the naukara with his thumb as he turned away from them.

'They'll keep. We might have a use for them. We might not,' Jean said it without apparent emotion, but Valko could feel strong mixed emotions emanating from her. She wouldn't be callous with the naukara, he was sure of it.

†††

They followed Denwar to a collapsed building — the rubble made up of older steel reinforced concrete rather than the smart plastics of the later built structures. Within the broken down and scorched blocks, they found the entrance to what must have once been an underground carpark. Unlike the basement level of the Empire State building, here the drainage had kept the under-levels clear of any flooding. Cars had become obsolete before the devastation — the preserve of wealthy collectors who'd had to pay huge sums of money to obtain the vehicles in the first place and then more to be allowed to drive them through streets that were no longer given over to the automobile. The identity of the building that formed the ruins above was a mystery, but the presence of seven dust-covered cars from different eras spoke of the wealth of its late occupants. Now, they were worthless: their fuel, whether petrol, hydrogen or deuterium, could no longer be replaced and there was no route through the rubble they could travel. So the vehicles lay entombed, like the mummified remains of a forgotten empire. Behind the corroding shells, there was a small, enclosed security booth, for the most part still intact. It was here that Denwar delivered them.

He gripped Valko's arm. 'No bang left tween us man, but no bad to ken and no bad to you, dig?'

Valko nodded his head, believing that it was an offer of, if not friendship with the Remnant clan, at least no hostility.

With a grin he said, 'Mass-mass, man.'

Denwar chuckled then turned and began to walk away. He paused as he passed Jean.

'Be treating them radded? Them cotton eyed? Bang edged tween us, Sister?'

'I will do what I can for them, but remember your debt is too great for easy repayment,' she said.

Denwar walked away, his back stiff. Valko watched the man leave then turned to Jean, setting his jaw and adopting his hard Moderator's gaze.

'Before we discuss anything else, tell me what happened to our companion? Last we saw he was being dragged off by one of the naukara.'

Her eyes flicked down, away from his gaze. 'I'm sorry,' she said. 'There were two of them that got away with him as a prisoner. By the time I finally cracked the encryption, they were out of the range of my ability to control them. One of Denwar's scouts told me that she'd seen them board a transport that looked like a Plenum craft. It sounded like a transpod from her description.'

'A transpod? Here? What the hell is going on?'

'There's a long history here that you need to know about Valko, to truly understand. I just don't think I have enough time to tell you all of it,' Jean said.

Valko moved to one of the desks that remained in the old security booth. He pulled out a chair and sat down, gesturing to Jean to take the other chair.

'Jean, you murdered Eugene Fisher. I need to know why. If I'm to trust you I have to understand. You murdered a man in cold blood. Tell me why I shouldn't have Satoshi arrest you?'

The hulking man didn't move from his place, leaning against the door frame, but he radiated tension as if he were ready to spring into action. She quirked an eyebrow at Satoshi.

'It wouldn't be quite as one sided as you expect but you're right, Val. I suppose you deserve an explanation, Satoshi too. I didn't murder Fisher. I only terminated one of his clones,' she said, in a cool, level voice as if it was nothing unusual.

Valko rocked back on his seat. 'His clones? What the hell are you talking about?'

'Fisher, the one you think I murdered, was merely a clone of the original. He had no separate life of his own, not really. He was no more than an extension of the Fisher who betrayed all of us in the Lunar colonies.'

'How is that even possible?' Valko asked, all the while trawling his memory for anything he knew about clones. He came up blank — they were old-tech, banned by the Temple.

'Fisher, like the rest of us, underwent full body synthorganic reinforcement. It means he doesn't age and has a tremendously enhanced lifespan, perhaps a limitless one. He's been using clones of himself to manipulate the Centra Autorita for decades now, maybe since the beginning, since Enclosure.'

'That can't be right,' Satoshi said. 'I met both Fisher's and they didn't look identical.'

'That's right, Satoshi, they wouldn't. Fisher had his clones' features altered. Some of them look nothing like him at all. Others have... shall we say, a family resemblance. Eugene Fisher was one of the latter.'

'Clone or no clone, you still killed him,' Valko said. How could she think that even an artificial human life was less valuable? Wait, cloning was a crime and clones themselves were treated like criminal property — they were recycled like all other waste. His head spun with the conflicting attitudes: what was right, what was wrong? He no longer knew.

'I expected you to be more ruthless but your implant has changed that, hasn't it?' Jean said. Valko didn't answer so she continued. 'Look, I'm sorry you feel that way, but Fisher's clones are not autonomous. They don't have any real free will. At most, they might have a surface personality and some fake memories to make them fit in better — under that they're little more than extensions of Fisher's own mind and will.'

'Like the brains in jars that Ari and Phil had?' Satoshi asked, though the scowl on his face remained, it was less angry and more troubled.

'Precisely. With synthorganics, it's fairly easy to create links to external tissues. Look at the way your implant works, Val. You no longer need to touch a person to connect to their minds, do you?'

'I don't know, I haven't tried.' It felt like a lie for he could already feel a faint buzzing from the minds near to him.

'Maybe you should, but not right now. The body I killed couldn't live without Fisher managing it. It was more of a tool: an extension of him, so he could continue to influence the Centra Autorita, without giving away his true identity.'

'Why should that matter?' Valko asked.

He folded his arms. The sincerity coming from her was almost as strong as if they were mindlinked but his distant echo of self, which doubted all, would not stay silent.

'The Temple,' Satoshi said. 'Think about it, Val. If the original Fisher were seen to still be alive and in control, the Temple would rebel.'

'That's right,' Jean said. 'Think what you will of them, they are, at least, committed to their beliefs.'

'And those beliefs would never allow for control by someone who'd used technology to try to cheat the natural cycle of things,' Valko said.

'Precisely.' Jean settled back in her chair, crossing her legs.

'But, why kill him? Why do you care if he'd discovered faster than light travel? It's useless except maybe as a weapon and anyway who is he going to use it against. It's not like there's a lack of weapons on the Mother, even now.'

'It wasn't the FTL. I don't really care anything about physics, it was never my field.'

'Well, what then?'

'He stole the implants from me. Yours, all those that are in the heads of every Moderator. Even the synthorganics Satoshi has. This was the final straw.'

'You made synthorganics?' Valko asked.

Despite what he'd seen in the Philosopher's memories, it was hard to believe that this young looking woman was responsible for a technology that was barely understood in these days and could only be replicated by the Plena whitecoats with the greatest of difficulty.

'Yes,' She said. 'And he perverted them. They were meant to be a protection not a weapon. A way to save lives not to make soldiers. Then your implant: it was meant to be a way of expanding human consciousness. To make us better than we were, to foster communication between people. All he did was use it to make better agents of control.'

'The Moderators,' Valko said.

'Exactly. Then, after all he'd taken from me, he found my lab. Sent in one of his agents to steal the last piece of my research.'

'Your lab — you mean the bunker?'

'No, that was a bolthole, but given he sent you there...' Jean said.

'Wait, he sent us there? I thought you'd set us up?'

'No, Val. Not my style. I was there to meet Actur. When I found you there, I made the mistake of thinking you were there to steal the last shreds of my research. Turns out he had a different plan.'

'So, you didn't kill Darius Actur?' Satoshi asked.

'What? No, he was working for me — he had access to things, could move unnoticed as just another drudge.' Jean said. 'I don't know what he'd learned that made him a target. Maybe he was just with Vinnetti at the wrong time.' A wave of uncertainty flowed out of her.

'Alright,' Valko said, deep in thought.

'Look, Val. Fisher's a ruthless egotist who'll use anyone — anyone — to get what he wants: more power; more control. The clone was just another one of his many tools.'

'And that's why you killed him?' Valko asked.

'Yes. But more than that. My research is dangerous, I had to stop him from being able to use what he stole to further pervert my life's work.'

'Which was what?'

'The means to fully activate the implants safely — to evolve one step towards transcendence,' Jean said. 'Up until now he'd only been able to force them to work at a low level, to be able to interpret thoughts and feelings when there was a hub connection. With the data that he's stolen, the key to my research, he could open every Moderator's powers up fully. Could give himself the same powers, if he wanted.'

'Why would that be a bad thing? It's made him a better person,' Satoshi said, gesturing to Valko. 'No offence, Val.'

'No, Satoshi. What's happened to Valko is that his implant

has been triggered to enter its ultimate state: what it was intended for. With my research, Fisher could avoid the raising of consciousness and just gain the ability to read people's minds — to strip-mine the memories of any one within range. Given that his ability to manipulate minds has exceeded what all of us from the Colonies could manage... Can you imagine what a tyrant he'd become?'

'The Moderators wouldn't go along with that,' Valko said.

'No. You're wrong,' she said. 'Remember what you were like before your implant was activated? Imagine you could have that cold control with none of the human empathy but with an even greater ability to dissect minds. You would've served him without question.'

'She's right, Val. When you weren't on NOTT, you were ruthless,' Satoshi said.

'So why bother with the NOTT at all?' Valko asked. 'The Philosopher said it was useless — just an addictive drug to leash the Moderators.'

'You've partly answered your own question. But that old fossil should keep out of things he doesn't understand — simply because he tried drugs at university, he thinks he knows. NOTT may have an addictive additive but its core component is tryptamine, specifically trimethyltryptamine or TMT. Tryptamines are non-addictive drugs that interact with the serotonin receptors in the brain, triggering hallucinations — sometimes thought to be shamanic experiences — and increasing empathy towards others. Tryptamines annihilate the ego, if you like, and make you feel part of everything.

Whether that's an illusion or not, it's the effect that tryptamines have on the inactive synthorganic brain tissue that's important. It allows them to work in a low-level state without becoming fully activated. Without NOTT you wouldn't actually have been able to use the basic abilities of the implant. Once it was activated, probably by a high energy shock to the tissues, NOTT became superfluous as the implant produces its own TMT, as it needs.'

'Is that why I had a toxic reaction to it? I overdosed because it wasn't necessary?' Valko said.

'What do you mean?' Jean asked.

'When you left us in the bunker. I had to take a shot of

NOTT by inhaling it as my wrist valve was broken.'

'He overdosed and began to fit. He only survived because they treated him at Apollo station,' Satoshi said.

'Really? You've been to Apollo station?' Jean said and Valko noted what appeared to be genuine surprise flash through her — she'd not reacted when they'd mentioned Phil and Ari's brains in jars. She carried on, interrupting his line of thinking. 'I suppose that too much nitric oxide would be harmful but there's no way that you'd have had enough in a single one of those vials.' The tip of her tongue protruded from the corner of her mouth. 'TMT couldn't cause an overdose, unless you'd consumed about a hundred vials and even then it'd be the dopamine agitator — the addictive additive — that caused it.'

'So what happened to me?' Valko asked.

'Ah… He knows. Fisher is nothing if not thorough. I thought he'd altered our conditioning of Satoshi as a trap for me or the others, but he must have been trying to kill you too.'

'What?' Satoshi shouted, lurching forward, fists clenched and eyes wild.

Jean stood and stepped forward to meet him, unintimidated. The big man towered over her, yet she met his gaze unblinking.

'Your Lunar War Syndrome. What we did to you and the others that killed everyone on the Moon. Try to attack any of us who were there and we take control of you.'

'But it didn't work,' Valko said, as — tentative for fear of triggering an explosion of violence — he took hold of Satoshi's shoulder. Even through the envirosuit he could feel the tension in the thick musculature.

Jean didn't break eye contact with Satoshi but she answered Valko. 'No, Fisher must have found a way to subvert it — that must be why he kept you all on ice for so long. It's the same reaction you get when the conditioning is accidentally triggered.'

Satoshi's had clenched his jaws so tight that it was hard to understand him. 'You messed with my head. You doomed my brother's in arms to die in psychotic rampages.'

'I and others like me. All of us who survived your coward's attack. Those child murderers you call your brothers in arms, we showed them mercy — the rampages are a sign of Fisher's tampering, attempts to subvert the conditioning. Count yourself lucky that you were brought back. If you are back?' The slender woman stepped forwards until she was looking up at Satoshi, nose almost touching his as he loomed over her. 'You're the go-to killer, so, why don't you try *me* this time…'

The moment lasted too long, but then Satoshi looked away and drew a ragged breath as he stepped back, returning to lean against the wall in silence.

Valko held back his own sigh of relief. 'You're saying that Fisher senior was trying to kill me by manipulating my friend?'

Jean broke eye contact with Satoshi and sat back down. 'Yes, putting you in a situation where his Lunar War Syndrome might trigger.'

'That's a hell of a gamble,' Valko said.

'Fisher can afford to take that kind of risk. After all if it failed, he must have figured you'd use a NOTT vial at some point after you'd left the Plenum. Do you have one on you?'

'Yes,' Valko said and reached into an internal pocket of the envirosuit, producing a handful of NOTT vials. Jean inspected them.

'Yes, each of these has the alpha symbol after the batch code. It must symbolise that they're different. Clever. The letter alpha is used to identify that the substance in NOTT is an alkaloid of Trimethyltryptamine, so it wouldn't raise any suspicions among one of the Plenum medtechs, but it's a way to mark the vials as different. He must've had a stockpile of ones, with a lethal dose of the dopamine agitator, to deal with troublesome Moderators, in a quiet way. Poison them and make it look like an overdose.'

The fleeting thought that Orla might have known what she was giving him reared up. It was ugly and every part of him rejected it. That only spoke of a more disturbing possibility — poisoning Moderators who had malfunctioning implants was standard procedure. If so, then what was happening to him had happened to others. The scale of this might be far greater. What Jean was saying bothered him in other ways. It didn't quite add up as the actions of just one person.

'Why bother with blowing up or shooting down the transpod? What about shooting the Martyr? I mean that was clearly an attempt on me. Surely it would have been easier to just destroy the transpod with a bigger bomb than hope I'd get poisoned before finding out something compromising or trusting to some sniper who couldn't hit the target.'

'You're right. There would be simpler ways. But what would they leave behind? Say your transpod had crashed in an area infested by nanodestroyers, yes, you'd be dead. But wouldn't someone ask how? Transpods have a very low failure rate, don't they?'

'Yes. Only one failure in the last twenty-five years and that caused a soft landing.'

'OK, so there'd be an assumption that you were shot down. Which means you couldn't be shot down in an active nanodestroyer zone. They could come later, wind borne, but no one could fire a missile from within an active zone.'

'Yes, so what?'

'So it would point to a bomb. That would lead to an inquiry. Isn't it far better to have multiple attempts, any one of which could fail but wouldn't lead back to him?'

'So why suddenly switch to using naukara?'

'I don't know. He must have concluded that you would be meeting me from your beacon movement. Why else would you be coming to New York?'

'Don't you mean you sent that transmission to me, knowing he'd monitor it?'

'Yes, alright. I suspected that he would, but there wasn't much choice. And at least you can see that he's tipped his hand.'

The question, *Surely, he'd know you could hack his naukara?* — formed in Valko's mind, but wouldn't travel to his mouth. A cloying feeling, a weight over his thoughts, pressed down. The question squeezed from his mind a drop at a time. A new question, an acceptable one grew in its place.

'But if the original Fisher is behind all of this, where is he?' Valko ran a hand through the stubble of his hair along the lines of old scars.

'That's what I was hoping to find out. I was waiting, posing as a lab assistant, in the hopes that I could learn his location or, failing that, his plans. That's when he discovered my main lab; I'd thought it was so well hidden. Took the one scrap of smart-paper I'd been stupid enough to write my formulae on.

He'd not had enough time to crack the code on the hardcopy, but I knew he would sooner or later.'

'And killing his clone — where he could see that it was you — you hoped that would draw him out?'

'Yes...' Jean began.

'So you look different from how he'd have remembered you, right? But he'd still know that it was you who killed his clone, even if he didn't know that you were his lab technician.'

Jean nodded, 'Yes. Xiang Rhea was a useful cover identity. Fisher never saw me looking this young.' *Then why did you look no different in the Philosopher's memory?* Valko asked himself. She continued, 'I was going to leave the area when he didn't reveal himself, watch remotely. Then, when I met you, I decided to stay.' She cocked her head, examining him.

'Because you wanted to see what would happen to your precious implant,' Valko said.

'No. No, I didn't even know it was active, Val,' she said. *Bullshit* he thought, then that cynicism evaporated as she smiled at him, coy, embarrassed, her lips evoking promises of a surrender to sensuality. 'Not until the hotbed. I don't know what it was. You remind me of someone I knew a long time ago — someone important to me — and I wanted to get to know you, to see you as more than just one of Fisher's pawns.'

'As simple as that?' His heart beat faster — why was he letting her affect him like this?

'I'm one hundred and twenty seven years old, Val. I know myself better than I ever have before, but even now, some things are a mystery to me. I needed to speak to you, in spite of the risk of discovery,' she said, shrugging.

The gesture conveyed nonchalance but her eyes were saying so much more. Valko could detect no falsehood in the emphasis she placed on the word 'needed' though he sought for it, through the clouding of emotions and the rush of hormones that went with them.

'Then,' Jean said. 'When I found out that your implant was active, fully active, I hoped I could help you. I tracked your communications until I learned you were going to the Hotbed. It was a safe space to check if I could do anything to stop what was happening to you.'

'Can you?' He asked.

She stared at him a long moment before speaking. 'You deserve the truth. If I could have gotten to you within an hour of your implant being shocked into its active state, it's possible I could have controlled it but now… Now it's meshed with your nervous system — linked with all of your brain. And it's growing. It'll develop to its full potential within a year. First erasing who you are — then killing you.'

Satoshi made a sound from his place by the doorway that was part groan, part growl.

'Why?' Valko asked. 'I mean, it's meshed to my brain, so why will it kill me?'

'The bonding is a typical synthorganic side-effect. In this case, however, you are a nutrient source for it, nothing more. The implant was never designed to exist inside a human host. It was meant to be protected in a stable, secure environment and be used by those with the appropriate synthorganics. Fisher has perverted my work by using it in ways that it was never intended. It is his particular genius to find new applications for the discoveries of others. I'm truly sorry but he signed your death warrant the day he made you a Moderator.'

Valko hung his head. She was telling the truth; he could feel it in her mind, read it in her emotions and hear it in her words. Like any man given a death sentence, he wanted to deny it. To plead. To rage. To wake up and find it was a bad dream. But it didn't matter: what he wanted made no difference.

'What about Vinnetti? What did she do to deserve her death? And Actur? You really didn't shoot him?' Valko asked, dreading the answer.

'I didn't kill her.' There was a glint of pain in her eyes, a slight emphasis on the word *her*. 'I assume Fisher had it done. He must have felt the death of his clone, may even have been riding him when it happened. Oh, I hope so, it would have hurt like hell,' she said. 'He must've realised that I was one of his clone's technicians and confused Vinnetti for me…' Valko thought about it — Jean looked enough like Vinnetti that they could have been related. Vinnetti was fairer, Jean darker — otherwise they were very similar in overall appearance. His attention returned to what Jean was saying, '…and he murdered her in the same way I killed his clone both to send me a message and to cover himself, if he was wrong. Clever and so typical of his way of thinking. As for Actur... he was in the wrong place at the wrong time.'

'But why could he possibly want to kill a young lab technician, without more proof that it was you? Why even think that it was you or Vinnetti? It could have been anyone,' Valko said. 'Or did Actur lead Fisher to Vinnetti, the way he led us to your bunker? Did he think you were actually Vinnetti too? Was he coming to warn her that the trigger code for the veterans was now a trap?'

'That must be it, Val.' She said.

Her willingness to jump on his theories and her own deductive leaps worried the investigator in him. All this certainty without evidence. And there was something she wasn't telling him. He could feel something of her emotional state bleeding out from behind the control — sympathy flooded him, pushing down his reasoning, but it felt... exterior in a way he couldn't grasp.

'Actur was a go between, but he didn't know what I looked like or my name. As I said, he was in the wrong place at the wrong time. As for Vinnetti. Well, that's one more thing for us to ask Fisher. One more thing for him to pay for,' she said, with a tone of finality.

Valko wanted to carry on but realised it would get him nowhere. Besides, the feelings pouring into his implant, told him that Jean had not murdered the young woman, though the serpent like knot of this natural self rebelled against his growing reliance on empathy. It hissed that Vinnetti must have been playing a part in all of this, but smothering sentiment stifled the question in his mind. He was left with the conviction that whether Fisher was responsible or not, he would find out and see punishment served on the culprit.

He changed the subject, 'Will my abilities keep on growing alongside the implant?'

'Yes, but not so much the seeming telepathy. You're probably at, or near, the limit of that now, though you may begin to experience the ability to alter the part of the electromagnetic spectrum, which your implant detects, to perceive not only brainwaves but other electromagnetism as well. You may even begin seeing electrical impulses the way your eyes see the part of the electromagnetic spectrum that is visible light. And I expect you'll begin to see deeper connections between people and places.

That's a side effect of the higher consciousness state. As we go along, you'll experience greater levels of absence. Probably when you are conscious rather than simply asleep or knocked out. I don't know what you've been experiencing up 'til now but whatever you've found, you'll remember more of when you wake each time. Hopefully, before the end, you'll simply not return from that state.'

'Is it real?' The question had been gnawing away deep inside him; now he knew she couldn't help him it came burrowing to the surface.

'Apart from the perception of electrical impulses? I don't know. My creation of the implant was influenced by old research into the shamanic drugs: ayahuasca, psilocybin and the synthetic ones like lysergic acid diethylamide. After I'd taken synthorganics to their physical limits, I achieved all that I'd ever intended. I felt a bit hollow but I recalled the Philosopher's ideas. He'd explored everything from the holographic universe paradigm to the theory of infinite quantum variance — what used to be called the many worlds theory. Not the science exactly but the philosophy behind the science. The 'what if' of theoretical science focused on its implications for the human spirit instead of the simple practical effect. He was the one who lead us away from holding to established scientific fundamentals.' She leant back in her chair. 'You've met the Arithmatician?'

Valko nodded.

Jean shook her head, smiling. 'He was willing to question whether causality was nonsense — spent ages trying to prove that it was time that was a constant and not the speed of light in a vacuum, just to avoid taking anything for granted. Well, with me the abandonment was evolution. I don't mean that I suddenly found God or anything, but he got me to look at things in a different way from the standard ideas. Not survival of the fittest but a force compelling an advancement to a higher state of being. Perhaps, that force was driving from without, perhaps, it was driving from within. Do you understand what I mean?'

'I'm not sure. What I experienced was seeing my existence as being transmitted into this body from elsewhere. Like I was some vast being sending myself as a signal into the flesh before you.' The words felt strange in his mouth — how inadequate words were.

'Fascinating. Who knows? Maybe that's the truth. But how could we ever test it? The whole point of my research was to find new ways of asking questions about our existence. Sure, I could make the human brain smarter. I raised my own IQ by over one hundred points. It didn't expand my consciousness any. The Philosopher made me question whether all the quackery — the pseudoscience as it was called when I was studying — might actually have some scientific basis. Oh, I don't mean all of it but I wanted to find out if there was a sustainable way of accessing an apparent higher dimension of thought.'

'And for that I will lose my life.' He couldn't keep the bitterness out of his voice.

'Yes. You'll join the ranks of those who've given their lives for knowledge. That's not all we are concerned with though, is it?'

The absence of emotion in her voice chilled him and his cynical core laboured in vain to reassert itself but emotive consciousness had won, leaving only a sense of unease in Valko.

'No,' he said. 'I don't know whether I believe you did the right thing by killing the clone, but Fisher has to be stopped.'

'I knew that we shared a connection Val, it must be that you're like me. You want people to be the masters of their own destinies.'

Warmth had returned to her expression and it was matched by the feelings radiating from her. Valko felt his concerns slacken, it was easy to forget that she was a typical whitecoat, logic governing all else.

'No. That's not it. I want the truth. All of it. Out there where it can be seen. There's been a crime, an unforgivable one, and I will see it punished.' For once both sides of him, the new and the old, were as one.

'Alright. We'll find a way to reveal him for what he is. I've arranged for transportation to Arcas Plenum, but it'll take time to get here. We may as well rest until then.' There was a glimmer in her eyes.

'Good suggestion,' Satoshi said. His stomach gave a deep rumble. 'Got any food?'

†††

They left the underground carpark and met up with some of the High Mesa Remnants. Their camp was a short way away. Denwar, avoiding Jean's gaze, invited Valko and Satoshi to join them there for rest and food. Valko wanted to take the crawler but it didn't take much to see that it'd been damaged during the fight with the naukara beyond their ability to repair. The black clad warriors were still standing stock still where Jean had left them. She touched the device strapped to her wrist and, as one, the naukara turned and began to follow them.

'How did you gain control of them?' Satoshi asked.

'Same way as we did during the Lunar War. All technology communicates using some form of electronic signal. We can interrupt that with a stronger signal and hijack it: reprogram processors to take control.'

'That's why synthorganics soldiers like me were necessary. You couldn't hack us, at least not at first.'

Valko stared at Satoshi, realising that he could see into his friend again. The memory of what Jean had admitted — that she had been among the survivors of the Moon massacre who had brainwashed him — burned in Satoshi's mind, but he was keeping it controlled, much like a glowing coal from one night's fire might be preserved to start the next night's.

Jean spoke to Satoshi as if their confrontation had never taken place. No hint of controlled anger simmering below her surface feelings leaked from her. Valko probed gently at the pressure of her mind, but unlike Satoshi, he could only feel the emotions that flowed from her, nothing more.

'Yes,' she said. 'You can be hacked, albeit we couldn't do it at range. But anyone could be if Fisher takes my research to the next logical step. Not just mind reading but mind control. We used neural reprogramming to build in the safe word to temporarily make you susceptible to our commands. It seems obvious now. They froze you until a way was found to overcome that. With Fisher able to subvert our programming, think what he can do with the power of the implants like Valko has.'

A thought came to Valko. 'I don't understand. If I accept that you and the other scientists didn't cause the devastation of the Mother, why didn't you stop the nanodestroyers? Couldn't you have hacked them?'

'No. That was part of the problem. When we hacked their naukara and diverted their missiles, the Super States got paranoid. They thought we'd turn their nanotech against them.' Jean's eyes took on a faraway look. 'So they built in a new system. Made each nanite, weaponised or not, have an adaptive encryption. Any signal received that wasn't immediately correct, would trigger a move to the next level of encryption.'

'So what?' Valko said, shrugging.

'Well you can't break a code with one lucky guess. It was a stupid idea really. It took only one error in their own transmissions to start the process. The code didn't work so they switched it to the right one, but the code had changed. Then it had changed again.' Jean shook her head. 'Then the nanites received different codes from different agencies. Those in control panicked and the nanites entered a lockdown state. Their programming became scrambled and suddenly, all these defensive nanites were interpreting the people they were supposed to protect as hostile. All life was registering as hostile: foreign invaders. It happened around the globe, but nowhere worse than United America. This is the end result,' she said gesturing to the ruins of Manhattan surrounding them. 'Thankfully, the nanites weren't set to autonomous reproduction. There's a finite number. One day they may all be cleared up.'

'How?' Valko asked — the thought of a world freed from the curse of nanodestroyers sounded like a fantasy, but if it could be done…

'I don't know,' Jean said. 'One of the other scientists, Aaida though we called her Nana given her field of expertise, was looking at developing nanites at a smaller scale and setting them to dismantle the nanodestroyers before shutting themselves down.' She noted Valko and Satoshi's puzzled expressions. 'Nanowarfare is all about whose got the smallest nanites. She was killed before her research was completed. Maybe one day, someone will finish what she started.'

Valko looked around the grim ruins before he returned to negotiating the rubble on the way to the Remnant's temporary camp. The decayed apple core of a city took on a malevolent feel as evening crept in: cracks and hollows filling with sly shadows.

Part IV

QUISQUE SUOS PATIMUR MANES.

EACH OF US BEARS HIS OWN HELL.

- PUBLIUS VERGILIUS MARO-

Chapter 15

They ate a hasty meal, scavenged from whatever the Remnants had found along their travels — dried roots, dried rat meat and flour made from ground cockroaches. The envirosuits' computers complained that the meals did not represent a balanced diet but otherwise detected nothing wrong with them. Valko's taste buds — and his stomach — disagreed. After eating in Apollo station and enjoying Shen's home cooking, this was horrible. He dreaded to think of what his reaction to Plena food would be now.

Jean sat across from him at the small fire they'd gathered round. Her eyes sparkled in the firelight and kept meeting his. She might be well over a hundred but she looked no older than he did. Younger if anything. Her presence both excited and calmed him. From anyone else, the story she'd told him would have been hard to accept. He'd have demanded proof. Would have wanted to strip-mine her mind for answers — probably still could but his instincts told him he didn't need to. When he tried to analyse the source of his certainty he found it inexplicable — there was no frame of reference in his experience of emotions. When he looked at her, he couldn't help but forget his fate and a broad smile kept finding its way onto his face. Now, his cheeks ached where muscles unused to the motion were seeing overuse.

A few scraps of material — some covered in patches but all frayed and old — were used to put up tents. The word makeshift would have been complimentary — the best fabrics went to the Remnants' patchwork envirosuits. None of the tents would completely keep out the cold wind but it was far better than sleeping unprotected. Denwar began to order a watch posted but Jean intervened, setting the naukara to do it. They formed a wide circle around the camp, each facing outwards, weapons levelled. Denwar's earlier pique had subsided and Valko assumed it was because Jean had begun treating the surviving Remnant soldiers.

'Don't they need sleep?' Valko asked, inclining his head in the direction of the naukara.

'Not like we do,' Satoshi said. 'Large parts of their brains were replaced, so the cybernetic parts are awake while the organic brain sleeps. Even then, the organic parts need less sleep. The waste products of their brains are more efficiently cleaned up than they could be naturally.'

'What a horrible fate,' Valko said.

He shuddered, such slavery must be worse than his own death sentence.

'Yeah. So many young men and women were tricked into giving up their lives. Maybe something can be done for them, like Ari told us, but I think giving them a dignified end would be kindest,' Satoshi said.

He yawned and entered the tent they'd been given to share. Valko lingered by the low burning fire; he didn't feel like sleeping.

For a long while, he sat gazing into the fire and poking it to rekindle its meagre warmth. The night was bitter with cold and he was grateful for the protection of his envirosuit. It clung to him in hot weather — wicking away sweat and helping to keep him cool — but in the cold the fabric expanded, drawing air in between its fibres to create an air layer next to his skin. The insulating effect was enough to see him through a cold New York night, even without tent and fire, but there was no reason to turn down added comfort.

Valko was beginning to rise to his feet when he saw Jean walking back into the camp and making her way over to him.

'Where've you been?' He asked, feeling serpentine cynicism skulk in the back of his mind.

'Getting away from the fire light so I could see the stars. I missed them while I was in the Plena.'

She hugged herself against the chill even though her matt black garment looked thick enough to protect her from the worst of the cold.

Valko glanced up and vertigo struck him. He was both looking up at the stars and looking down from them. Fearing another departure into an altered state of consciousness, he wrestled his gaze from the heavens and settled his eyes on Jean.

'Jean,' he said, wanting to say much more.

'Shh.'

She held one finger to her lips then lowered her hand and

held it out to him. He took it, struck dumb, and she led him out beyond the ring of naukara. She'd pitched her tent away from the others and no one had questioned her desire for privacy. Jean opened the tent flap and pulled Valko inside, her strength overwhelming his. Her kiss reached down into him, igniting a fire in his chest — the heat swelled between them until it threatened to burn away their world.

Passion overcame them and they lay together — the first sin of Man and Woman: the spreading of the disease called People.

He revelled in her lithe and muscular body, its hardness yet tempered by a soft smoothness of skin. She gripped him with fervour — her gasps a susurration in his ear — and he wondered at her indulgence in his gaunt and pale body.

This was so different from Valko's other carnal experiences — few and far between as they'd been. Before, he'd never made love. Just sex — he'd used, he'd never shared. Here, his feelings went beyond the priapic. At the peak of their shared pleasure, he felt himself begin to slip away. She was there, with him — he was inside her being as much as he was inside her body. She clung to him and their minds and spirits intertwined. His sense of self eroded as she shared thoughts, feelings and memories with him and he reciprocated, feeling no shame and no fear. Her life lay before him and he drank in the intensity of the sharing.

They took flight upwards. The experience of ascension was now familiar to him but he could feel Jean's apprehension, so he let his confidence wash over her, as they took each other inwards and outwards. Their greater selves entwined — missing parts of his spirit filled by her, gaps in her own being filled by him. It was then that he saw himself through her true essence for the first time and understood the context of his life. He saw it and tried to hold onto it — to remember it and bring it back. There were uncomfortable truths that needed to be known. Then the pull of his body demanded his return and, try as he might, the enlightenment slipped away and ignorance washed over him again.

✝✝✝

They were woken early by the thrumming of high powered turbines. Valko peered through a gap in the tent to see an old style scramjet aircraft landing in the middle of the camp. The down draft from its low altitude turbofans, though controlled, was uprooting the tents. Most of the High Mesa Remnants were running around, desperate to collect their precious gear before it was blown away. Several others were waving their fists at the pilot and yelling obscenities.

After a moment, the craft landed and the pilot popped the canopy before jumping down. She ignored the swearing Remnants and made her way over to Jean, who was smoothing her skinsuit as she exited her tent. Valko watched through the gap, embarrassed and wanting to choose his moment before emerging.

The pilot swaggered over to Jean and they engaged in a short conversation, while the Remnants bustled about. The remaining tents were struck and the High Mesas began to ready themselves to leave. Valko took the opportunity to creep from Jean's tent. Feeling like a sheepish teenager, he cringed when Satoshi came over and clapped him on the shoulder.

'What a beautiful morning, eh Val?' The big man's eyes were sparkling with amusement.

'Did you save me some breakfast or do I need to write you up for failing to take care of your Tantei?' He'd be dammed if he was going to be the butt of some joke his Sergeant was no doubt trying to think up.

'Not much, there's a pot of some reconstituted mush still warm by this morning's fire.'

'Thanks,' Valko said without much enthusiasm.

'So who's our pilot?' Satoshi asked.

'No idea. Does it matter? We don't have time, we need to get back to Arcas Plenum as soon as possible. There's a chance we can track Davidson's beacon and whatever is going on there, we need to know about it.'

'I hope Sadiq is alright.' Satoshi's amusement fell away replaced by a look of guilty realisation.

Jean walked over to them with the pilot. She shared a brief secret smile with Valko then introduced the woman by her side.

'This is Harula, she'll take us to Arcas Plenum.'

Harula stood with her weight over one hip and her right hand resting, with casual ease, on a holstered pistol strapped to her thigh. Her left hand held a lightweight flight helmet, the faceplate still flickering with data streamed from the idling aircraft. She was chewing something, but didn't seem to be ready to swallow it.

'Pleased to meet you,' she said in a rich drawling tone. 'I hear you folks have got to get a move on. We'll be taking a shortcut so, don't you worry, I'll get you there in time.' Harula met both of their gazes, one after the other, then smiled to herself and turned back to her craft. She pressed something at her wrist and the aircraft's rear compartment opened. Jean lined the naukara soldiers up and walked them in.

'What are you waiting for?' Harula called back to them.

Valko and Satoshi looked at each other, clearly both thinking the same thing.

'Are we riding with the naukara now?' Valko said under his breath.

They began to move towards the rear door of the aircraft but Jean walked between them taking each by the arm and guiding them to the passenger cabin mounted behind the cockpit.

'Credit me with some style, gentlemen, please,' she said.

They boarded the aircraft and hardly had time to settle in before Harula had the turbofans roaring once more. Take off was smooth, then they were pressed back into their seats by a burst of acceleration as the craft leapt into the sky. To Valko it was a reminder of the discomfort of their trip to Apollo station and back but their pilot seemed to relish the jolt — her whoop of joy was audible even over the engine sound.

'What did she mean by the short cut?' Satoshi asked Jean.

'It's nothing to worry about. We're going the direct route rather than flying the long way round.' There was no trace of concern in her voice.

'The direct route?' Both Satoshi and Valko said together, incredulous.

'Relax. Harula knows what she's doing. She's been flying since before either of you were born.'

'Either of us?' Satoshi said but received no answer.

Valko began to feel trapped by his restraints. 'But the

direct route's going to take us through the Atlantis Project storm front. We'll never make it.'

'Relax Val. This is a Hawkmoth, not a transpod. Once we get to the right height, we'll burn straight over the storm front. Satoshi, you must have heard of one of these before?'

Jean's face showed little sign of the physical stresses they were all experiencing — her voice was easy and clear.

'Yeah. They'd been phased out for more modern tech when I started training but I remember their reputation.'

'What reputation?' Valko asked.

Satoshi turned his head to look at Valko. 'Old guys used to call them mules. Hawkmoths could carry tons of equipment at high speeds but the name came from the kick they give when the scramjets engage.'

'Ten seconds,' Harula called over the intercom. 'Stop your grinnin' and drop your linen!'

The kick when it came was bad. Without the benefits of an acceleration couch, Valko was slammed into his seat with stunning force. His ribs ached but didn't break and after a few seconds the pressure eased off. The whole vessel vibrated but the noise of the engines decreased.

'We're flying at nearly twice the height of a transpod's maximum operating altitude. Safe from the influence of the Atlantis effect,' Jean said.

'How fast are we flying?' Valko asked. 'It seems so quiet.'

'Thinner air and fewer moving parts than the turbofans. Plus we're moving faster than the sound waves created behind us. Believe me, if we flew past you, you'd be deafened,' Jean said.

'This is old tech,' Satoshi said, his voice a low rumble that almost merged with the engine sound. 'Old even before I was born. It's like flying in an antique.'

'An antique?' Valko asked, taken by the unfamiliar word.

'Something people used to collect to feel a connection with the works of the past — same as a *gǔdǒng* or heirloom but without the need for a family link. A bit like Davidson's affinity for the old vids,' Satoshi said.

†††

The entry into the Plenum was going to be tricky. They'd landed about a quarter of a mile away from the outer skin of the green-gold structure that reared out of the landscape like the trunk of some twisted and decaying tree, grown to gargantuan proportions. Harula had told them that the Hawkmoth was radar neutral and would have evaded detection: at least, detection by the standard systems used to keep track of the comings and goings of the transpods, but Jean seemed uneasy and the naukara remained on board.

'Always an idea to have backup when necessary. Harula will standby for the next forty-eight hours before departing,' Jean said.

They bid farewell to Harula, who raised one hand to her forehead, palm down.

'Fisher may have more sophisticated detection systems than radar,' Jean said.

'We should assume he knows that we are here then,' Valko said. 'That is, if he's inside.'

'Where else would a spider be than at the centre of his web?' Satoshi asked.

'Hiding nearby, Satoshi,' Jean said. 'I've studied biology for my whole life. Arachnids vary greatly in their behaviour. Some will hunt not squat in a web. Anyway, Fisher is far more cunning than some arthropod.' Her patronising tone made Satoshi narrow his eyes. 'He's not stupid enough to believe that hiding in plain sight would be any protection.'

'Evidence,' Valko said, looking at Jean.

'What about it?' She asked.

'Evidence will lead us to Fisher. Not guesswork or metaphor.'

'What about trying to draw him out?' Satoshi asked.

'No, he's too clever for a simple trap. Besides, he'd send one of his slaved clones.' Jean turned back to the Plenum. 'We need to get in first, then we can see if we can find you some evidence, Val.'

Valko paused a moment, considering her words. 'Agreed, but criminals often think themselves too clever for simple traps while walking straight into them.'

They hiked the short distance to the Plenum's outer

surface. Up close, it was smooth and uniform — a dull metallic surface that rippled almost like cloth. The apparent imperfections of its shape were only noticeable at a distance. Unlike the other buildings that they'd been in, even Outpost Theta, the Plenum's outer surface was as fresh as it had been on the day of Enclosure. Gentle sunshine bathed the colossal, crooked structure and the verdant landscape surrounding it in defiance of the moribund world, yet here they were seeking to creep back into the melancholy of Enclosure.

It didn't take long to find one of the pipelines that took excess organic waste out into the surrounding soil. When they'd flown into land, Valko had stared at the megastructure — filled with warring emotions. Seen from above, the Plenum was at the centre of a spreading stain of green on the uniform muted brown and grey of the landscape. That green had spread for ten miles in every direction but it was still no more than a foothold. Like most Plena, Arcas had survived being enveloped in nanodestroyers, while all the surrounding area had been stripped of life, down to the microscopic level. It'd taken decades — and thousands of lives — to burn the molecule sized death machines back, enough to establish the small stain of green in the blasted landscape. That was why Martyrs were sent out beyond the zones of the greatest devastation, where one man or woman could bring life back to an area one hundred miles in diameter. Some pipelines extended great distances underground to provide local preserves with resources but they also allowed smugglers a way of entering the superstructures. It wasn't easy, but so long as what was being brought in carried no contamination, it was possible.

'The Plenum defences were designed to allow uncontaminated humans to enter with relative ease. It's getting out that's hard.' Valko strode ahead of the other two.

'Let me guess, Val. You learned about this working smuggling cases.' Satoshi grinned at him.

'Precisely. Come on, follow me. We should be able to gain entry to the under-levels this way.'

Valko lead them both along one of the pipes, to where the pristine skin of the Plenum enveloped it. It felt good to be back in familiar territory, where he was the one in the know.

They approached the skin and an imperfection became apparent. The pipe blocked most of it, but they could see the material around the pipe was bulging in a roughly hemispherical shape, the flat edge neat with the ground. Valko held out his hands and dug his fingers into the material. With a ripping sound, he pulled his hands apart and the material ripped in a long, straight tear. He stepped through, but held the opening while Jean and Satoshi followed him. They found another similar curtain of material in front of them. It remained stiff until Valko released the layer they had passed through, the edges meshing together once more so they were seamless.

'You must have come this way before, Jean,' he said.

'No, Val. I never even knew you could. I came into the Plena by way of one of the Outposts. Their security seemed so much easier to breach.'

'Hence the wei-zhuce,' Satoshi said.

'Yes, the smugglers do tend to keep their little secrets. If too many people knew about these entrances more would be done to block them. Most entrances to Plena are covered by half a dozen security monitors. The ones here are out for *maintenance* and have been for at least the last five years.'

'If you know about it, why let them get away with it?' Jean asked.

'Without their vices, people rebel. Plus vice is a good way to ID potential troublemakers so the contraceptive dose in their food and water can be increased.'

Valko repeated the procedure with the second layer, grateful for something to distract himself from the uncomfortable secrets he was privy to. Caring about other people was costing him too many pangs of conscience. They stepped through, the rip closing behind them with a sound of silk sheets whispering over each other.

'Ah, the heady aroma of processed air,' Satoshi said with a sigh.

There was nothing life threatening for the envirosuit's filters to block out so the breathing masks were open, giving Valko and Satoshi the full effect of the stagnant air in the under-levels.

Satoshi turned to look at the sealed rip and asked, 'Er, Val. What's happened to the wall?'

The material behind them appeared to be just dirty

discoloured grey metal, the same as all the surrounding walls.

'This side is impenetrable,' Valko said. 'Once you come in this way, there's no going back out, except through the upper-level exits or those doors that have been made permanent.' He left out mention of the route they'd sent Joey Koewatha down: best to keep to a habit of not talking about what they'd done — get too comfortable referring to it casually and who knew what ears would hear.

'How'd they get the pipes out then?' Satoshi asked.

'They didn't. They brought them in,' Valko said.

'Such a security risk,' Jean said.

'Not really — as I said we know it's there. Anyway, the material responds to orders from the Centra Autorita computers. If a large number of people approaching sparked concerns of a hostile invasion, they'd have been met by an impenetrable wall, instead. But, we do need to hurry. Our ingress will have been tracked, and without our beacons we'll be tagged as wei-zhuce at the next monitor we pass.'

'What are we going to do about that? It's a crime to remove your beacon.' Satoshi's voice echoed in the chamber, but the concern in his tone remained clear.

'True, but we did have a legitimate reason for doing it. Odegebayo will understand, once he has the full picture. We'll need replacements and I don't think we want to get them from the Justeco Centro. If Fisher's clones truly do permeate the Centra Autorita hierarchy, we'd be making ourselves traceable again.'

'I got mine at Outpost Gamma when I entered Plenum society, it's legitimate. What're you going to do?' Jean asked.

'We know the right man, Jean. Oshi, let's go and pay our old friend Slim Jan a visit,' Valko said.

Chapter 16

They took great care as they negotiated the under-levels of the Plenum. After the harsh air of the outside world and the piercing light of the Sun, the dark and dreary interior seemed even more oppressive than usual. Valko couldn't help notice the taint of pollutants in the air and the subtle miasma given off by g-plants.

Rain was falling but it wasn't the same as the black water he'd seen and felt in New York or the crystal sparkles that had fallen on him near Shen's hallowed home. That had carried with it a cleansing quality giving hope that fecundity might return to the Mother. The New York rain had felt like the Mother was mourning, crying burning tears. The Plenum equivalent just wetted him with greasy water.

They removed the most obvious parts of their envirosuits — the hoods and masks — trying to look less conspicuous. Jean stripped off the armoured sections of her skinsuit and — absent its haze of light distortion — she didn't look out of place, though the lines of her striking and powerful femininity were made obvious. They might attract some odd looks, if anyone could be bothered to pay attention, but moving through the less frequented areas and then diving into the soup of the overcrowded ones would keep them anonymous. All too soon, they were boring their way into the press of people.

For the first time, Valko found it uncomfortable, an invasion of his personal space. Satoshi's bulk and strength allowed him to keep close to Valko, and Jean had even less difficulty. When a surge in the crowd threatened to move her, she scythed through it, whereas Satoshi had to wade through the tide of humanity. Valko raised his eyes at their behaviour.

Overcoming the abnormal discomfort he'd begun to feel and settling back into the familiar rhythm, he flowed with the people, merging with them as if they were one great organism. Everyone he touched passed their senses to him and soon his mind was expanding through the whole crowd. It was a heady experience, a feeling of communion. There was sorrow and frustration but underneath it, were the embers of hope. That final bastion of the human soul had not yet been ground out of these people. Reaching out, through all of the minds he touched, he blew a gentle breath on that ember and saw it flare. The mood of the crowd changed and there was a literal buzz of positivity. Each person in his path helped Valko along and he soon outpaced both Satoshi and Jean, despite their far greater physicality.

After another half an hour of the pressing crowds, they arrived at Slim Jan's shady boutique. Valko pushed inside, Satoshi and Jean flanking him. Nothing had changed about the shop, save that this time there were a couple of customers. They were dressed in bodysuits not wearalls — it marked them out as a long way above common drudges. They were obviously in the lower echelon of the elite, with rec allowance to spare. The man and woman looked up at the new arrivals, and exited in a hurry.

'Ah, Tantei Gangleri. What a pleasure to have you, once more, in my small shop. Have you come to buy? You know what they say: small shop, small price.' Jannick Del's affected lisp once more grated on Valko's ears.

'You deal with the wei-zhuce. I want to know who can provide them with fake beacons. Now!' Valko said.

'Why Tantei, whatever makes you say such a dreadful thing? Surely no one can forge a beacon.' Jan was doing his best to act surprised.

'Cut the act, Jannick. I won't have you charged — if you provide me with information.'

Valko drew out his old icy tone. Then it occurred to him, if he wanted to, he could reach out and take the information from the man's mind, but the thought of doing so repelled him. Invading an unwilling mind suddenly felt like a crime to him. That and the cesspit conditions of the inner world of a man like Jannick Del would be enough to repel a naukara.

'Ah, there are, of course, things that I know. One can't help but hear things. Who would hold me responsible for things I've heard in passing?' Slim Jan's well-greased words slid from his mouth.

'I would. Tell me now.'

Valko put a sense of dangerous finality into his last word and reached out with his mind, projecting a flavour of fear from his aura. Jean and Satoshi both stepped back while Slim Jan's ample body quivered.

'Yes, Tantei. I will tell you everything that I know. Please have mercy on a humble merchant.' Just as last time, the fake lisp had evaporated. 'Please, follow me.'

Slim Jan waved a wobbling arm, festooned with cheap trinkets, at a curtain behind him. They made their way into a back room that was suffused with a cloying odour of some perfume or narcotic.

'I will not be held accountable?' Slim Jan asked.

'No. You have my word,' Valko said, this time seeding his aura with confidence and sincerity.

'Alright then, Tantei. Beacons cannot be forged — they require a continuous uplink with the Centra Autorita Core computer and a database of all the Enclosed remains securely encrypted. However… there are two ways to get hold of a beacon, or so I've heard.'

Satoshi let out a low rumble reminiscent of a growl.

'My sergeant is growing impatient, Jan.' Valko smiled inside, pleased at Satoshi's contribution.

'Yes, I understand. I know of a man who can provide… how do I put this? Recently liberated beacons. If you're a bit squeamish or want a genuine identity, I know someone who works in the Office of Registration. She will provide a new, unique identity but her price is considerably higher.'

'Recently liberated? You mean from the dead?' Once Valko would have seen the crime and felt nothing more, but now distaste rose in him as a nauseating wave.

'Well, those who are terminally ill or have received fatal injuries that don't immediately kill them. Shortly before they expire, their beacons are removed and tricked into a diagnostic mode before they're given to their new owner. The whole process is rather time sensitive as a result and supply dictates availability. I'm sure he wouldn't go so far as to arrange accidents on purpose, of course.' Slim Jan licked his rubbery lips.

'Oh, of course,' Valko said. 'Presumably, the recipient of the beacon is then lumbered with an identity that can only be used for a short period of time. Tell me more about the woman in Registration. What's the catch and what's the price?'

'The price, Tantei?' Slim Jan's eyes narrowed and a shrewd look came over his face.

'Yes, I want to know how a wei-zhuce could ever afford such a process,' Valko said, trying to cover his slip.

'Ah, but of course you do, Tantei. The catch is that the new registration risks alerting the kensakan of the anomaly, unless the Registration is for an infant.'

'You mean you either have a beacon that could immediately alert the kensakan or you have one that declares your age to be that of a new-born?' Valko asked.

'Ah, yes. It really is a difficult system to work around you see. Not many wei-zhuce can afford it. Those wei-zhuce who are willing to take on a dead Enclosed's identity, for a couple of years at a time, can often reach an agreement where they pay with commodities taken out of their future rec allowance. Owe favours, that kind of thing — the standard Hotbed trade. I'm afraid the lady in Registration is somewhat less willing to consider long term investments. She requires payment upfront in the form of luxury goods or a very large, direct donation of rec allowance.'

'How could she ever use it? Surely, she has to work with favours like everyone else in the black market. There's no easy way around the rec allowance system, so she'd have to be tied into the Hotbeds,' Valko said.

'I don't know but imagine — she can create identities. How difficult would it be to make one of those a dummy she can use to access her wealth? Now, was there some other way that I may be of service, Tantei?' Slim Jan asked, sweat beading on his forehead.

He'd exposed himself to quite a bit of danger by revealing all that he had — the people he dealt with would not forgive this if they ever learned of it. The effectiveness of the threat Valko posed surprised even the experienced Moderator. The man was indeed a weasel.

'Yes, give me the identities of these two brokers and their locations,' Valko said.

'Er, Tantei…' Slim Jan began, wringing his hands.

'No hesitating, Jannick. Now!' Valko shouted.

Slim Jan began to open his mouth to speak but then stopped. He assumed an apologetic expression. 'Tantei, I've given you what you asked, but I must ask for something in return for this. If you were truly investigating this, no doubt you would simply have dragged me in for interrogation or stolen the thoughts out of my mind. No?'

Valko remained silent, knowing the game was up.

'As I thought.' Slim Jan straightened up, assuming a more dominant stance.

'Don't forget yourself, fat man. I could still snap you in two with one hand.' Satoshi growled.

'Then you would never have the answers you seek. Make no idle threats to Slim Jan.' The soft looking man had a spine after all.

Valko decided to try another tack. 'You assume to know the workings of the Moderators? I have authority to conduct an investigation in any way I see fit. Satoshi, prep him. I will extract all of this maggot's filthy secrets and we'll have what we need.'

Satoshi began to move towards Slim Jan.

'Now, now. Let's not be too hasty. I ask only very little. I'm willing to help you, if you keep my name out of it. Promise me that I've nothing to fear from any other Moderator. Let me tell them that I work for Tantei Gangleri and everything I do is for the sake of giving you intelligence for your investigations and those of your kensakan. Have I not already assisted you once, in the matter of that stinking wei-zhuce?' A wheedling tone had re-entered the man's voice. He was a man who changed his attitude swifter than the wind changes direction in a tornado.

'Done,' Valko said.

He had little to fear from future blackmail. With an inwards grin, he recalled Denwar Koewatha and spat in his right hand before holding it out to Slim Jan. To his surprise, the effete man did likewise and grasped the outstretched hand with unexpected vim.

'Done indeed, Tantei. The brokers are Jodie Skellan and Tenebrous Vaskin.'

He picked up a stylus and wrote something on a sheet of old hardcopy that lay strewn on his table. Valko watched, fascinated. It wasn't even smart-paper but actual, real, organic starch paper — like they'd used after wood and cotton based paper became obsolete. Jan passed him the note.

'Their locations.' He noted the expression of wonder on Valko's face. 'Oh, the paper. It isn't genuine. I know an enterprising whitecoat who can manufacture it using the processors.'

'Tampering with processors is a serious crime. Best not to boast about your link to it,' Satoshi said with a grim look.

Valko studied the paper and considered which would be easier to reach. If they could gain access to the Registration records, they might be able to use them to obtain information that would lead to Fisher. Add that potential lead to the greater ease of tracking Davidson's beacon from within and it was a straightforward decision. Marketing the soon to be dead's beacons was an outrage — the thought of it made Valko's gorge rise — he vowed that he'd set in motion an investigation into this Tenebrous Vaskin. The name sounded too much like an alias to be a reliable way of tracking the man but it was a place to start nonetheless.

They left Slim Jan's, Jean not having said a word. Once they were outside she blew out a long breath, 'What an awful man.'

†††

The approach to Jodie Skellan was straightforward. The Office of Registration was easy to reach and lacked any major security control of access to the building. The couple of times they needed to pass through doors that required beacon access, Jean took the lead and got them through — it all seemed too easy but, as far as Valko could see, they attracted no attention. Then it was a simple matter of locating the cramped workspace that Skellan was assigned as her office.

That she had an office — even though it was barely large enough for a small desk and two small chairs — spoke of her seniority within the administration of Registration. Finding her was easy enough. Valko had taken a guess that she'd work during the standard A day cycle rather than B or C cycle, given the less urgent nature of Registration. Most work that required constant attendance of a worker would have one assigned to A cycle, one to B and one to C. Cycle A was the worst for most of the Enclosed, because it meant that all the other Plenum services, like Registration, would be closed to the A cycle worker during their down time. That's why B cycle or C cycle cost part of a drudge's rec allowance.

The guess paid off, she worked the standard shift — no hardship when all the services she'd need were in the same building. No one questioned the three as they made their way to her office. Each in their way radiated an aura of purpose and authority that put paid to any thoughts of interference.

Entering the office, Valko noted the quality of the woman's clothing first: it was nothing out of the ordinary. In fact, Jodie Skellan looked normal in every way. She was plain of appearance, not ugly but not pretty either. Her face showed her age to be late thirties but the slump of her shoulders and the cords that stood out in her neck made her look a little older. No sign of retrogening here. No sign of an excess of rec allowance. There was nothing to give her away — except the smell. Not a smell in the olfactory sense, but the way Valko's mind interpreted the impressions he got from her. He smelled fear. Which, given he'd always been told that his appearance screamed Moderator, meant that she was afraid of him. Afraid that her time was up.

'Jodie Skellan?' He asked.

'Yes, what can I do for you, sir?' Her voice remained calm and even.

'Satoshi, close the door,' Valko said, then returned his attention to Skellan. 'You can assist me in an investigation.'

'You are a… a Moderator, sir?'

'Yes, this is my Sergeant,' he said indicating Satoshi. 'And this is a whitecoat who is assisting me.' He indicated Jean.

'Whatever I can do, please tell me, sir. What is the nature of your investigation?' A slip, the woman's nerves causing her to reveal too much interest.

'Your criminal activities, in aiding the wei-zhuce to obtain beacons and fake Registration, are not the subject of my investigation. I work murder. Help me and perhaps we can keep your dirty little secret to ourselves,' he said it in an even tone, careful not to threaten — this criminal was clever and subtle. If he wanted her help he needed to persuade her.

Skellan hunched further into herself. 'I knew this day would come,' she said, almost to herself, then looked up, resignation in her gaze. 'What do you need from me?'

'Confidential access to secure Registration records. Two

duplicate adult male beacons and, finally, your assistance in locating an active beacon.'

She looked at him sharply. 'That's quite a lot to ask, Tantei. I'm not even sure that I can do all of it. Why don't we start with what I know I can do? Whose beacons are to be duplicated?'

'Mine and my sergeant's. From the records — not a simple copy of the ones we have installed.' Valko resisted the urge to hold his breath after he'd said this. Now was the point where what seemed to be a smooth interaction could go wrong in a hurry.

'Difficult. But doable. What are to be done with them? Implantation must happen within fifteen minutes of activation.' Her question seemed genuine enough and not an attempt to probe.

'All that you need to know, is that this is an...' He groped for a word — thoughts of Davidson sprang to mind as did an appropriate metaphor. 'An undercover operation.'

Whether the answer satisfied Skellan or not, she gave no indication, instead, making a few entries onto her terminal. After a moment or two, she picked up a datapad and told them to follow her, leading the three of them down to an archive room crammed with ancient looking data storage stacks.

'It's all on an old crystal storage matrix. Makes data loss extremely unlikely, but it has its flaws. Tell me your full names.' They did and, after consulting her datapad, she popped a crystal wafer out of one of the banks and took it to a nearby terminal. 'Here, I can read the hardstate record of your beacons from their last backup.'

'Backup?' All three said together.

'Oh, you wouldn't be aware of it happening, but every few weeks, your beacon is connected to the archive and its current memory is backed up. It's really very little data: location pings and health alerts — nothing to get excited about.' There was a thin smile on her face, as if Skellan were enjoying their discomfiture. 'The backup will also be triggered whenever the beacon re-establishes contact after being out of range. That's rather rare, of course.'

She made a few entries on the device and then returned the wafer back to the stacks. 'Who did you want to track?' She asked.

'Dr Eugene Cimbrian Fisher,' Valko said, then after a moment 'And Jack Arnold Davidson.'

'One name so familiar to me, the other not. An interesting selection. One moment.'

She repeated the process and, this time, withdrew two separate wafers. One had a quite different appearance from the other — far newer and better maintained. She led them deeper into the archive, to a storeroom with shelves stacked with small bronze coloured discs about the size of a fingernail, contained in sealed injection packets. She selected two and handed them to Valko.

'These need to have the identities transferred to them and then be inserted into the subject's neck at the sixth vertebrae, within fifteen minutes. Any longer and the injector becomes disarmed again as a security measure.'

'I understand,' he said and turned to Satoshi. 'Sergeant, if these are primed now can we get them to the subjects in time?'

'Yes, sir, can do, sir,' Satoshi said.

'We'll ask you to prep them once the rest of our business is concluded. You have the data on the two beacons?'

Skellan nodded.

'How do we use it?' Valko asked.

'I'll transfer it to your hubs. You do understand that the data on this Jack Davidson will not be real time?'

'Yes. Thank you.'

Something might have happened to Jack — was it only his malfunctioning implant that made him care? Whatever the source of his feelings, this was the best chance for finding where the kensakan had been taken — if he'd been brought back to one of the Plena. This system — a record of every Enclosed's comings and goings — fit with the overall philosophy of Plena life. He was very familiar with active beacon tracking — had used it on a number of occasions — but he'd never suspected the records would be kept in a solid state for the lifetime of an Enclosed. This unexpected evidence trail, might give him a way to locate Davidson, without needing to rely on the Justeco Centro — without alerting Fisher.

'Administrator Skellan, please upload the identities to

these beacons, now.' He held them up.

'Certainly. You may find that there is some difficulty with your own beacons when I do. Duplicates will cause the monitoring system problems. If it thinks you're in two separate locations, you might find your access to certain Plena systems restricted. Also, travel between Plena will be problematic for you while your original and its copy are both active.'

'These things are of no concern to you,' Valko said.

He felt bad for being so harsh on the woman, but it was necessary — a quiet voice inside asked him why he wasn't outraged at the crimes this grey faced administrator had committed. He turned from the question, unwilling — unable — to answer.

Skellan gave a curt nod and fiddled with her datapad. There was a beep from each of the packaged beacons.

'They're now active. The fifteen minute timer has commenced,' she said. 'Insertion is simply a matter of placing the package on the neck at the sixth vertebrae and pressing the tab at the bottom of the package.'

'Thank you. That will be all for now,' Valko said, starting to turn away.

'Please, before you go. What will happen to me?' She was struggling to keep from pleading.

'As agreed, I will not alert anyone to your involvement but I may need further assistance from you in the future. Otherwise, you can relax for now.'

Valko turned on his heel and left without waiting for a response. Even so, he could feel her worry — she didn't believe him.

They waited until they were out of sight then dashed down the narrow corridors at the heart of Registration, to a nearby refresher. There was room for both Valko and Satoshi inside the cubicle, if they squeezed tight together, so they managed to help each other install the beacons. The pain was intense: Valko hadn't healed from his less than surgical removal of his original beacon. He missed his auto-hypnotic pain suppression now more than ever — the price of having his mental conditioning stripped away so his eyes could be open. When it was his turn, Satoshi didn't so much as wince.

They were back on the grid — traceable but also granted access rights to the Justeco Centro and other restricted areas. With any luck, there'd be no consequences for the removal of their beacons. With a whole lot more luck — if Fisher had been tracing them — he would have given up after realising their beacons had been removed. Of course, that would take more luck than Valko believed they were entitled to, let alone would receive. He and Satoshi cleaned each other up — grateful that no one was around to see it — then left the restroom.

Jean was standing in the corridor outside, studying the information on the datapad.

'This is incredible,' she said. 'Fisher's clone had a very specific movement pattern — I don't think he ever left Arcas Plenum. If this data is accurate, it must mean the original is here.'

'Why would he need to stay close?' Satoshi asked, coming to stand behind Jean and looking at the stream of data on the 'pad.

'Neural connections between extra-cranial, synthorganic implants and their user have a maximum effective range,' she said. 'That range is a function of the waveform of organically stimulated electromagnetic transmissions.' She paused, considering their blank faces. 'Sorry, force of habit. It means if he's connected to his clones, all, or at least some of the time, then there's a range limit. Even synthorganic cells can't generate enough power to transmit a reliable link further than about a kilometre.'

'So the bastard is here,' Satoshi said, with a grin. Then his expression dropped. 'Valko, he's this close. What if he's done something to Sadiq? I've got to go and check on him.'

'Go, Oshi,' Valko said. 'We'll be at the Justeco Centro trying to get a live feed on Jack.'

Valko patted him on the shoulder and watched as his friend rushed out. A cold spear of rationality thrummed through him: this was nothing more than emotion getting in the way of the needs of the case. He shook it off — how had he ever been able to live with himself being like that?

'If I understand this data correctly, your friend Davidson was brought to this Plenum, straight from New York. This record though, it seems to be far more detailed, like a constant check on his every movement since I killed the clone,' she said it without a trace of emotion, like someone talking about a triviality. Like she had been discarding an unwanted lab sample.

'Hmm. I wish we'd checked our own records. If Fisher or one of his clones was keeping track of Davidson, maybe they were tracking all of those involved in the investigation.' Valko felt cold wash over him. 'Is that why Fisher had us targeted? To stop the investigation?'

'That, or he was interested in signs that your implant was activated. I suppose that wouldn't explain tracking your kensakan though,' she said.

'In my experience, there are usually many different motives for criminal actions,' Valko said.

Jean paused, considering him. 'Yes, I suppose you're right. Whatever the motivation, I think this data shows something else. I'm sorry but since his arrival back in the Plenum, there's been no further update.'

'What do you mean?' Valko's anxiety crept over him — an unfamiliar and unpleasant sensation.

'It suggests that his beacon has since been deactivated. Like he was killed.' Jean looked at him and he felt sympathy welling in her. To his eyes, she was now surrounded by an ambient field of energy — strongest around her head — and he could *see* the colour of her thoughts. The momentary optical effect disappeared and his focus returned to her words.

'No, I don't agree. If he'd been killed, there should be an alert in the data. We've got to check the live tracking data from the Justeco Centro.'

'Alright, but I think you should prepare yourself. I'm sorry. I know how it is to lose friends.' He stared at her, wondering what made her think that Davidson was his friend. Was he? He'd never liked the man before but now felt indebted to him more than anything else — no, that wasn't true, Jack mattered to him. Valko changed the subject, uncomfortable with the close analysis of his feelings.

'What about data on the Fisher clone? Anything else you can glean from it?'

She began an absentminded drumming of her fingers on the back of the datapad. 'Possibly. It occurs to me that one person's vital signs tend to reveal a clear enough pattern over time to allow for identification.'

'Like a fingerprint?' He asked.

'Yes, though with the biometric data being comparatively limited, it wouldn't be anywhere near as reliable. Regardless, it might allow us to identify his other clones.'

'I see, they may have been altered cosmetically but their internal characteristics would remain the same,' Valko said, seized by the possibility.

'Theoretically. I mean, we might get a lot of false positives. I don't know. I've never tried a comparison myself.' Somewhere buried deep within him, there was a rumble of discontent. He ignored it.

She was rubbing her right temple with two fingers probing into the hollow there. A stray strand of hair had fallen loose. Valko reached out and brushed it back.

'We've got a lead. We just need to chase it down,' he said and leant over to give her lips a gentle kiss.

Jean looked up at him and smiled. 'Hope will keep us going. I've learned over the years that its value is making you see something through to the end.'

'That doesn't sound reassuring,' he said.

'Sorry. At my age, you gain a different perspective.'

'When we made love, I saw some of the things you lived through. I think I understand you, at least better than I otherwise could have.'

'I know. It was a… singular experience. I hope we have a chance to explore the possibilities again.' She winked and he felt his blood warm.

'That's something to look forward to,' he said.

They left the administration building and negotiated the crowds on their way to the Justeco Centro. The route was choked with people as usual, but Valko held Jean's hand and the way opened up before them.

Chapter 17

Satoshi hurried along. Should he stop by the Temple first? It would be about this cycle that Iona would be taking Sadiq in for his advanced indoctrination classes. Why didn't she see the truth of the Temple? He tried to make himself believe that he couldn't blame her, but deep down he couldn't get over his irritation at the woman. No matter what he tried, she always set his teeth on edge.

He thought better of going into the Temple; it might lead to a major delay if someone recognised him from his last visit. Since they'd ruled out Temple involvement in the murders — with Fisher as the main suspect for Vinnetti, and thus Actur too, and Jean apparently justified in killing a barely sentient clone — the process of infiltration he'd started had slipped from his mind. Now, it threatened to undermine his efforts to find his son.

Thoughts fixed on Sadiq, he plowed through the press of bodies in the corridors leading to his habitation section. Like most veterans — those that had stayed sane — he'd been granted a better living space than his rank and rec allowance would permit. A combination of gratitude for their sacrifices and a desire to keep the unstable Veterans happy.

He'd never understood how these people could lie to themselves that they'd done away with the drive for material acquisition, which had caused so much destruction in the world. They were like the old communists — living in an idealistic but impractical idea that covered up the same old lies.

Those with power lived as they wanted; those without were grateful for what they got. Any meagre improvement in their lives was a blessing and they accepted the system at face value. A system shored up by the racketeering of the Hotbeds and their web of favours that were as good as money. He remembered how it'd been in the World, back when he'd been growing up.

At least, this place no longer had vapid celebrities and fat businessmen while poor children starved. Here, those who lived in the best conditions did, at least, make the biggest contributions to the society of the Plena. It wasn't a true meritocracy but, perhaps, despite all the inherent flaws, this was the most just society the world had ever seen? He shuddered at the thought.

†††

'Jean, I've been wondering…' Valko said as they climbed the steps to the Justeco Centro's rear entrance.

'What?' She glanced at him but remained focused on avoiding the oncoming press of people coming down the stairs.

'How exactly did you end up getting help from the Remnants and some of the Koewatha family in particular?'

Valko had tried hard but he couldn't fight his long honed inquisitorial instincts. Something wasn't quite adding up for him.

She flashed him a look. 'You've waited until now to ask me? Shit, Val. Have you still been questioning whether you can trust me this whole time? After I opened myself to you?' Her voice didn't rise but the tone became cutting and tinged with anger. He could feel waves of hurt coming from her — what a fool he was being.

'No, Jean. I don't doubt you, not now. It's only… well, call it my Moderator's side. I can't leave a question unanswered,' he said, knowing it was scant justification for undermining their pristine trust.

She stopped, which almost caused the people behind them to stumble into them. Then — aware of the congestion she was causing — she grabbed Valko and dragged him to one side, into a small alcove that allowed access for maintenance drudges to get at some of Plenum's local sub systems. Her fingers dug into his arm — there was no way that he could resist her strength. It was disconcerting that this woman, who had the appearance of a slim twenty something, was both so much older than him and so much stronger. He felt as helpless as he might if Satoshi had grabbed him, like a mischievous two-year-old being dragged to one side to be admonished by an embarrassed mother.

'You want to know the connection? Fine Val. I'd hoped you'd trust me after all of this, but whatever. I've made myself useful to various Remnant groups over the years. They're exposed to radiation, toxins and nanotech all the time. Mutation is a real risk. Happens to their children all the time. They're born with birth defects, most are so serious that they don't survive long.

Older Remnants get cancers. Did you see why I started my work? When I laid myself bare to you? Did you see?' She was hissing this as at him, clearly wanting to shout but also wanting to keep this spat private.

'I saw a knot of pain, I didn't look at it beyond that.' He said, feeling a mix of chagrin at the situation, shame at doubting her and fear that he might have ruined something wonderful in his life. The near silent, cold sliver of his old self said differently. It applauded his choice to question and demanded satisfaction.

'Then let me tell you. I was pregnant once, a long time ago. This was on Mars, back before the colony was fully established. Lots of radiation and other problems with air filtration. My unborn daughter was affected. She died during birth. I was already studying genetics and I'd been accepted into a research program with the Cydonia Lab. That's where I first invented synthorganics. A way to protect the genetic data stored in each cell and prevent mutation from radiation damage. The sort of thing nanotech never managed to achieve. I used my expertise to help the Remnants, to help their children be born without defects.'

She held her head up high, challenging him to question her further. He wanted to stop — was desperate to stop — but that relentless voice kept on.

'It's just such a huge coincidence that it was a Koewatha. That Denwar had spoken to Joey.'

He tried to make it sound like an observation, not a question but she saw straight through him.

'You think I was spying on you? I told you, I was interested in you, was keeping track on you but I didn't know what you'd done for Joey. Who by the way was a 'Koewatha', but not a 'High Mesa'. Remnant clans are a local thing. You don't even know what 'Koewatha' means, do you?'

Valko began to stutter an answer, but she cut him off.

'The clans all have one. It's a religious title, not a name. Denwar contacted me...' she gestured to herself with a thumb '...when I put the word out that I needed help rescuing a Moderator. He asked me who it was and I told him your name. He told me what you'd done and pledged his clan to help. Satisfied?'

She folded her arms and speared him with her gaze.

Valko, on the receiving end of a level of intensity that matched the best he could produce, looked down. 'Jean, I'm sorry. I had to ask.'

'But the interrogation is now over, right?' Her voice dripped with vitriol.

Valko glanced up and met her furious stare. 'Yes. Yes. Look, I trust you, but surely, you can understand? It's in my nature to question things.'

Hurt remained deep in her eyes. After a moment, she pushed past him and continued up the steps, 'Let's find Fisher.' She said.

Valko watched her go for a moment. Old instincts whirred into gear as he analysed her reactions to his questions. Then — with every one of those instincts screeching at him — a thick wad of padded emotion rammed down, muting and then silencing the objections of his authentic self.

Their entry to the Justeco Centro went unchallenged. Valko's reputation made kensakan and techs alike look away, not wanting to attract the Moderator's gaze. So he led Jean, as good as invisible, into the under-levels where data monitoring was conducted. He sat at a terminal, and it flashed through him that this was Davidson's terminal or, at least, one he'd spent time using. There was an echo of feeling: frustration and something else. Fear.

'We should be able to locate his beacon if it's still active,' Valko said.

'Is he the priority here? I mean, isn't it only a matter of time before Fisher realises we're on to him and scurries off to some hiding place in another Plenum?'

'The equipment is old, but it should be able to handle tracing Jack while looking for active beacons transmitting similar biometrics to Fisher's clone.' There was a sharp edge between them now but he hoped it would fade.

'Fine. What do you need me to do?' She rested her hand on his shoulder, and that touch seemed to reconnect them.

'Forgive me,' He said and gazed up at her.

'Forgiven.' She smiled at him. 'Now seriously, Val. What do you need me to do?'

'Upload the biometric data from the datapad to that

terminal.' He indicated a nearby workstation. 'You should see an option to track by biometrics. Select it.'

'Useful.'

'Yes, the system has every Enclosed's fingerprints and DNA on file. Sometimes, we need to identify a suspect by voice recognition or biometrics. It's not often used, but some of the living quarters use biometric entry systems. They were popular before the War. Some of that data is the kind of thing measured by beacons, some isn't. The whole Justeco Centra has probably solved two cases using this in the last ten years.'

She set about the task, while he tried to locate Davidson. The system was slow but it was solid: streams of data filled both their screens but Valko's resolved first into an obvious pattern. Davidson's beacon was sending an intermittent signal that was flitting from location to location — within Arcas Plenum, at least, but the signal was scattering all over the place.

'I've got Davidson, but his beacon's signal is suffering from interference. What about you, any matches yet?'

Jean ignored him for a moment as she adjusted the terminal's controls with single-minded focus. Then she grinned.

'I've got something. Two matches. One of them is a bureaucrat in the administration department the other is in the Justeco Centro.'

'You have got to be joking,' Valko said. 'It's not Odegebayo is it?'

'What makes you say that? No, it's not him. Someone called Hampton.'

'Hampton? Oh shit...' For a moment, the whole world dropped away. 'Is that why the Old Man has disappeared? Look Jean, this is serious. If Fisher controls one of the Pravniks then he's had access to all my reports. He'll know all about each member of my team. He'll know about their families. Mother's Tears, I've got to warn Oshi.'

┼┼┼

Satoshi reached the door to his quarters and braced himself. There'd be a long argument over why he'd been away so long without contact. Then he stopped. Instincts switched on full:

the door had been forced — he could see the signs. They might have been too subtle for the average person to notice; it wasn't as though the door had been kicked in. No. There'd been a precise application of force to overcome the door's locking mechanism. He'd done the same many times himself. Both as a kensakan and from his old life, back when he was an ITF agent. There'd been times when it'd been a case of blow the doors in — or the walls — and then there'd been times when a quiet approach, one that left little sign, was called for.

He reached for his omni-pistol. In all the fuss, he'd still not recharged the gun's capacitor and was left with six rounds of turbo penetrators. Not much need for it. If anyone was still inside, it'd be a close-quarters fight. Their bad luck.

Satoshi eased the door open in the same way that it'd been forced. What might have taken another kensakan some time and equipment, he had the strength to manage with his fingertips. The door released, but he held it — preventing the gentle whirring slide that would give his presence away. When he entered it would be in a rush — he wanted there to be no warning.

Remembering that strength wasn't the only virtue of his synthorganics, Satoshi strained his ears. The simple act of focusing on them activated a greater degree of sensitivity: he could hear the creak of the structure of the Plenum and the conversations of the inhabitants of the nearby quarters.

No sound from within. No breathing. No heartbeat. He'd been wrong before — that time long ago in the Panasian forward camp — so he prepared for a confrontation. Taking a deep breath down to his core and finding the still place within — behind his surging emotions of anger and fear for his family — Satoshi rammed the door open and was through it. He rolled into the room and came up with his gun trained, then covered all of the corners.

There was no one. He checked the bedroom, ready to fight but there was no sign of movement. The room to the refresher was open; he crept to it and flung it wide, gun trained. A shape huddled in the cubicle. He pulled back the screen and let his gun fall.

It was Iona. She'd been stripped and bound. A wad of her clothing was stuffed into her mouth as a gag but it was no longer necessary. She would never scream or shout again. The dark red wound in her throat gaped, an obscene mouth that cried of death's swift naissance.

More tender than he'd ever been with her in life, Satoshi reached in and embraced the shell that had been Iona. Lifting her out of the cubicle, he cradled her in his arms, ignoring the coldness of her skin and the stiffness of her limbs. He carried her to the bed, removed her bonds and pulled the gag from her mouth — gentle, so gentle — before setting it aside.

A quick look in the refresher's cubicle showed him that was where it had happened. The blood had been washed out and little remained. His hands tightened as they gripped the walls of the refresher and the metal crumpled and buckled under the pressure but he didn't notice. Didn't care. He stared at her lifeless body and tears carved his cheeks. If this were Fisher then he would tear the man's heart out with his bare hands.

The demon claw of Lunar War Syndrome gripped his mind — brought to full wakefulness. Pulse pounding in his temples he leant against the wall for a moment, passing a hand over his eyes. He felt transported again into memory. The same feeling of fury, of powerlessness as when his unit was being slaughtered on the Moon. His control was slipping.

A memory bubbled up from the depths and, as it broke the surface, he was back there: hearing the radio chatter as he lay near death, among the broken remains of the lab they'd been storming, in the aftermath of the scientist's weapon exploding.

++*Control, this is strike team Charlie Niner. Repeat, strike team Charlie Niner. Device is deployed. Heavy casualties suffered. Officers and senior NCOs all dead. Request evac co-ordinates. Control, do you read? Over.*++ *Static whined loudly on the comm channel.* ++*Control this is Lance Corporal John Kamdar, International Task Force, strike team Charlie Niner. Serial number…*++ *more static nearly deafening him* ++*…dead, evac shuttles are not landing, repeat the shuttles are not landing…*++ *Bursts of static in his ears or was that whining noise coming from his suit? He couldn't be sure, he couldn't move, could hardly breathe.* ++*Control, God damn you, where is our evac? Those bastards aren't com…*++ *The signal broke with the high pitched screech of explosive decompression, he didn't know if it was his death coming or the strike team's. Then there was a tapping noise. It sounded like it was coming from the airlock. Tap. Tap. Tap.*

Satoshi came back from his daze slowly, realising he'd

slumped down against the wall with his head knocking backwards against it — over and over and over again. The flow of his tears hadn't slowed, but he stood, went over to the bed again and sat, one hand reaching out to touch Iona's cold arm. Stilling his mind, he stopped weeping — and was filled with purpose. Vengeance. Then another thought came, obvious and yet only now penetrating the fugue of his anguish. Sadiq!

┼┼┼

Valko arrived to fins Satoshi sitting on the bed, hands clenched so tight the cords on their backs stood out like steel cables. The scene told Valko the bitter ending to Iona's story.

'Oshi, Mother's Tears. I'm so sorry.'

Satoshi glared at him. His eyes were clear and focused. Though there were the tracks of tears on his face, it was clear that no more were flowing. There was only fatal intensity.

'Where's my son, Val? Does Fisher have him?' Satoshi asked, voice more the growl of an animal than the throat of a man.

'I don't know. I've been trying to contact you, to warn you. Hampton is one of the clones.'

Satoshi stood. 'She did this?' Every word scythed through the air, red hot.

'I can try to find out from Iona… if you want,' Valko said.

He'd never felt so awkward at the thought of using his abilities — the wisdom of raven's, carrion bird's ken. A look of disgust bloomed on Satoshi's face, then washed away to be replaced by resignation.

'Do it,' he said.

Valko approached the corpse, readying himself for the journey into the deceased mind. He stopped short, feeling… an echo. His vision took on the overlay of energy trails, scintillating spirals of Mind that flowed around Satoshi's head. There he could see a wisp of a connection to Iona's body from somewhere else, like the lingering touch of a departing loved one. He closed his eyes and allowed the world around him to dissipate. There it was. A presence, like his own. Like Satoshi's. Vast and near infinite, yet, until recently, limited as he was. He stopped himself from detaching from his earthbound consciousness and tried to press his mind into the being he saw before him. It wouldn't work. He needed to go further but, if he did so, he would risk not remembering anything he learned. Set against the scope of the experience, his mundane concerns would be trivial. He broke off his meditation, there was no choice. This would have to be done the old fashioned way.

Satoshi hadn't moved, and it was unclear whether seconds, minutes or hours had passed. Unpredictable dislocation from time seemed to be symptomatic of entering a higher state of consciousness. The time for such ruminations was later, however. The mute reminder of urgency, lay twisted on the bed.

Valko took out his Moderator's hub, feeling a mixture of emotions at stepping backwards to a more primitive means of mindlinking, but without the artificial stimulation of the hub there was no electrical activity in the brain for his implant to read. As he affixed terminals to Iona's head, compassion for the watching man guided his careful hands. He'd never known her, only understood that there had been trouble between her and his friend.

The link completed. Cellular decay was limited, Iona's memories were there for him to access. Guilt flowed over him at sifting through the intimate sentiments stored in her short-term memory — he raced through her desperate efforts to find out what had happened to her bondmate and saw her encounter with Davidson. He felt her disgust and doubt as to the man's intentions. Valko was troubled; he'd have to warn the vulgar kensakan off mentioning Iona — if Davidson survived all this. Then she met with Rennard and tried to contact Odegebayo himself. The Old Man, showing his unpredictable nature, had blanked her. No, maybe whatever had taken Odegebayo off the case had already happened.

Normally, he would have found himself amid the most recent brain activity first, but without knowing why, he'd skipped back deeper into her mind. Mindlinks were not predictable — unlike Jean seemed to believe, memories were not localised in the brain. You couldn't simply pick a point and delve in. They would flood up as they saw fit and only skill and experience would allow a thorough sifting. In many ways, looking into another's mind — particularly a deceased mind — was like looking into a gemstone.

You saw different scenes as you turned this way and that, looking at different facets.

Then Valko found Iona's last memories before the murder, before he could begin a surface read of them he was drawn in — his mind becoming hers.

Iona started awake, but the quarters were silent. Moz Rennard had told her he would come over, as soon as he had news but he'd not contacted her yet — three days of waiting when Satoshi had already been gone over a week. She didn't know how she'd take it if something had happened to him. The other kensakan — the slimy one — had come by a couple of days ago to reassure her that all was going to plan and that he would be heading out to provide backup. It hadn't reassured her. It seemed like no one knew what was going on. She'd tried to contact Pravnik Odegebayo again but so far she'd been met with silence from his office.

Her gaze went to where Sadiq had been working on some small and quiet project. It involved nurturing a bud of g-ivy to make it grow into a small tree. Where the boy got such strange ideas from she could only guess, it must have been his father's influence. Sadiq had said little about Satoshi's absence. He stayed focused on his studies and when she tried to talk to him — to comfort him — he'd told her in a quiet, serious voice that it would be all right. He'd told her not to worry about his father: that of all men in the Plena he could be counted upon to look after himself.

How strange. Her, a grown woman, being comforted by her young son. All thoughts of pushing his status within the Temple had left her. All she wanted was to see Satoshi's giant frame filling the doorway to their quarters once more and to hear the sigh he always made when coming home.

He was the most irritating, obstinate and old fashioned man she'd ever known. At first, selection as bondmate for a veteran had seemed a privilege. There'd been the fear — the understandable fear — that bonding with a veteran carried the risk of becoming their first victim if the Syndrome should take hold. But then, she'd met him. Despite his intimidating physique, there was a gentleness about Satoshi that she'd never expected to find. The first time they'd slept together, he'd behaved as if it were his first experience. Puzzled, she'd not dared ask him but, as time passed, she'd understood — he'd no memories of lovemaking with anyone else.

Their initial tenderness had affected her deep down: it was wrong — against everything she believed. The teaching of the Temple said so. Humans were not meant to be content: joy must submit to guilt for the sins against the Mother. She'd focused her attentions on their child — turning from Satoshi to keep from the sin of happiness. Found fault with all he did to keep her love for him at bay.

Their son made her proud: he understood the need to seek atonement — impossible as it was to attain. So, she'd poured her being into him, into encouraging him to live according to the needs of the Mother. She hadn't dared share her hopes with Satoshi — he could hardly hide his disdain for the Temple. Instead, she cloaked her dreams with the semblance of ambition and saw the man she fought not to love drift away from her.

She admitted that tender feeling now, knowing that by doing so she'd damned herself.

The door chimed: a visitor. Was it Rennard with news? Pulse racing, wild and sick with expectation, Iona ran to the door. It slid open with a whir. She saw the face of her visitor and her own face fell, assuming the haughty mask she hid behind. Inside, she begged the universe for good news, but all she felt was a scintilla of fear curl up in her belly.

Valko hit a blank wall of Mind. This wasn't the nullity he'd struck in Vinnetti's destroyed brain but something else. The presence he'd felt when he'd tried to reach out without his hub was intruding, blocking his efforts to look further or deeper. He was wide open to the grander Mind — it'd never been like this before, he'd always been too closed. Now he could feel Iona holding him back from her last moments of anguish.

Why? What didn't she want him to see? A gentle caress of thought touched him, she was stopping Satoshi learning the true identity of her murderer, protecting him from something worse than the fact of her death. A shred of sensation burst from the dead memories, a single perceptive shard. Iona had experienced an intuition, an echo from beyond her body-bound consciousness, which told her of the will behind her murder. Whether the hand that had done the deed had been a woman's or not, the will that drove it had been.

Valko sent what he could of his perceptions — the disembodied fragments of the scene — into his hub. He wanted something to show Satoshi, there was nothing he could show that needed shielded from his friend. Preparing to disconnect, he once again felt the touch of that disembodied consciousness. The player behind the mask of flesh. He reached out to her, to it. She used him, used the established mindlink as an anchor and he allowed himself to flow outwards and inwards. Together they felt Satoshi's tortured spirit and drew him into the link, allowing his friend to see and feel the love Iona had held for him — still held for him.

After time immeasurable yet instantaneous, Valko pulled himself back to the physical and detached from the hub. Satoshi stared down at him, eyes shining with tears, but there was peace there too.

'Val, what did you do? Was that real? Was that her?' He asked in an awed voice.

'I don't know for sure, Oshi. It's the kind of thing I've been experiencing. But how can it not be real?'

Valko couldn't lie and claim certain knowledge of the truth of his experience. There was a part of his mind, that old snakelike core, which warned they could be hallucinations no matter the extraordinary abilities that went along with them.

'It felt real,' Satoshi drew a deep shuddering breath. 'I always thought she hated me.'

His face returned to a grim visage, but the hint of grief driven insanity, which had shone in his eyes, was transmuted. There was still fury there, but it was counterbalanced. Measured. Stronger and more terrifying, perhaps, for being more clearly directed. 'Who killed her, Val?'

'I'm sorry, Oshi. Her murderer came from behind. She never saw the face even while she was being bound,' Valko said.

Why was he lying? Ah, it wasn't just his reluctance to seem mad, to admit that the spirit of Iona had refused to give up the face, though she'd known it — the refusal of a ghost. Satoshi would only be hurt more by it and then there was whatever horror the echo of Iona was trying to protect her bondmate from.

The lie carried on being spun by his mouth, almost without the need for his conscious input. 'The impression she had was of revulsion for the touch of the killer, not merely shrinking away from an assailant but a deep distaste for feeling those hands on her. Her murderer was stronger than she was, she didn't have much chance to struggle but I had a sense, like there was an echo of the will driving the murder. I can't explain why but that will felt female.'

'Hampton,' Satoshi snarled.

'Maybe. It wasn't clear that the will behind the murder was present in the murderer. I know that doesn't make much sense and I'm sorry to be so vague, but without a visual memory it's the best I can do.'

Valko held back further explanation: this deceit was against all he'd stood for his whole life. But the lie was justified, wasn't it? Satoshi didn't need any more weight added to his woes. At Valko's heart, the small piece of him that fought so hard to stay free from his implant's influence, howled in pain.

'Can't you find out from that other place? Isn't the truth there to see?' Satoshi asked.

'I don't know, Oshi. I usually don't remember specifics. I'm not sure we could trust the answer, anyway and when I'm in that state, it's hard to remember what's important to us right now. It gives a perspective where all of this is... less significant.' He'd wanted to say meaningless, but it wasn't entirely true and would not be understood — it might just drive the hurt deeper into his friend.

'Then we'll get the answer from Hampton or Fisher the hard way. Whatever else you want from them, you need to know that if he killed her... I'm going to tear his heart out.' The look on Satoshi's face made it clear that he wasn't speaking figuratively.

Valko went to lay a hand on his friend's back, but seeing the aura of barely restrained violence that kept pulsing beneath the exterior calm, he held back.

'I understand. Let's get the truth first, then make sure you get your revenge.'

'Where's Jean?' Satoshi asked.

'I left her tracking Hampton's movements. It may tell us if she was here and lead us to her, too.' Valko kept his tone neutral.

Satoshi's expression shifted again, this time he looked sick with worry. 'Val, I don't know where Sadiq is. What if Fisher has him?'

Projecting confidence into his every word, Valko said, 'We'd best get back to Jean. We can trace Sadiq's beacon. If Fisher has him we won't get an exact location, but at least we'll know. If not... well, you can make sure he's safe before we make our move.'

Satoshi looked as if he was having to try hard to focus on what Valko was saying. Necessity outweighing his discomfort at intruding on the privacy of his friend's mind, Valko studied him with perceptions wide open. He could see the creeping insanity waiting just behind the dark pall of Satoshi's emotions, the Lunar War Syndrome ready to send his friend spiralling into unrestrained violence. It was taking all Satoshi's self-control to push that dark demon back. For now, sanity prevailed. Valko looked away.

'OK,' Satoshi said. 'Lead on. I'm with you.'

✝✝✝

Valko tried to get hold of Rennard but the kensakan's hub was on standby, accepting messages only. It did little to settle his worries. Instead, he had to settle for an anonymous message to the Justeco Centro to inform them of the homicide. Iona's body would be recovered and frozen pending closure of the case. Then he linked with Jean.

«*Jean, bad news. Satoshi's bondmate has been murdered. We think by Hampton. Can you trace her movements around my current location?*»

There was a brief wait for her to respond.

«*Val, she's been there, and recently. I'd say within the last two hours. She's been moving around the Plenum a lot. No movement from the other clone though.*»

«*So... she is the murderer, or rather Fisher is.*»

The shrinking part of Valko's essence that remained callous and calculating refused to accept the logic. Why would Fisher want to murder Iona? If leverage over Satoshi were needed, why not kidnap her instead — hold her and the boy? But what Jean had found in the beacon tracking data was clear — there was no other suspect.

«*Must be.*» Jean sent, her lack of doubts did little to allay his own. He loved Jean — *no you don't* — , could trust her — *no you can't* — so he dismissed his misgivings — *don't be a fool!* Valko let volatile emotion conquer phlegmatic reason.

«*Any closer to locating Fisher?*» He asked.

«*Maybe. I've had an idea, but it best wait until I see you face to face.*»

«*Alright. Before you leave the Justeco Centro, I need you to do one more thing.*»

«*Name it.*»

«*Track Sadiq Tomari, registration number...*» He broke off and looked to Satoshi.

'Do you know Sadiq's Registration number?'

'It's 47X193 Psi,' Satoshi said without pause.

«*Jean, 47X193 Ψ.*»

«*Copy that.*» There was a momentary pause. «*No, there's no return on his beacon.*»

«*It's scattering like Davidson's?*»

«*No, it's just blank, no return.*»

«*Understood. Change of plan, we'll come to you, keep monitoring.*»

«*Alright.*»

He broke off the communication.

'Where's my son?' Satoshi asked, desperation seeping from every pore.

'Jean can't get a return signal from his beacon,' Valko said, trying to say more but Satoshi interrupted him.

'He's dead?'

'No. No, Oshi. It's likely he's somewhere the signal can't get through — doesn't mean he's with Fisher. Plenty of places in the Plenum where beacon tracking is obscured by machinery. Think of where we find Hotbeds. And remember Jack's signal scatters, but it's still detectable. If Sadiq were with Fisher, wouldn't his do the same?' He tried to keep the tone of his voice firm and confident to hide the haziness of his deduction.

'Val, what are we going to do?'

Satoshi had fallen into despair — his face twisting and his words choked from his throat. He was bouncing through emotions at high speed. Every time he seemed settled on a focused state of mind, some new fearful torment showed in him.

'Jean's got an idea. Come with me.'

Valko guided Satoshi out of the rooms, feeling the skin prickle at the back of his neck as he caught the wave of roiling emotions suppressed by the big man's iron will, as they rushed to meet Jean.

╫

Halfway to the Justeco Centro, they saw a large contingent of kensakan heading in their direction. The kensakan — giving no sign they'd spotted Valko or Satoshi — were heading to the crime scene the two had left less than five minutes before. They were equipped for riot control rather than a murder investigation.

'You think they're coming for us?' Valko asked.

'Let them come.'

Crowds melted out of the way of the riot gear equipped kensakan. Each was armed with close combat stun batons or wide-angle knockout guns and was wearing body armour covered with electro capacitor cells — anyone coming into contact with the armour would receive a painful shock.

'At least they're not armed to kill,' Valko said.

'Doesn't make any difference. If you incapacitate your opponent, it's an easy matter to restrain him in a way that he can't breathe and claim it was an accident. Crooked police officers have been doing it for generations. The kensakan have it down to an art.'

Satoshi had never sounded so world-weary and cynical before; Valko tried to reach out to him, to send a feeling of hope. He was met by a chasm of emotion — carved by despair and filled with roiling fury.

'I won't argue with you, Oshi. Whatever they want we need to get out of here and meet up with Jean.'

Valko did his best to fade into the crowd — an effort made harder by the widespread panic of everyone else, frantic to get away from the kensakan. Most of the seething mass no doubt thought they were caught up in a civil disturbance — every Enclosed had heard the stories of the swift and brutal justice enacted on previous mobs. It wouldn't be the first time that innocents had been swept along in riots they wanted no part of — not that it would matter to the kensakan.

'All it takes is for one of them to look this way and we're in trouble,' Valko said in a low voice as he tried to match the movements of those around him — anything not to stand out.

Satoshi just gave a feral grin but his desire for the easy distraction of violence was not fulfilled. The kensakan were focused on getting to their destination and not on surveying the crowd. They passed within ten metres of Satoshi yet did not notice him — even though he was a clear head above everyone else in the crowd and far wider at the shoulders than any of them. They marched past, unaware of the hostility radiating from him.

Valko was beginning to feel sparking flashes of a migraine; he was pretty sure it was being so close to the intensity of Satoshi's emotions and their rapid shifts.

They made good progress — once the crowd had settled back into its routine surging to and fro. Individuals who'd seen the kensakan hurried along to their destinations like a ripple in water. Their passage carried with it disturbance and fear but this soon settled down as they went on their way, trying to navigate the churning mass of humanity.

╬

Though overshadowed by grief and the palpable lust for vengeance coming off Satoshi, Valko found the return to the Justeco Centro smooth and easy — no one checked them, no kensakan guarded the entrances. They entered the back way and no one paid them any notice. Skellan's beacons must not have been flagged. Jean was where Valko had left her: seated at an archaic terminal, crunching data. She looked up at them when they came in.

'I'm so sorry, Satoshi,' she said, sympathy shining from her. 'Fisher is sadistic — but he does nothing without purpose. If he has Sadiq, he'll make demands. Don't trust him. He's probably hoping to compromise you or push your Syndrome over the edge. Be strong.'

It was so achingly genuine that Valko had to blink back tears, but his Sergeant glared at her with suspicion. Valko thought back to what he'd experienced with Iona's memories and what had happened countless times before. Something clicked into place.

'Anything new, Jean?' He asked.

He wanted to take the focus off Satoshi and allow the emotions to settle into the background so he could ask Jean a question that would, without a doubt, trigger another argument. It was there though, nagging at him. The question. He had to ask it.

She talked them through her findings: a pattern of movement by Hampton, who was now in the same building that they were on one of the higher levels. Satoshi nearly needed to be restrained from storming up to confront her, but he responded well to Valko's calm warning not to jeopardise their lead on the true villain — the lauded saviour of humanity — Fisher.

'Neither she, nor the other clone, seem to move far from these central administrative buildings,' Jean said, indicating a map of the Plenum on the screen and circling the heart of the Centra Autorita.

'So he *is* hiding in plain sight?' Satoshi asked.

Blood rushed to Valko's cheeks — he'd scoffed at the idea as had Jean. She didn't seem to bothered, just inclining her head.

'Maybe,' she said. 'Wherever he is, puts a limit on their range of movement but he could be at the base of the Plenum or at its apex. Or anywhere in between.'

'How does this help us?' Valko asked and began massaging his forehead where it felt like a drudge was pounding away with a hammer.

'Neither she, nor the other clone, ever move within a certain area either.' Jean highlighted a section of the data stream. 'Except recently. About the same time as Davidson arrived in the Plenum, Hampton's beacon record goes crazy, but before it did she was heading into that same area.'

'Where?' Valko asked, leaning forward: intent, the throbbing pain behind his eyes forgotten.

'Somewhere between the Lab and the Conclave.' She scowled at him. 'I may have been right on top of him or beneath him all that time.'

Satoshi began pacing. 'So Fisher was very close to where you killed his clone? How does he stay hidden? Could there be a chamber below the Lab area?'

'Maybe.' Jean looked thoughtful. 'Remember, the clone was going to the Conclave from his own lab. They're not directly on top of each other.'

'Yes,' Valko said. 'It did look like he'd been taking a short cut. You presumably followed him from the lab.' Valko did his best to keep an accusatory tone out of his voice.

Jean shifted in her seat before she answered, 'Yes, he arrived at the Lab in a fluster and then went about gathering up papers from his private office. Stormed out with that briefcase the original always used to carry.'

'Little details, Jean. They can give great insights in an

investigation.' She scowled at Valko's superior tone but he continued. 'That briefcase, you'd seen it before?'

'Yes. Erasmus always had it back when we were on the Moon and he was the Chief Scientist. He liked to pretend he had something important in it — never let it out of his sight. Even when we were scouting a location for a third base, he had it with him in the buggy.'

'Third base? I never knew there was a third base,' Satoshi said, seeming taken by the casual reference to a time that now lived nowhere but the distant memories of his fellow refugees from the past.

'Yes. Collins base. Named in honour of the third astronaut on the historic mission. He may not have landed but without him the mission would have failed. We had a particular respect for the unsung heroes of science. Armstrong was built first, then Aldrin and we were about to start construction of Collins when Fisher betrayed us.' She'd brightened at the memories of better times in a safer world, but bitterness crept in the moment Fisher was mentioned.

'You hate him don't you?' Valko asked.

'Yes,' she said, no hesitation in her voice, only absolute clarity.

Valko still didn't quite understand where that wrath came from — he'd seen the barest traces of it when she'd shared her feelings with him. They'd been so bound up in other emotions that he hadn't explored much of what there was to see in her memories; it hadn't seemed necessary. Now his curiosity was an itch, demanding to be scratched.

'Jean, the briefcase. Had you seen it with Fisher's clone before you killed him?'

'No, I don't think so. Why?' She stared at him.

Valko found himself hooked by the look in her eyes; her face was so expressive, each emotion revealing different shades of her beauty. Then like interference clearing from a signal, the needs of the investigation snapped back into focus.

'It must have been something he'd only been given before he went to the Lab. Check the beacon records.'

She performed a quick search. 'Yes, there's a short period where there's a glitch. The sort of thing that must happen all the time, but here it's significant, isn't it?'

'Yes,' Valko tapped the readout. 'The clone has to have been with the original Fisher. This shows he was in the Lab, out of it with a glitch that lasted maybe half an hour, then back in the Lab again.'

'So he was a short walk away,' Satoshi's voice rumbled from the position he'd taken leaning against the entrance, one eye as always on their security.

'Precisely. If we can give Hampton a reason to go to him, we can lie in wait near the Lab and follow her,' Valko said.

'What can we possibly do to make her do that?' Jean asked.

Valko took a deep breath, this was going to be the hard part.

'Jean, memories are not specifically located in only one part of the brain. That is to say: if you damaged a part of the brain, you couldn't selectively destroy memories. I think that you know this. If you wanted to destroy the brain, you'd have used a gun and shot him in the head.'

'OK. Where's this going?' She was beginning to get exasperated with him again. Satoshi shifted his weight. He was keen to get moving, to find Sadiq and to exact revenge.

'Bear with me. You chose to use the nanowire because you knew it could target a particular part of the brain with surgical precision. There must have been a reason.'

'Yes.' Her eyes bored into his and a chill ran through him.

'You wanted to attack the part of the brain that was linked to the original Fisher, didn't you?' It was the only conclusion that made sense to Valko.

'Yes. Alright, it wasn't only about stopping memories. So what?' There was a dangerous tone to her voice.

'Would it have hurt him?'

He couldn't escape the feeling that he was in imminent danger from Jean. She took on the aspect of a coiled serpent about to strike, and Valko wanted to alert Satoshi to the waves of menace flowing from her. Like a mouse caught by a cobra, he couldn't break eye contact.

'Oh, yes,' she said, biting off each word and beginning to lean towards him.

Valko tried to clear his throat but found he couldn't. It took a great effort for him to croak, 'More than a simple shot to the head?'

Jean stopped her slow advance but her eyes maintained their fearful grip on his. 'Yes, any fatal trauma causes a failsafe in the synthorganics that breaks the link before the synthorganics are destroyed. Usually.'

'But by targeting it first you'd cause him the full pain of the experience?' The idea was becoming clearer and clearer in his mind, while the oppressiveness of Jean's stare receded.

'Yes.'

'You hate him that much?'

'Yes, dammit Valko.' Despite the impatience evident in her words and the tone of her voice, the dangerous edge had dissipated.

'He hates you the same way?'

'I don't know. Yes, I think so.' Her apparent uncertainty left him wondering whether he'd imagined the previous intensity.

'Is he the kind of man who would want to make an enemy suffer or the kind who'd want to kill them swiftly?'

'What kind of a question is that?' She asked.

'An important one, Jean. What do you think?'

'He'd like to make it long and painful, if he had the chance. If he had hold of me, he'd want to extract all of my knowledge. I'm sure that wouldn't be a pleasant experience.' She was projecting a hint of fear and with that Valko was flooded with concern for her.

Part of him wondered at the rapidity of the change, but again he overrode it.

'Then we have our way to him,' he said.

Jean sat back, eyes widening. 'You can't mean…'

'We're running out of time, I think it's our only option,' Valko said.

'What are you two talking about?' Satoshi asked, a confused scowl twisting the hard lines of his face.

'Valko wants to use me as bait. Get Hampton to deliver me to Fisher, in person. You and he will swoop in to save me, like the cavalry.'

'The cavalry?' Another one of their Old World references

that left Valko feeling ignorant.

'I'll explain it later, Val,' Satoshi said. 'So you want to go with the plan that Fisher was apparently too clever to fall for?'

'In the absence of a better suggestion what else can we do?' Valko said. 'He has Davidson, maybe he has Sadiq too. Once he realises that we're back on the grid he'll trace us through our beacons. He knows we've met because of the naukara, they'd transmit a signal of what they were seeing right?'

Jean nodded.

'So he'd know that they'd been disabled. He has to assume that all of us are now aware of the truth. That we're united against him. We're a threat that grows the longer he leaves us. Logic demands he squash us as soon as he can. In every way, our time is running out.'

The words resonated deep inside Valko, the candle of his life burning now faster and brighter. Satoshi's face had darkened at the mention of Sadiq, he set his jaw and gave a sharp nod. Jean blew out a long breath.

'Alright,' she said. 'We'll do it your way. Give me a chance to prepare myself. I'll meet you back here in twenty minutes.'

She rose without waiting for a response and hurried out of the room.

'Doesn't she want to know how we're going to deliver her to Hampton?' Satoshi asked.

'Apparently not.'

Valko stroked his chin, troubled. He began to hold up the shreds of doubt that he held about Jean, but, even as he tried to encompass them, they flew from his mind on a wind of feeling — a sentiment that said he was doing the right thing.

Chapter 18

They waited outside the Lab. It was based on the lowest of the middle-levels, without access to those above it save by a circuitous route. The old elevator shaft at the bottom of the Plenum had been a far faster way for Eugene Fisher to go — never knowing he was only rushing to his death. The Lab building itself was innocuous enough: part of the well-planned structures of Arcas Plenum, it was covered by the ubiquitous g-moss. Unlike the medical centre, there was no particular odour of antiseptic released by this genus; the sterile environment inside would be controlled on an experiment-by-experiment basis.

It was symptomatic of the pervading attitude to science that the vital work of the whitecoats in Arcas Plenum's Lab was kept down here — out of sight. Not quite in the uninhabitable areas, where no one but drudges on maintenance duty would go, yet still hard to get to. The average Enclosed wouldn't have a reason to come near the Lab, it had been sited away from areas of regular thoroughfare on purpose. Was that a Temple decision? To keep science out of sight and out of mind? Or did it suggest that Fisher had arranged for his work, and that of his clone, to be in a location which might be overlooked? Where the Temple's own strategy would work against it as much as much as against the masses. It mattered little now.

'Do you think she believed him?' Satoshi asked, as he fidgeted with the mobile beacon tracker they'd 'requisitioned' from Justeco Centro stores.

'We'll know soon enough. I think Rennard will be persuasive. After all, he doesn't know what he's really doing,' Valko said and grinned at Satoshi.

It'd been easy enough to arrange for Rennard to receive an alert calling him to an attempted sabotage of the Lab. He'd arrived not long after they'd sent the anonymous tip off about a former technician trashing the place. Jean had been relaying an audio feed from a headset-hub when he arrived — good old, naïve Moz Rennard. Straightaway, he'd arrested her for attempting to undermine the efficiency of the Plenum — a serious enough offence that he'd needed to call it in to ask the

Justeco Centro for backup — they'd send a Moderator. A short vid recording showing Jean was the suspect Rennard had apprehended would have been attached to the message to make sure that any records of her identity and past offending would be with the Moderator as soon as possible. Fisher must now know who Jean was; there would be a flag on possible sightings of her. He'd want any threat to his research dealt with fast — there was a high chance that Hampton would come to deal with it.

'What do we do if this doesn't work and Jean's just arrested? She'll be executed and recycled for this. Worse, if they bother with a mindlink it'll all come out,' Satoshi said.

Absentminded, the sergeant kept clicking the selector on his omni-pistol between energy and ballistic settings — now fully charged, fully loaded. He'd still complained that they lacked sufficient firepower. They had no choice; there was no way to traverse the Plenum armed with anything more substantial without attracting attention.

'Easy, Oshi. Relax.' Valko flooded his voice with a calm he didn't feel — the burden of command. 'She'll take the bait. Either here or later, once Jean is in custody. She can't afford for Jean to be mindlinked by a Moderator, any more than we can. All we need to do is to follow Hampton when she takes Jean to Fisher. The clone taking the enemy to its master.'

'Do you really think that Fisher is that predictable?' Satoshi asked, shaking his head.

'No, not the man — the emotion. Hate will make people act both stupidly and predictably.' He mentally added, *I hope.*

'What if he just decides to have his clone do it?' Satoshi asked.

'"What if"s" are no help to us at all,' Valko said, 'Pull yourself together.'

There was none of the old harshness to his tone, but Satoshi reacted as if there had been. He reverted to obedient sergeant almost without thinking. Valko saw the shadow over Satoshi, but obedience to the chain of command seemed to ease the insidious skulking of his Lunar War Syndrome. If Fisher had meant to push Satoshi over the edge by killing his wife and taking his son, he'd come close. Killcrazy was no further away than a single slip of Satoshi's willpower.

It didn't take long: Hampton arrived on her own. They

listened as she spoke to Rennard, dismissing him and taking custody of the prisoner. Then they heard the sound of Rennard departing and the audio followed him.

'He must have forgotten to hand the hub over. Rennard, you baka,' Valko said, wondering whether it was the old kensakan trick of forgetting evidence they could trade or if the man were just preoccupied.

'It's alright, there's only one exit from the Lab,' Satoshi said, confident now that their gamble seemed to be paying off.

They waited. It was taking too long.

'What the hell are they doing in there?' Satoshi asked.

'I don't know,' Valko said, rubbing the back of his head where a dull ache had started up. 'Could there be another way out?'

'Maybe. Should we take a look?'

'What and risk giving this away? No, let's wait another fifteen minutes, then we go in.' Valko massaged the bridge of his nose, trying to dull the needlepoints driving into the back of his eyes.

They waited for ten minutes before Hampton emerged, dragging a large canister behind her — the kind the kensakan might use to store a corpse in, on the way to the Justeco Centro's forensic lab. At first, it looked like a show of incredible strength — Jean must be inside — but then Valko saw the wheels at its base: there was a powered traction unit doing all the hard work.

Flitting from shadow to shadow, they followed Hampton as she began to disappear into the murk. Jean's beacon was showing up bright and clear on the tracker.

'We'll know we're getting close when we start seeing that scattering effect,' Valko said.

'It may come on suddenly, or it may not affect us at close range. Don't rely on it. This is pre-War tech, it'll function in ways you're not familiar with.'

Satoshi had drawn his omni-pistol and held it in a loose grip. In his hands it looked light and small in size, but Valko recalled its weight and how it was so large it looked ludicrous in his own.

Hampton walked at a steady pace and cast the occasional glance around her but in the same natural way anyone walking along would. She showed no sign of any awareness of being followed. Her route took them down a ramp, then another and in less than five minutes they were at the lowest level of the Plenum where the reek of foul water washed over them.

'This really is a short cut. Most of the time you'd need to walk much further to find a ramp or F-shaft and then wait in line to get to the next level,' Valko said.

'That's because the mass elevators and rapid access chutes were closed down at the time of Enclosure. All about preventing too much rapid and uncontrolled movement by the populace,' Satoshi said, as if he'd been there. On reflection, Valko corrected himself: Satoshi probably had been there.

'We're not too far from where Eugene Fisher was killed,' Valko said. 'So maybe after the clone visited the original, he went directly to meet the Conclave.'

'He could have doubled back to the Lab first. It's not that far — but this would be the way he'd come if he were in a hurry,' Satoshi said, then stopped — ducking further into the cover of a nearby cluster of pipes. Valko did the same. It was so easy to secrete himself amongst the tangle of pipes and old machinery, he could understand how wei-zhuce were able to evade the kensakan.

Hampton had stopped and was now peering around, studying each approach to the area she'd entered — a meeting of five passages through the inner workings of the Plenum's vitals. She still didn't seem to notice them — her caution appeared to be more habit than out of any sense that she was being followed. After a moment, ostensibly satisfied, she thrust her right arm in between some of the pipework near her, and did something with her hand. The action was too well hidden by the pipes and the dripping water running down off everything but whatever she did triggered a reaction from the ground beside her.

There was a quiet shifting sound, an almost inaudible grind and rattle of metal on metal as an opening appeared. Shallow puddles of oily water drained into the hole. Hampton manoeuvred the canister next to the opening and then moved it over the hole. Instead of dropping, the canister floated in place for a moment before lowering out of sight. She watched it go, reached into the same nest of pipework and did something again. The hatch closed and the surrounding puddles of water, formed from the internal Plenum precipitation, filled up, concealing its presence. Hampton peered around one last time, then turned and walked off — not a care in the world.

They waited for a moment until she was out earshot — even from Satoshi's enhanced hearing.

'We follow the canister, right?' Valko asked, feeling the mounting tension in his friend spilling over into his awareness and adding to his own uncertainty.

'And let Hampton get away?' The big man growled, fist clenched tightly around the grip of the omni-pistol.

'She's nothing but a puppet for the original Fisher. She's obviously been altered dramatically to be female and look so different, but you saw the readout from her beacon. The biometrics are a 99.999% match for Eugene Fisher. Forget the difference in gender and appearance, they're the same person.'

'You're right,' Satoshi let out a long sigh and returned his sidearm to its holster, slung on his bulging right thigh. 'And if you're not I'll deal with her, it — whatever she is... later.'

They crept to the place where Hampton had stood moments before. There was nothing to suggest a change in the floor surface. Dirty water had flowed in to cover the closed hatchway and whatever was concealed in amongst the pipework was not visible from outside the snaking cluster of tubes and cables.

'What if it's some kind of DNA scanner, or a passcode?' Valko asked, gripped by worry. 'What if she used a key?'

'Now who's using "what if"? Problems like that are what this is for,' Satoshi said, patting the omni-pistol. 'With a full charge it'll cut straight through the hatch. The metal can't be that thick. Give it a try, Val.' He gestured to whatever device was hidden by the pipes.

Feeling an inexplicable trilling in his nerves — fearful of hidden jaws about to close on his wrist — Valko reached in between the pipes. Filthy water streamed over his hand, he felt the roughness of metal that had corroded over decades from the constant downpour. With his arm pushed into the gap up to his shoulder, he finally felt it: a featureless, smooth pad that felt warm to the touch. Hoping it wasn't a handprint analyser or some other biometric lock, he pressed it. There didn't seem to be any give and his heart jerked in his chest as a low whining sound came from where his hand rested — no shock of electricity. A muted click sounded from the floor where the hatch had begun to open.

Satoshi had his omni-pistol in one hand and a long blade in the other, held reversed so the back of the blunt edge of the knife was pressed to his inner forearm. Valko hadn't seen him take the knife and wasn't sure where it had come from. Crude and vicious, the blade was blackened but with a swirling pattern to it. An uncomfortable creeping sensation made its way up Valko's spine — he recognised that blade, its dark brutal edge seemed to whisper of the lives it had drunk. No... it was just his imagination.

'That's the knife you had on the Moon, isn't it?' Valko asked.

'Yeah. I didn't remember before, but it was with my gear when I woke from storage. I kept it in my quarters but never knew why until now. This blade's been with me since I joined the ITF — seems appropriate that I'm going to use it to cut Fisher's head off.'

'I thought you were going to tear his heart out,' Valko said.

Satoshi regarded him slowly. 'I'm going to cut his head off right after I tear his heart out.'

There was no trace of any humour in his tone; the ruthless certainty there sent a shiver through Valko. As much as he'd changed, Valko could see that Satoshi had been altered too. Gone was the sensitive soul, who'd so riled him all those years. Now there was just a killer with a thin skin of ice over a roiling lava flow of wrath.

Shaken to his core by the insight, Valko passed a hand over his eyes. When he moved his hand back, Satoshi, just plain old Satoshi was standing there again. Valko pointed in the direction of the hatch. 'How are we going to close it after us?'

Satoshi strode to the opening. 'Why bother?'

The previous grinding noise grew more strident as Satoshi blocked the mechanism; his strength was incredible — no strain showed in his body or face.

'Might want to get down here before the mechanism breaks, Val.'

Valko hopped down the hole, landing on a concealed lift plate that had already started to descend. Satoshi held the hatch back with one hand while he lowered himself before dropping onto the narrow platform beside Valko. The hatch, no longer obstructed, snapped shut and they were plunged into darkness. Combined with the sensation of descent, it made Valko's heart race. The tube took forever to descend — his nerves making time drag — but it was a descent of, at most, fifty metres.

'This must have been constructed as part of the original city.' Valko whispered. 'Sinking a shaft this deep would have been impossible to conceal after Enclosure.'

'I've seen something like this before,' Satoshi said, his voice low but not a whisper. 'The ITF loved to hide secret operations bases in places like this.'

'I always saw the ITF as the military arm of the UN World Government.'

'No — we had a wider ambit. Most of what we did was trying to keep the Superstates in line, stopping them from finding, or making, reasons to go to war with each other. It was always convenient to have a concealed base in the major cities. We were surprisingly successful at keeping them hidden. Arcas Plenum was originally a UNWG prototype city — it's no surprise we had a base here.'

'Would the depth explain the signal scattering?' Valko asked, though he realised he already knew the answer. He wondered why he'd bothered to ask. Shame flushed to his cheeks — it was to cover his nerves. Clenching his jaw muscles tight, Valko vowed that he wouldn't let cowardice — artificial and flowing from his implant — claim him.

'No, I'd have expected fifty metres to effectively block the signal. If this was an ITF facility, there'd have been a lot of communications links to the surface. Relays and the like. The beacon must be using the same system but, without the correct encryption, the signal is scattered so it can't be located.'

Valko felt his self separate into Satoshi for a moment — *he scratched his cheek — two days' worth of stubble irritating his usually clean-shaven face. He longed for the days when he'd been able to shine a light on his face and switch his beard off for six months — but that tech was lost with so much else. The stupid rules of the Plena meant that even the small amount of hair taken every day from men's faces was a resource to be recycled. This screwed up world was no different from the old one. The rules didn't apply to the elite in the same way as for everyone else; even something as simple as growing a beard being a sign of status. No change, just a different symbol. Now, when he got his hands on Fisher...* Valko pulled himself back into his own headspace, gasping. His control was slipping. Satoshi seemed oblivious and now started saying how obvious it was that there'd be an ITF base here, and that Fisher would have known about it.

'Why didn't you mention this before?' Valko asked.

His intermittent headache had faded in the aftermath of the unwanted flash of insight, but every now and then he'd get a sudden pulse of pain that made him wince.

'I didn't think of it as a possibility. I may have my memories back but they're not organised, I need something to jog a memory, most of the time.' A touch of his usual good humour returned. 'I'm an old man, remember?'

They reached the bottom of the shaft and found a smooth and empty corridor in front of them, lit with low-energy red lighting. There was a strange mix of sounds coming from ahead: the bubbling of liquids, clicking of machines and a sound like rasping breathing.

Both men had drawn their sidearms. Valko knew that the tranqgun he carried — even set to lethal — wouldn't have much effect should they encounter naukara. Satoshi's omni-pistol might prove more useful in such tight confines, where larger weapons were almost as much of a hazard to their wielder as to their target. But having the reassuring weight of a frag gun in his hands would have made Valko feel much better.

They reached the end of the corridor and peered out — eyes and ears straining. The light was dim and it was hard to make out the layout and purpose of the room they looked into. The source of the faint glow came from the base of the walls revealing the shape of the room but keeping its contents obscured.

'No sign of Jean,' Valko whispered.

Valko stepped into the room, senses pricking. He was aware of Satoshi stalking forward beside him, muscles bunched like a predator ready to strike at the first sign of prey.

The room was large by Plenum standards but filled with all manner of equipment of unknown purpose. Ahead, Valko could just about see the canister's motor unit. It'd been detached and left near the entrance — so who'd carried the cylinder with Jean inside. Another unlit corridor exited the room directly across from them and Valko began to cross to it, Satoshi following a step behind.

Valko was in the lead; the moment he set foot in the dark passageway, doors — which had stood unseen in the low light — slid open in the left and right-hand walls. Valko turned back to look into the room. There were now four corridors opening into it. Out of each of the two most recently opened, there came a figure. The lights in the room flared on and blinded Valko, but he'd seen enough of the forms to know they were naukara — the same sort as those that had attacked them in New York.

Satoshi had already raised his gun by the time Valko's vision cleared enough to see. The sergeant fired a flaring blast of energy into the head of his leftmost foe followed by one of the ballistic turbo penetrator rounds. There was an explosion of gore and micro component parts. The naukara collapsed in a heap but the other one, spared by the demise of its counterpart, had time to pounce on Satoshi.

Valko raised his tranqgun to fire a shot — for all the good it would do — but as he did so the door he'd stepped through slid down. Illumination flared from every surface of the corridor until it was like being in a tunnel of light. Then that blinding whiteness filled with dark figures reaching for him. He fired off maybe eight rounds from his tranqgun before it was knocked from his hands — had he done any damage at all? Cold hands, clawed hands, gripped him and dragged him out of the blinding corridor of light into darkness — he felt a prick in his arm and numbness bit at him, stealing the world away piece by piece.

†††

Valko came awake, his stomach rebelling and his mouth dry and sore. There'd been no transcendence this time. Nothing save unconsciousness — a void of unknowing. He was upright and restrained at his wrists, upper arms, head, and at his legs above and below his knees. The light hurt his eyes but, as his vision adjusted, he realised it was a normal Plenum level of illumination, like that of an overcast day. He wasn't alone. A figure sat at a comfortable desk covered with old style terminals; he drifted into focus — Odegebayo. The Old Man was leafing through hardcopy files, appearing to assimilate their data in an instant.

'What are you doing here?' Valko tried to ask him but the words rasped in his throat. Valko coughed and tried to swallow but it didn't help. He couldn't even gather enough saliva to spit. Odegebayo didn't even look up.

To either side of Valko, other figures hung, he could make them out by straining to look from the corner of his eyes. Jean dangled to his left; Davidson sagged in his restraints just past her. At the end, Satoshi hung, blocking any view of what lay beyond. They were all there, bound as he was. Odegebayo stood, walked to the door of the room and disappeared into the dim, red-tinted hallway.

'He's on the way to the refresher — again. One of the pleasures of growing old the natural way, parts of your body breaking down — you never escape the unpredictable need to pee.'

The speaker's voice chimed out, resonating through the chamber. He stepped into view. Who else, if not Fisher? Youth and charisma combined to make the man, but more than that he sparked with vibrancy. Despite skin tanned to rival a Remnant, he was the spitting image of Eugene Fisher — the clone Jean had murdered. Valko corrected himself, the clone she'd terminated.

'What is he doing here?' Valko managed to croak.

'Odegebayo? Just a short stay while matters are resolved. He'll return to his post soon, none the wiser for his little sojourn here.' Fisher walked round in front of Valko and turned to face him.

'Why was he ignoring me?' Valko asked.

'He thinks he's in a medcentre after being treated with some more retrogene therapy. Thinks he's reading reports and managing things at a desk in the convalescing room. When I'm done, he'll wake up in a real medcentre just in time to be discharged.'

Fisher raised a datapad and input a commands. The binding around Valko's head released a degree and a clear plastic tube curved around into his mouth. Cool, clean water trickled from its end and, as he sated his thirst, his throat began to clear.

'What are you doing, Fisher?' Valko asked.

This was it — the moment he'd learn if they were to live

or die. He cursed inwardly. They'd known Fisher was too clever to fall for a simple ruse. Where had the overconfidence in their plan come from? Had his last shred of judgement been smothered by the sandstorm of his emotions as the rest had been worn away and buried, bit by bit?

'I'm trying to work out what to do with you and your friends.' Fisher smiled; it wasn't sinister or smug but nonetheless it filled Valko with dread. 'You've created something of a problem for me. You and that woman.' His tone became biting at the mention of Jean.

'What have you done to them?' Valko asked, coughing so hard his whole body shook the chains that held him, leaving them clanking and rattling.

'They're just unconscious, for now. Perhaps, you can tell me what the hell you think you're doing, breaking into my sanctum?' His voice snapped through the air with a whip crack.

'Rescuing Satoshi's son, finding Jack Davidson and revealing the truth.' Valko glared defiance at his captor.

Fisher rocked back and rich laughter effervesced from him. 'The truth? All this time and I never knew you were a comedian at heart, Valko. You've been listening to Jean's truth and the truth as peddled by that crackpot who calls himself the Philosopher, haven't you.' Fisher scoffed. 'Do you believe they've been telling you the truth? One word of it? I had my eye on you, long before all of this. The most logical of *my* Moderators — a man who doesn't rely on guesswork. A man free from the constraints of petty emotion. A man with no compunction about doing what he must. Has that malfunctioning implant robbed you of your own identity?'

Valko was stunned — there was truth in these words. He'd expected lies.

'No doubt, they blamed me for all the world's woes while vindicating themselves? Told you how I stole all their precious research and perverted it. Yes, I can see from the look on your face I'm close to it.' The handsome face twisted in scorn. 'What about her? What lies did she tell you to make you work with her? What promises did she make? What favours did she bestow? You do know she's a murderer, don't you?'

'Killing a non-sentient clone has never been called murder, Fisher. Not in the Plena you built. From what I hear you're the one who deserves the title murderer.' Valko said, his anger swelling — but oh, how close to the mark Fisher was getting.

'A non-sentient clone? Is that what she told you? That's just like her. Jean knows all about clones. Oh yes, Eugene was a clone, but non-sentient? What piloted by my consciousness, I suppose? Under my direct control was he? His father too?' Fisher came close to Valko's face and sneered — there was pain behind the expression, seeping out around the edges.

Valko, voice still hoarse, strained to shout back, to stop the erosion of his new paradigm. 'I've linked to her mind — I've seen the truth. I've linked to the Philosopher's mind and seen his memories. In either view, you're a monster responsible for the death of billions.'

'You think one man caused all of this?' Fisher asked, waving his hand as if encompassing not just the room but the whole world. 'Wake up, Gangleri. They're using you.'

'If you're the one telling the truth then let me see it in your mind,' Valko said, feeling a surge of hope at the thought of Fisher making the fatal mistake of letting him in.

'Yes, why don't I let you see? The drug you were given should have worn off enough for you to try.' Fisher sat back on the desk, quite calm — it couldn't be this easy, could it?

Valko closed his eyes and reached down inside himself, his mind growing along with his perceptions but, before the physical world retreated like a curtain pulled aside, he stopped himself. This was the apex of his ability in the physical world. Yes, he could try to see Fisher as he truly was — in that void beyond the veil of illusions — but then this would all be meaningless to him. Instead, he found the discipline inside himself to hold onto his physical perceptions — an anchor point of uncompromising and ruthless logic still there, deep down — and reached out with his mind, probing for Fisher's. There it shone, a web of such density it appeared solid, to have weight: he plunged inside.

Valko saw three spheres of memory. As he tried to navigate between them, confused and seeking for what was real, his mind was swept into the first and he lived it. It was all inside him. Fisher was his father. Valko watched his own birth and raising at the hands of a firm but caring man. They lived in a small apartment in New York and Valko went to school there. He saw his whole life unfolding up to the present moment. No War had happened, no bombs had fallen and nanites were still just a distant dream. The Moon had not been scarred by nuclear fire. The memory was so real — so true — that Valko had to fight with every grain of his being not to believe it. Every thought and recollection was so convincing and genuine. His father loved him and would only ever protect him; Dad was shielding him from the mental health laws, keeping him at home to treat him away from the state asylums. Dad was risking everything for him, he couldn't fail him. Just take the medication, one dose at a time, it was working. He was getting better. Now, one part and one part only of Valko resisted. The remote and sceptical nucleus which was the true him said 'This cannot be!' The medication wasn't working, they were taking him for the lobotomy…

The next life of memories flooded in submerging what had come before. The Mother was devastated and the Plena were full. Valko had become a Pravnik, bondmated with Orla and they'd been ordered to produce a child. It was a son. They called him Eugene. He watched the boy grow and knew all of a father's pride for an accomplished son — a son who looked more and more like him every day. At night, he dreamed of a different life, but it was slipping away. Suddenly, brutally, his son was murdered. Fury filled him. He knew who had done it, knew the twisted touch of her hand, a hand that revelled in causing him agony. The still waters inside Valko granted him sanctuary — there he found memories of the real world. Innocuous details like the dirt under his nails when he cleaned his tranqgun, the numbers on the NOTT capsules and the discomfort of sweat rashes when he'd worked the case in Singa Plenum. They were real. The bubble of memory broke but before he could take control, Valko was plunged back into Fisher's life seen through a final facet of the mind.

This time Valko kept himself, sitting as an observer, outside memories as complete, whole and vivid as the other two. Fisher was an immortal. He was a being called Lucifer who had taxed humanity from before the creation of the World. At the same time, He was someone who'd been called Jesus — or was it Ieshua — the hope and redemption of all. He was Siddartha Gautama — becoming the Buddha by denying Mara and his own existence as 'I'. And Hitler consigning the Jews to the gas chambers with sadistic pleasure. And Gandhi turning peace into the greatest means of liberation. The names meant nothing to Valko but he lived through the memories and knew each of the beings in intimate detail. He understood the contradictory nature of the memories. The spark of self inside him was fading, near exhausted. It tried to rise up, to liberate him from what could not be: it failed.

All of it was true. Fisher loved him and hated him. He was the world's greatest foe and its greatest saviour.

Fisher released him; with a gasp Valko opened his eyes and retreated from his expanded consciousness.

'What the fuck have you done to me?' He screamed at Fisher.

Fisher was standing watching him, faint amusement evident in his eyes. 'Why don't you take seven breaths — it'll calm you down.' Fisher winked. 'Now, I've just shown you how someone with sufficient mental architecture can present a false memory to you. Although perhaps one of those memories has a hint of truth? Perhaps, not. Do you understand?'

Valko had no choice but to retreat from this epiphany into his logical mind — now nothing more than a cold pebble at the base of the landslide of his emotions. 'You're telling me that anyone with synthorganic brain tissue could manipulate me through a mindlink, show me false images?'

'Yes, that is if they had enough extra capacity. Anything I, or that so called Philosopher or even Jean shows you could as easily be a lie as the truth.'

Fisher radiated love and understanding tinged with vicious loathing. The effect was nauseating in its contradictory intensity but Valko began to feel his own emotions resonating — they shifted, matching those Fisher was projecting into him.

'As for emotions,' Fisher said. 'I can project whatever I like. Given time, I could use those same emotions to manipulate you — make you think your own were reacting naturally. Don't you think they could too?'

'But... I can go beyond the merely physical. I can see things as they truly are,' Valko said, desperate to fight back against this assault on all his beliefs and assumptions.

'*If* it is real. *If* it is not just one amazing trip caused by the drugs you've been given. If it's not just an hallucination caused by the tumour you have. Maybe you do see beyond the veil, some grand plan behind this shallow reality, but do you remember it? All of it? Be honest.' There was an absence of expression on Fisher's face and no hint of mind emanated from him — no emotive signals of any kind.

The cool detachment soothed Valko more than anything else could have right at that moment. It was fresh water from a mountain spring to a desert pilgrim.

'No,' he said. 'There's so much, I can't choose what to hold onto.'

'Valko, I must apologise for doing this to you — Jean and I have been involved in a… cold war against each other for decades now. She still blames me for what happened on Mars — she thinks I didn't share her grief. That on its own wouldn't have been enough to foster our mutual hatred. It was just a spark. We've done such things to each other over time.'

Fisher paused and Valko turned the question over in his mind, *was Fisher the father of Jean's daughter?* Before he could settle himself enough to ask, Fisher continued.

'What brought this to a head? It was my fault, I took Jean's implants and her latest research. But it was for good reason: she had sabotaged my own stock of synthorganic implants and caused no end of problems. She has this belief that, since she discovered synthorganics, no one else is allowed to advance the field — least of all me — even if they only want to use her precious discoveries for the good of humanity. Her ego used to rest upon intellect, now it is supported by the twin pillars of ignorance and arrogance. I was using her discoveries to better the lives of all of us… to give humanity a better world.'

'To save yourself, you mean.' There was no anger in Valko's voice, in spite of his suspension in chains, his sense of dignity was creeping back.

'No, Valko. They — those who have turned you against me. They take the individualistic view — while I look to the needs of the species as a whole. They worry about today — I worry about tomorrow and about a thousand years from now. There is much you don't remember about your past, which is natural given the implantation process but, deep down, you've never changed as a person.' Fisher stroked his chin. Valko saw the movement as staged: someone in such control of themselves could not act without thought.

'Maybe that's true, but I know enough to disbelieve you. You killed Vinnetti and, ultimately, Actur too. They'd uncovered what you'd done to the veterans, hadn't they? Subverted them so they'd go killcrazy whenever someone tried to activate them. So you sent an assassin to deal with them. Make it look like the same MO as your own clone's death, to throw off the scent.'

'Excellent, Valko,' Fisher smiled but it reeked of smugness. 'Excellent. But you're not quite there yet.'

'You admit you killed them?'

Fisher stepped back and held his hands out to his sides, palms up. 'Yes, I admit it, I did — or rather one of my agents did. You know that a single human life or two, are nothing when set against the species as a whole. One death — for the right reasons — might be a good thing. History would support me on that. Though if Eugene's murder at Jean's hand was not truly murder then neither was Vinnetti's. Perhaps even less so. And Actur wasn't much different.'

'What do you mean?' He said, the Moderator's tone that had gone a long way to giving Valko so much of his reputation returning to his voice. He was finding it easier to set aside the emotive overload he'd been suffering — his rightful self coming to the fore — how long could it last?

'Do you think that I am the only one with clones? At least, I allow mine to have some autonomy. There are others who have mere extensions of their own will. Who do you think was puppetting Vinnetti? Iduna Vinnetti. Xiang Rhea. Iduna and Rhea. Jean was always such an egotist.'

'You're saying Vinnetti was her clone?'

Fisher raised an eyebrow and smiled but stayed silent.

'I suppose you expect me to believe that Eugene Fisher was sentient? Not just your puppet.'

Valko's lip curled in derision, though he was now unsure of his previous judgement of this man. The stories he'd heard throughout his childhood of Erasmus Fisher — his selfless heroism and ingenuity in preserving millions of lives in the Plena — reverberated through his mind. Maybe this man was in the right? Valko's logical mind snapped back to the key requirement: evidence.

'Yes. He thought of me as Grandfather. Well, not this body, but the one I let him see. He didn't even know the truth of his situation. So what if I sent messages to his subconscious mind on occasion? I never took control of him — I didn't interfere when he wanted to pursue his fool's quest in defiance of physics. My other offspring — clones if you insist — some know, some don't; I let them make their own choices.' Righteous anger was in the words and Fisher paced up and down in front of Valko, but there was still the nagging feeling that it was staged.

'You mean Hampton?'

Fisher stared into his eyes for a moment, allowing a slow smile to spread across his face. 'Her too. This is all beside the point though. Regardless of whatever Jean has told you, I have no desire to kill you, but nor can I let you — any of you — leave. It is a quandary.'

Emotion clawed its way back to the forefront of Valko's being — the clean air of his mind fogged again by emotions: synthetic and fraudulent. 'Why not let them go? If you mean us no harm like you say.'

'Did I say that? No… I do mean you harm. That meddling bitch deserves what's coming to her. Your moron subordinate, what is it? Oh yes, Davidson. He deserves a fitting punishment. You and Satoshi, though. I have no particular problem with you. The attempts on your lives were conducted by Hampton not me. Eva made two errors — using a cretin and assuming you were acting against my interests. But you survived and Actur's escape served its purpose. Besides, I wouldn't waste such useful… instruments.

Eva is the most aberrant of my clones. I'd hoped to control her by placing her in a position of some authority where she could feel that she was in possession of real power.' Fisher shrugged. 'It was the classic error. Give someone a little of what they want and they just want more. She took it upon herself to remove Odegebayo thinking to give me a stronger position. You've been caught up in her little power play. Such is the way of children — she doesn't deal well with competition. It's taken me valuable time to undo what she wrought.' Fisher threw up his hands in frustration. 'Ah, what's the point? If I free you and Satoshi, he'll try to kill me because of what he thinks Eva did and because he thinks I have his son. After me, he'll kill her. I'm not going to let that happen — she's the closest thing I have to a daughter. Even if she is a conniving psychopath. I must give serious consideration to changing her mind. Not all clones turn out close to their progenitor, more's the pity. Don't you agree, Valko?'

'So what are you going to do?' Valko was beginning to feel a sinking feeling in his stomach, a weight that swung this way and that, trying to find escape — downwards.

Fisher locked gazes with him and said, 'You and Satoshi will undergo another period of re-education; I hate to waste resources. Davidson, well I'll have to think of something noteworthy for that waste of skin. It's a pity time travel is impossible or I'd have had his parents neutered.' He grinned with such malevolence that it carved his face anew — a different aspect, a different man. 'Jean, well that depends on whether I've got the original... oh, I do hope so. The face may be different...' The thought of how it had been the same face he'd seen in the Philosopher's memories jumped into Valko's mind — manipulation of him even then? His attention returned to Fisher,'...but it never was much to look at, anyway. Regardless, I'm going to take all of her secrets as a small recompense for the pain she's put me through. After that, well I'll see what's left of her consciousness. Now, if you don't mind, I have a mess to clear up.'

Fisher reached up and pressed something to Valko's neck. Consciousness fled almost as fast as the pain of the breaking of his skin could reach him.

Chapter 19

Valko woke again, this time to true darkness. It wasn't just the time it was taking for his vision to recover from whatever narc Fisher had injected him with, he was in a room with the barest hint of light. The sound of liquid dripping onto a hard surface echoed around him. Water or some, more viscous, liquid. There were other sounds — not as close: harsh rasping breathing and a sound of something tearing wetly, interspersed with occasional sounds of fluid being sucked up by a machine. Pain still scythed through his head and his mouth , yet there was a clarity that had not been there before — a balance between his competing facets.

A question burned in his mind, sudden and unexpected. A product of his subconscious mind, or something his physical, limited being had taken from his greater consciousness — it didn't matter. The question gave him a chance. Not only to get out of this, but to know the truth. He had to know if Jean had been deceiving him. Too much of what Erasmus Fisher said made sense to him. What was worse — he couldn't find the lie in the man's words.

Valko ran through the evidence: Jean's reluctance to be questioned; the ease with which she had tracked him and Satoshi; and her access to the naukara in such quick time. She'd been involved in whatever brainwashing had been done to Satoshi, albeit whatever she'd done had been superseded. By Fisher? There were no other candidates — so she had to have been telling the truth about that.

What about the access to clones? She had the knowledge to be able to create clones; if everything he had been told about her was true, she was the leading geneticist of her generation — of all the generations since DNA had first been discovered. It would be a simple matter for her to create a clone or several clones. She'd known about Fisher's clones and understood their limitations. Was that from practical experience or the theoretical? She had a callous attitude about clones — naukara too — but was Fisher playing him? Weakening his will to make brainwashing him easier? What he'd implied about Actur — the smug smile Fisher had flashed him when he'd told him he was close to the truth.

Actur, who'd been trying to say 'Benedict Arnold' before he died...

Another thought began to plague him, how many of his recent decisions could he trust? Why had they been so confident in walking in here, right into the trap? It was so obvious that someone like Fisher would be waiting for them, would have the resources to do this to them. It pointed to some element of mental conditioning. Was that what Fisher had meant by 'another period of re-education'? Had he been programmed to fail, some leftover from his Moderator's training?

Or was Jean the manipulator? He recalled all the fractured thoughts he'd found suppressed by some smothering sentiment. Free again — for now — of the cataract of emotion that drowned his doubts, he could put together the lost fragments: her contradictions and the sense that there was another intent being imprinted over his own whenever he questioned her motivations. Had she blinded him with passion?

Other questions boiled up. Why was she so calm? Was this just a way of learning Fisher's location, the body that she sent in with them nothing more than a hollow shell and as expendable as they were? It made a perverse logic when he adjusted his thinking to that of a near immortal with multiple bodies. And yet, there was the breathless apex of their passion that had transported them — moving in unison — to the existence behind the veil of physicality. How could such an experience be faked?

Jean had soon reverted to her logical scientist's view of the world, but he'd seen it in those moments looking into her eyes when they'd first returned to the mundane world of flesh. The wonder and awe in her gaze. Could she be so good at faking emotions? To what end? Why not show him a series of convincing memories and keep it at that? Fisher had shown that he could create any memories he liked in his synthorganic mind. Why not create the sense of the greater consciousness? Play up to his hallucinations, if hallucinations they were.

Something else began to nag at him: Vinnetti had been homosexual — with, what a mere three per cent likelihood of a shift to breeder status. Was that inherited by clones too? If so, then was Jean using sex, using love as nothing more than an act, binding him to her with it when she felt nothing for him, when he was the wrong gender to be her type? No... she'd been pregnant

— but did that change anything? Was he fooling himself? His love for her was real... wasn't it?

Valko's instincts called from some primal depth — he shouldn't be awake, his consciousness at this time was unintended. It gave him a chance but, before he could act, he needed to work through all of the conflicts in his mind. Whatever he did had to be right — there'd be just one chance. It all came down to what he chose to believe. Part of his mind was normal, human, flawed: the seat of an emotionless, ruthless being. The other part was artificial: not the pure processing of a computer but the capacity of brain cells that operated far beyond the human.

Fisher, the Philosopher and Jean had altered their brains to raise their intellects and the capacity of their minds beyond that of common humanity. Not one of them had his implant — the artificial tumour that was his death sentence. It bestowed upon him, not great intellect, but some of their artificial powers of mind it was true, yet its true purpose was clear — Jean had admitted as much. It had been created to allow the normal frail minds of the physical being — natural or artificial, baseline or enhanced — to perceive the realm of higher consciousness. A radio receiver provided with a new and powerful dish, he had the bandwidth to receive so much more of the signal of his greater being. How could that be faked? Drugs? He didn't think so. He didn't know.

The reptilian part of his mind, his true self, railed against this line of thinking. Of course, it was hallucination: everything around him was real. He agreed with it. The physical world was real, but just because it wasn't an illusion didn't mean it was all that there was to existence. The serpent mind snapped at him that he was being a fool but he saw it now for what it was. Yes, a part of him — but not the whole of him. Valko let go and plunged into the deeper reality, his analytical mind yammering away at him in futile resistance.

†††

Stars and planets wheeled past him; they were real, but small. Significant — not all encompassing. He held onto himself, because, in truth, there was no separation. There was nothing to fear here. Yes, he could see that the physical world was not the greater part of existence — as it had always seemed before — but it did still matter. He saw inside himself gaps, pieces missing in a puzzle he had to answer. He saw within himself the immaculate, rational core — saw its value but knew its limitations: logic could not lead him to the true reality. He poured as much as he could of what unfolded before him into that rationality and saw it swell and warm, fed in a way that it had never been by the pursuit of pure, mundane truths.

Teenage yearnings to remember his past boiled over and, now, reaching through the veil of time, that had no meaning to the spirit, he saw his origins and made peace with them. He drank the well of soul dry, quenching the blazing questions within his being. He saw his existence as a raindrop striking the surface of a pond. The force of its fall made a ripple, but the water merged into one.

There would be a price for this. Enlightenment, seized in this way, could not be bought cheap. It mattered little to him.

He asked himself the question, 'Is this real?'

Heard it echo through the eternity of his being. What did such a question matter, after all?

Sending his awareness outwards the Mind sought Others. It was a journey of millennia and light years uncountable, yet it took but an instant — they were there all around him. They were within him and he within them. There, he found the shard of being that was Jean — saw her greater self, locking out all other perceptions to see through the eyes of the body and feel physical reality. He found the shards of Mind that were Satoshi, Davidson and Fisher.

Floating at the centre of all things, wrapped in a fold of the void, their sins were laid out before him. Sins of the world — meaningless here, beyond the boundaries of body. A dreamlike echo, what had seemed so important, intruded on his apotheosis. Purpose.

The many fractured pieces of Fisher, bound as links in a chain, beckoned to him. Here was the Mind's final need — here within this being. His reasoning, his fear and his hatred. There was his greed and lust for power too, tempered by the conviction that he was doing what was right — they mattered little. Fisher, like him and all the Others, was seeking, ever seeking, for an end to division — yet in binding the splinters of his soul together, he had only succeeded in welding a blade of sorrow to drive ever deeper into his own heart.

Looking at him in this way, the Mind could see Fisher linked to many bodies yet all leading back to the One. Like a tortured reflection of the Others who were many people at once throughout time or had chosen to seek meaning within the consciousnesses of a flock of birds, Fisher spread questing tendrils wide into Life. They diverted him from his true purpose. The wisdom of his greater self was lost, so deep was he focused on trivia. It was a familiar problem, as many of the Others showed. The Mind saw a way to bring succour to Fisher.

The Mind groped in the void for Jean, to bind up the wounds in her essence, to lock knowledge of her truth to his mortal core. It was futile. Here, where he extended beyond the fragile delusions of time and space, she was lost to him. His singular purpose had set him on a solitary path. Still, his love for her triumphed over his reason, even now.

He took what he knew of the one known as Fisher into himself and knew, with a deep knowing that defied rational thought, what he had to do. The Mind reached out and, feeling his own connection to the physical world, used that connection to unhook all of the links in the chain that was Fisher, bar the one original. With profound sadness, the Mind shrank back into the insubstantial world, diminished and became Valko Gangleri once again.

†††

The scream, hoarse and croaking, snapped Valko back to consciousness. A wet bubbling voice cried out its dismay. Light shone in straight pillars to the cold hard floor, slick with blood and other fluids. Valko hung within one of those pillars of light, restraints pulling his arms and legs back while his head was held over a metal tray.

His vision was overlaid with sparkling traces — Jean had warned him that seeing electrical impulses in the world around him would start when he was close to the end. He could barely make out surgical implements to one side on a metal table beneath him. They'd been used and were coated in dark blood. One, some sort of round saw, still had pieces of bone stuck between its teeth.

The knowledge of where he was and what was happening already coursed through his mind — this was where Fisher would tear the last shred of his free will away. The pain in his head had gone, replaced by a mounting pressure. Valko knew what it presaged: it didn't matter, not anymore.

All that Fisher had shown him was in preparation for this: Fisher would twist the technology of his implant to reveal the secrets he'd seen in Apollo Station, all he'd learned from Jean's mind. Then he'd be cut open and a sample of his implant would be removed for *research*. Re-education would be some form of neural programming, creating a seamless fiction in his mind.

To him, Fisher would be in the right and Valko would submit to living out his remaining days — short as they were — helping with the man's research. He'd never see Satoshi, Davidson or Odegebayo again. They'd be sent back into the Plena, not brainwashed but worse: part of their brains replaced by some of Fisher's cloned material. They wouldn't be puppets exactly, but their free will would be curtailed and out from their eyes, Fisher would gaze.

The ultimate means of tightening control over the Plena — if it could happen in Arcas, he could duplicate the process elsewhere. Valko recalled the name the Philosopher had thought of Fisher by, the one that spoke of his special expertise: the Visionary. Fisher had been a polymath and valued for his ability to combine different fields of research to create astounding breakthroughs and technologies — he'd lost none of his skill in turning the work of others to his own, surprising, new uses.

The screeching continued. At first, Valko thought it was Jean, fearing some horrible torture was being done to her but he could see her hanging to his left. Her body at least, his eyes, which saw the tracks of life — nerve impulses and the body's electric fields — saw no spark running through the husk of Jean.

She'd been opened down the back and her spine cracked apart. The split ran all the way up to her skull. The slick furrowed mass of her brain with its white, branching cord suspended below now floated in a large clear container to one side.

Fisher hadn't lied: he'd not killed her. Indicators on the container showed neural activity and the tissue's vibrant mix of grey, white, red, and black spoke of a living brain, not the dull colours of a preserved sample. She wasn't dead, but maybe she wished she was. Valko could see the lines of fire — intense and angry — zigzag their agonised way through the brain and spinal cord. She pulled at him — seeking the sensory input his contact could give, but he withdrew. He wanted to soothe her, but he risked losing himself in her agony. Reason spoke, with a soft voice, to compassion and Valko turned away, to focus on what had to be done.

Forcing his head against the restraints, Valko looked round: the screaming came from a hunched figure — a man's torso contained in a clear tube with wires and cables running from it in multiple directions. The head and arms were not contained, a softer flexible material sheathed the neck and upper arms, keeping the cylinder sealed from the air. The cylinder itself was filled with a swirling liquid of a vague, reddish tint. The head was thrown back in a scream, which stopped only long enough to draw another ragged breath in. Lines of power, bright and flashing with shocking bursts of energy, were visible to Valko as they coursed over the man and radiated from him in many directions.

This was Fisher. The Original — not a clone, not a puppet. A survivor of nanodestroyers. The handsome young man, who had spoken with Fisher's voice, and had worn Fisher's expressions on his face, lay on the floor beside the ruined man trapped inside his jar. The clone body was twitching in the way a corpse will sometimes move; there was no volition behind the movements, only stray and fading nerve impulses. The thin arms that emerged from the Original's cylinder thrashed about, spattering the blood that covered them all around. Flecks hit Valko as he hung several metres away.

Valko jerked his head away from the sight, finding the restraints had just enough play to let him look around a half head-turn to left and right. He couldn't see Satoshi but felt he was close — their previous link made it easier for Valko to find his friend.

Satoshi was unconscious — powerful drugs designed to incapacitate even one with his level of synthorganic reinforcement pumped through his body. Valko recalled the purpose of the drugs, from some dark well of memory lurking inside him. They would trigger Satoshi's mind to enter the auto-hypnotic state, which allowed for his programming. Programming he — no they together — had defeated before, by plunging into memories from before the conditioning had bound Satoshi's mind in talons of forgetfulness. Valko lunged outwards and drove his splinter of mind into his friend's psyche deeper than ever before — the distance between them forcing him to stretch his will to breaking point to make the connection.

†††

Valko watched as Satoshi was once again in that room with Cooper beside him as they burst in on the torture of the young woman. But it was different. There was no torture, just standard interrogation — not by a lone officer but by several soldiers. The memory of who the woman was came clear — a Lunar Terrorist possessing knowledge the ITF had to retrieve.

She looked up and said, 'Benedict Arnold.' All perception drew down to a pinprick, Satoshi was a puppet, trapped in his own body. She'd used him, used Cooper too, to slaughter her captors and take her out of the compound. Then she'd set them both on a revenge mission. The details were a haze, a pain of memory that Valko couldn't find. Satoshi's mind hadn't been able to breathe past the control of the medical nanites clamping down on every synapse. There'd been blood and death, but silent and controlled — not an insane rampage. Only Satoshi had come back to her — an obedient slave — and she'd told him a story, weaving a memory to patch over the hole in his mind, before sending him to wait, a sleeper agent, in the heart of Fisher's domain.

Valko followed the thread to a memory of discovery — Satoshi being disabled along with the other veterans, taken down before they could be activated. A single memory of a whitecoat leaning over and saying, 'They've been hacked. I need more time... Freeze them.' Then dank, cold sleep.

Fetters of control remained, tied to many different memories — so many of them bore a different flavour, the tampering of a different will.

Valko plunged between them, seeking one that remained clear of the taint — clear of Lunar influence, clear of Fisher's subversion. An old memory smouldered in the depths of Satoshi's mind. No steel web of nanites held it in bondage. He thrust into it.

Satoshi rolled back to his feet. His strong, fifteen-year old body had taken the shock of falling well. Now, he looked down at the old man before him. His grandfather, always fond of sake and sweet potato moon cakes, had succumbed to the temptation of a western diet. It'd taken its toll on him, as his ample belly showed. It hadn't mattered. Gritting his teeth, Satoshi attacked again, frustrated by the failure of his superior training — he was the inter-school champion, wasn't he? His grandfather, looking unconcerned, allowed the young man to grip his thick forearms. Satoshi twisted, seeking leverage, to find his grip insufficient as his grandfather — with a small repositioning of his feet — kept shifting out of the joint lock. No matter how hard he gripped, the old man's skin slipped through his hands as if oiled. He knew that this was just a question of mind and focus. His grandfather had explained to him time and time again that visualising slipperiness in his arms was all he needed to do. The young man — a good student and a believer in the clear progress that science and rational thought had provided — rejected this throwback to the ancient superstitions and misconceptions. Nonetheless, the wrinkled old arm slipped through his grip every time.

He tried a different approach, seeking to bend the arm but found it impossible. His grandfather's arm was not locked but instead flexed slightly and would give just a little. Again, every effort to bring his youthful force to bear was diverted by a small shift of the old man's stance — an exercise in visualising energy flowing through the arm. More nonsense.

In frustration, Satoshi threw himself into the task of twisting the old wrist.

'Oshi, have you learned nothing? Even if I allow your hold...' His grandfather did so, and with a rush of triumph Satoshi pressed his grip, twisting the old man's arm with no thought to the harm it might cause. '...it is worthless'

The old man relaxed, going with the pressure and using it to flip over in the direction of the torsion, landing on his feet, resuming a position of ease. For an overweight old man in his eighties, it should have been an impossible feat.

'Stop using that rubbish they taught you on the mainland. It's just foolishness for school children.'

His grandfather punctuated the remark by laying the fingers of his free hand on Satoshi's chest, then delivering a nonchalant strike with the heel of that palm. The blow knocked the young man clean off his feet, his grip broken.

Satoshi lay dazed and winded; his ego had absorbed the blow as much as his body. For a moment, focus on where he was and what he was doing escaped him and he lost himself watching the motes of dust floating in a sunbeam shining through the dojo window. Adrift within thoughts of the resemblance of life to the course of a speck of dust caught on the warm air, he didn't notice the shuffle of his grandfather's approaching feet.

'Show me what I taught you instead, boy.' The old man's voice was calm and even but the reprimand in it was clear. He would tolerate no more foolishness in his dojo.

Satoshi stood and proved he still knew the forms — each kata smooth and flowing, so different from the stiff and stilted style he had learned at his school on the mainland. The familiar movements, long unpractised, had taken on a life of their own in his subconscious mind and now sprang to the surface, unhindered.

'Good... now, strike me.' The old man indicated his round stomach.

Satoshi hesitated a moment, drew back his arm to his hip and with a loud cry slammed it forward with all his strength, his hip flicking in at the last moment and his other hand pulling back to the opposite hip. The punch connected but did little more than cause the old man to shift backwards a half-step. He fetched Satoshi a clip to the ear.

'Properly, boy... like I showed you. Don't waste your energy with all that movement.'

Satoshi, chastened at the failure of his punch to so much as wind his grandfather, reached deep inside to find the timeworn teachings. He held his arm softly, using the barest effort to hold it up, a short distance from the rounded gut. Awareness of the flow of energy through his body bloomed and he it drove up from his stomach and through his arm. The force of his blow was an order of magnitude greater than the previous strike but his grandfather shifted aside before it connected.

'Hmm, perhaps you haven't forgotten as much as I'd feared.' The old man said.

Satoshi straightened and bit back a remark. He could feel the truth of what his grandfather had been telling him, there was no use denying it. The modern way was inferior: no longer bound to the true spirit of combat, it had become no more than a sport — hollow and brittle.

†††

Valko returned to his own mind, the scale of what had been done to Satoshi was hard to grasp — the manifold alterations. Valko's own mind blanked out, thoughts unable to encompass what he'd seen and felt. Unable to form around the scope of the deceit. A roar from the other room told him that he'd at least been successful in bringing his friend out of his stupor.

There was a sound of breaking machinery and Valko knew that synthorganic muscle had triumphed over the restraints. A whirlwind of rage, Satoshi swept into the room, taking in the situation all in one go.

'Val? You alive?' He asked, his voice a hoarse growl.

'Yes, Oshi,' Valko croaked. 'It's Fisher, the real Fisher. Sadiq isn't here, Fisher doesn't know where he is, but he did kill

Iona.'

The last was true... after a fashion. Hampton was as much a part of Fisher as his right hand — whatever the Original might have said. Even though she had not done the deed with her own hands, his lingering doubts overridden by his passion, Valko knew that she'd caused it. That made her — and her clone father — culpable.

She couldn't still be alive, not with her link to the greater consciousness of Fisher severed. While — to the Original — she might have seemed to have autonomy, Valko had seen with vision beyond mere sight, that she was chained to her clone father — her spirit no more than an extension of his own and her consciousness using his as a relay to their shared soul. It was as clear a fact to Valko as any he'd reasoned out in all his years as a Moderator.

His words galvanized Satoshi, who, needing no further prompting, spun to face the screaming ruin of a man. Valko saw the boiling emotions inside Satoshi burst free as the sergeant attacked Fisher's cylinder — clearly intent on carrying out his promise to rip his enemy's heart out. The tank resisted the blows, it couldn't be made of glass after all but something far harder. The Moderator still buried deep within Valko speculated it was aluminium oxynitride — the so-called transparent aluminium — even as his dominant passions howled for blood.

Fisher stopped his screaming and brought up his hands, one still gripping the blood spattered surgical tool he'd used on Jean. He slashed at Satoshi with surprising speed and Valko knew then that he'd misjudged the situation: whatever was happening with Fisher, he was far from helpless. But that wasn't the greatest danger. The activity around the man's torso, within its fluid filled tank, bore all the hallmarks of nanodestroyer infestation. To survive their assault he must have reinforced his body with synthorganics — so the fluid was a nutrient bath for their constant growth.

Waves of nanodestroyer activity surged up the torso. A constant seething of the micro machines devouring Fisher's flesh upwards from the waist, while it was being rebuilt with equal speed downwards with the most resilient cells available — synthorganics. Hard to believe though it was, Fisher had found a way to survive nanodestroyer infestation. Then the scale of the risk he posed became clear to Valko.

'Oshi, you mustn't breach the cylinder!' Valko shouted even as his friend engaged in death's waltz with the broken man.

Fisher quickly revealed the cybernetic appendages surrounding him, which had lain dormant and impossible to see in the darkness as he'd screamed his soul's agony. His life support cylinder was held up by a trio of metal legs that lent him a surprising degree of agility. He used his multiple mechanical limbs to flail at Satoshi, never quite getting close enough — the sergeant's reactions and training protected him.

Another titanic blow to the cylinder by the superman, rocked Fisher backwards, knocking the front legs of the contraption off the ground. Satoshi seized the opening and whipped out a low, vicious kick to the single leg remaining in contact with the ground. The kick was precise — one of the great pistons that drove the leg ruptured, its pressurised fluids spraying out in a wide arc, leaving the floor slick with lubricant. Fisher staggered away trying to regain his balance on the slippery ground with the two legs remaining to him. All the while he was slashing out with claws, drills and scalpels.

'Oshi, listen to me' Valko pleaded — distracting his friend could be fatal but if he didn't warn him of the danger they were all undone. 'He's infested by nanodestroyers! If you break the cylinder we'll all be torn to pieces. It's the only thing holding them in check.'

He couldn't tell if Satoshi had heard and understood him, as the two combatants circled, thrashing at each other. They were moving out of his line of sight and Valko craned his neck to watch.

Dark shapes flooded into the room — naukara, answering the call of their master. All was lost: they outnumbered Satoshi four to one.

It was over.

Satoshi ignored a whining bone saw, which slashed across his chest, sprang past the biological arm that wielded it and seized Fisher's head in both hands. With a wrench and a sickening cracking sound, Satoshi broke the withered neck.

He didn't stop there. Even as the arms — biological and cybernetic — spasmed, Satoshi flexed his massive shoulders and dug his fingers hard into the skull in his hands. He twisted, jerked back and blood sprayed out as he pulled Fisher's head clean off.

The body fell away, clattering to the ground, while blood spurted from the torn neck in slowing pulses as the heart driving it died.

The naukara were still advancing, weapon arms extended and ready for the kill. It must mean their master was not yet dead — Valko could see the ghost-line whispers of the severed head's communication with the drone soldiers. Satoshi seemed to realise that mere decapitation was insufficient for a creature like Fisher: he hefted the head — its eyes still fixed on him and its lips mouthing obscenities — and, roaring, cast it with crushing force at the nearest naukara. The head struck, cracking open on the hardened carapace and knocking the cybernetic soldier over.

Satoshi's ferocity abated and he stood, making no sound, save for the deep whooshing inhalations of his breath. The naukara lowered their arms, reverting to standby now no directives came from their master. Satoshi looked over to Valko and raised a hand in salute.

'It's the last time he kills by remote control,' the blood soaked sergeant said, grim satisfaction on his face.

He approached Valko and, releasing the restraints, gathered him into his arms, heedless of the gore that now coated them both. Valko found that his limbs didn't work: he couldn't stand or even hold onto Satoshi. Before he had time to worry over this, Satoshi was embracing him, breath hooping as the huge man wept.

'Val, I'm so sorry. It's finally come clear in my mind. It's me, it's my fault.'

'What are you talking about?'

'He was my controller. He programmed me just like I was one of those naukara. Every time I had a check-up I'd be getting orders burned into my subconscious. All that time I thought I was practicing kata, entering a state of mushin. All that time wasn't a blur from some trance state. I was out killing for him. The procedures that were used on me — you saved me from them, set me free. But oh, Val. What I did at his command.' Violent sobs wracked the big man. 'Vinnetti. It was me that killed her. And Actur. He was there, tried to intervene. I had orders not to kill him just to wound him and let him go. But he knew the words of the trigger and it threw me off. I shot him him but I was too far under Fisher's control to go killcrazy. It stunned me instead of turning me into a puppet. It must have been what he was trying to do when we found him — paralyse me again. Maybe that's what he was doing in the bunker... trying to warn Jean that she couldn't control veterans any more. Or bring her some other intel. I don't know.

It doesn't matter now, he's dead just like the others. I was Fisher's retribution. Set up before Eugene was killed, like he was just waiting for it to happen. I was there in Berlin when he activated me — sent me to kill Vinnetti — he thought she was Jean. It makes no sense. It was all lies, from the start. He used what was done to him as a cover for the murder of an innocent woman and I was the tool.'

'Oshi, you're not responsible for something you didn't have control over. I think Vinnetti was Jean — in a way — a clone of her. He had to use you, she'd be too deadly for anyone else to stand a chance. And I think he was controlling both of us all along and maybe all the Moderators and surviving veterans. I think part of me broke free because of my accident at the scene of Vinnetti's murder. I know you. You're a good man — you didn't choose to do it, you didn't know what you were doing.'

'No, Val, oh no. Part of me knew — part of me enjoyed the killing I did during the War and after. He chose me because of it. Of all the veterans, my psyche would hold up to his control best because I didn't object to killing. Not really. I'm a monster — I nearly killed you too — if you hadn't stopped me...' Satoshi sobbed, tears flowing down his cheeks in torrents.

Valko wanted to return the embrace, but couldn't — his arms wouldn't work.

'No, Oshi. You're not a monster. Fisher would never have pointed you at me — your friendship couldn't be subverted like that. He knew it. I know it. He couldn't know that the conflict between the Lunar Scientist's programming and his own would drive you over the edge any more than Jean could — she was wrong about that. I think she was playing us, I can't believe I bought it, but her words, Oshi. They reach into me and rewrite what I'm feeling. We've both been pawns in some cold war.

I can't blame you for something you did when you were completely out of your mind. And what about Iona? You reacted like a man — like a good man — would. You grieved. Then you did what you could to stop it happening to someone else — to Sadiq. You took revenge only because you cared so much for her, because you wanted justice for her.'

'No, you're wrong. I took revenge for myself — because I wanted the pleasure of tearing him apart,' Satoshi said it with savage passion and Valko wondered what to say to bring his friend back from this.

'No, Oshi, you've been used. Your son. Think of Sadiq. You're reeling from the brain conditioning breaking apart — confusing Fisher's will with your own. Fight it. Be what you were always meant to be — free your own mind. You've got strength in your soul, Oshi. Rise up against all he did to you. You can do it.' Valko felt his words take on a force beyond their simple meaning. 'Take your pain and turn it into a force to break free of the last of the conditioning. You're not a drone, not a naukara.'

'Val… I…' Satoshi let out a deep bone weary sigh, and set his friend down. Valko began to collapse, he'd no control of his limbs. Satoshi laid him gently on the surgical table. 'You're right, Val. I know, I will fight, but first I need to get you help.

NON SEMPER EA SUNT, QUÆ VIDENTUR; DECIPIT
FRONS PRIMA MULTOS: RARA MENS INTELLIGIT
QUOD INTERIORE CONDIDIT CURA ANGULO.

THINGS ARE NOT ALWAYS WHAT THEY SEEM; THE
FIRST APPEARANCE DECEIVES MANY; THE
INTELLIGENCE OF A FEW PERCEIVES WHAT HAS
BEEN CAREFULLY HIDDEN.

-GAIUS JULIUS PHAEDRUS-

Epilogue

Valko watched as he was prepped for transport to a medcentre — strapped onto a board with the jelly like mass of a respirator ready should his breathing begin to fail. Kensakan by the dozen and the remaining Moderators — those who'd not collapsed after Fisher's control over them was broken — joined in searching the hidden facility. Fisher's body had been the first thing they'd dealt with — the deadly container had been purged with incinerators, the only sanctioned use of fire allowed in the Plena. The medtechs came them, forced to carry Valko on their shoulders in the cramped conditions, until they eventually made their way to the medcentre, where Orla waited.

After he'd been fussed over, the medtechs had left Valko in peace while they struggled to understand what was happening to him. Lying in bed, he felt eased by the familiar smell of the g-moss. He'd grown up in the Plena and — despite his love for the outside world — it was right to be home again.

'Gangleri. I will overlook your breaches of the Moderator's code... we owe you, and Satoshi, much it seems.' Odegebayo leaned over his bed, his face once again concealing his true ruthless nature behind the lie of a kind smile. 'You will excuse me while I turn my attention to seeking out how far this worm of manipulation has burrowed through our society.'

The Old Man left and Valko sighed in relief. Orla bustled around several medical devices in the room. She seemed broken by the news from the latest scan. His efforts against Fisher had triggered a massive growth spurt in his implant and his life was nearing its end. They had few words for each other. What could he say? There was nothing she could do to save him and, despite the tenderness he sensed she felt for him, he loved another. He contemplated sharing his visions with her but knew, with that deep knowing he couldn't challenge, that Orla needed no help from him.

The door to his room slid open and Jack Davidson walked in, sweating reluctance, hands clasped in front of him like a nervous petitioner. The lines of energy flowing through him confirmed the knowledge Valko had brought back with him.

'I know all of it, Jack,' he said before the nervous man could speak.

'You do, Boss? How?' Davidson said, shock driving out the apprehension of moments before.

Valko could read him with ease. Davidson had been playing with the idea of confessing all, but whether he ever would have was academic. To Valko, contrition was irrelevant.

'Sit down, Jack.' Valko indicated the seat beside his bed.

Davidson did as he was bid and Valko seized his arm with fever strength. He bit down a grunt of pain and stared the flabby man straight in the eye.

'I can see right through you, Jack. You're a dirty, sleazy, corrupt man who always dreamed of being something different, a hero of the law. None of that matters now.'

'Boss, look I can explain. Please, I'll do anything you ask.' Davidson was blubbering.

'I want you to come with me for a moment, Jack. Leave your fear behind, it has no place where we're going.' Valko closed his eyes and reached out beyond himself, dragging Davidson with him.

'What the fuck...?' he heard Davidson say before the world around them faded.

They ascended to the higher state of consciousness, hurtling upwards and shedding all sense of body as scraps of ethereal skin. The Valko Mind was freed from its pain and the Davidson Mind was freed from its guilt, deep though it was. They rode the tides of existence together until, breasting the final wave of perception, they flew free of all trace of their individuality.

Speech was irrelevant at this level of consciousness, instead Valko led Davidson, in unity, through the chasms of his soul. They watched the ragged peaks and the rank swamps of his life. The experiences of a sordid man — the light of his being dwindling every day into further decay, now took on forms grand and terrible, for all their ephemeral bleating. Valko reached into the wounds of spirit revealing them to be illusions, distractions from the truth. Even the vilest depths of Jack Davidson held lessons for the luminous and transcendent being, which had pored over the bad excuse for a life since its beginning. The two Minds, Valko and Davidson — now alloyed through their shared understanding — knew the insight would not survive their return to limited consciousness.

The Valko Mind showed Davidson a way. It required a sacrifice, but the guilt-ridden heart longed for it. What desolate shreds of essence that might be lost, had taught all the lessons that any soul could ingest from such wretchedness. Valko began drawing them spiralling downwards to the physical and felt the reluctance of the other Mind. They both knew it must be this way: life had to be lived. It should not be prematurely ended — to do so, would be to fail in the search for the answer to the primordial question: the why of their quintessence. The Minds tore apart from each other, and, in their separation, became nothing but men again.

Both of them sat in silence while tears streamed down Davidson's face.

'Is none of what I was still with me?' He asked Valko, in awe.

'Some of you has changed forever, Jack. You changed it. What you do with that wisdom is up to you.'

'Yes Boss, what you've done for me... I won't forget it. Ever. I swear it.' Davidson stood and walked out — a look of serenity on his face.

'What the hell is wrong with Jack?' Satoshi asked, as he came in.

'He's had something of a change of heart.'

Valko didn't want to reveal too much. It wouldn't matter in the long term and he hadn't opened Davidson's mind to see him facing a one way trip to a recycler.

'I see,' Satoshi said, his voice subdued.

'Any news on Sadiq?' Valko asked, here near the end of his journey, his concern for the boy was genuine.

Satoshi brightened, 'Yes, he's safe. He's back in my new quarters.'

'I'm glad Oshi. Where was he?'

Satoshi radiated embarrassment. 'The Temple had sent someone to watch him when it learned I was gone. Something about safeguarding one of the potential future leaders. They took Sadiq to a safehouse when he ran from our quarters, after finding her lying there.' The big man stopped for a moment, choked up. 'Kept him safe until they saw me.'

'So the Temple isn't all bad then?' Valko asked gently.

'No, I suppose they were the one organisation that

remained free of Fisher's control.'

'Somewhat ironic, given what I think we've both come to believe about them.' Valko shifted in the bed — seeking a comfortable position but not finding it. 'Oshi, we need to talk about the future.'

Valko resisted the upwelling of his emotions. He knew or, at least, believed he knew what awaited him after death, but the fear and sorrow were still there. He couldn't allow that to show.

'We'll find a way,' Satoshi said, though his tone belied the hollowed look of his eyes. 'Orla's smart, she's doing everything she can. Maybe, if we send you back to Apollo station, they can help?'

'Oshi, you're like a brother to me. There's no point hiding from the truth of this. You know what's going to happen. Listen, while I still have time, I want to ask you a favour. Actually, three favours.'

'Anything, Val,' Satoshi said without hesitation.

'Jean, she's not dead is she?' Valko asked.

'No, but... What Fisher did is worse than death.'

'Oshi, all her cells were synthorganically reinforced. She could be given a new body. Fisher was preserving her brain and spinal cord for a reason. Not simply as torture. If anyone can help restore her it's those on Apollo Station.' Satoshi listened to Valko, face grave.

'I'll try. But you should know the results of the test that Orla was running on Jean shows that she's suffered serious neural damage. Fisher may not have killed her but she's in a vegetative state.' Satoshi broke eye contact and looked down.

'Oshi, Fisher told me that Vinnetti was Jean's clone — just her puppet. Problem is, I know that he was capable of deceiving me even with my... abilities, so I don't know if it was true or not. I don't know if Vinnetti was simply a clone or just another body for Jean to pilot at will.'

'But he did kill Vinnetti right? I mean he used me to do it, didn't he?' Satoshi grimaced at the memory, Valko could see the horror in his friend skulking like a fanged creature of shadow and mist. Satoshi's actions were like a dark dream as his mind tried to heal from the trauma by shutting the memories away.

'Oshi, there have been too many lies — too much

manipulation of both our minds. I don't know for sure that he used you to kill Vinnetti, in spite of your memories. But I think he did. I don't know for certain if she was a clone of Jean or not. But I think she was. The point is: Jean may have had other clones. There may still be a way to save her.' He didn't say what they were both thinking. Couldn't such a process save him too?

'I'll contact Apollo Station and see if they'll help.' Satoshi promised.

'Good. When I'm gone... you must take my body to them. They will help you to tell everyone — all the Plena, all the Remnants. Tell them all that we've learned, all that I've told you and shown you.'

'Shown me?'

'Yes, Oshi. It's the last thing I need from you. Take my hand.'

†††

Satoshi did as he was bid. Valko's grip became inescapable and Satoshi felt dragged outwards yet, at the same time, inwards into himself.

Perspective changed and Satoshi saw. He saw how every human being was no more than a receiver for their consciousness and that consciousness was a greater thing than could be contained in a body. He saw how ideas of good and evil, wrong and right, lost their meanings. He saw how each consciousness lacked something — some key part. Then Valko was there beside him, showing how life provided lessons that fulfilled some of that want. He saw how living the wrong way, making the wrong choices, could hold back other consciousnesses and hold back the self — but not always by obvious things. Last, Valko showed him how each of the consciousnesses was connected to each other and everything else, and how — learning this — many of the missing parts within, which could not be filled by mere experience, were made perfect.

Satoshi saw himself, Iona and all those he knew. He saw his grandfather. He saw Valko. Saw him as he truly was.

Then they were receding back to the world of the senses — the world of the body with all its limitations, now made too clear.

The vision persisted a while though it became diluted. Satoshi was left with a sense that he had *known* and had *seen* but he could recall that greatness only through a dim veil — an echo of the dream.

Satoshi blinked and settled himself back into the chair beside the bed. Was it real? Was it hallucination? He didn't know. There had been too much manipulation of his mind in the past for him to trust such a vision.

'Val, it's not true is it? It's just a shared hallucination spreading from your implant, isn't it?' He shook his friend's shoulder when there was no reply.

'Val? Val, I need to know.' Satoshi was desperate now, he called for Orla. He *had* to know. Had to but Valko had already slipped back into the dream eternal.

Ω

About the Author

Luke Hindmarsh was born in Oxford before being dragged all over the world by his parents, courtesy of the armed forces. Before starting to write full time, he worked as a Criminal Barrister in London for ten years. He now lives in the Scandinavian wilds with his wife and their half-viking children. When not writing, Luke teaches Shinseido Okinawan Karate and drinks far too much coffee.

Acknowledgements

Hal Duncan, Editor Extraordinaire (and one of the best authors out there!), who has taught me more about writing than anyone else.

Fellow authors Phillip Pass and Louis Mastrangelo for their wise counsel as 'Uber' Readers.

Tony Asquith and Roger Sheldon for their kind reading of the earliest drafts and for all their guidance over the years. *Domo arigato,* Sensei and Sensei! The Okinawan way is best!

Chris Apps for taking time out of parenting and programming the AI which will one day take over the world to read the 2nd draft and give me frank comments.

Peter O'Connor at BespokeBookCovers.com for making this book look good.

Thank you to all the Hubsters for encouragement and criticism in the true meaning of the word. Best wishes to all of you!

Moccamaster for making sure I had enough quality caffeine to keep going until 2am all those nights.

Printed in Great Britain
by Amazon